D0848360

LOUIS L'AMOUR

LAW OF THE DESERT BORN

A GRAPHIC NOVEL

LAW OF THE DESERT BORN

A GRAPHIC NOVEL

LOUIS L'AMOUR

Adapted by **Charles Santino**

Script by **Beau L'Amour and Katherine Nolan**

Based on the short story by **Louis L'Amour**

Produced by **Beau L'Amour**

Illustrated by **Thomas Yeates**

Lettering by **Bill Tortolini**

BANTAM · NEW YORK

Law of the Desert Born is a work of fiction. Names, characters, places, and incidents are the products of the author's imagination or are used fictitiously. Any resemblance to actual events, locales, or persons, living or dead, is entirely coincidental.

Published in the United States by Bantam Books, an imprint of The Random House Publishing Group, a division of Random House, Inc., New York.

BANTAM BOOKS and the HOUSE colophon are registered trademarks of Random House, Inc.

ISBN 978-0-345-52812-4
eBook ISBN 978-0-345-53856-7

Illustrations by Thomas Yeates

Printed in China by C & C Offset on acid-free paper

www.bantamdell.com

2 4 6 8 9 7 5 3 1

First Edition

Book design by Bill Tortolini
Production consultation by Marshall Holt Entertainment

To Kathy L'Amour,
who has made so many things possible

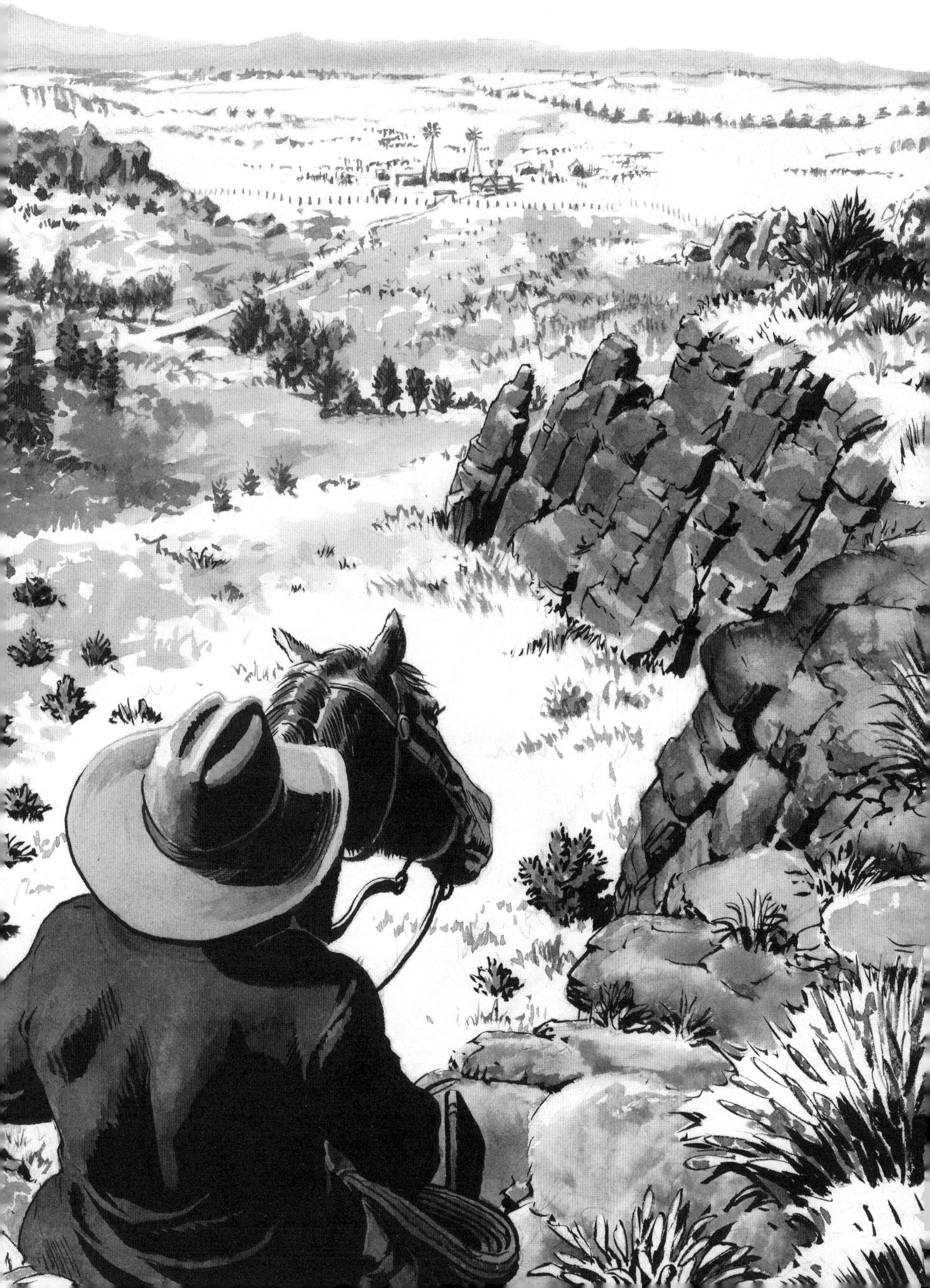

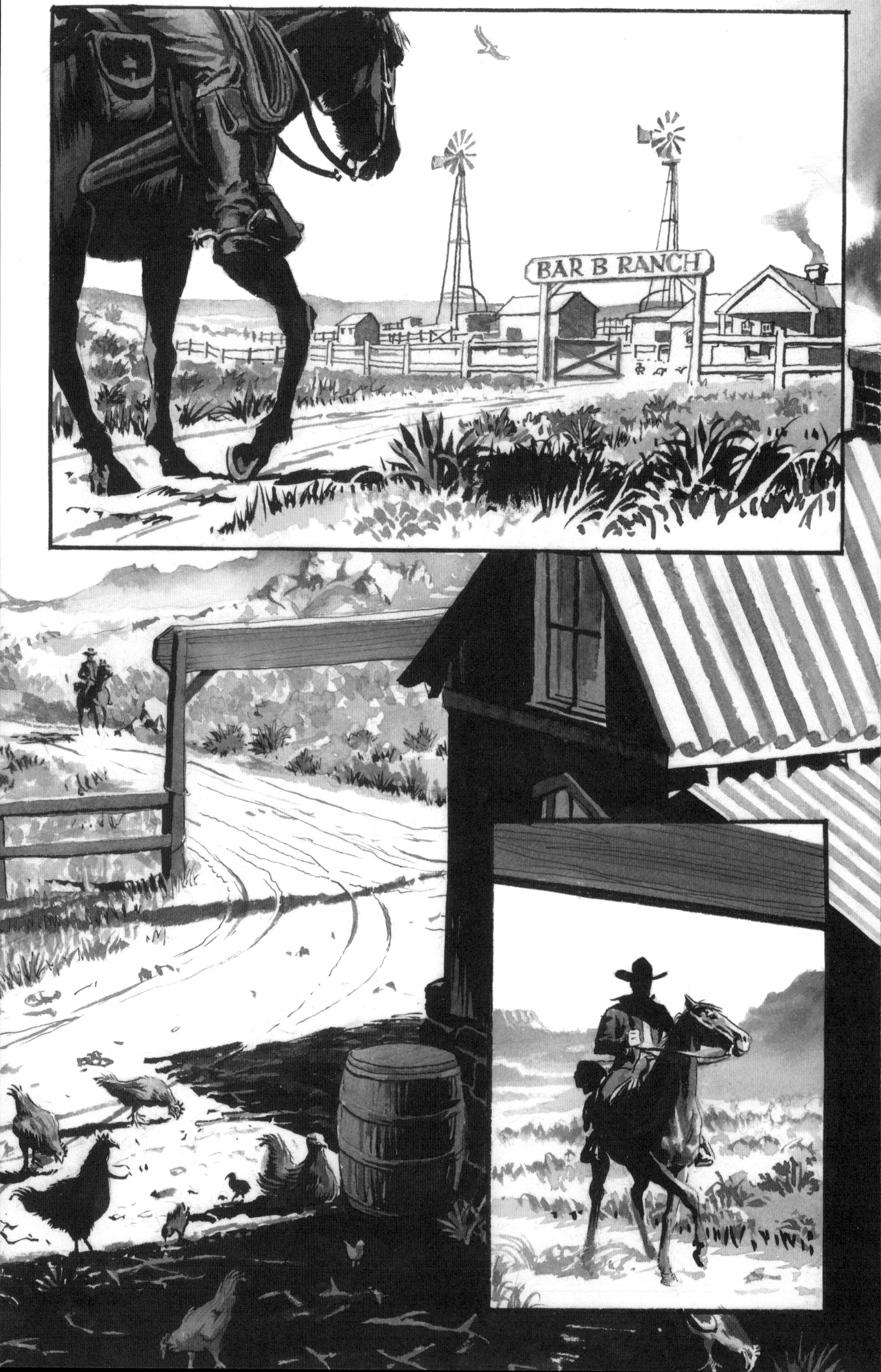
BAR B RANCH

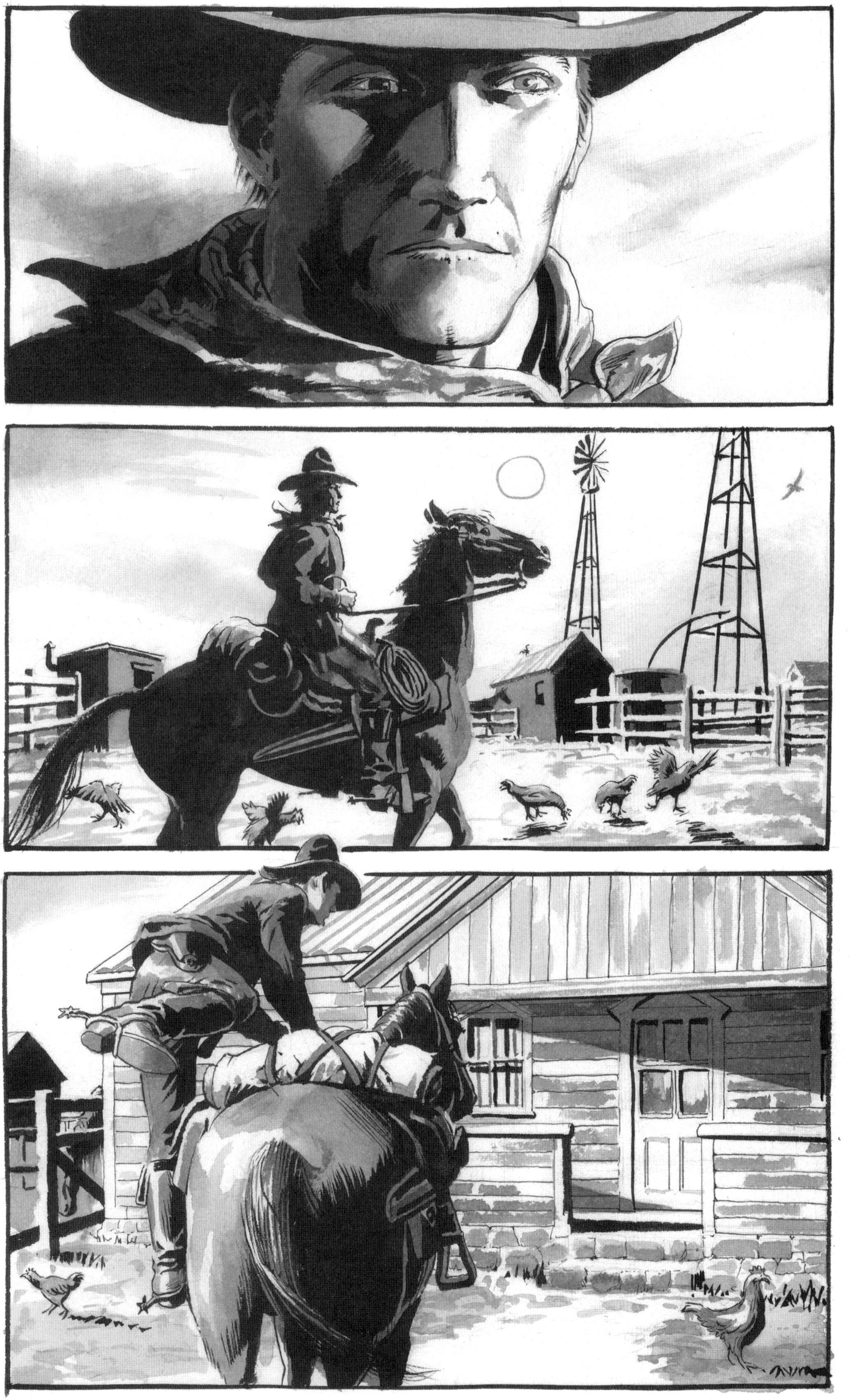

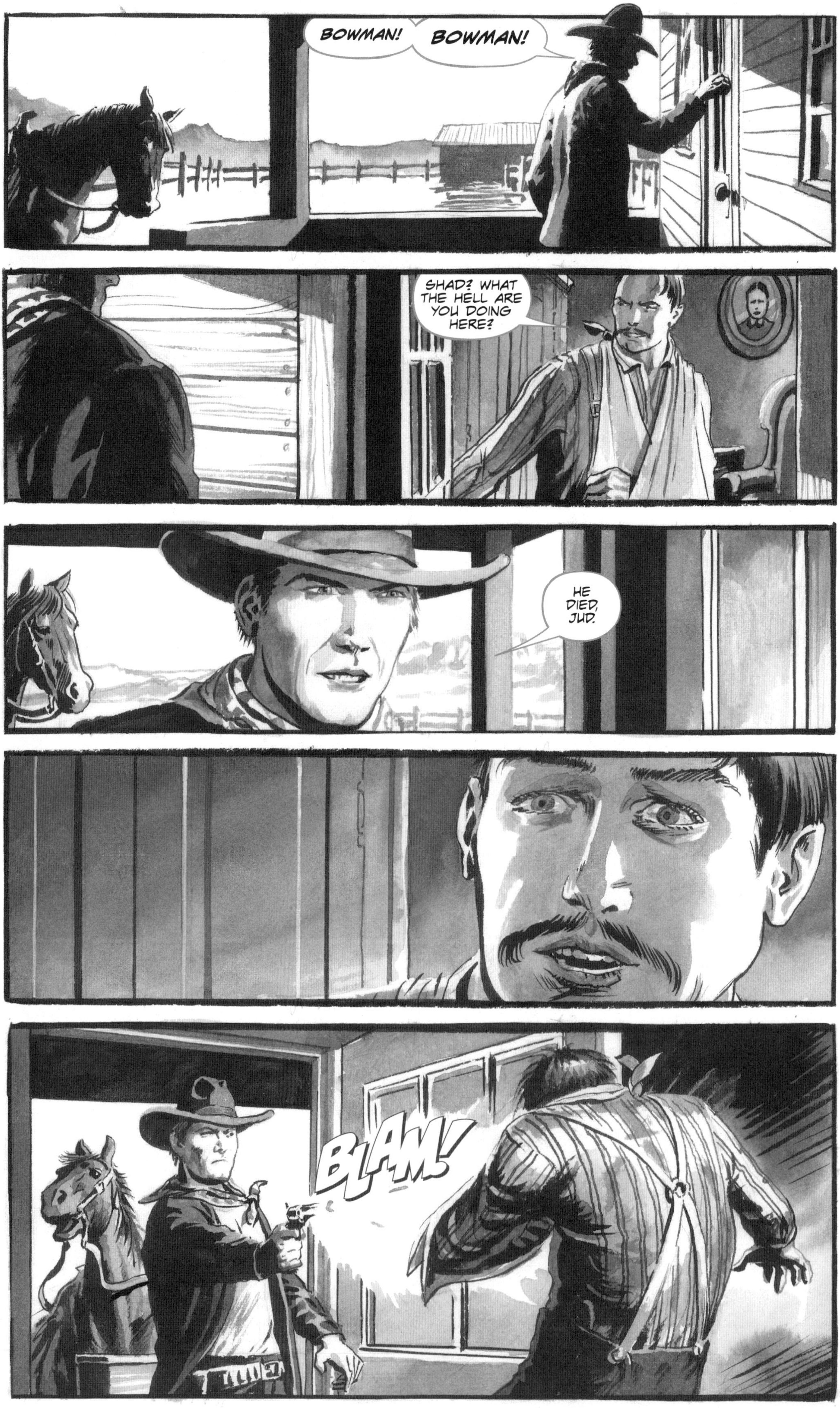
BOWMAN!
BOWMAN!
SHAD? WHAT THE HELL ARE YOU DOING HERE?
HE DIED, JUD.
BLAM!

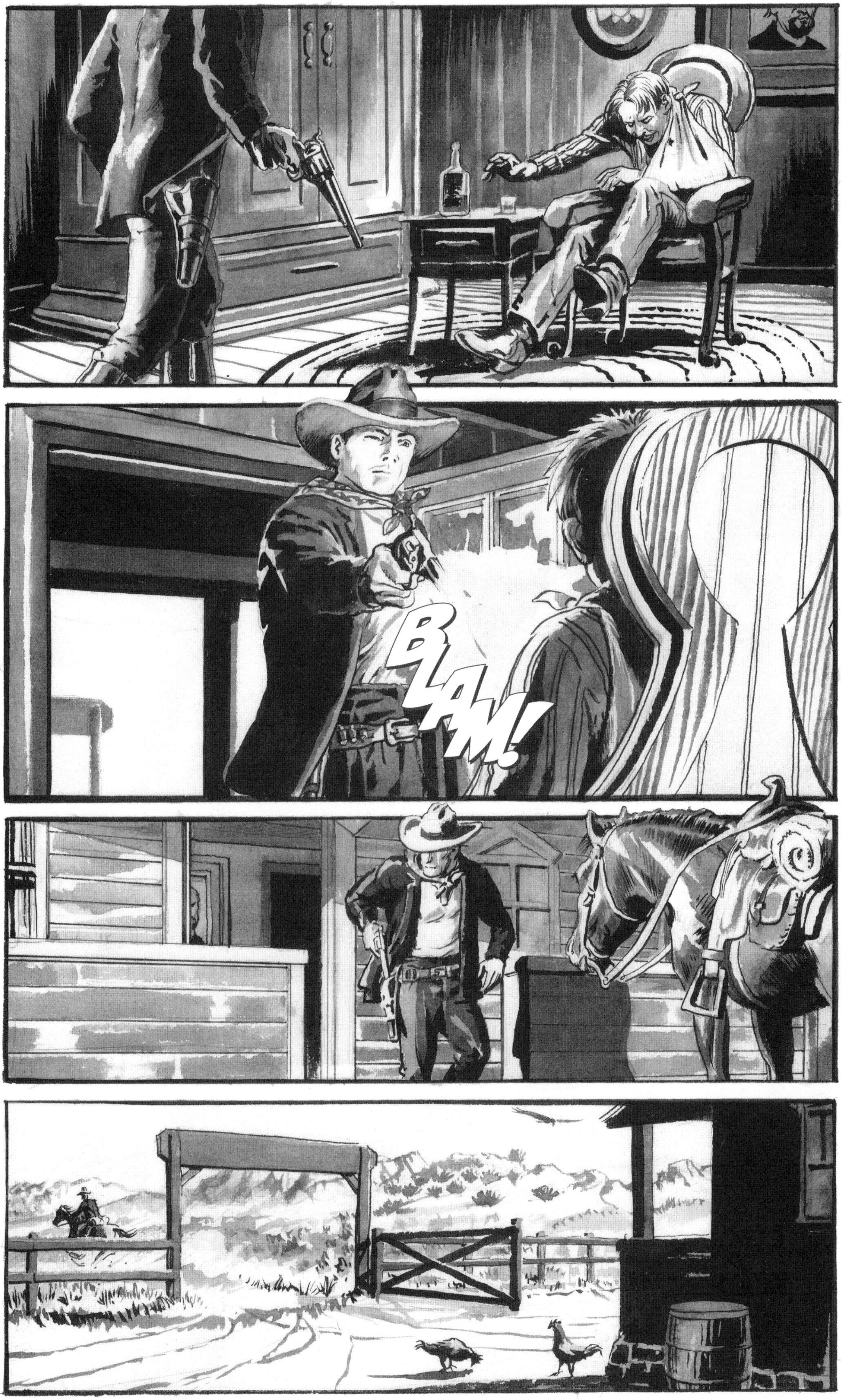
BLAM!

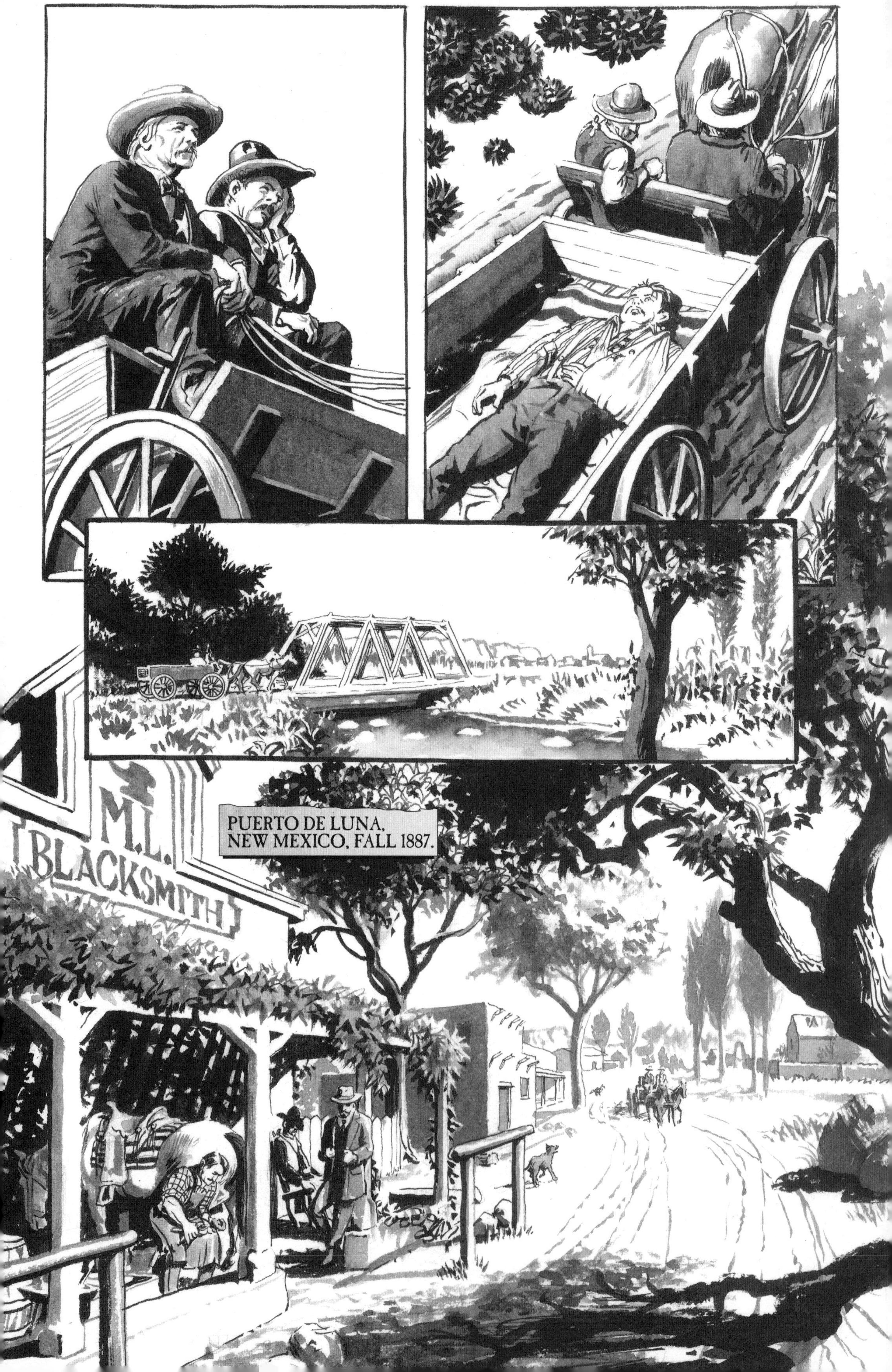
PUERTO DE LUNA,
NEW MEXICO, FALL 1887.
M.L.
BLACKSMITH

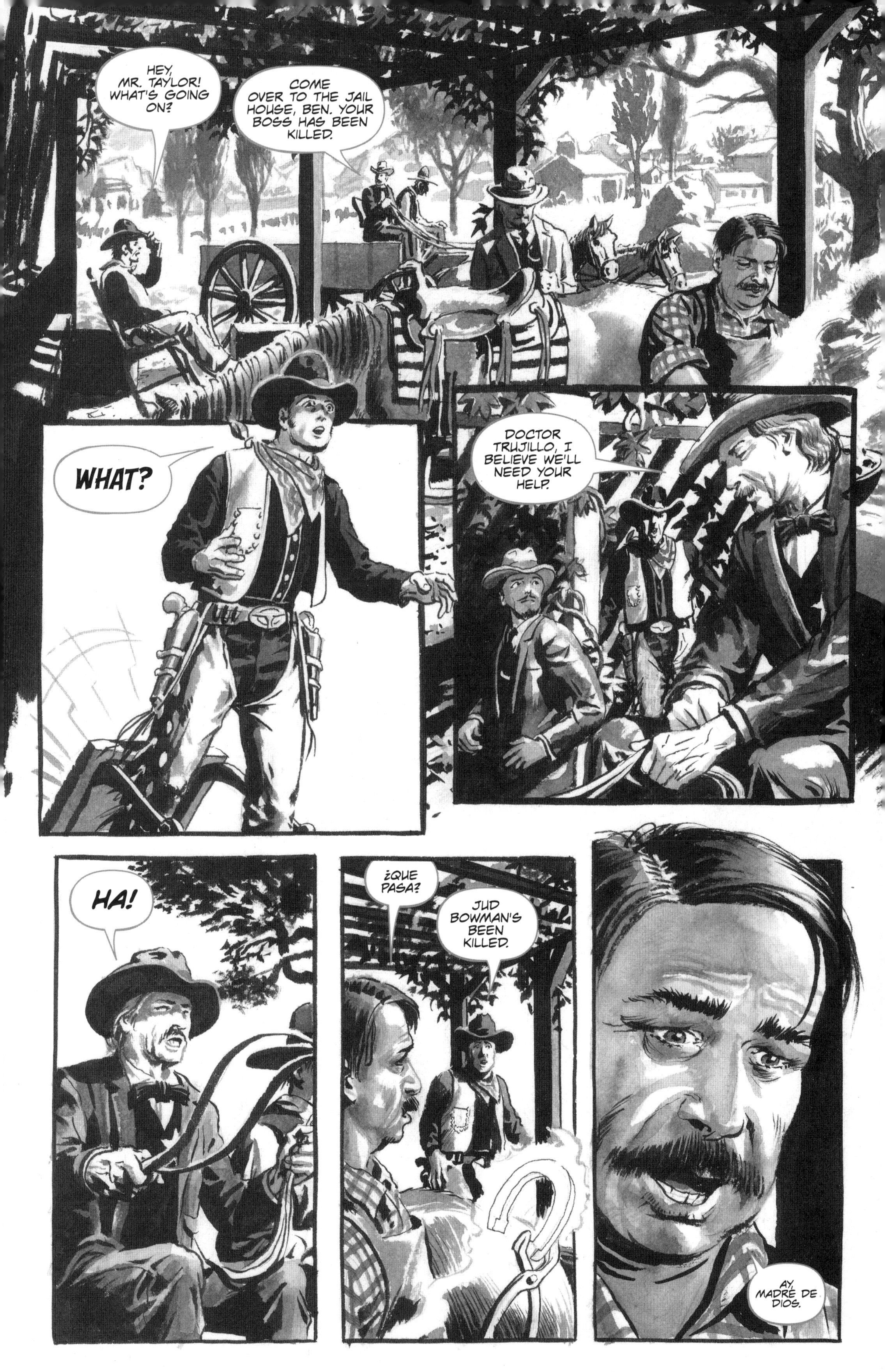
HEY, MR. TAYLOR! WHAT'S GOING ON?
COME OVER TO THE JAIL HOUSE, BEN. YOUR BOSS HAS BEEN KILLED.
WHAT?
DOCTOR TRUJILLO, I BELIEVE WE'LL NEED YOUR HELP.
HA!
¿QUE PASA?
JUD BOWMAN'S BEEN KILLED.
AY, MADRE DE DIOS.

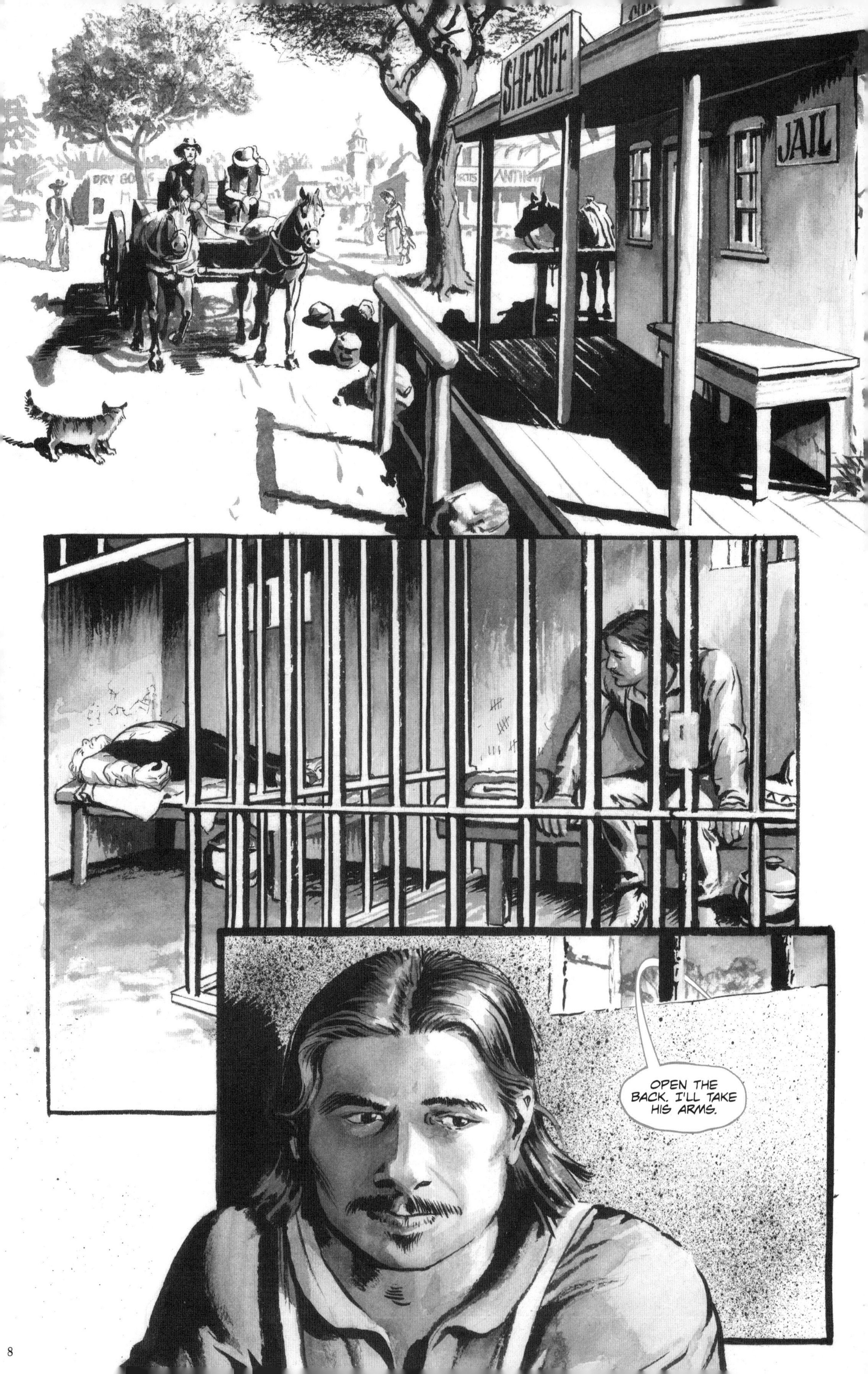
SHERIFF
JAIL
DRY GO
OPEN THE BACK. I'LL TAKE HIS ARMS.

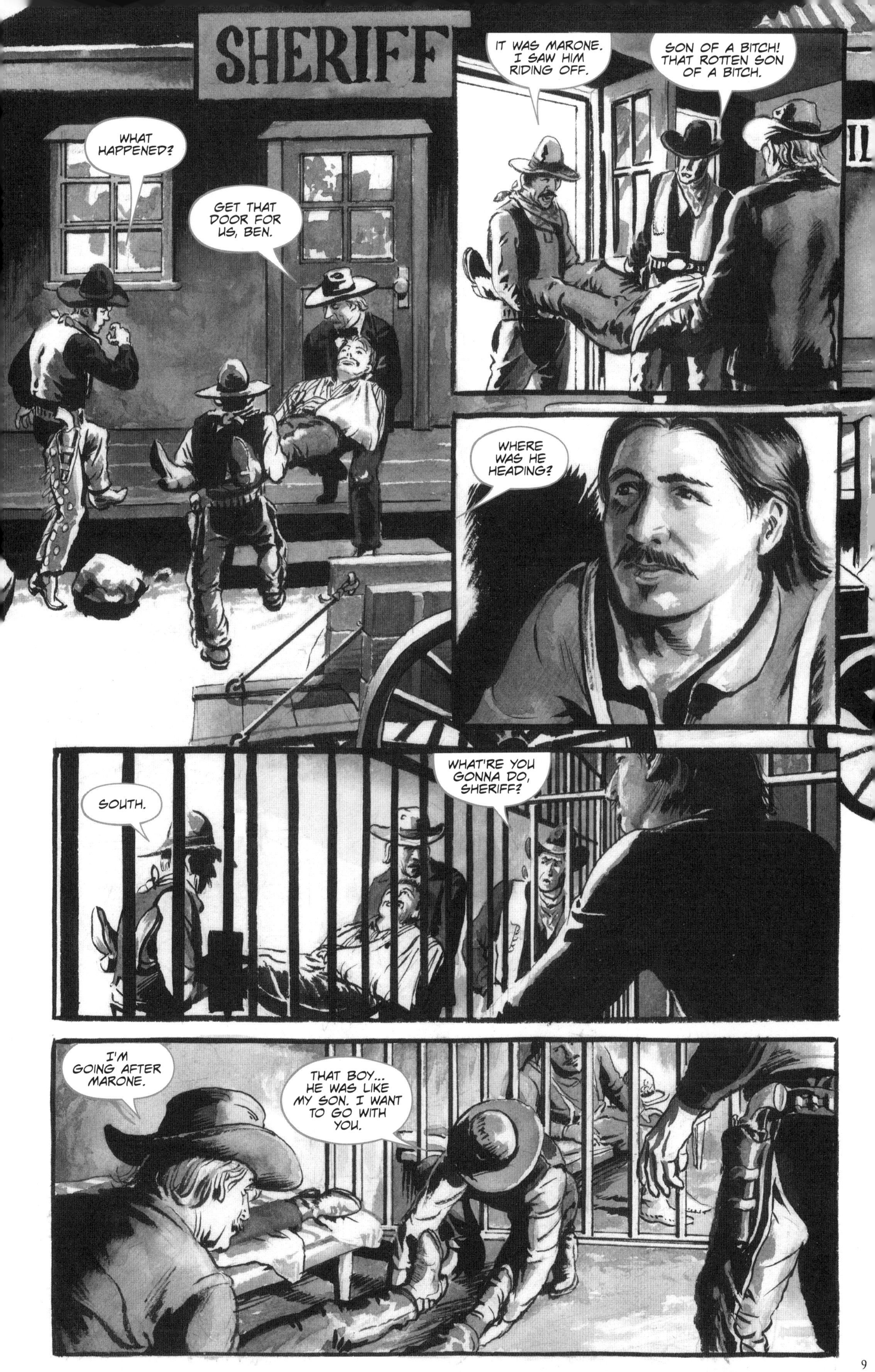
SHERIFF
WHAT HAPPENED?
GET THAT DOOR FOR US, BEN.
IT WAS MARONE. I SAW HIM RIDING OFF.
SON OF A BITCH! THAT ROTTEN SON OF A BITCH.
WHERE WAS HE HEADING?
SOUTH.
WHAT'RE YOU GONNA DO, SHERIFF?
I'M GOING AFTER MARONE.
THAT BOY... HE WAS LIKE MY SON. I WANT TO GO WITH YOU.

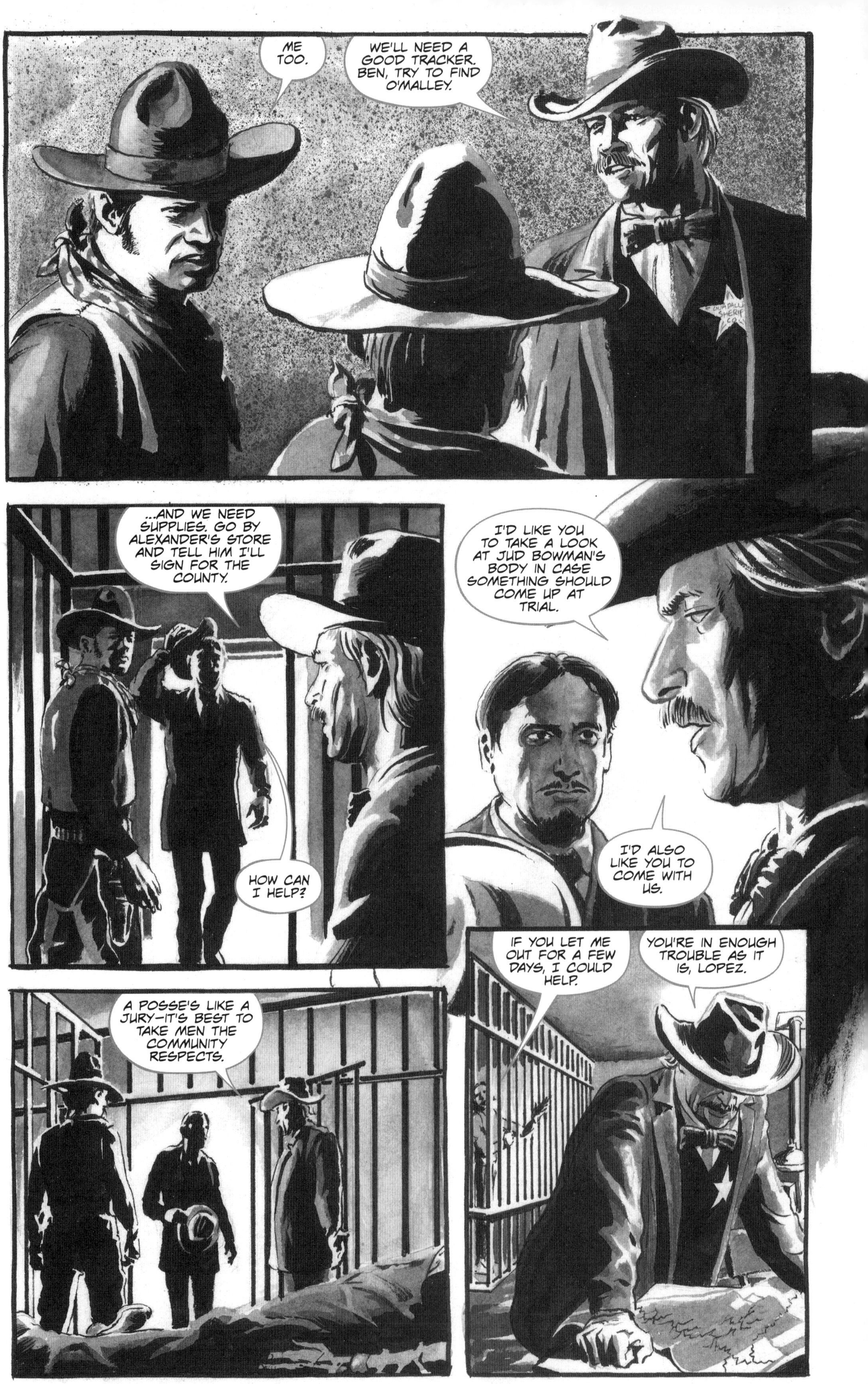
ME TOO.
WE'LL NEED A GOOD TRACKER. BEN, TRY TO FIND O'MALLEY.
...AND WE NEED SUPPLIES. GO BY ALEXANDER'S STORE AND TELL HIM I'LL SIGN FOR THE COUNTY.
HOW CAN I HELP?
I'D LIKE YOU TO TAKE A LOOK AT JUD BOWMAN'S BODY IN CASE SOMETHING SHOULD COME UP AT TRIAL.
I'D ALSO LIKE YOU TO COME WITH US.
A POSSE'S LIKE A JURY—IT'S BEST TO TAKE MEN THE COMMUNITY RESPECTS.
IF YOU LET ME OUT FOR A FEW DAYS, I COULD HELP.
YOU'RE IN ENOUGH TROUBLE AS IT IS, LOPEZ.

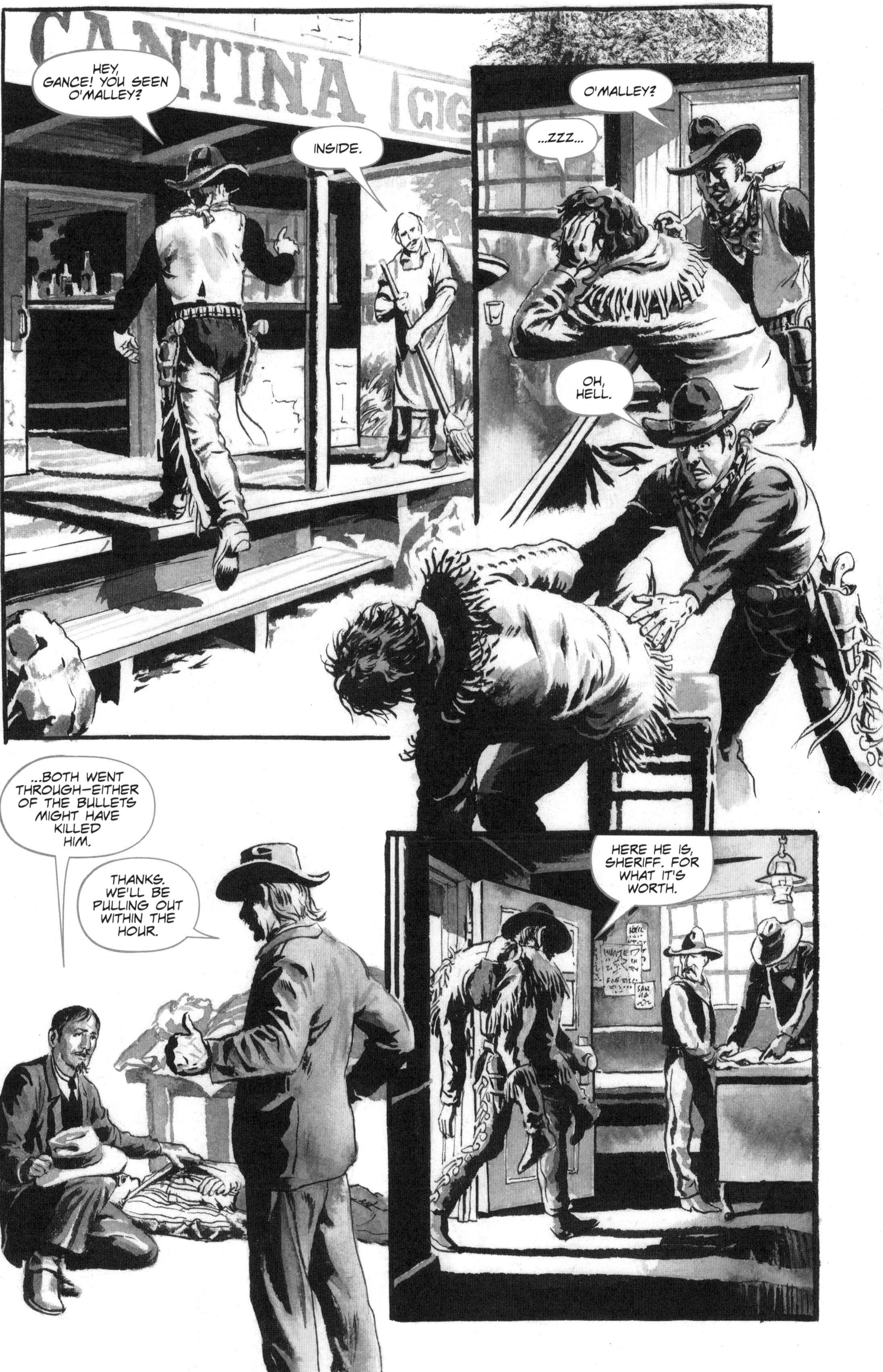
CANTINA
CIG
HEY, GANCE! YOU SEEN O'MALLEY?
INSIDE.
O'MALLEY?
...ZZZ...
OH, HELL.
...BOTH WENT THROUGH—EITHER OF THE BULLETS MIGHT HAVE KILLED HIM.
THANKS. WE'LL BE PULLING OUT WITHIN THE HOUR.
HERE HE IS, SHERIFF. FOR WHAT IT'S WORTH.

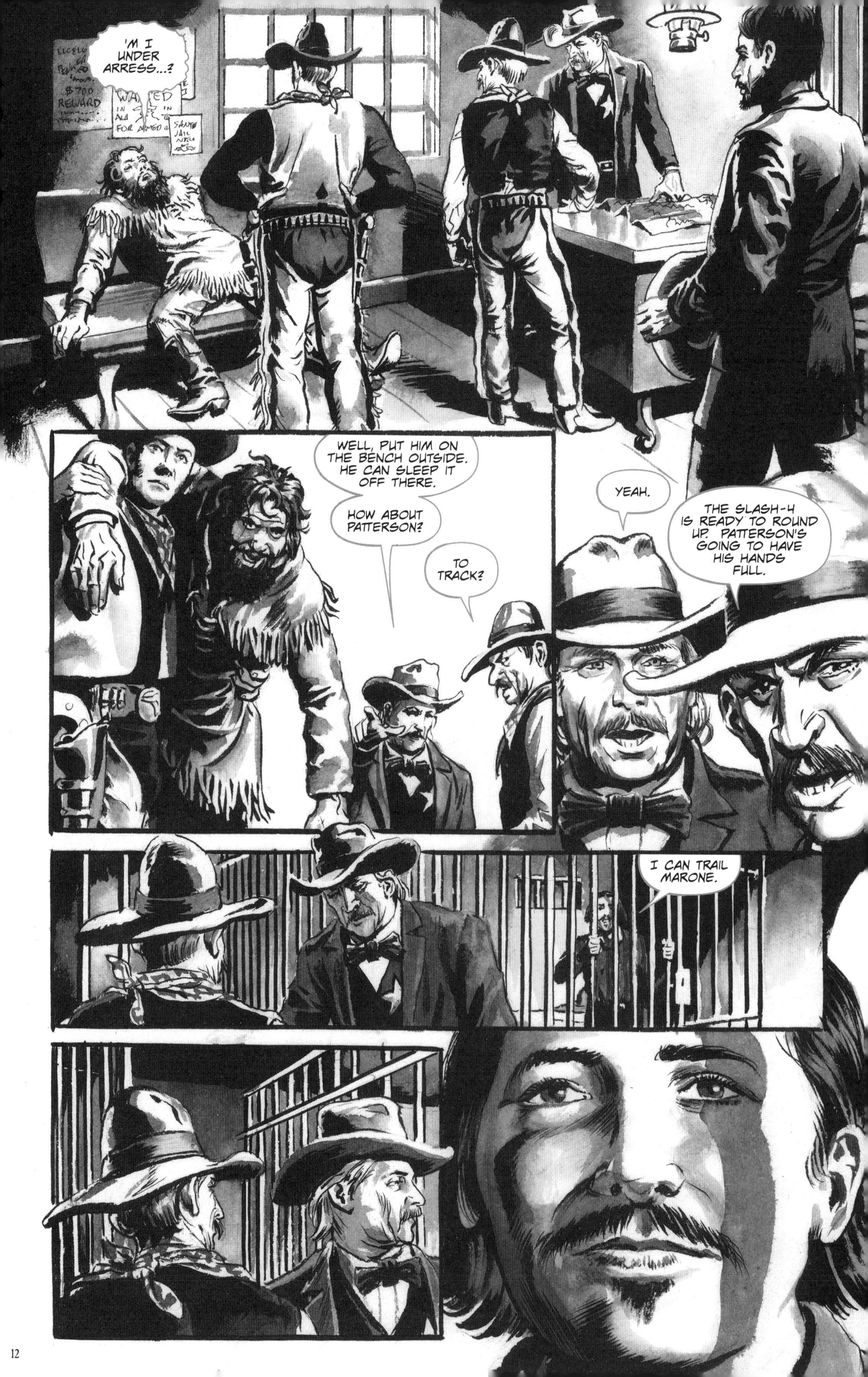
'M I UNDER ARRESS...?
WELL, PUT HIM ON THE BENCH OUTSIDE. HE CAN SLEEP IT OFF THERE.
HOW ABOUT PATTERSON?
TO TRACK?
YEAH.
THE SLASH-4 IS READY TO ROUND UP. PATTERSON'S GOING TO HAVE HIS HANDS FULL.
I CAN TRAIL MARONE.

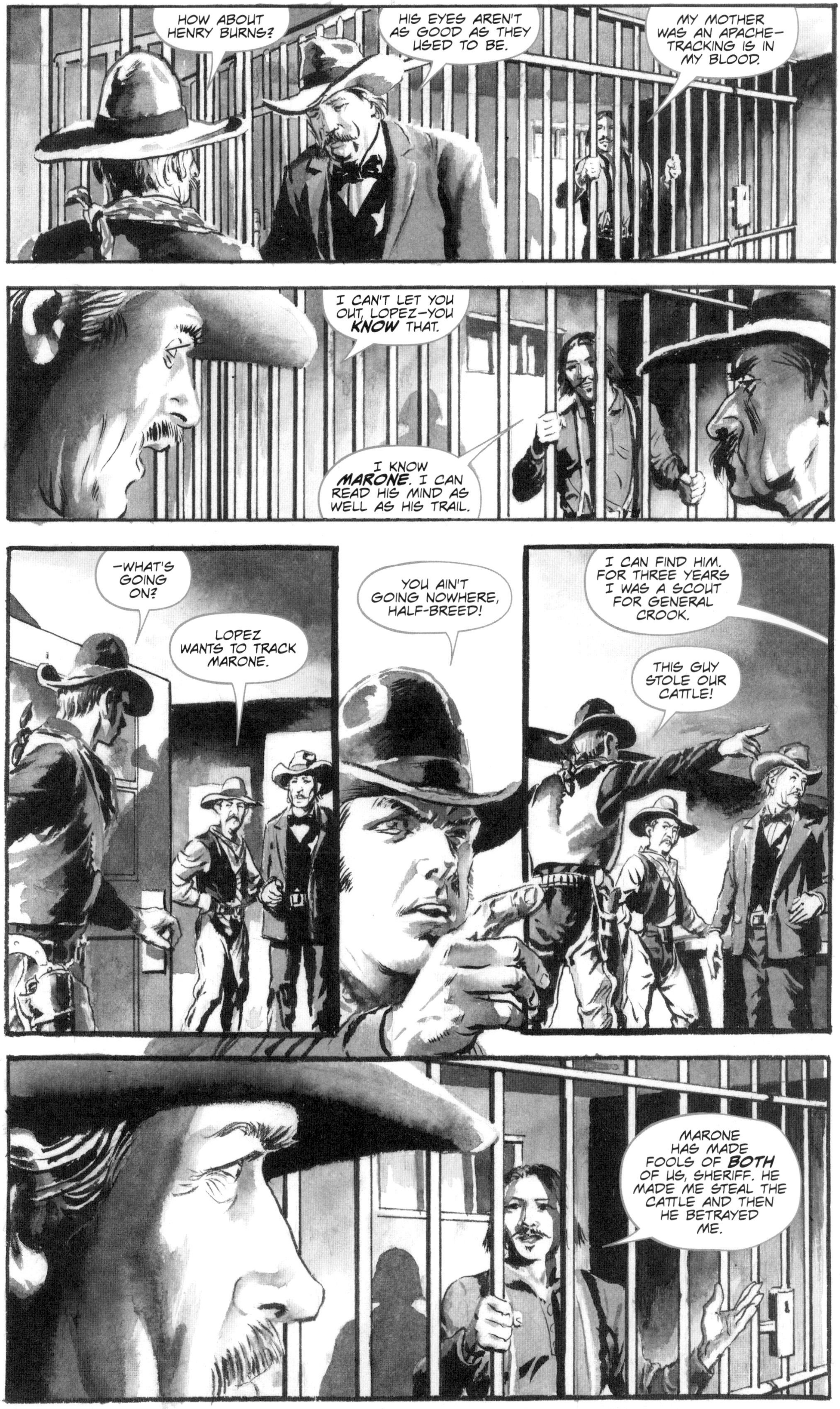
HOW ABOUT HENRY BURNS?
HIS EYES AREN'T AS GOOD AS THEY USED TO BE.
MY MOTHER WAS AN APACHE-TRACKING IS IN MY BLOOD.
I CAN'T LET YOU OUT, LOPEZ—YOU KNOW THAT.
I KNOW MARONE. I CAN READ HIS MIND AS WELL AS HIS TRAIL.
—WHAT'S GOING ON?
LOPEZ WANTS TO TRACK MARONE.
YOU AIN'T GOING NOWHERE, HALF-BREED!
I CAN FIND HIM. FOR THREE YEARS I WAS A SCOUT FOR GENERAL CROOK.
THIS GUY STOLE OUR CATTLE!
MARONE HAS MADE FOOLS OF BOTH OF US, SHERIFF. HE MADE ME STEAL THE CATTLE AND THEN HE BETRAYED ME.

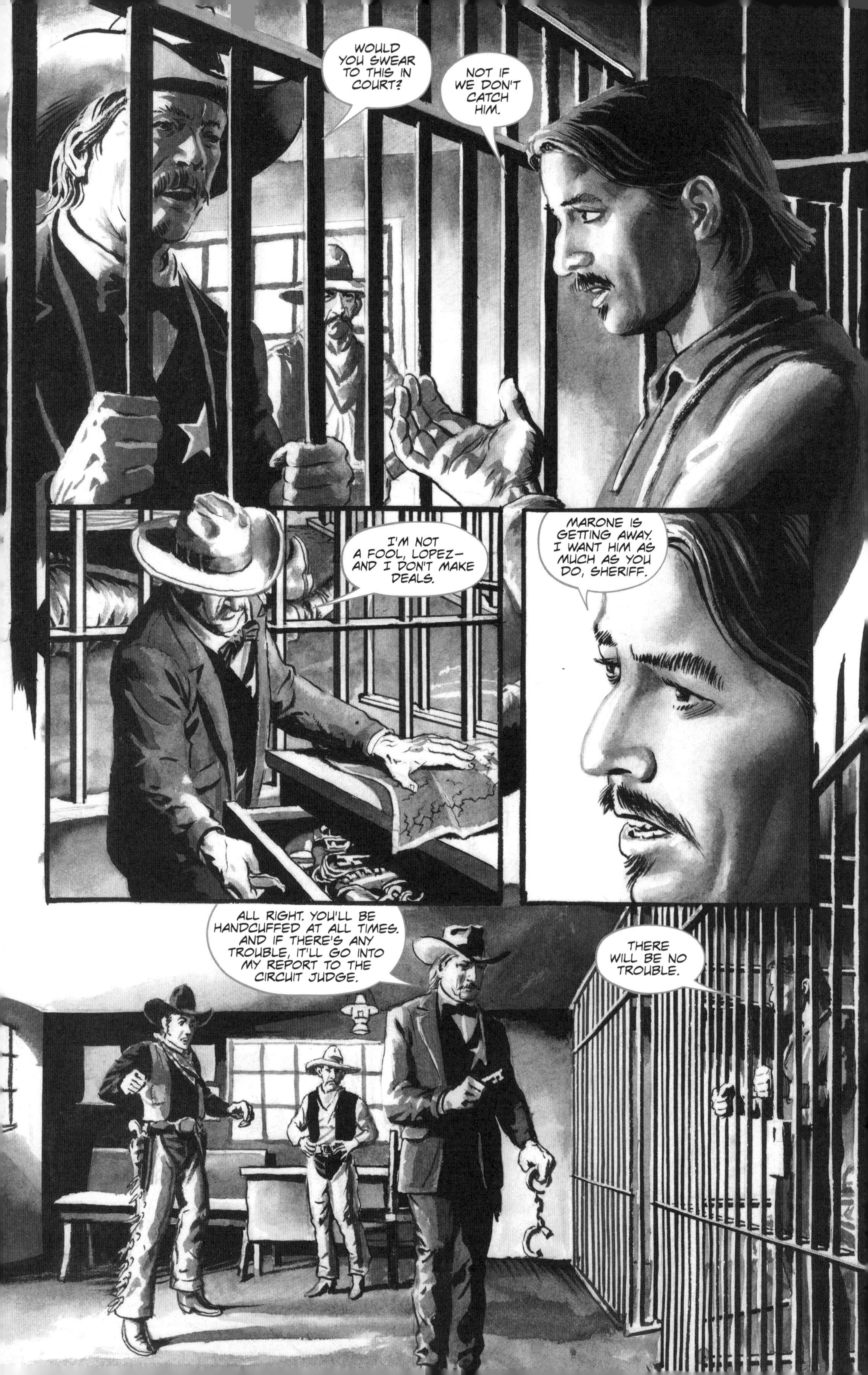
WOULD YOU SWEAR TO THIS IN COURT?
NOT IF WE DON'T CATCH HIM.
I'M NOT A FOOL, LOPEZ— AND I DON'T MAKE DEALS.
MARONE IS GETTING AWAY. I WANT HIM AS MUCH AS YOU DO, SHERIFF.
ALL RIGHT. YOU'LL BE HANDCUFFED AT ALL TIMES. AND IF THERE'S ANY TROUBLE, IT'LL GO INTO MY REPORT TO THE CIRCUIT JUDGE.
THERE WILL BE NO TROUBLE.

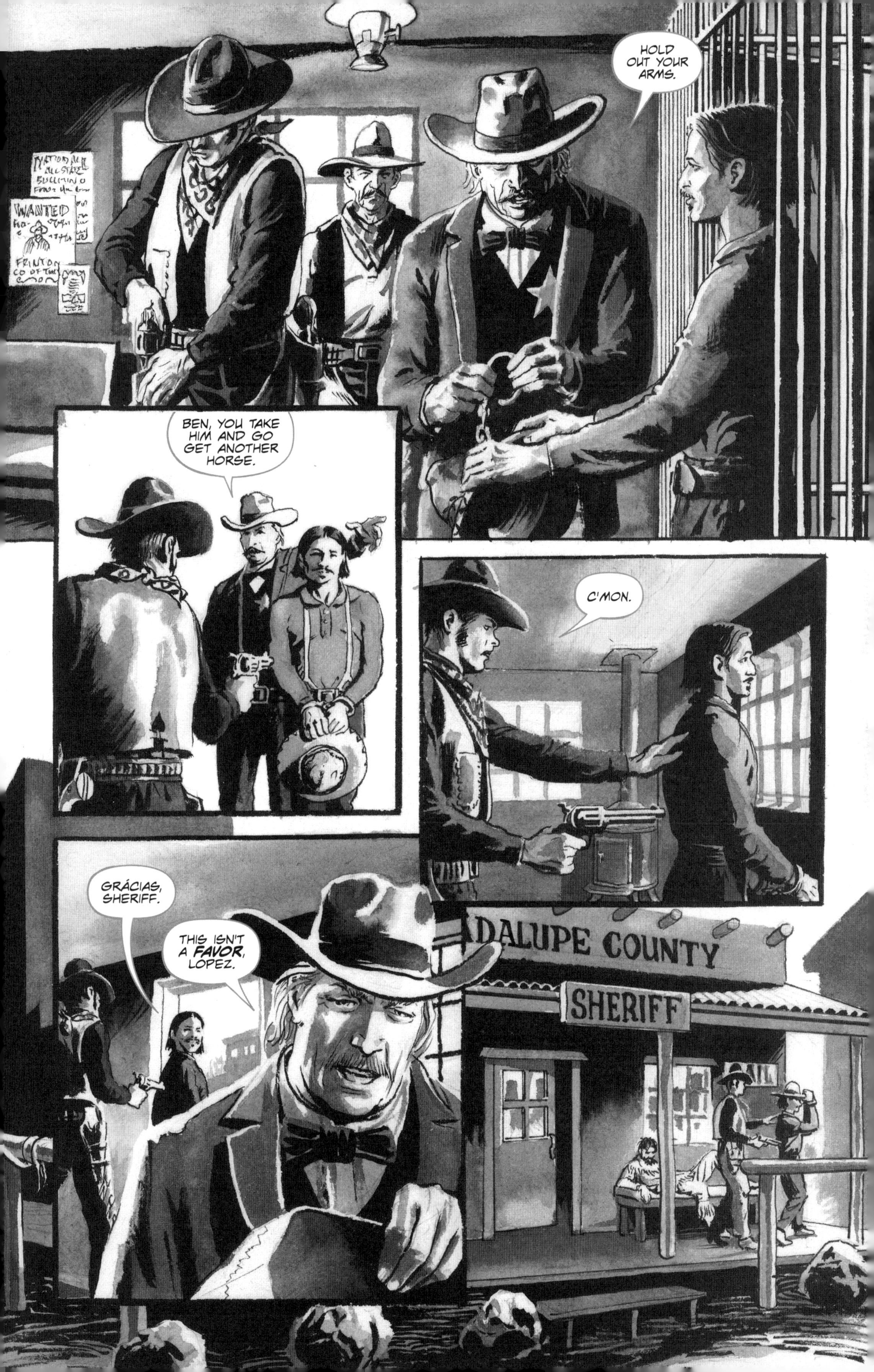
HOLD OUT YOUR ARMS.
WANTED
BEN, YOU TAKE HIM AND GO GET ANOTHER HORSE.
C'MON.
GRÁCIAS, SHERIFF.
THIS ISN'T A *FAVOR*, LOPEZ.
ADALUPE COUNTY
SHERIFF

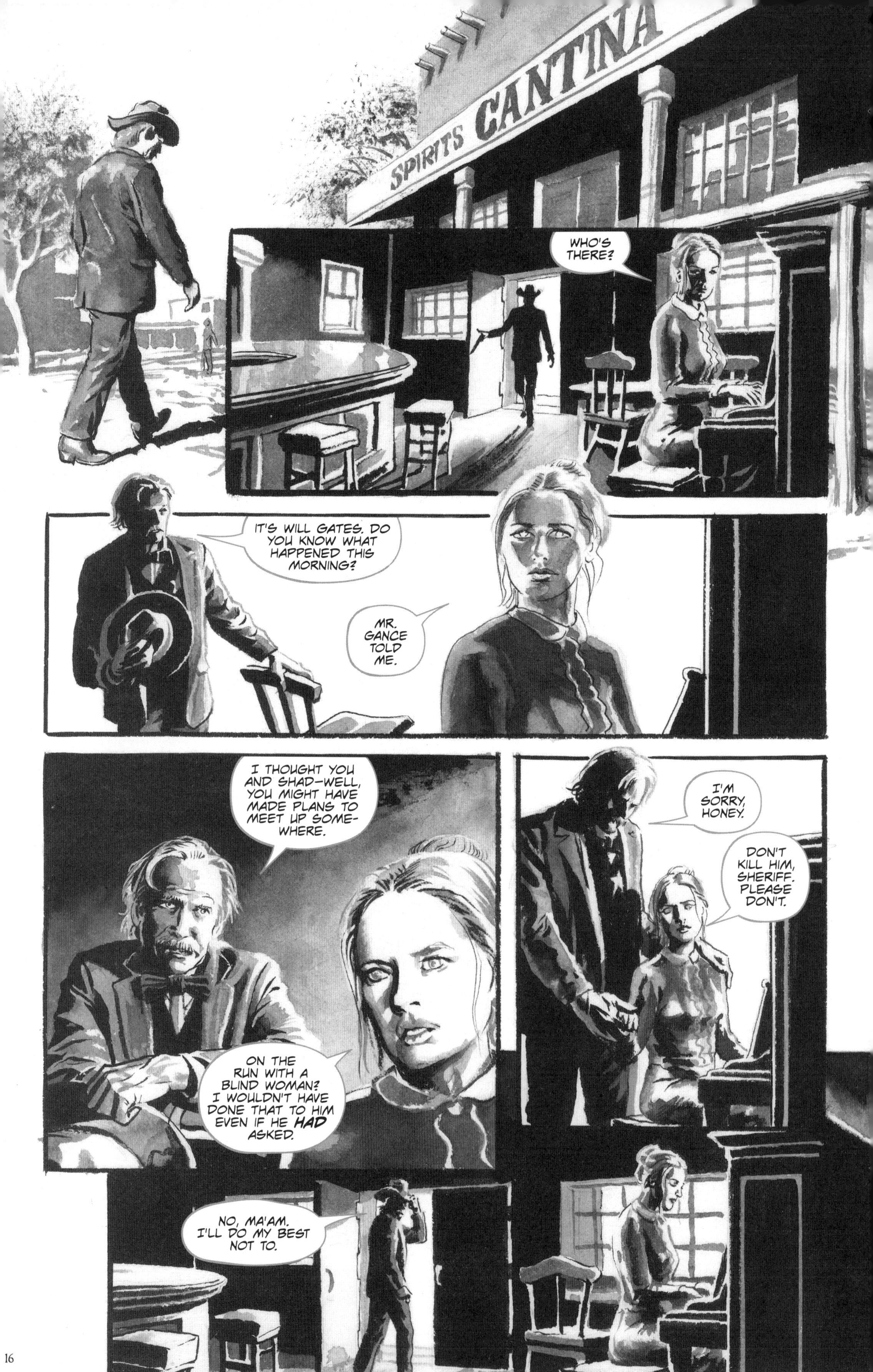
SPIRITS CANTINA
WHO'S THERE?
IT'S WILL GATES. DO YOU KNOW WHAT HAPPENED THIS MORNING?
MR. GANCE TOLD ME.
I THOUGHT YOU AND SHAD--WELL, YOU MIGHT HAVE MADE PLANS TO MEET UP SOME-WHERE.
ON THE RUN WITH A BLIND WOMAN? I WOULDN'T HAVE DONE THAT TO HIM EVEN IF HE *HAD* ASKED.
I'M SORRY, HONEY.
DON'T KILL HIM, SHERIFF. PLEASE DON'T.
NO, MA'AM. I'LL DO MY BEST NOT TO.

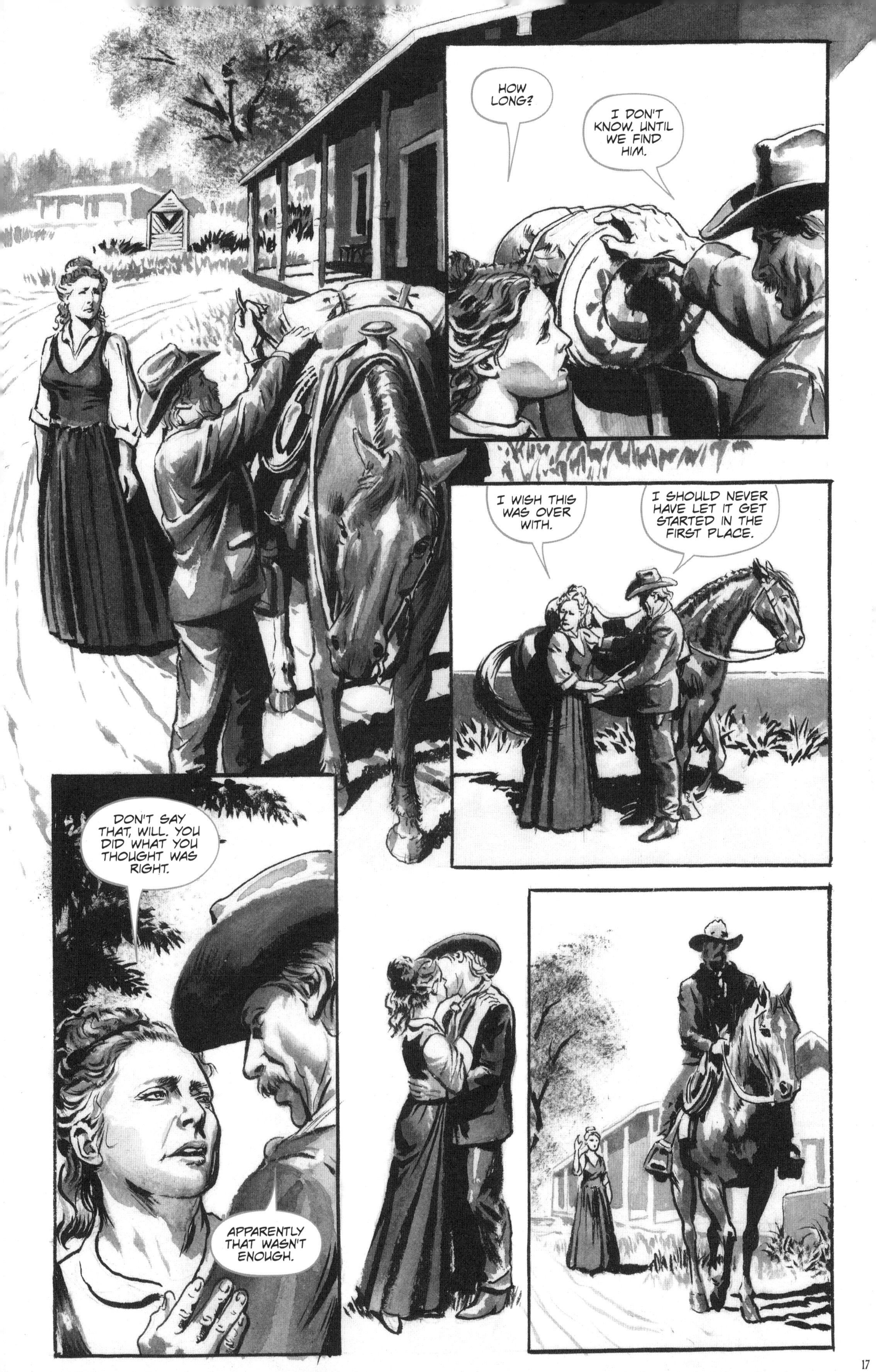
HOW LONG?
I DON'T KNOW. UNTIL WE FIND HIM.
I WISH THIS WAS OVER WITH.
I SHOULD NEVER HAVE LET IT GET STARTED IN THE FIRST PLACE.
DON'T SAY THAT, WILL. YOU DID WHAT YOU THOUGHT WAS RIGHT.
APPARENTLY THAT WASN'T ENOUGH.

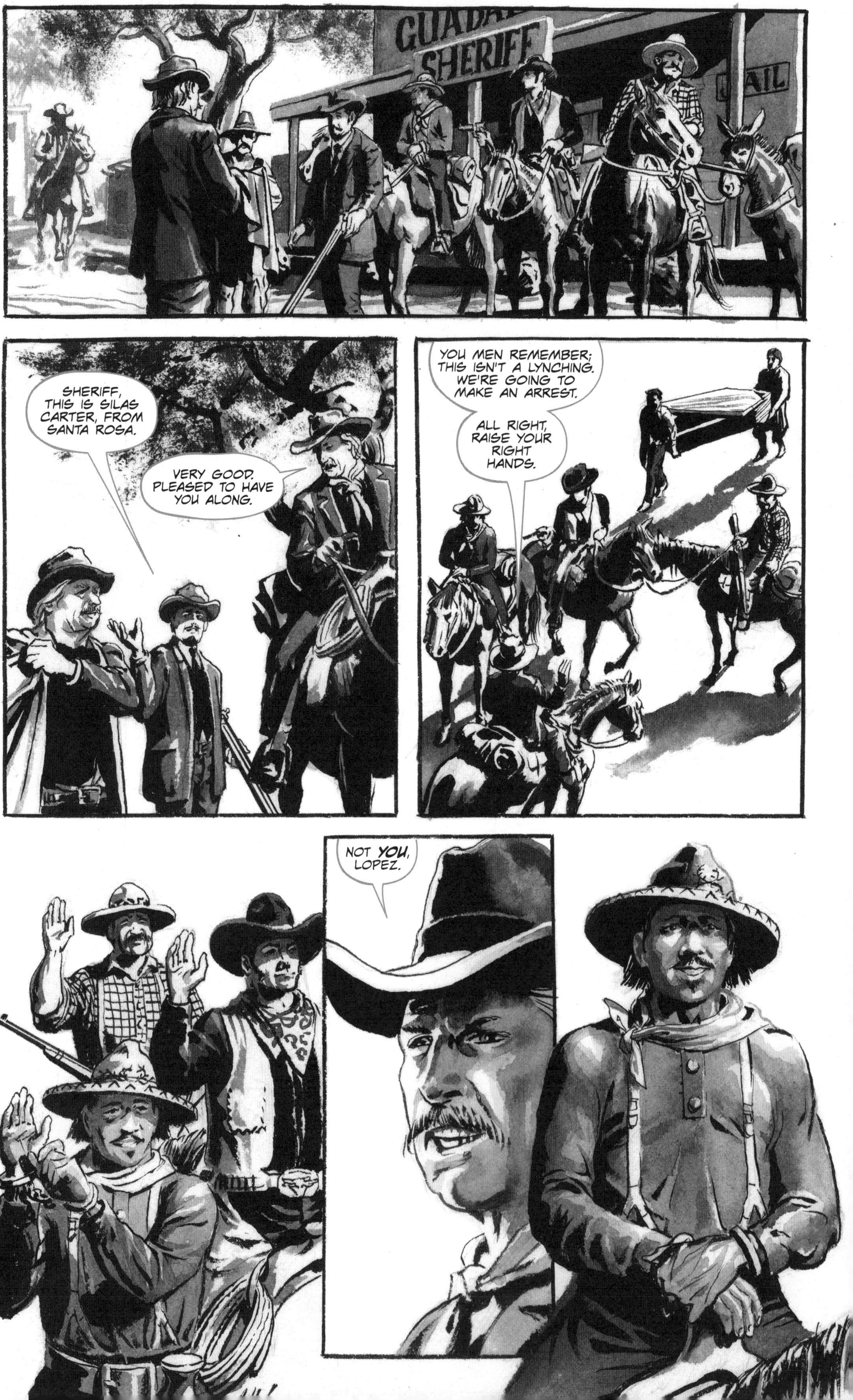
SHERIFF
SHERIFF, THIS IS SILAS CARTER, FROM SANTA ROSA.
VERY GOOD. PLEASED TO HAVE YOU ALONG.
YOU MEN REMEMBER; THIS ISN'T A LYNCHING. WE'RE GOING TO MAKE AN ARREST.
ALL RIGHT, RAISE YOUR RIGHT HANDS.
NOT ***YOU***, LOPEZ.

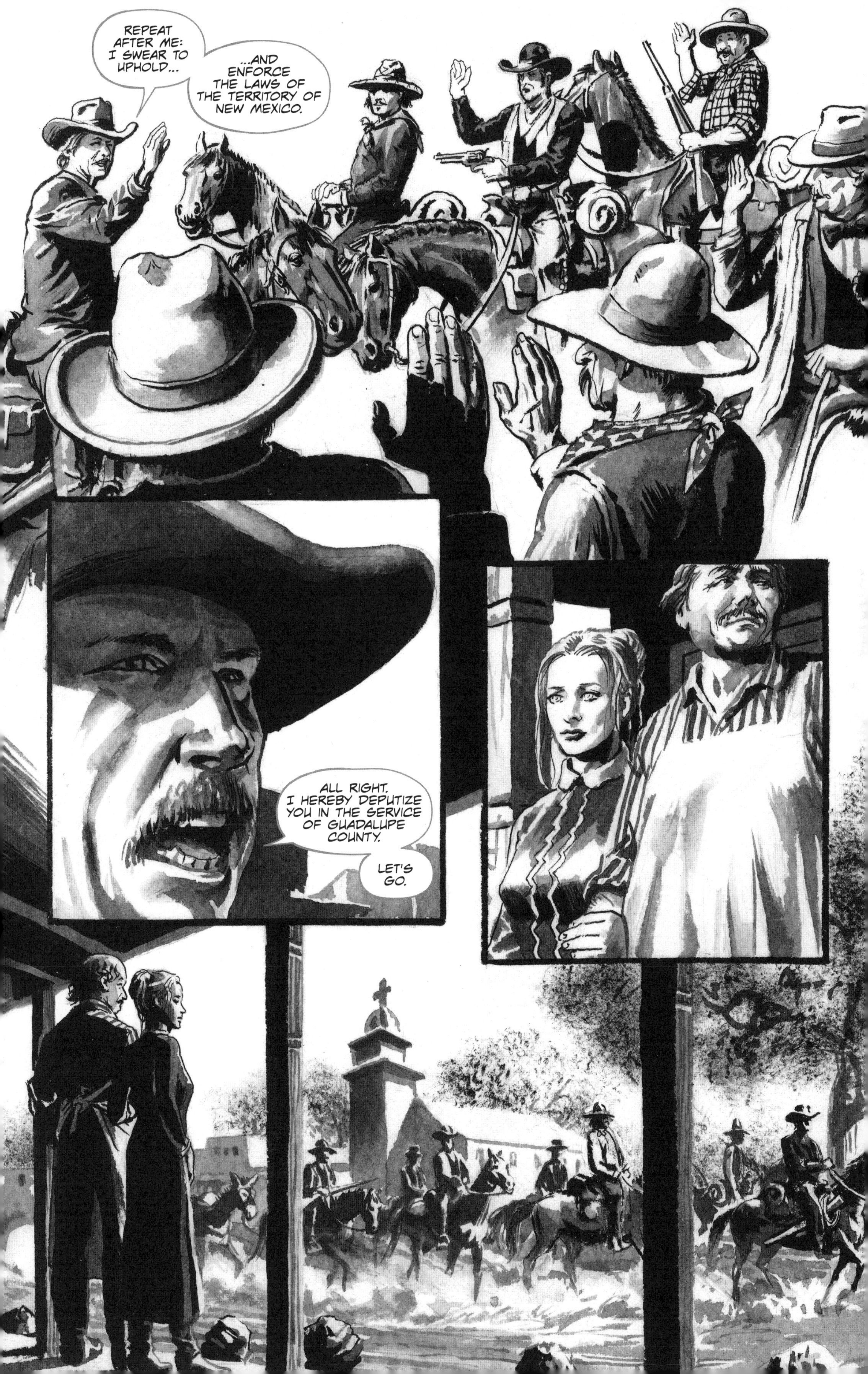
REPEAT AFTER ME: I SWEAR TO UPHOLD...
...AND ENFORCE THE LAWS OF THE TERRITORY OF NEW MEXICO.
ALL RIGHT. I HEREBY DEPUTIZE YOU IN THE SERVICE OF GUADALUPE COUNTY.
LET'S GO.

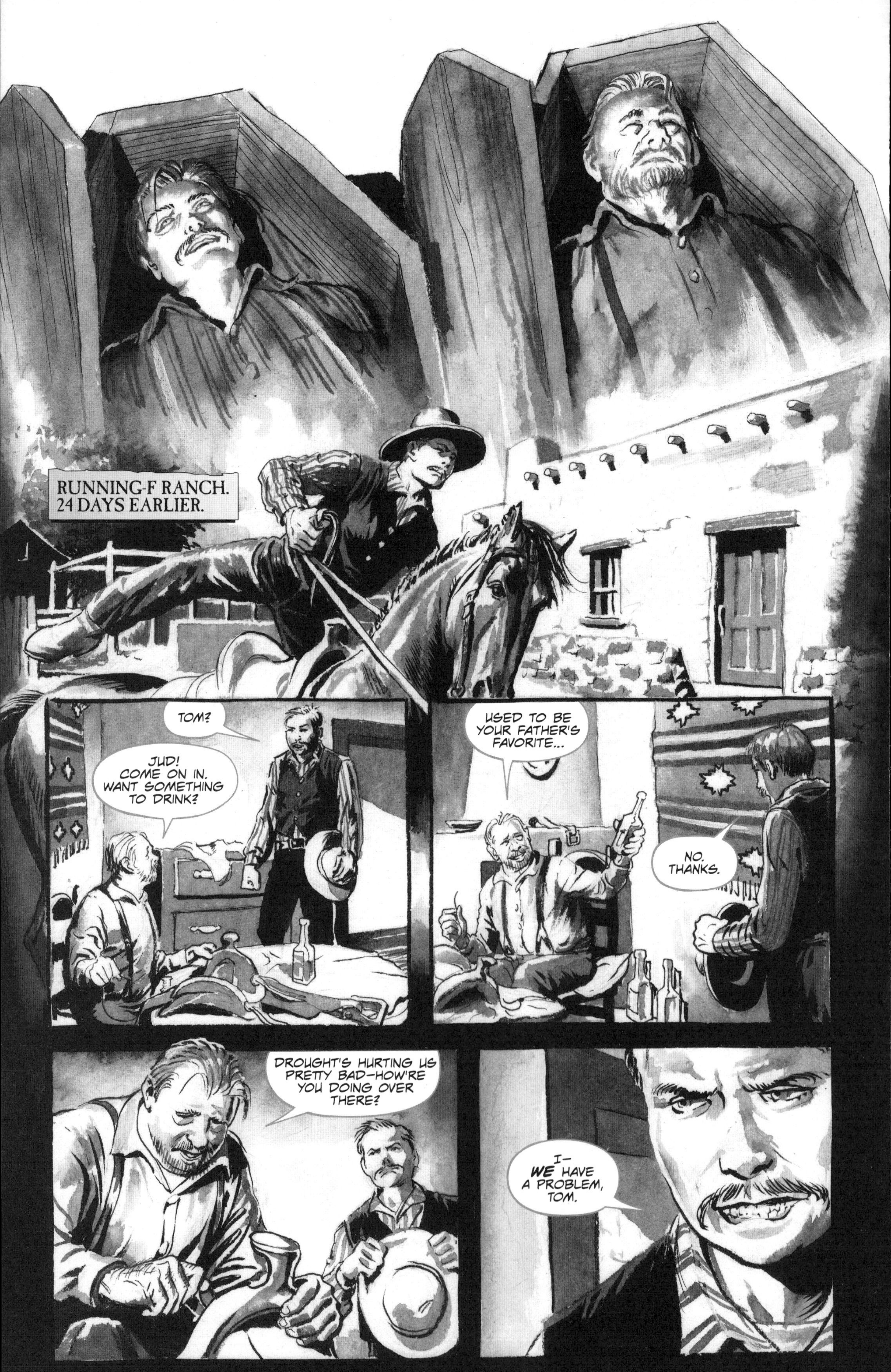
RUNNING-F RANCH.
24 DAYS EARLIER.
TOM?
JUD! COME ON IN. WANT SOMETHING TO DRINK?
USED TO BE YOUR FATHER'S FAVORITE...
NO. THANKS.
DROUGHT'S HURTING US PRETTY BAD--HOW'RE YOU DOING OVER THERE?
I-- WE HAVE A PROBLEM, TOM.

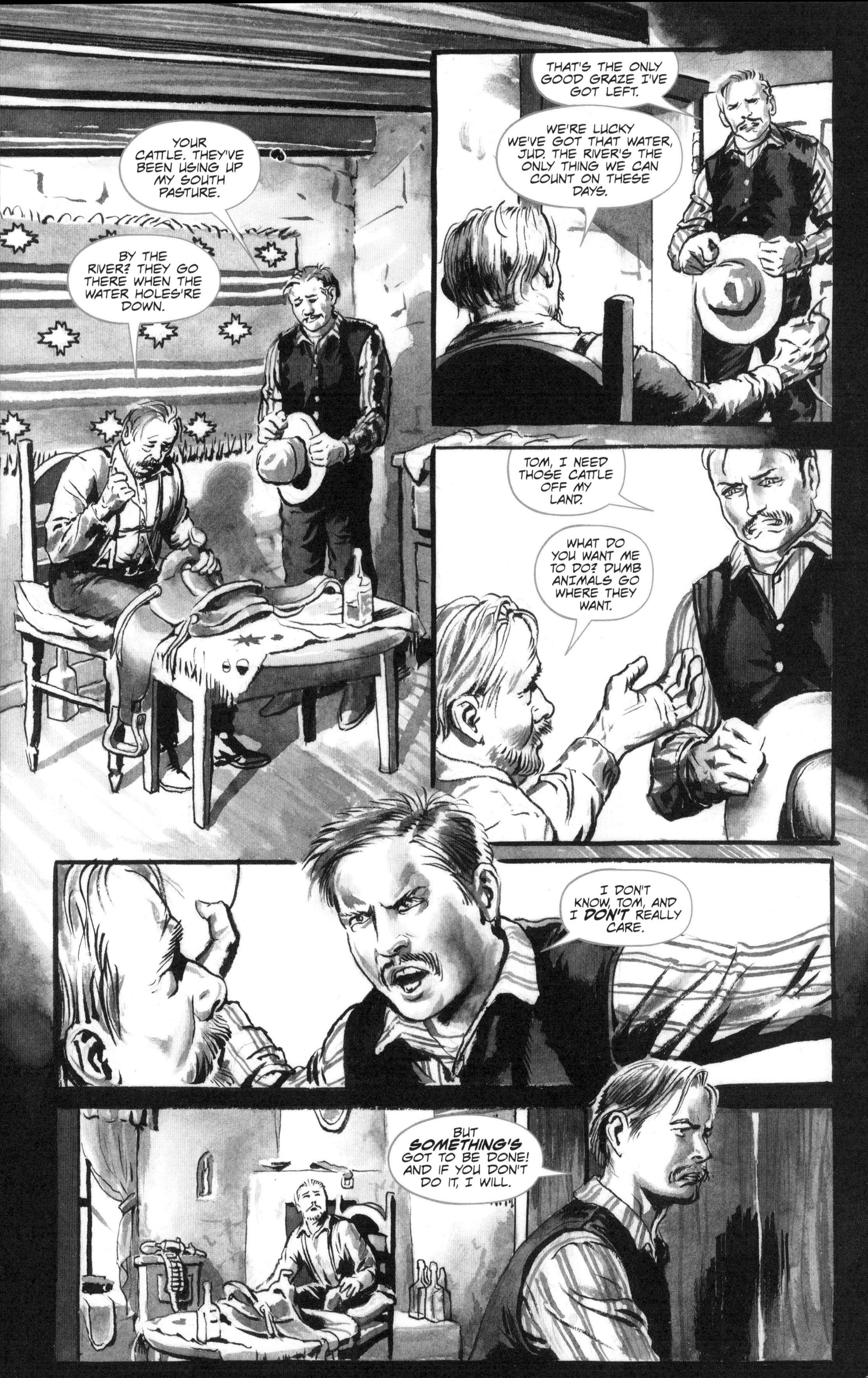
YOUR CATTLE. THEY'VE BEEN USING UP MY SOUTH PASTURE.
BY THE RIVER? THEY GO THERE WHEN THE WATER HOLES'RE DOWN.
THAT'S THE ONLY GOOD GRAZE I'VE GOT LEFT.
WE'RE LUCKY WE'VE GOT THAT WATER, JUD. THE RIVER'S THE ONLY THING WE CAN COUNT ON THESE DAYS.
TOM, I NEED THOSE CATTLE OFF MY LAND.
WHAT DO YOU WANT ME TO DO? DUMB ANIMALS GO WHERE THEY WANT.
I DON'T KNOW, TOM, AND I **DON'T** REALLY CARE.
BUT **SOMETHING'S** GOT TO BE DONE! AND IF YOU DON'T DO IT, I WILL.

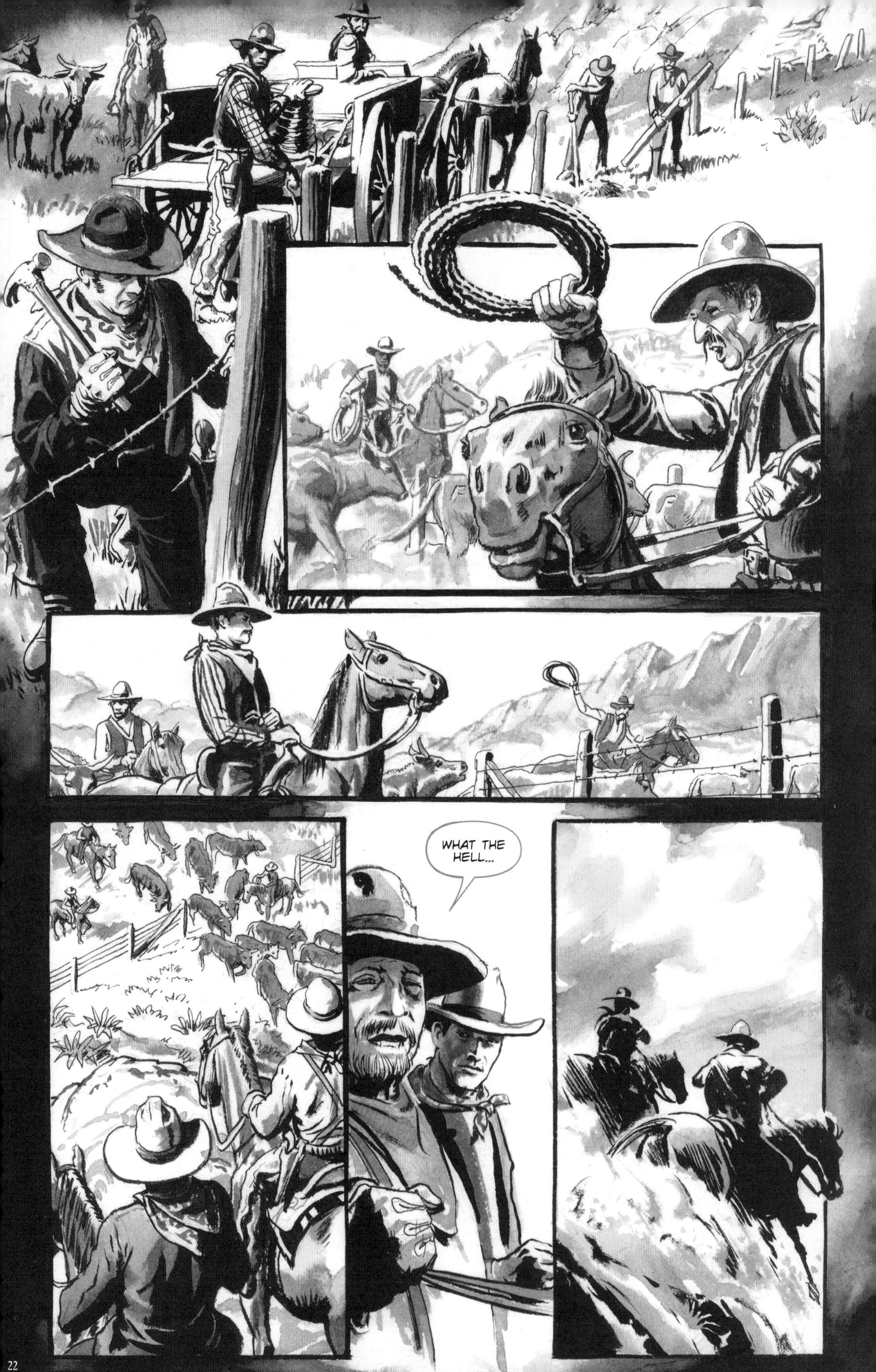
WHAT THE HELL...

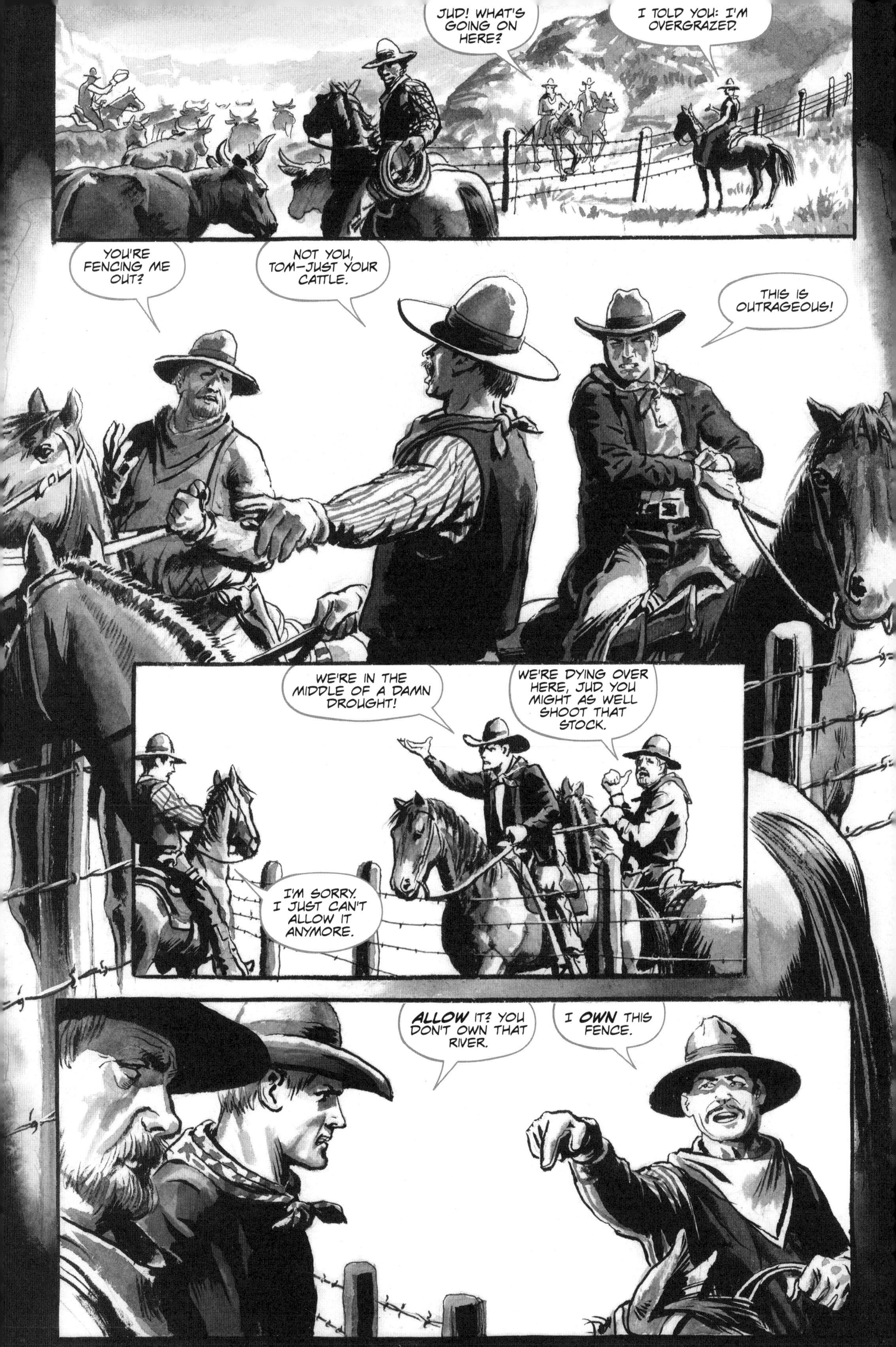
JUD! WHAT'S GOING ON HERE?
I TOLD YOU: I'M OVERGRAZED.
YOU'RE FENCING ME OUT?
NOT YOU, TOM—JUST YOUR CATTLE.
THIS IS OUTRAGEOUS!
WE'RE IN THE MIDDLE OF A DAMN DROUGHT!
WE'RE DYING OVER HERE, JUD. YOU MIGHT AS WELL SHOOT THAT STOCK.
I'M SORRY. I JUST CAN'T ALLOW IT ANYMORE.
ALLOW IT? YOU DON'T OWN THAT RIVER.
I OWN THIS FENCE.

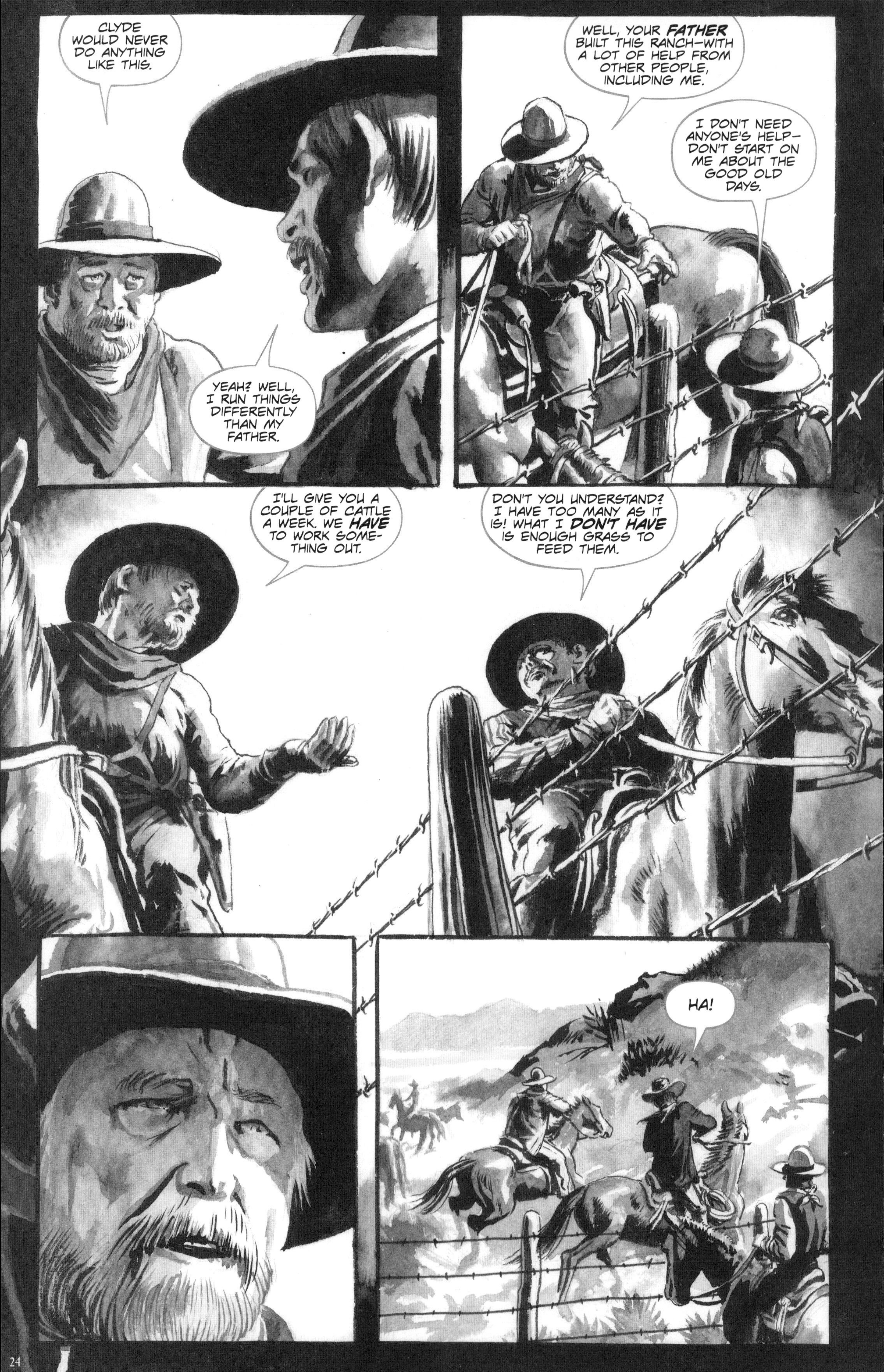
CLYDE WOULD NEVER DO ANYTHING LIKE THIS.
YEAH? WELL, I RUN THINGS DIFFERENTLY THAN MY FATHER.
WELL, YOUR FATHER BUILT THIS RANCH—WITH A LOT OF HELP FROM OTHER PEOPLE, INCLUDING ME.
I DON'T NEED ANYONE'S HELP—DON'T START ON ME ABOUT THE GOOD OLD DAYS.
I'LL GIVE YOU A COUPLE OF CATTLE A WEEK. WE HAVE TO WORK SOMETHING OUT.
DON'T YOU UNDERSTAND? I HAVE TOO MANY AS IT IS! WHAT I DON'T HAVE IS ENOUGH GRASS TO FEED THEM.
HA!

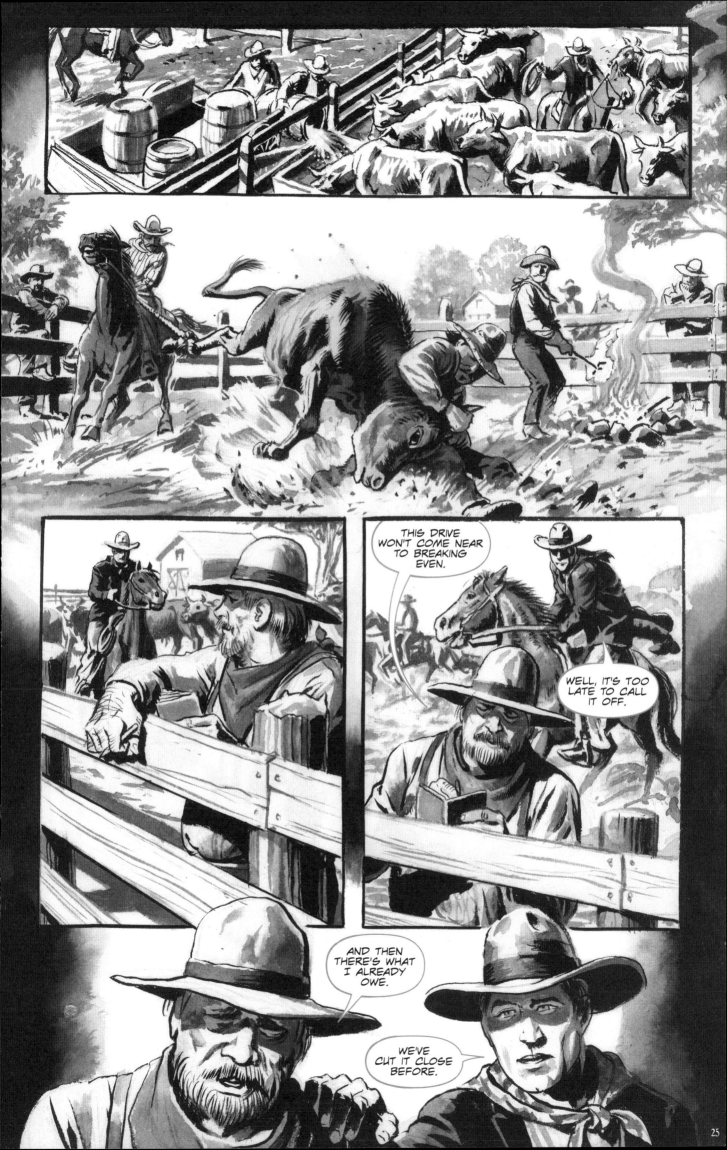

THIS DRIVE WON'T COME NEAR TO BREAKING EVEN.

WELL, IT'S TOO LATE TO CALL IT OFF.

AND THEN THERE'S WHAT I ALREADY OWE.

WE'VE CUT IT CLOSE BEFORE.

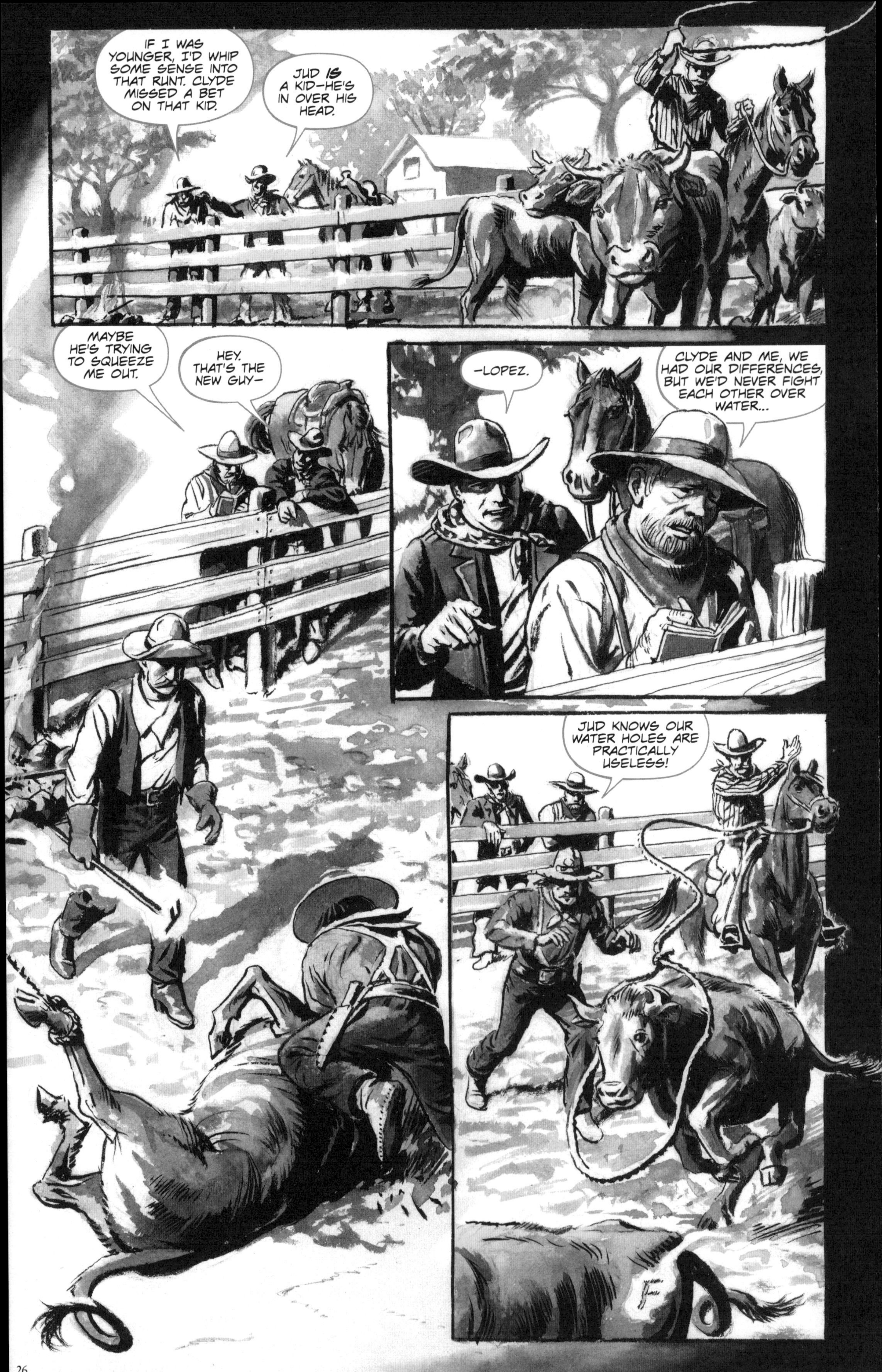
IF I WAS YOUNGER, I'D WHIP SOME SENSE INTO THAT RUNT. CLYDE MISSED A BET ON THAT KID.
JUD **IS** A KID—HE'S IN OVER HIS HEAD.
MAYBE HE'S TRYING TO SQUEEZE ME OUT.
HEY. THAT'S THE NEW GUY—
—LOPEZ.
CLYDE AND ME, WE HAD OUR DIFFERENCES, BUT WE'D NEVER FIGHT EACH OTHER OVER WATER...
JUD KNOWS OUR WATER HOLES ARE PRACTICALLY USELESS!

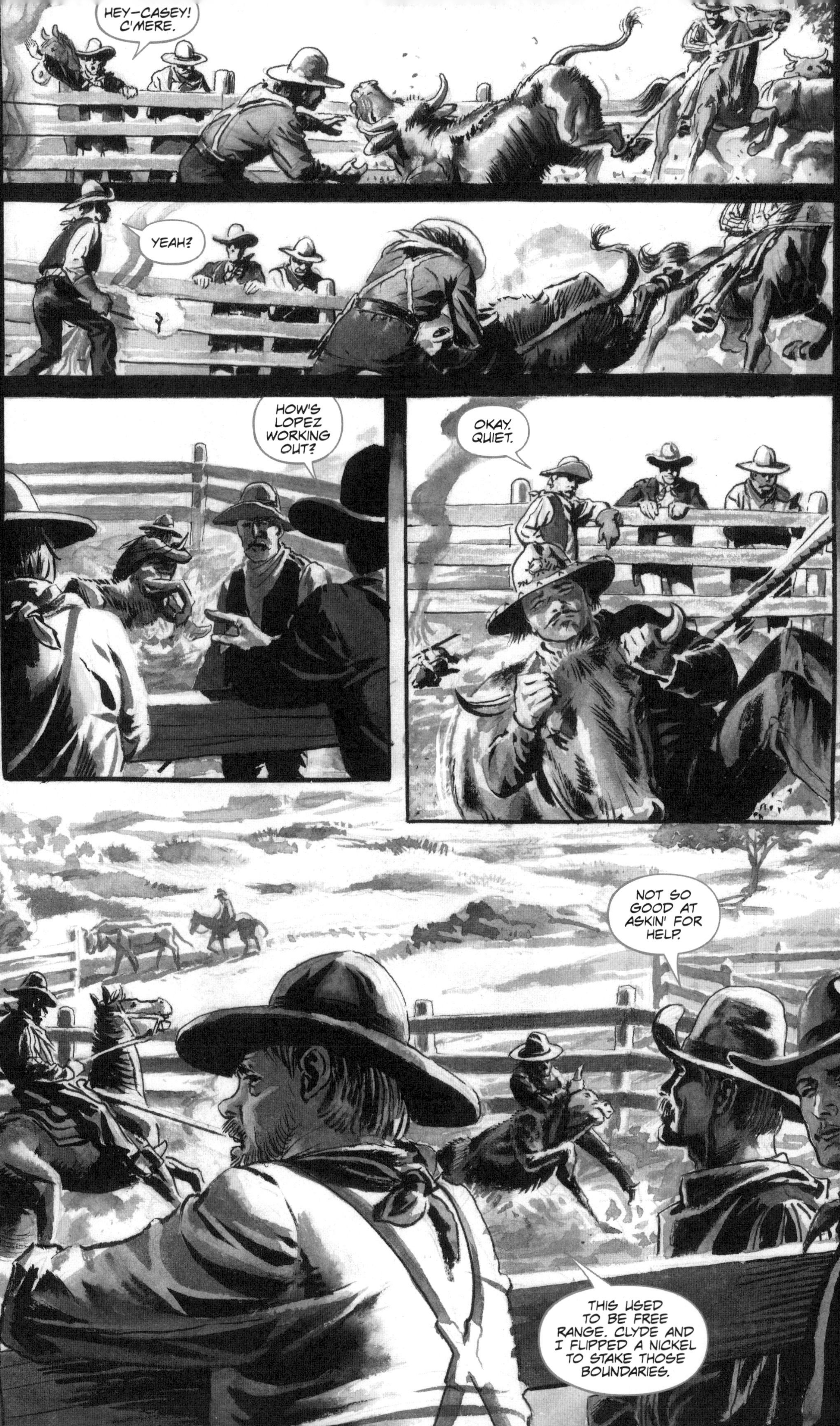
HEY–CASEY! C'MERE.
YEAH?
HOW'S LOPEZ WORKING OUT?
OKAY. QUIET.
NOT SO GOOD AT ASKIN' FOR HELP.
THIS USED TO BE FREE RANGE. CLYDE AND I FLIPPED A NICKEL TO STAKE THOSE BOUNDARIES.

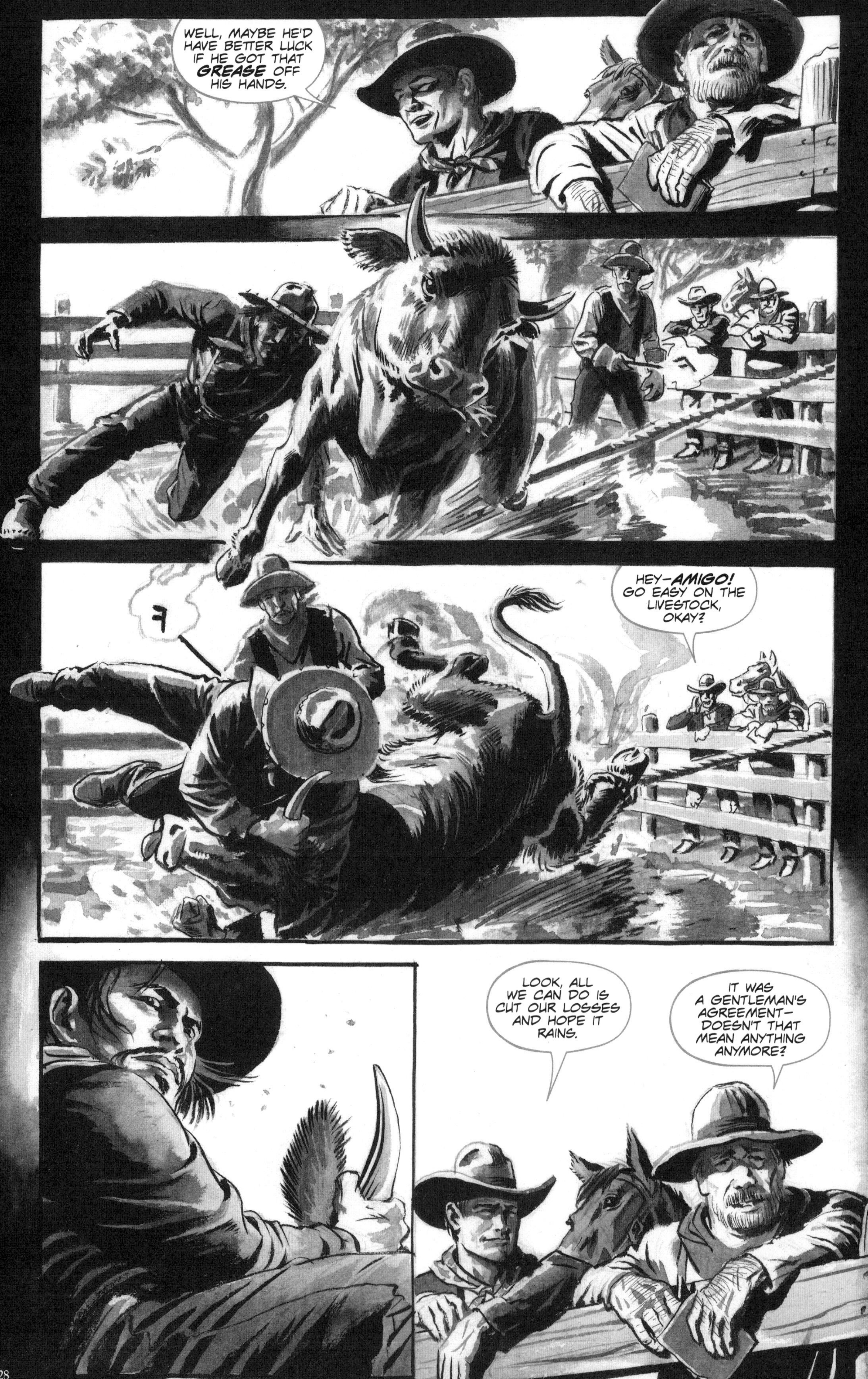
WELL, MAYBE HE'D HAVE BETTER LUCK IF HE GOT THAT GREASE OFF HIS HANDS.
HEY–AMIGO! GO EASY ON THE LIVESTOCK, OKAY?
LOOK, ALL WE CAN DO IS CUT OUR LOSSES AND HOPE IT RAINS.
IT WAS A GENTLEMAN'S AGREEMENT– DOESN'T THAT MEAN ANYTHING ANYMORE?

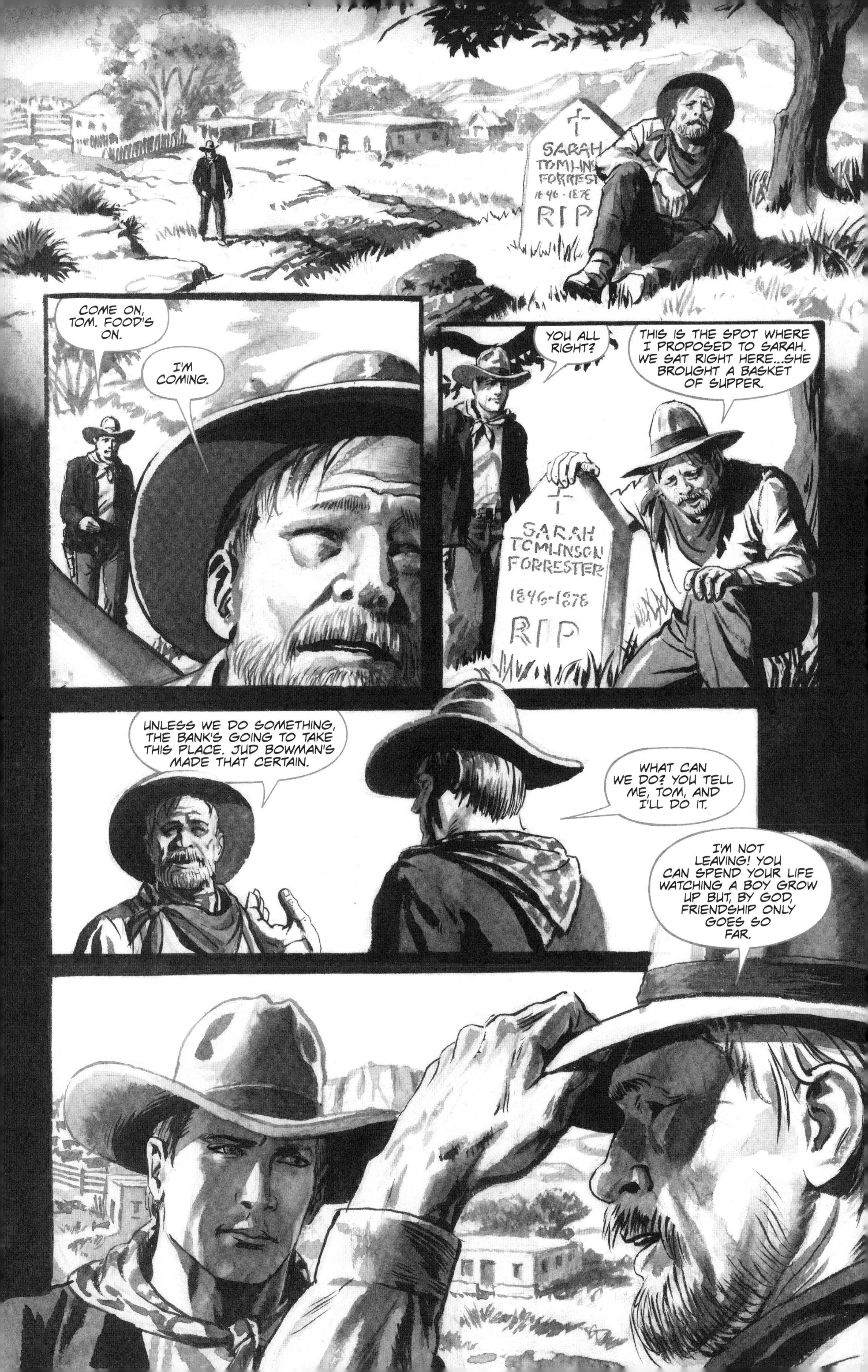
SARAH TOMLINSON FORRESTER 1846-1876 RIP
COME ON, TOM. FOOD'S ON.
I'M COMING.
YOU ALL RIGHT?
THIS IS THE SPOT WHERE I PROPOSED TO SARAH. WE SAT RIGHT HERE...SHE BROUGHT A BASKET OF SUPPER.
UNLESS WE DO SOMETHING, THE BANK'S GOING TO TAKE THIS PLACE. JUD BOWMAN'S MADE THAT CERTAIN.
WHAT CAN WE DO? YOU TELL ME, TOM, AND I'LL DO IT.
I'M NOT LEAVING! YOU CAN SPEND YOUR LIFE WATCHING A BOY GROW UP BUT, BY GOD, FRIENDSHIP ONLY GOES SO FAR.

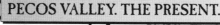

PECOS VALLEY. THE PRESENT.

WELL?

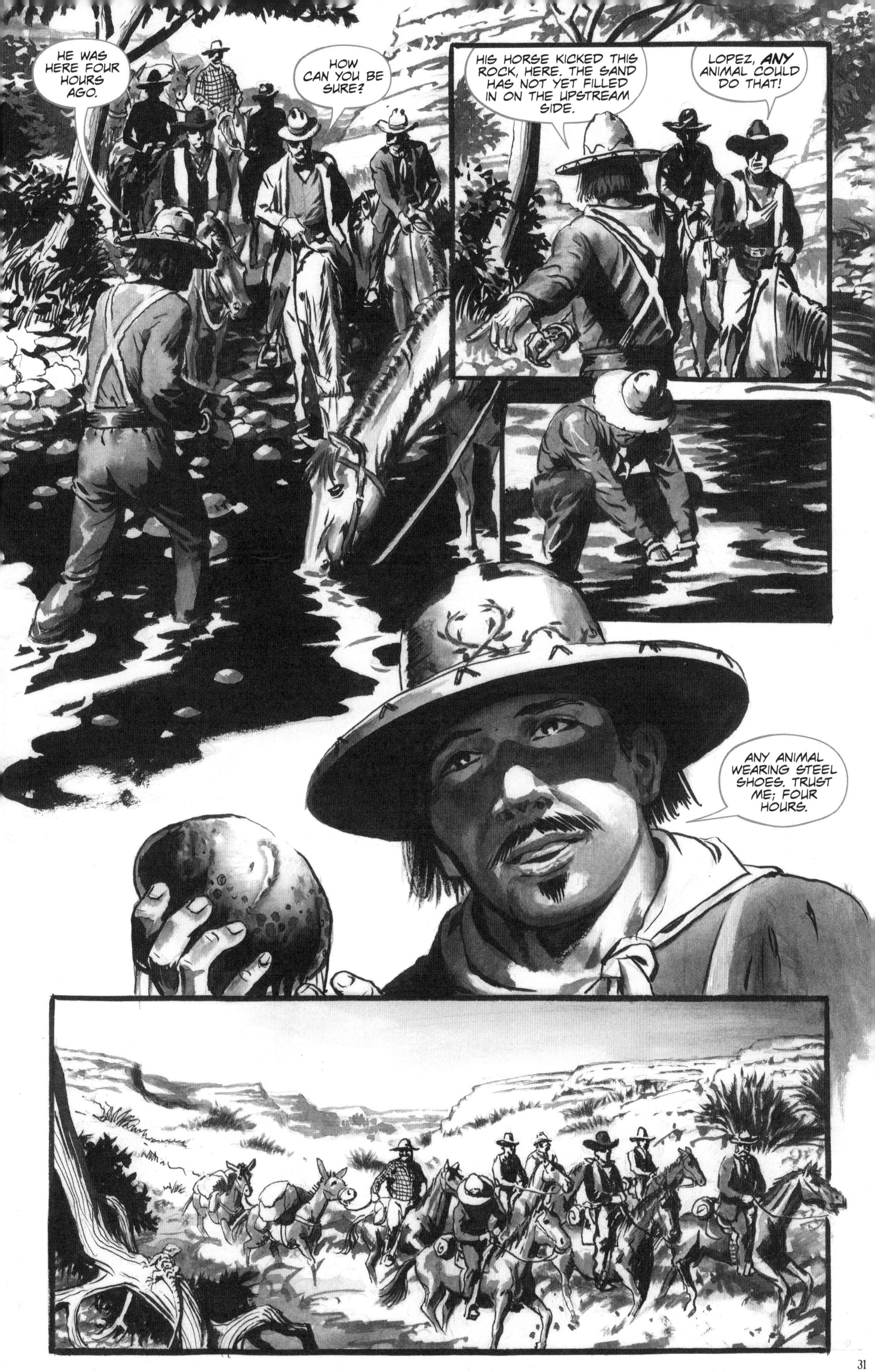
HE WAS HERE FOUR HOURS AGO.
HOW CAN YOU BE SURE?
HIS HORSE KICKED THIS ROCK, HERE. THE SAND HAS NOT YET FILLED IN ON THE UPSTREAM SIDE.
LOPEZ, ANY ANIMAL COULD DO THAT!
ANY ANIMAL WEARING STEEL SHOES. TRUST ME; FOUR HOURS.

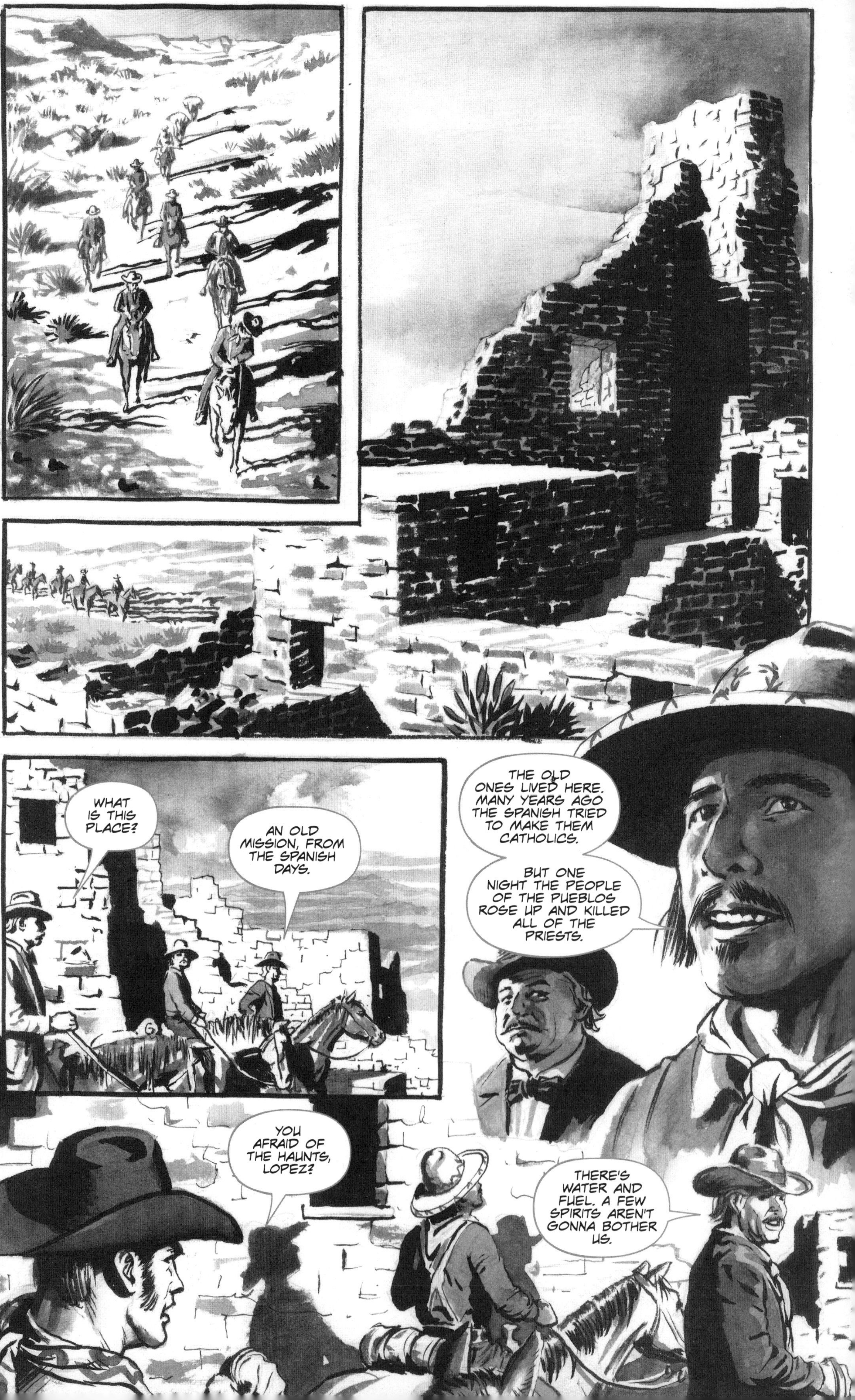
WHAT IS THIS PLACE?
AN OLD MISSION, FROM THE SPANISH DAYS.
THE OLD ONES LIVED HERE. MANY YEARS AGO THE SPANISH TRIED TO MAKE THEM CATHOLICS.
BUT ONE NIGHT THE PEOPLE OF THE PUEBLOS ROSE UP AND KILLED ALL OF THE PRIESTS.
YOU AFRAID OF THE HAUNTS, LOPEZ?
THERE'S WATER AND FUEL. A FEW SPIRITS AREN'T GONNA BOTHER US.

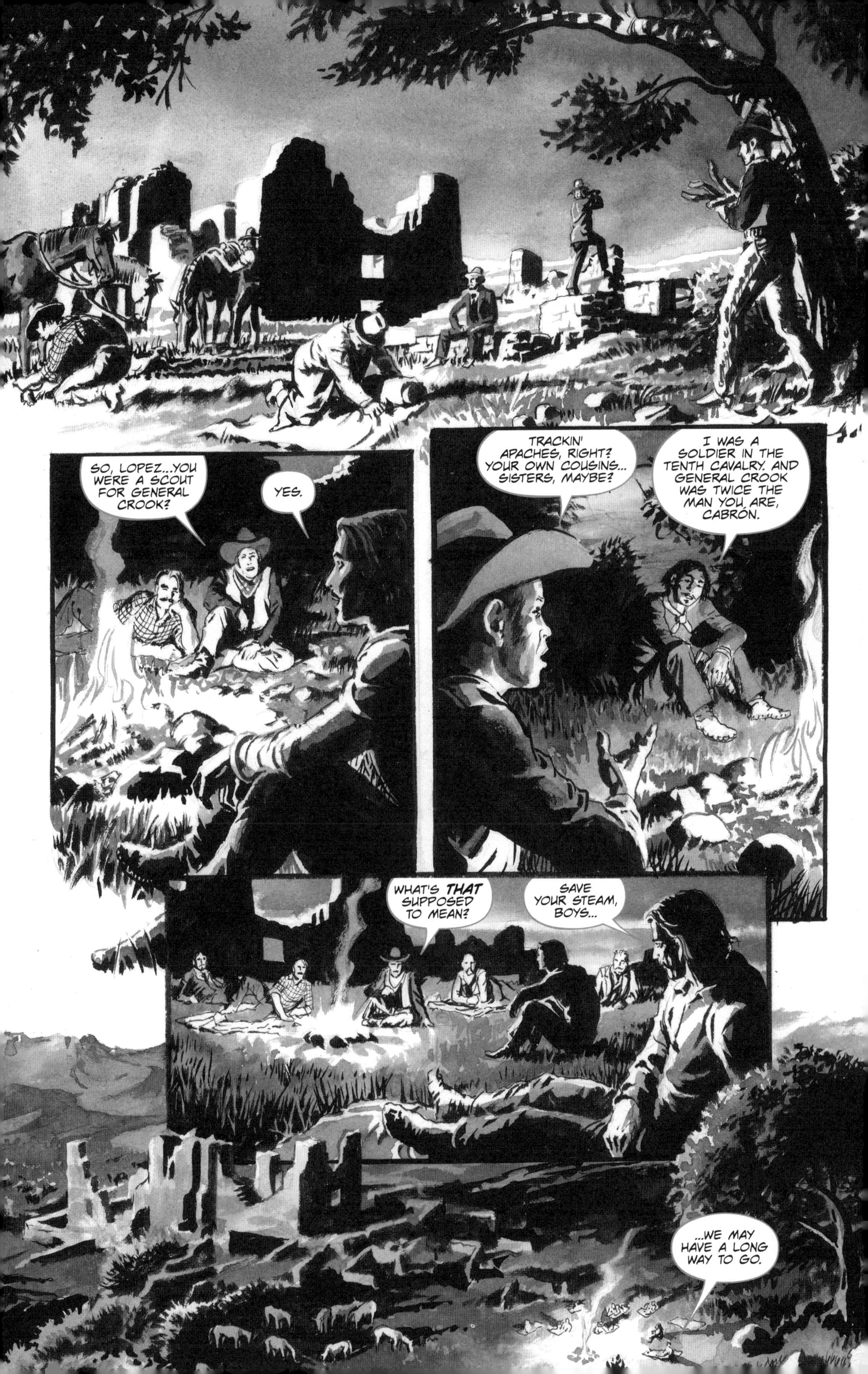

SO, LOPEZ...YOU WERE A SCOUT FOR GENERAL CROOK?
YES.
TRACKIN' APACHES, RIGHT? YOUR OWN COUSINS... SISTERS, MAYBE?
I WAS A SOLDIER IN THE TENTH CAVALRY. AND GENERAL CROOK WAS TWICE THE MAN YOU ARE, CABRÓN.
WHAT'S THAT SUPPOSED TO MEAN?
SAVE YOUR STEAM, BOYS...
...WE MAY HAVE A LONG WAY TO GO.

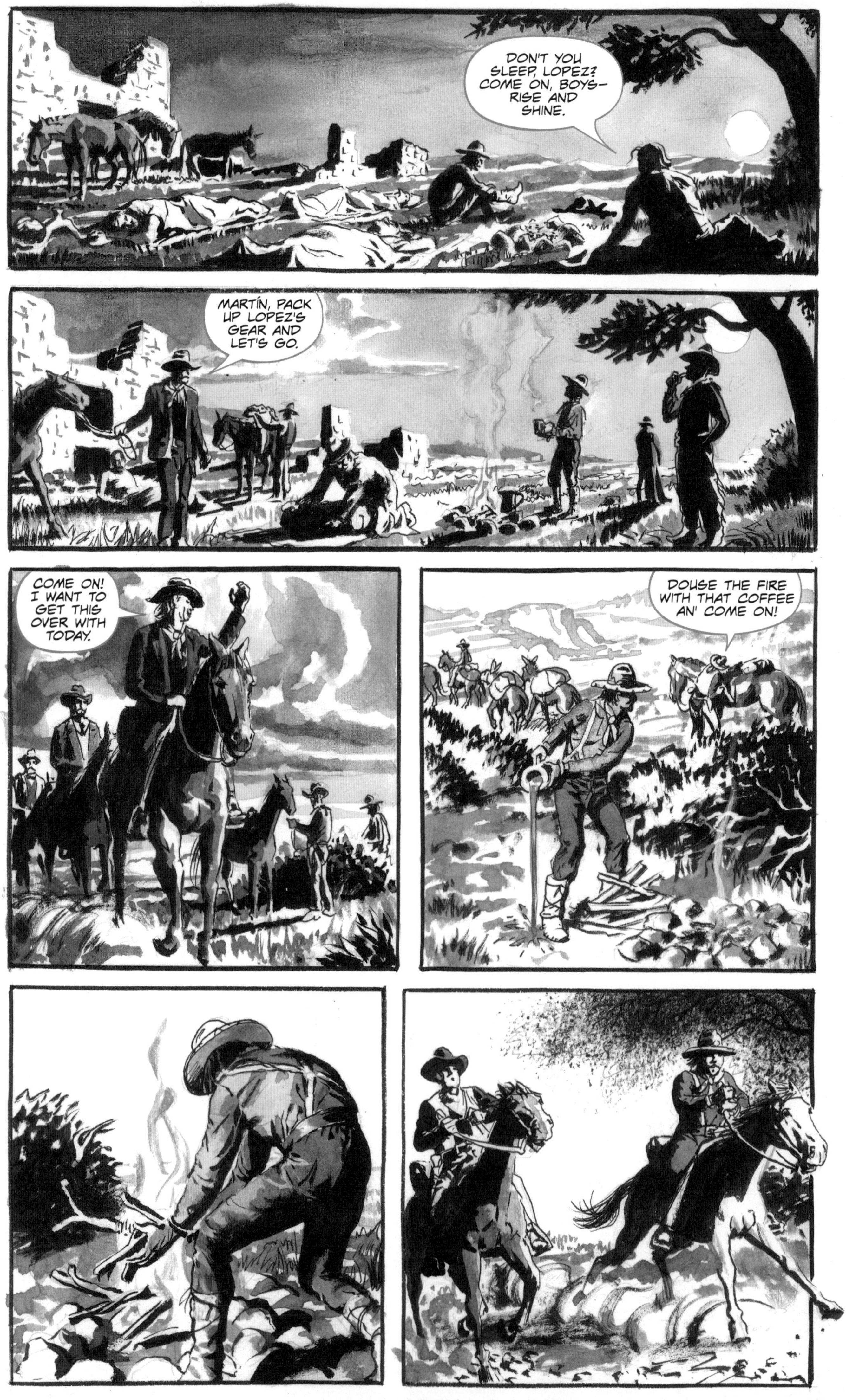
DON'T YOU SLEEP, LOPEZ? COME ON, BOYS-- RISE AND SHINE.
MARTÍN, PACK UP LOPEZ'S GEAR AND LET'S GO.
COME ON! I WANT TO GET THIS OVER WITH TODAY.
DOUSE THE FIRE WITH THAT COFFEE AN' COME ON!

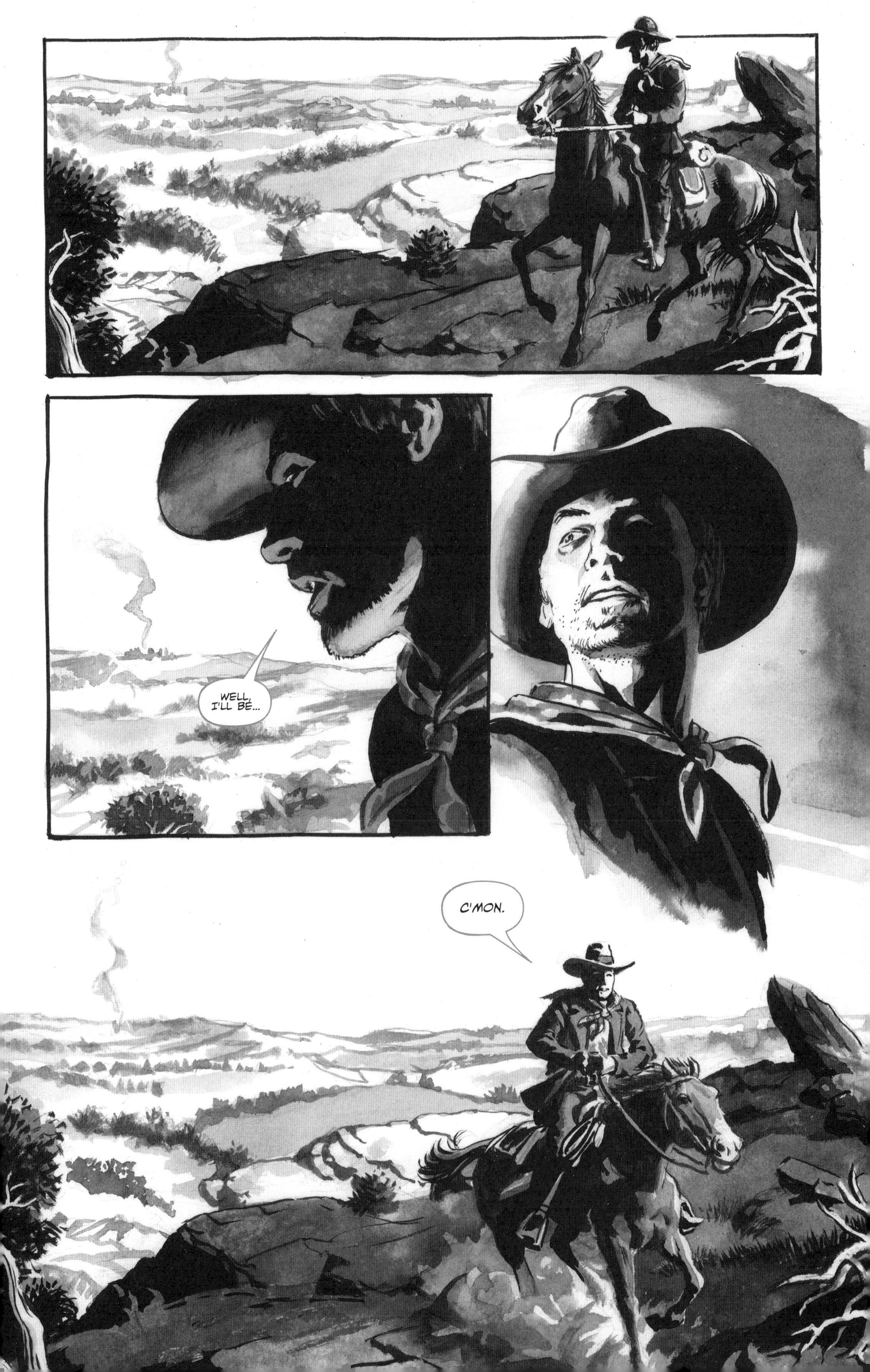
WELL, I'LL BE...
C'MON.

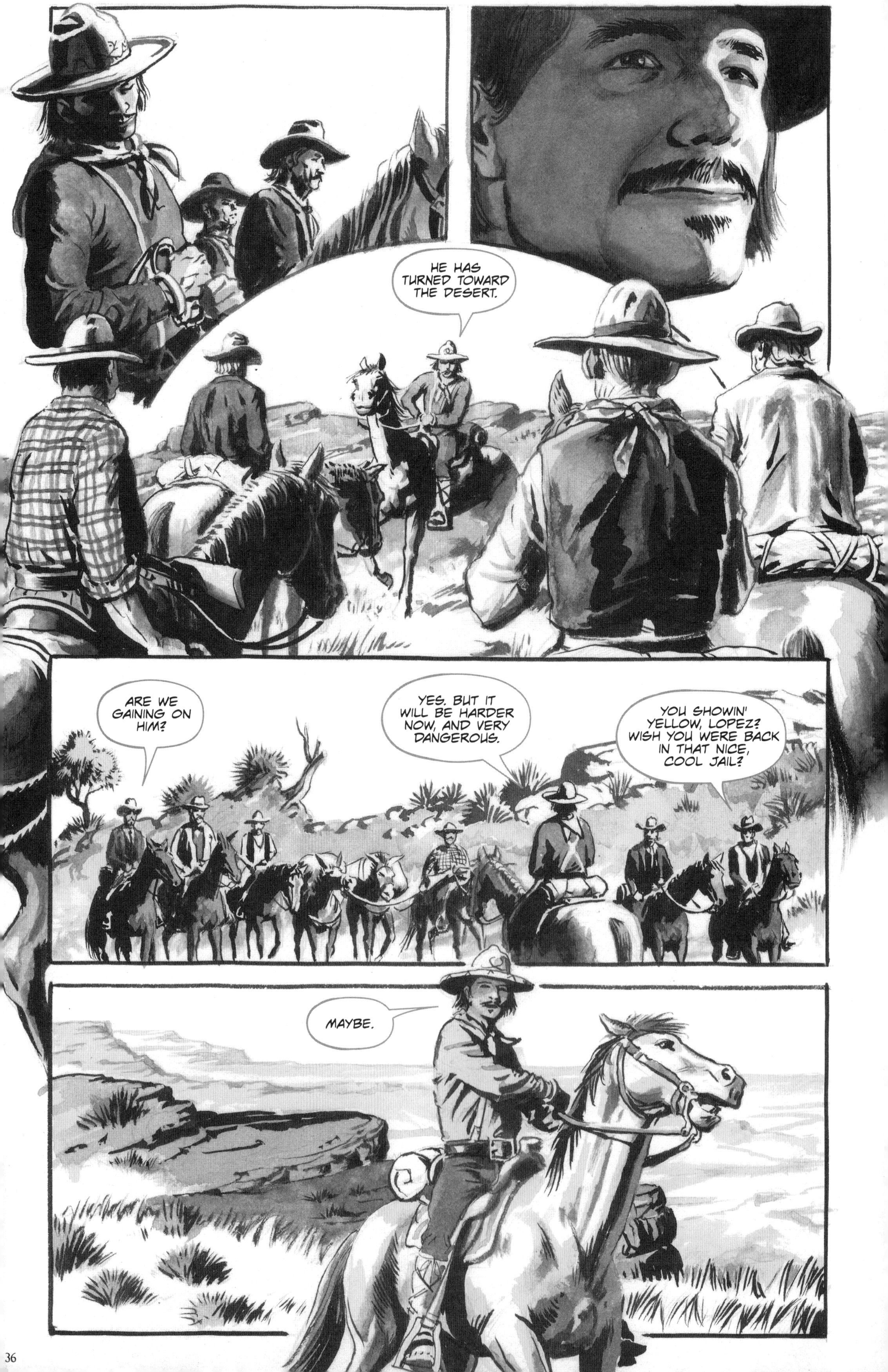
HE HAS TURNED TOWARD THE DESERT.
ARE WE GAINING ON HIM?
YES. BUT IT WILL BE HARDER NOW, AND VERY DANGEROUS.
YOU SHOWIN' YELLOW, LOPEZ? WISH YOU WERE BACK IN THAT NICE, COOL JAIL?
MAYBE.

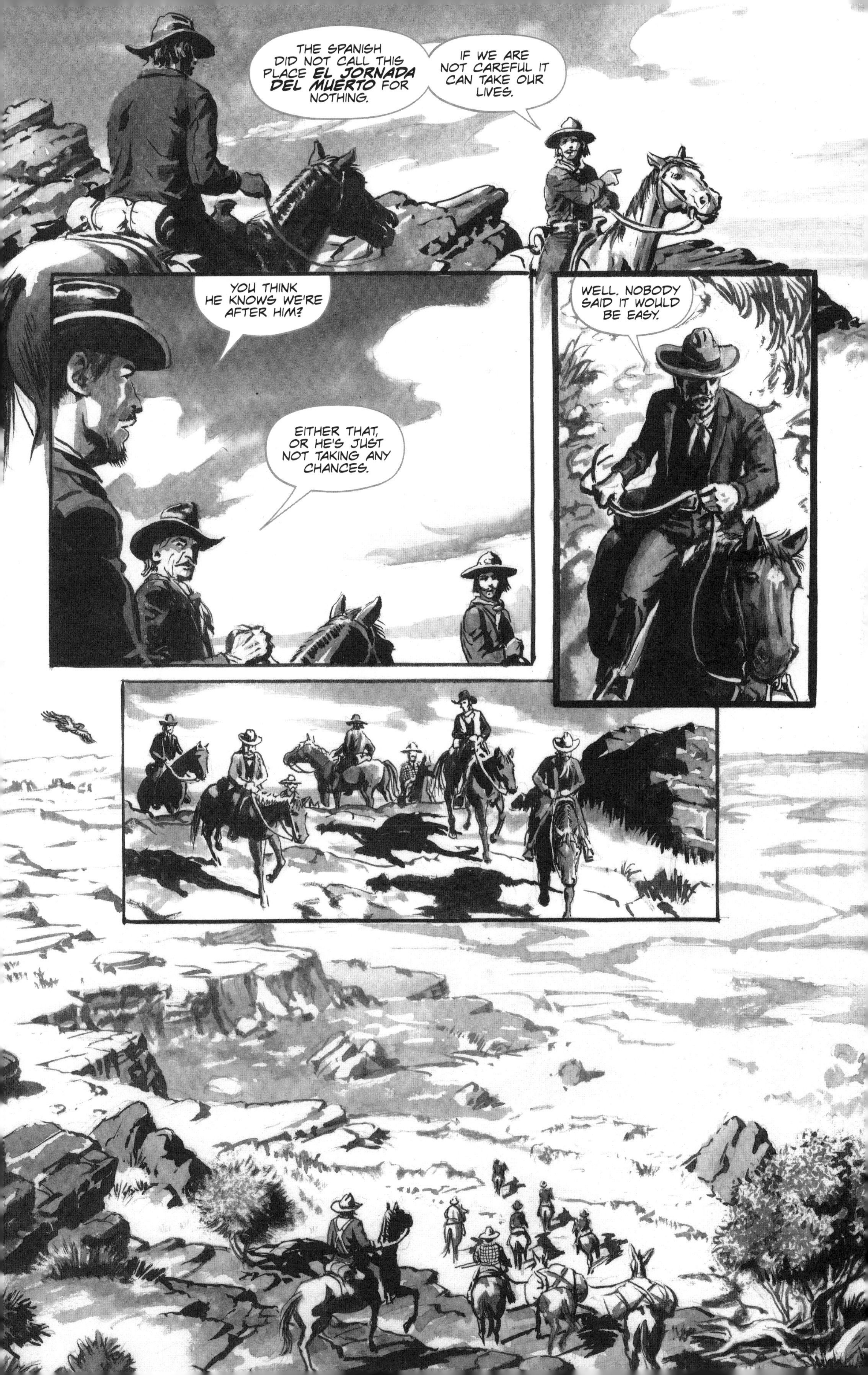
THE SPANISH DID NOT CALL THIS PLACE **EL JORNADA DEL MUERTO** FOR NOTHING.
IF WE ARE NOT CAREFUL IT CAN TAKE OUR LIVES.
YOU THINK HE KNOWS WE'RE AFTER HIM?
EITHER THAT, OR HE'S JUST NOT TAKING ANY CHANCES.
WELL. NOBODY SAID IT WOULD BE EASY.

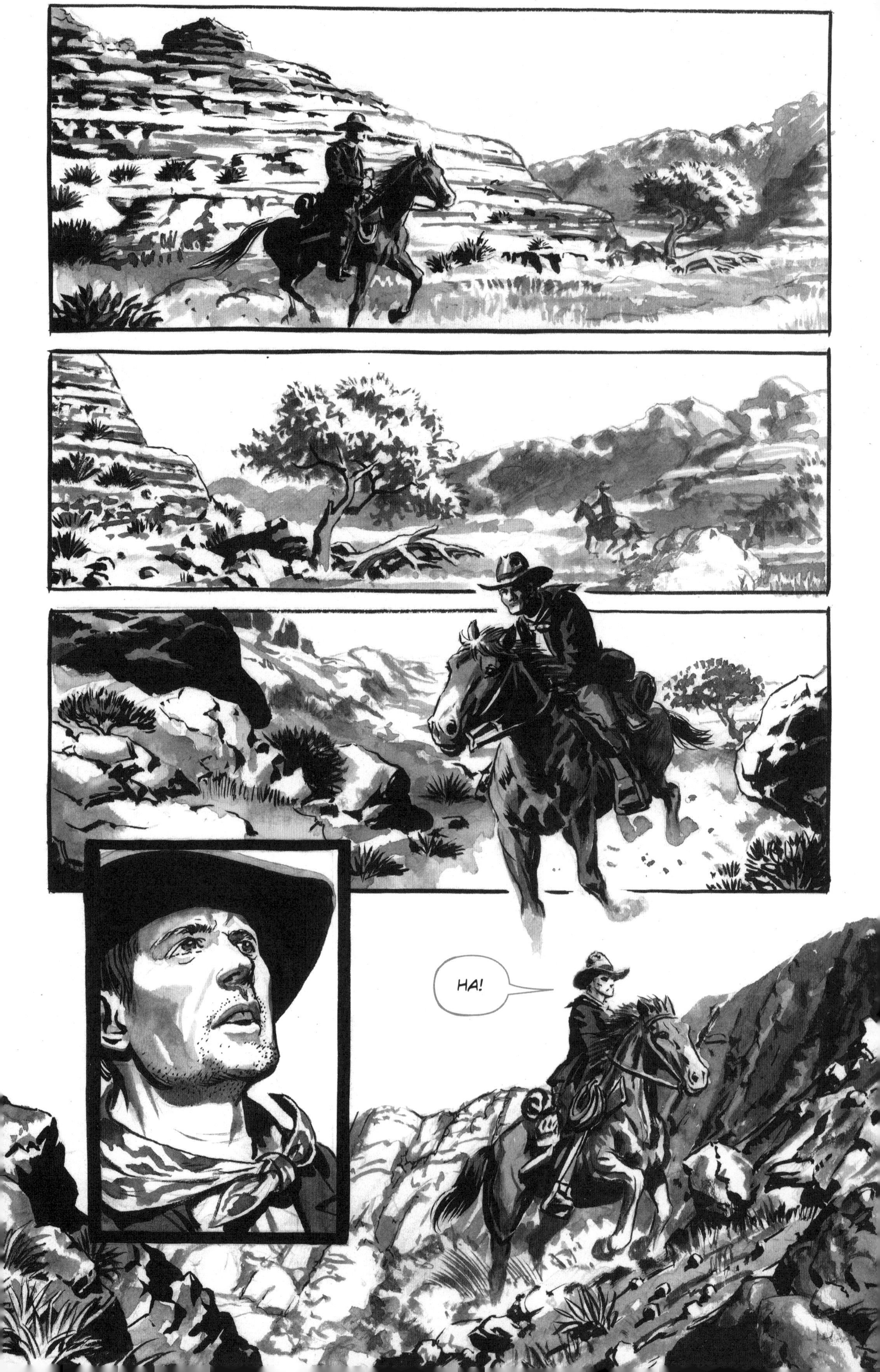
HA!

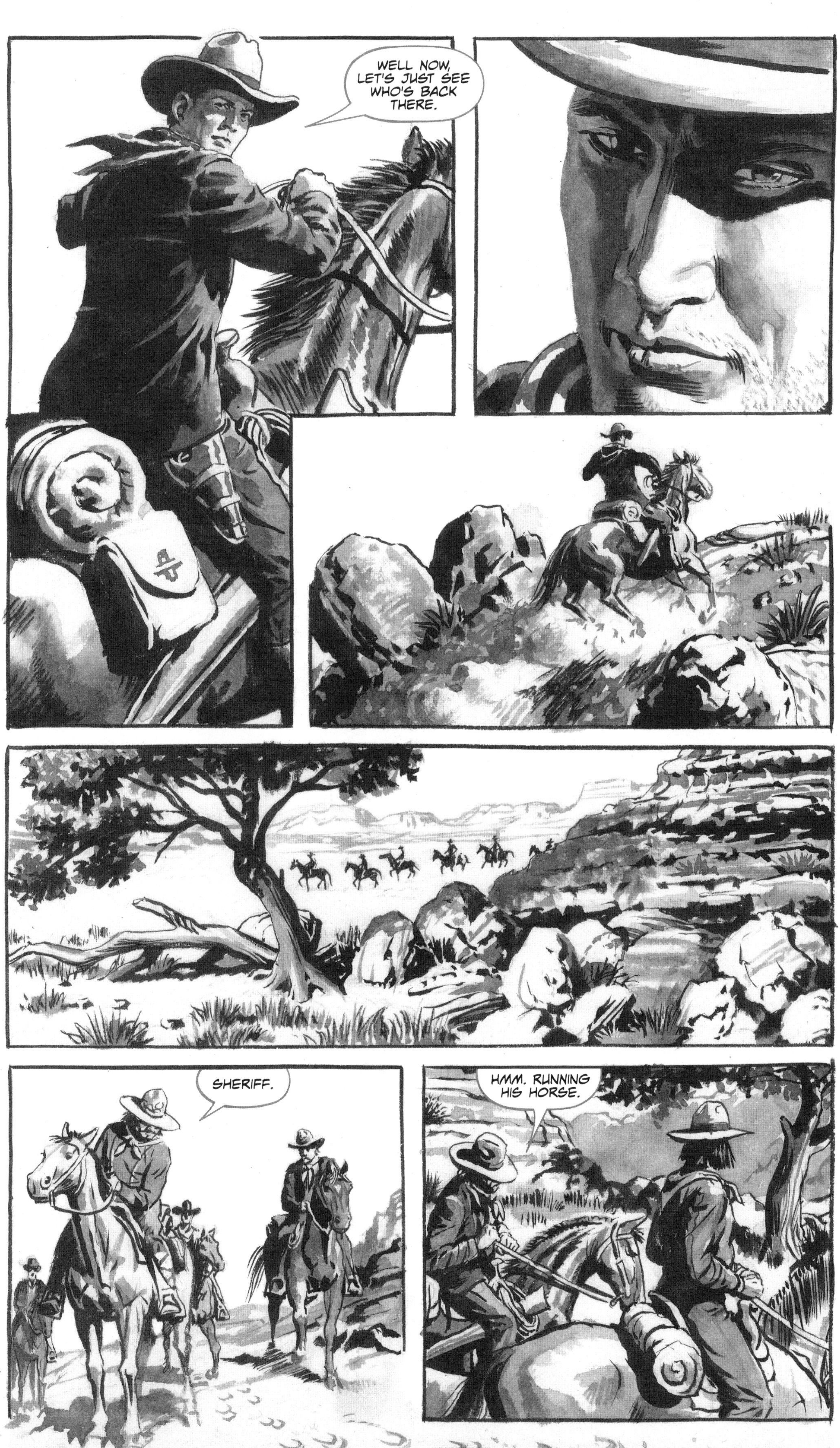
WELL NOW, LET'S JUST SEE WHO'S BACK THERE.
SHERIFF.
HMM. RUNNING HIS HORSE.

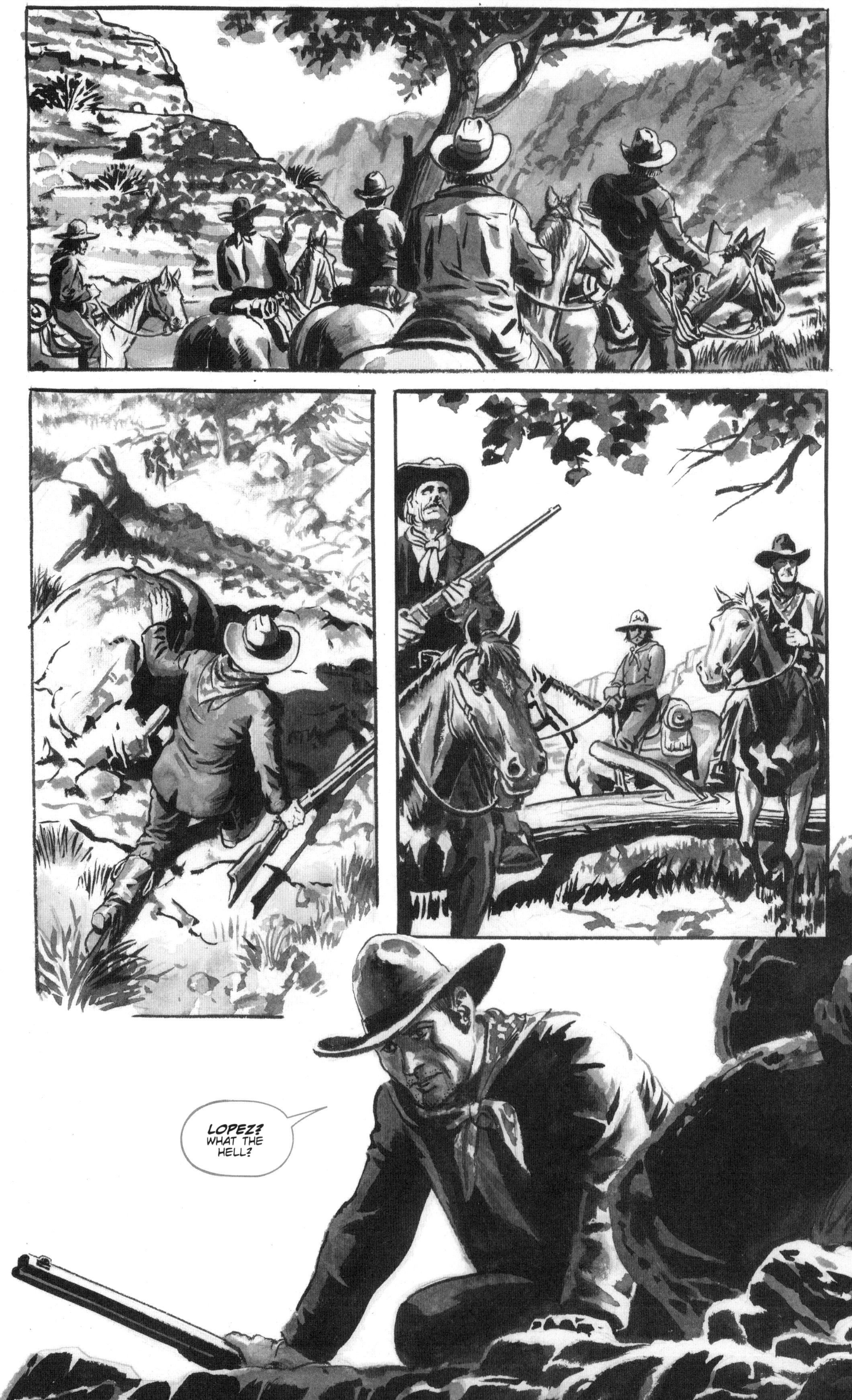
LOPEZ? WHAT THE HELL?

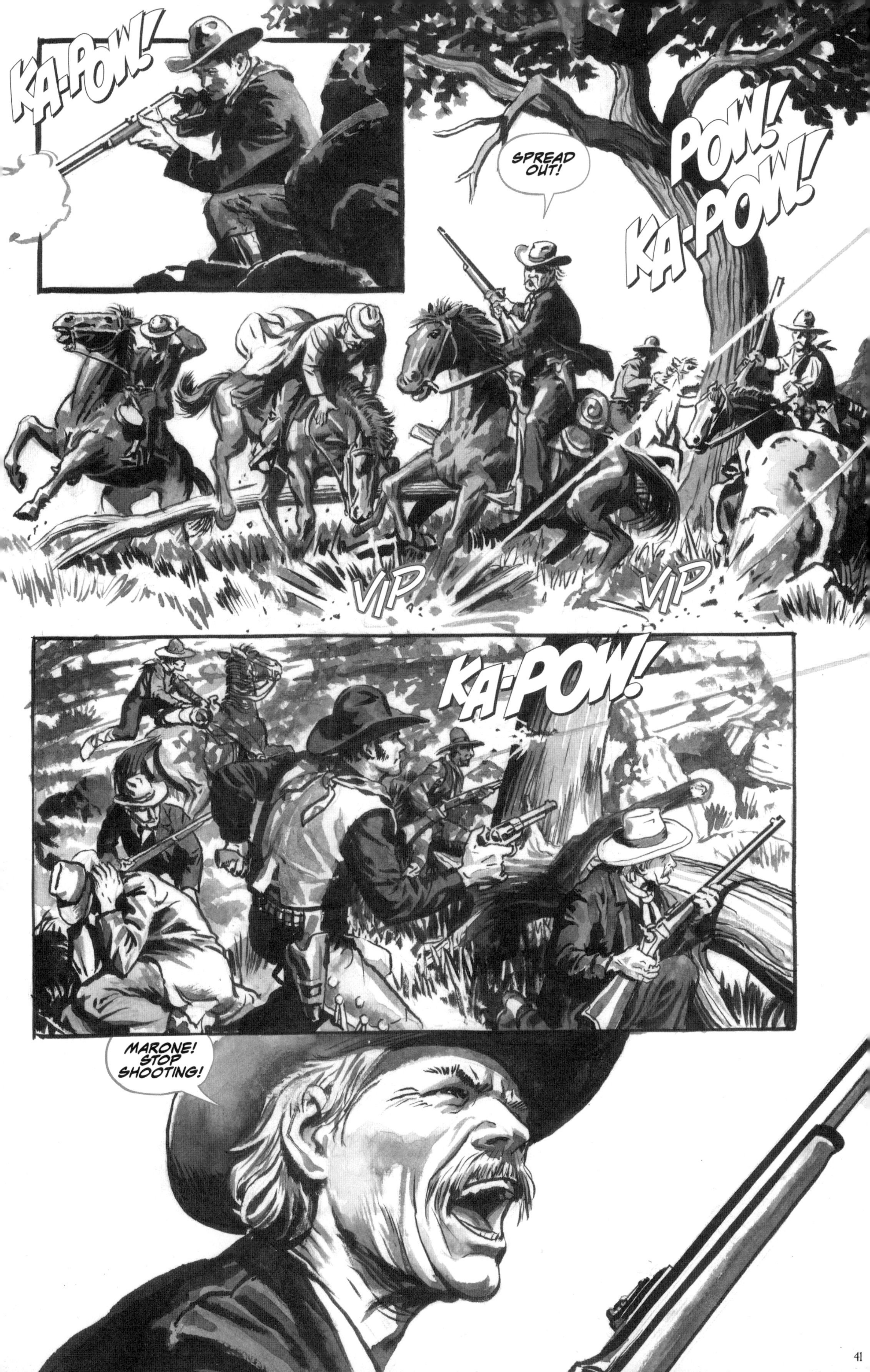
KA-POW!
SPREAD OUT!
POW!
KA-POW!
VIP
VIP
KA-POW!
MARONE! STOP SHOOTING!

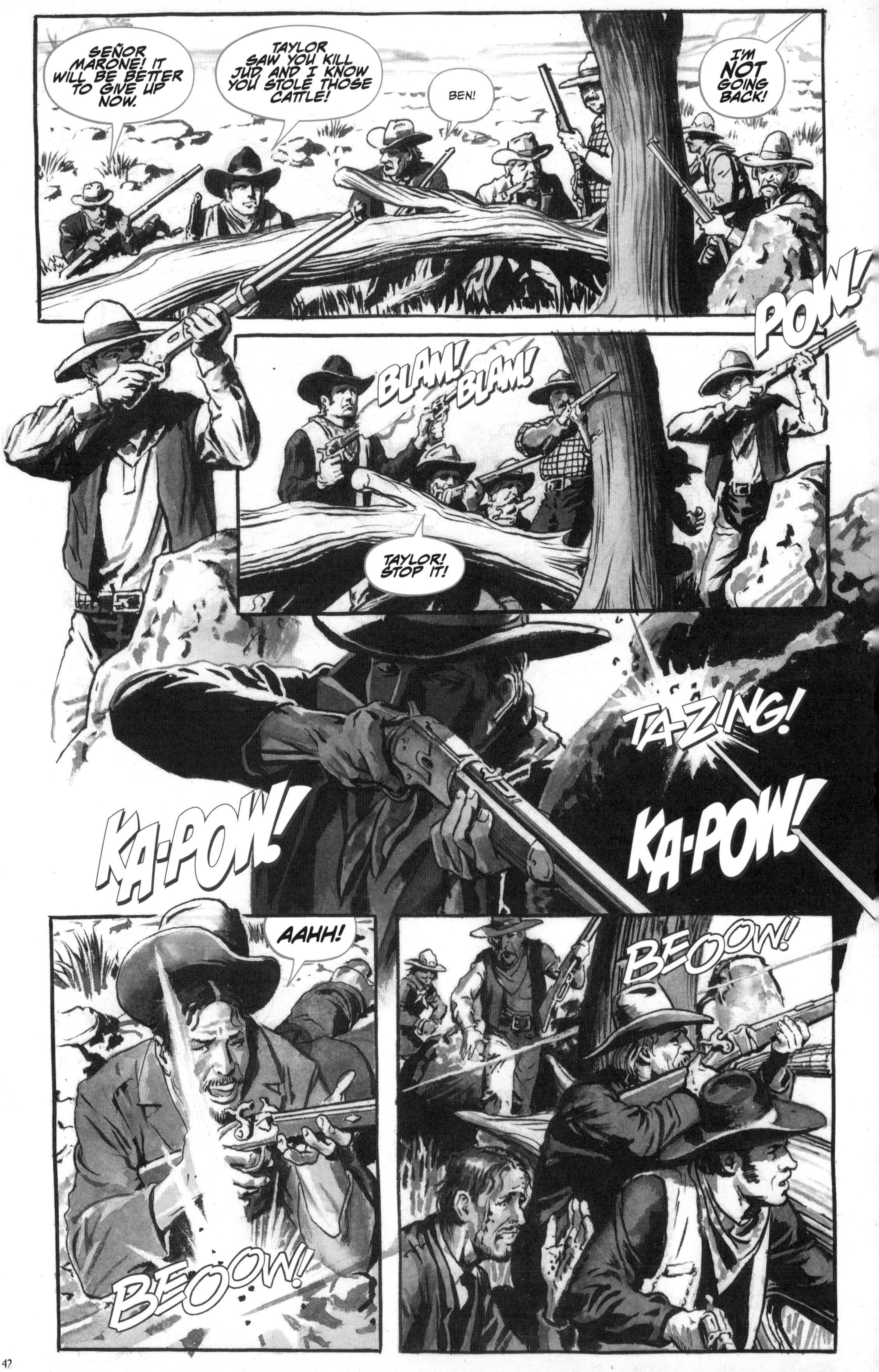
SEÑOR MARONE! IT WILL BE BETTER TO GIVE UP NOW.
TAYLOR SAW YOU KILL JUD AND I KNOW YOU STOLE THOSE CATTLE!
BEN!
I'M NOT GOING BACK!
BLAM! BLAM!
POW!
TAYLOR! STOP IT!
TAZING!
KA-POW!
KA-POW!
AAHH!
BEOOW!
BEOOW!

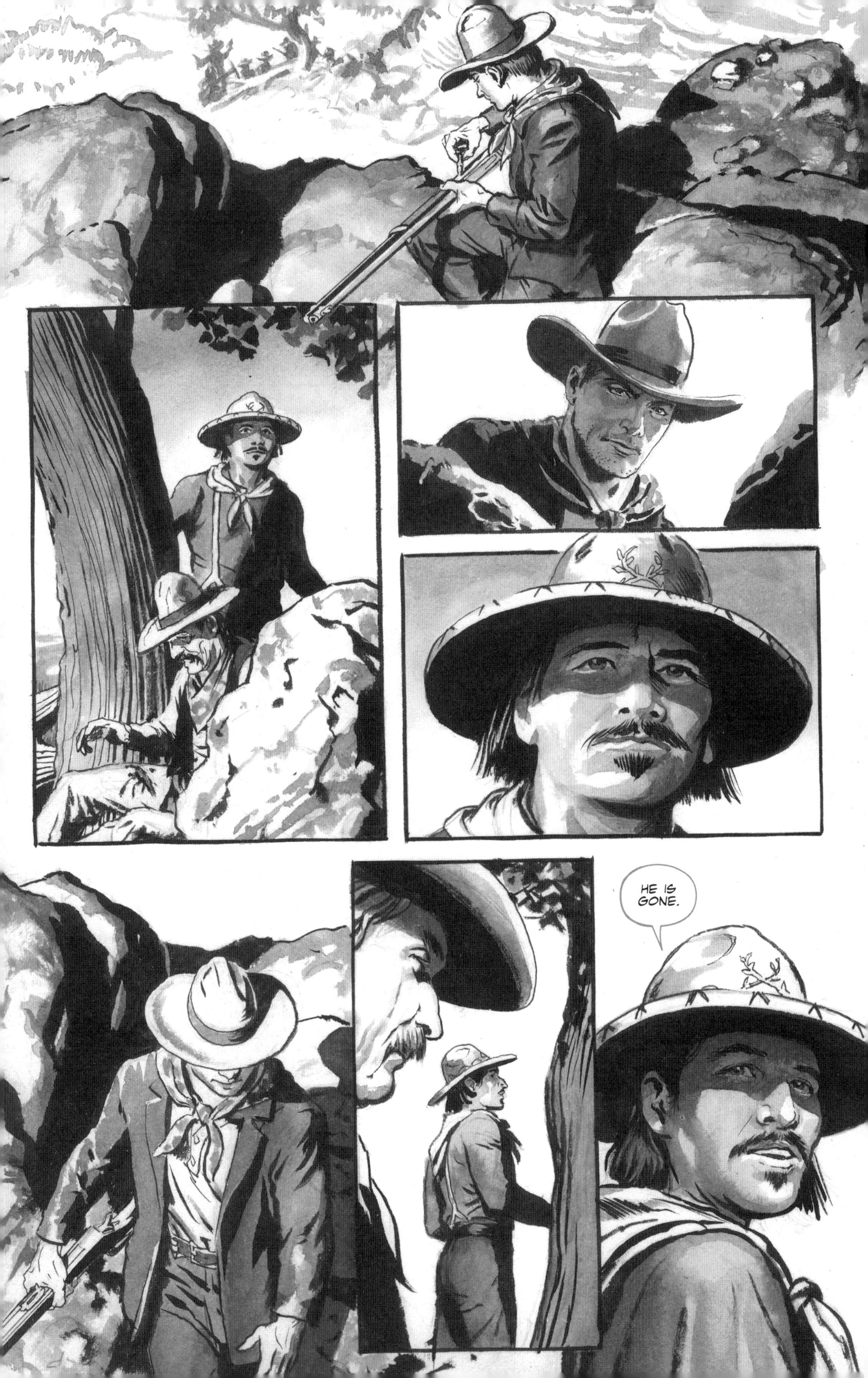
HE IS GONE.

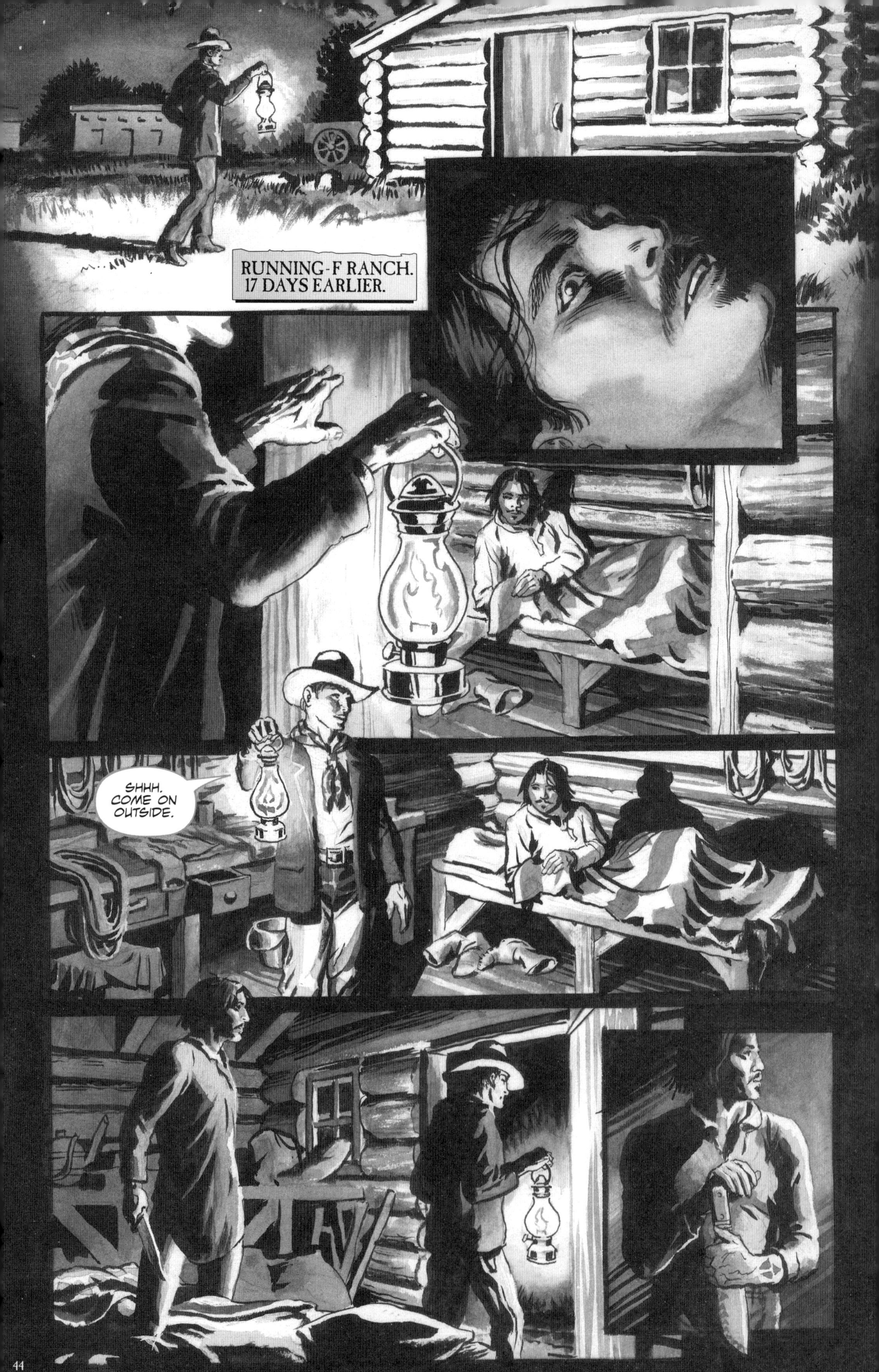
RUNNING-F RANCH.
17 DAYS EARLIER.
SHHH. COME ON OUTSIDE.

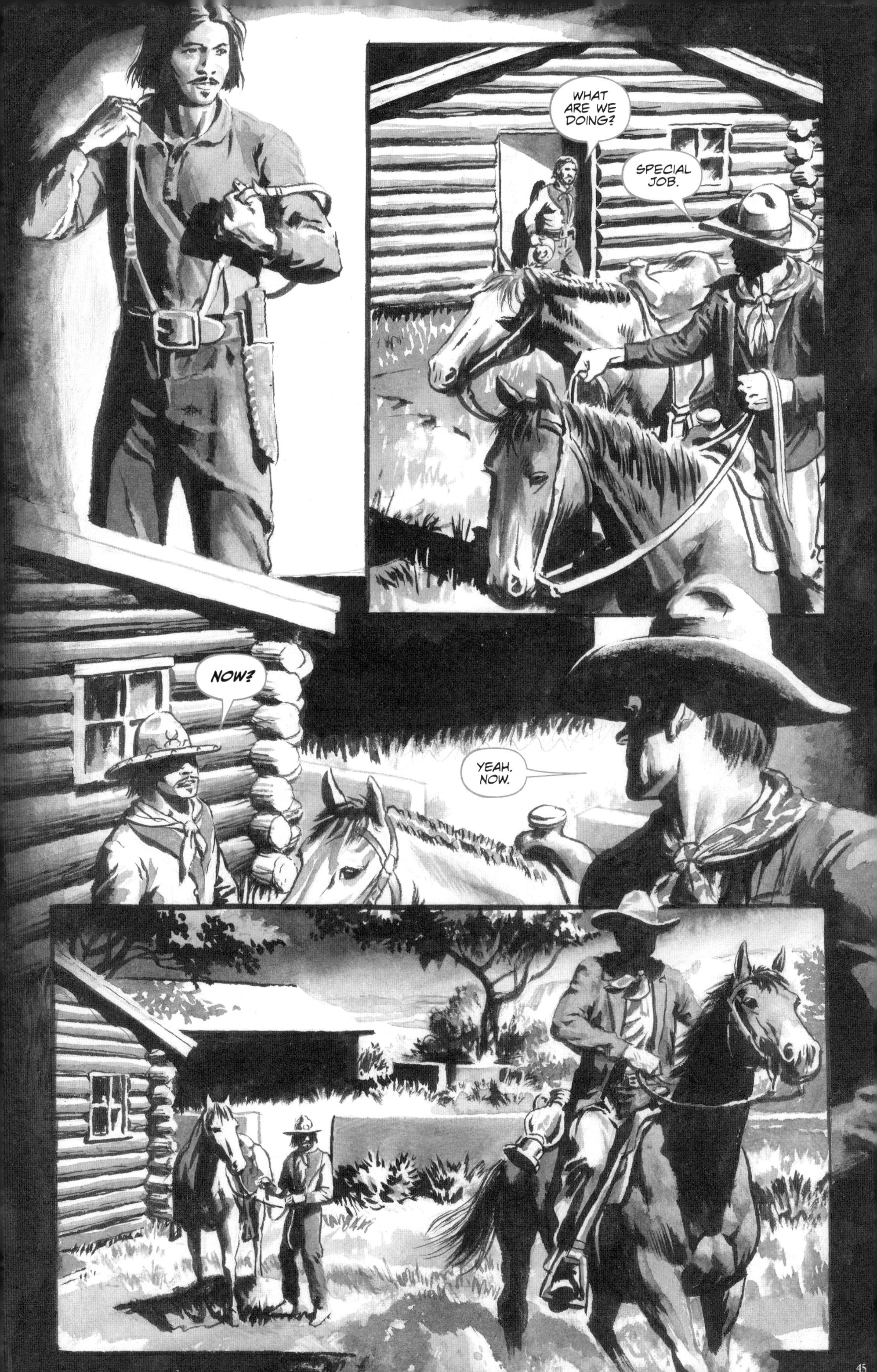
WHAT ARE WE DOING?
SPECIAL JOB.
NOW?
YEAH. NOW.

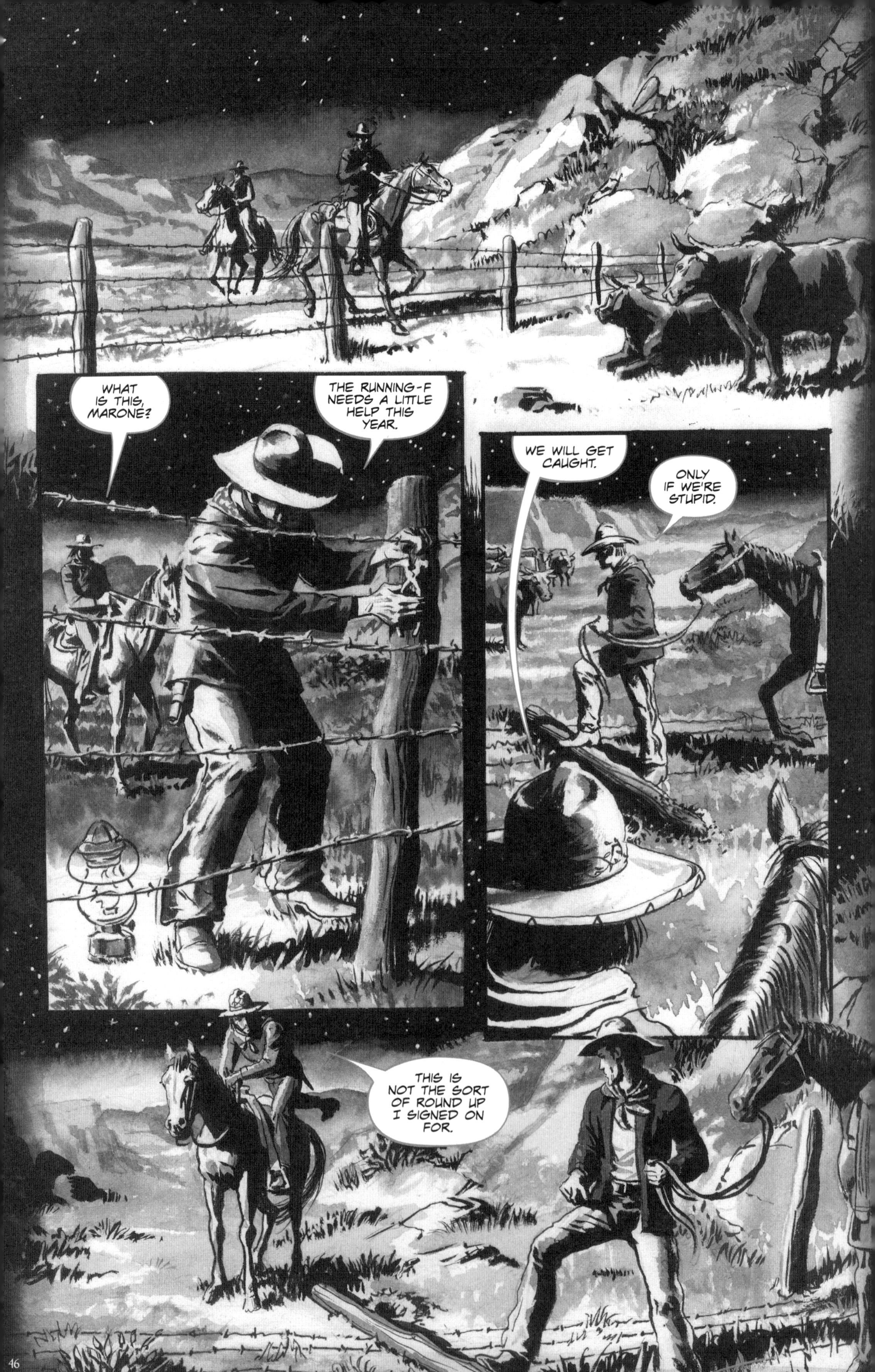
WHAT IS THIS, MARONE?
THE RUNNING-F NEEDS A LITTLE HELP THIS YEAR.
WE WILL GET CAUGHT.
ONLY IF WE'RE STUPID.
THIS IS NOT THE SORT OF ROUND UP I SIGNED ON FOR.

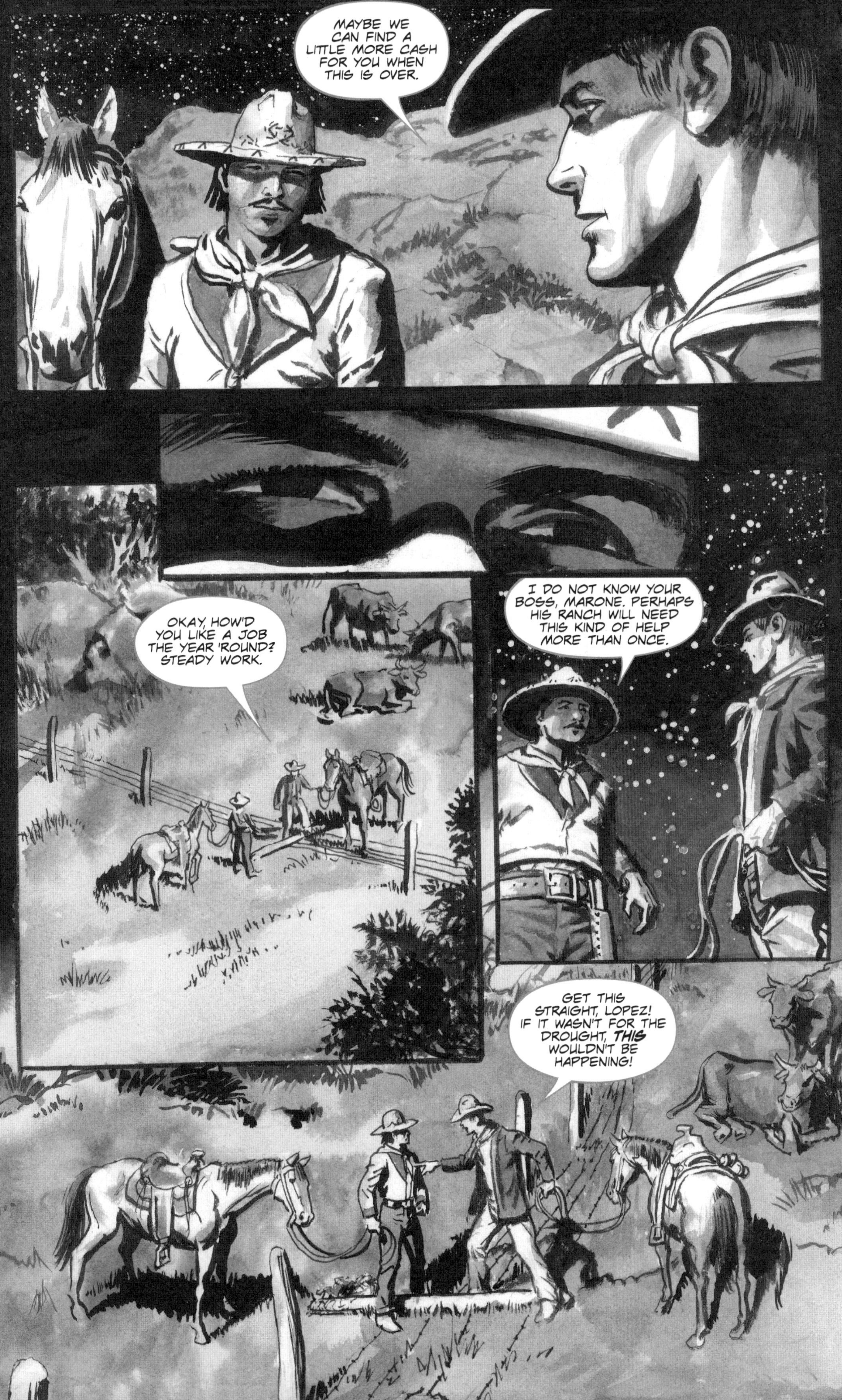
MAYBE WE CAN FIND A LITTLE MORE CASH FOR YOU WHEN THIS IS OVER.
OKAY, HOW'D YOU LIKE A JOB THE YEAR 'ROUND? STEADY WORK.
I DO NOT KNOW YOUR BOSS, MARONE. PERHAPS HIS RANCH WILL NEED THIS KIND OF HELP MORE THAN ONCE.
GET THIS STRAIGHT, LOPEZ! IF IT WASN'T FOR THE DROUGHT, THIS WOULDN'T BE HAPPENING!

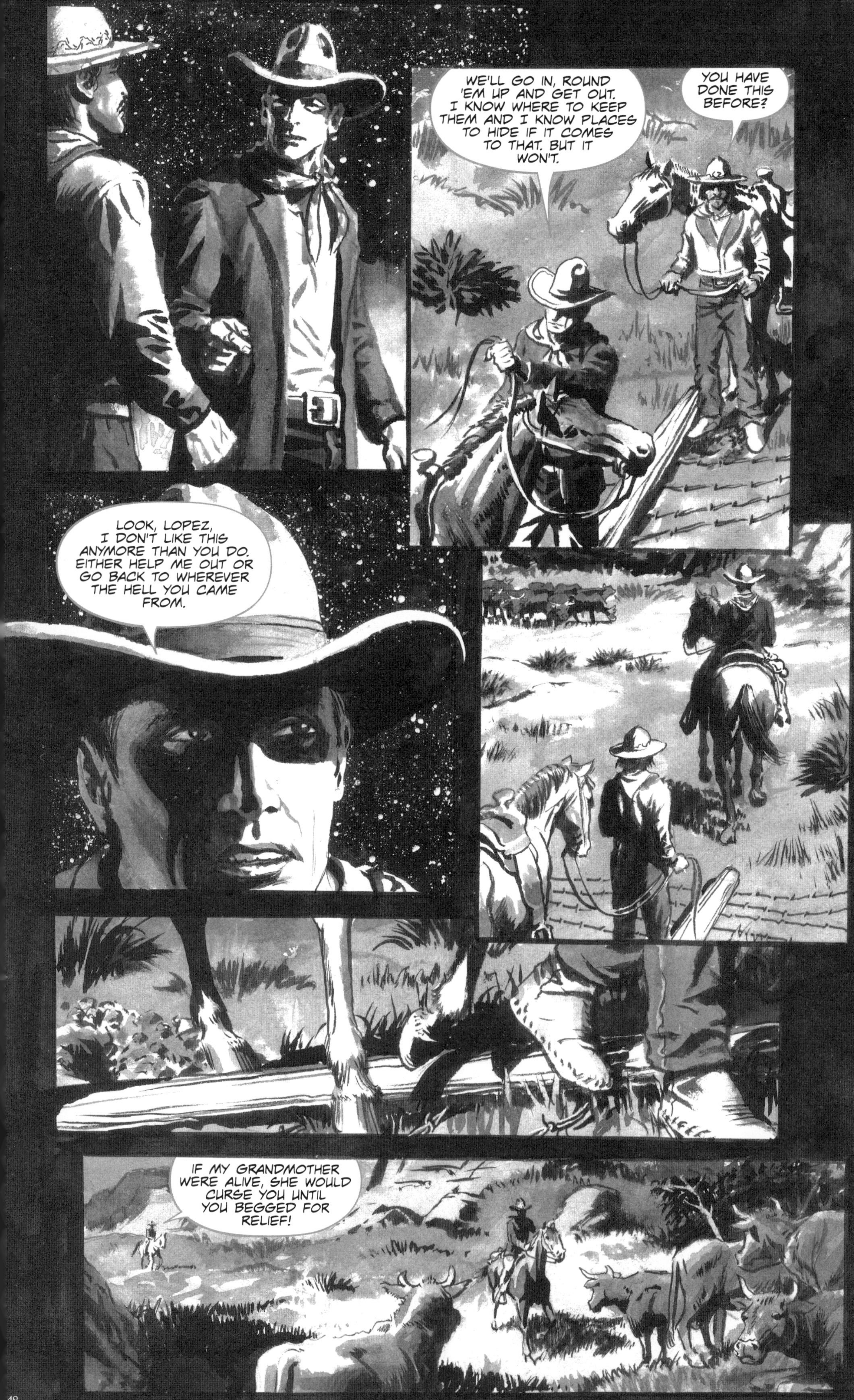
WE'LL GO IN, ROUND 'EM UP AND GET OUT. I KNOW WHERE TO KEEP THEM AND I KNOW PLACES TO HIDE IF IT COMES TO THAT. BUT IT WON'T.
YOU HAVE DONE THIS BEFORE?
LOOK, LOPEZ, I DON'T LIKE THIS ANYMORE THAN YOU DO. EITHER HELP ME OUT OR GO BACK TO WHEREVER THE HELL YOU CAME FROM.
IF MY GRANDMOTHER WERE ALIVE, SHE WOULD CURSE YOU UNTIL YOU BEGGED FOR RELIEF!

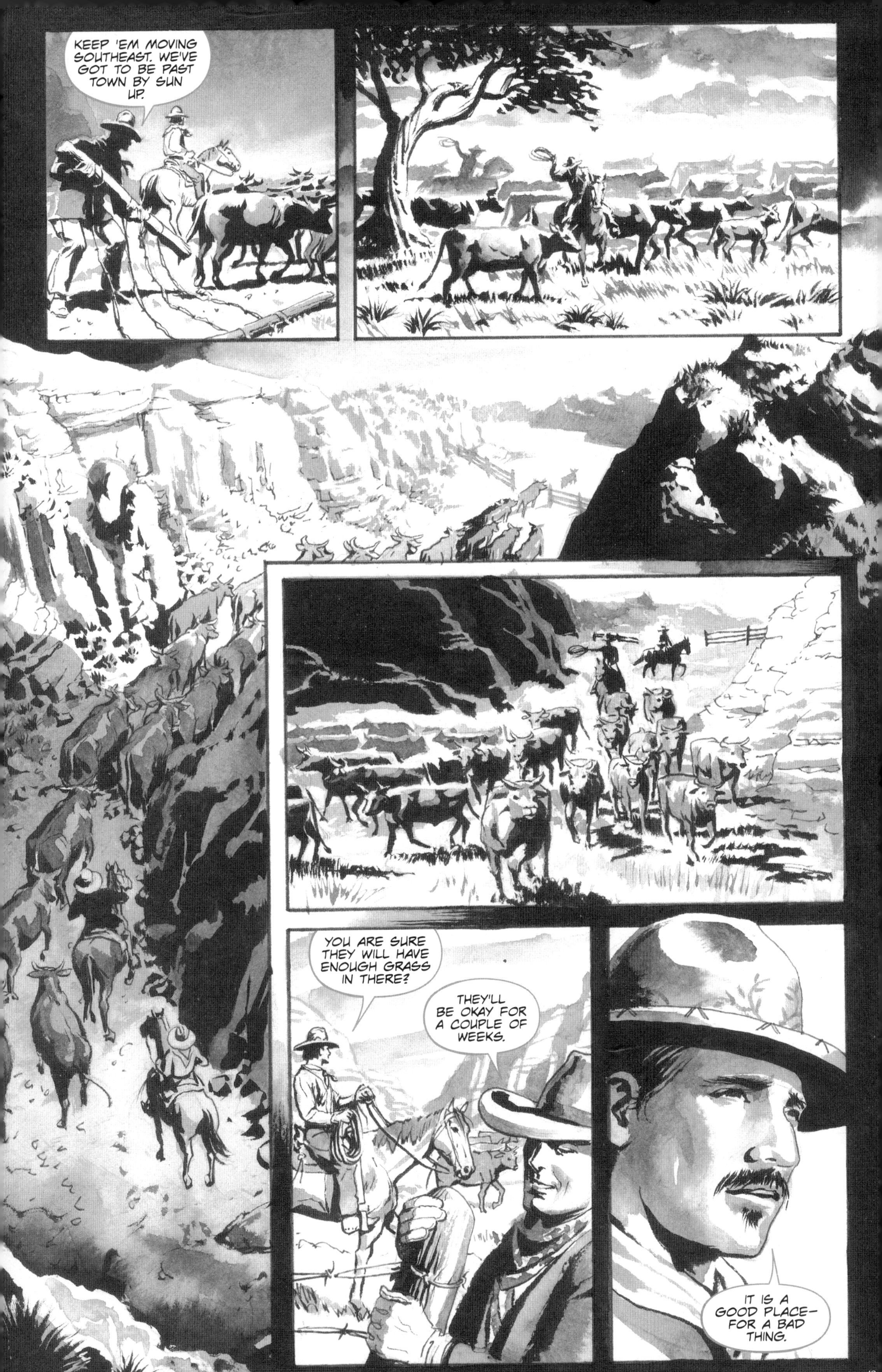
KEEP 'EM MOVING SOUTHEAST. WE'VE GOT TO BE PAST TOWN BY SUN UP.
YOU ARE SURE THEY WILL HAVE ENOUGH GRASS IN THERE?
THEY'LL BE OKAY FOR A COUPLE OF WEEKS.
IT IS A GOOD PLACE— FOR A BAD THING.

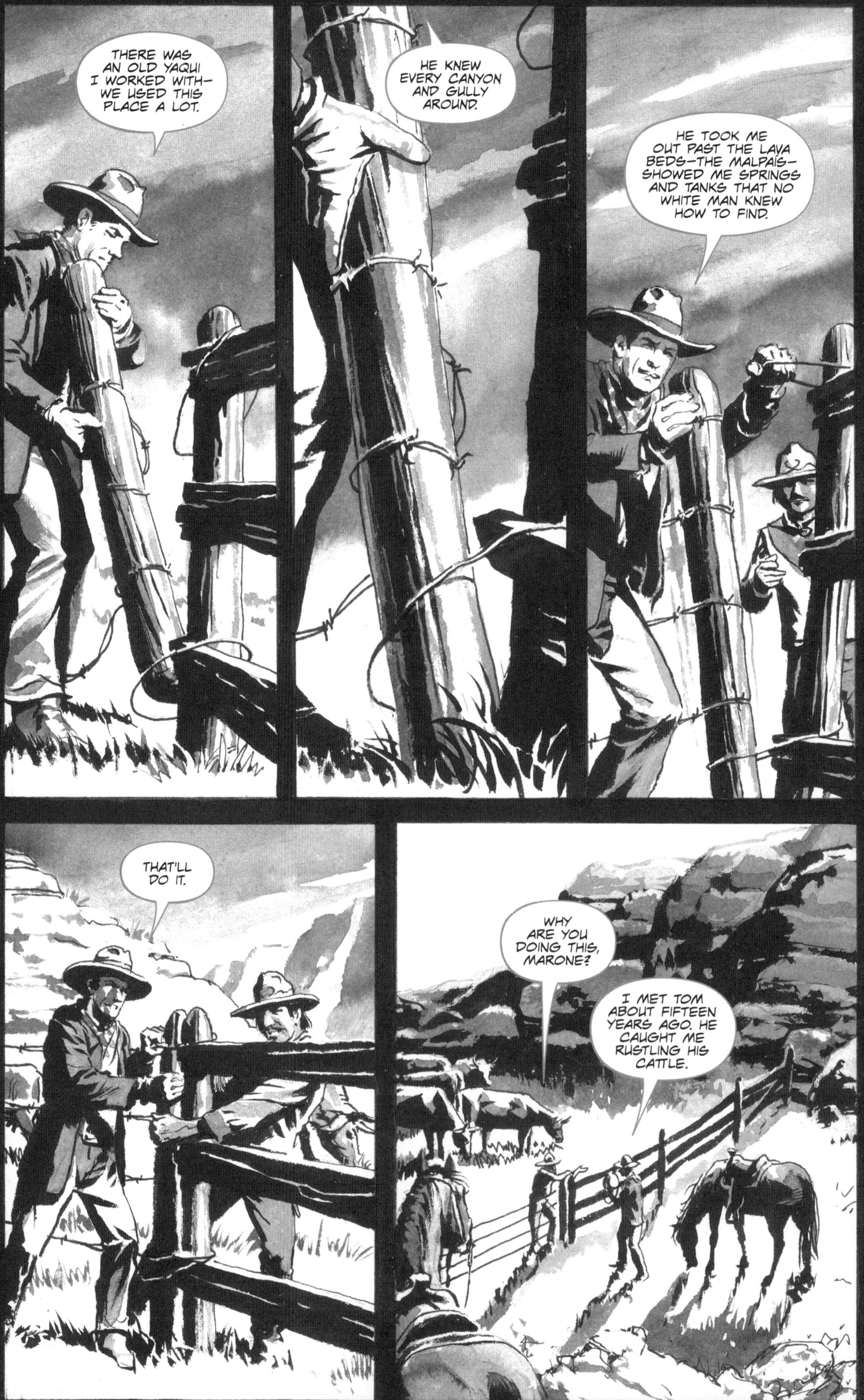
THERE WAS AN OLD YAQUI I WORKED WITH—WE USED THIS PLACE A LOT.
HE KNEW EVERY CANYON AND GULLY AROUND.
HE TOOK ME OUT PAST THE LAVA BEDS—THE MALPAÍS—SHOWED ME SPRINGS AND TANKS THAT NO WHITE MAN KNEW HOW TO FIND.
THAT'LL DO IT.
WHY ARE YOU DOING THIS, MARONE?
I MET TOM ABOUT FIFTEEN YEARS AGO. HE CAUGHT ME RUSTLING HIS CATTLE.

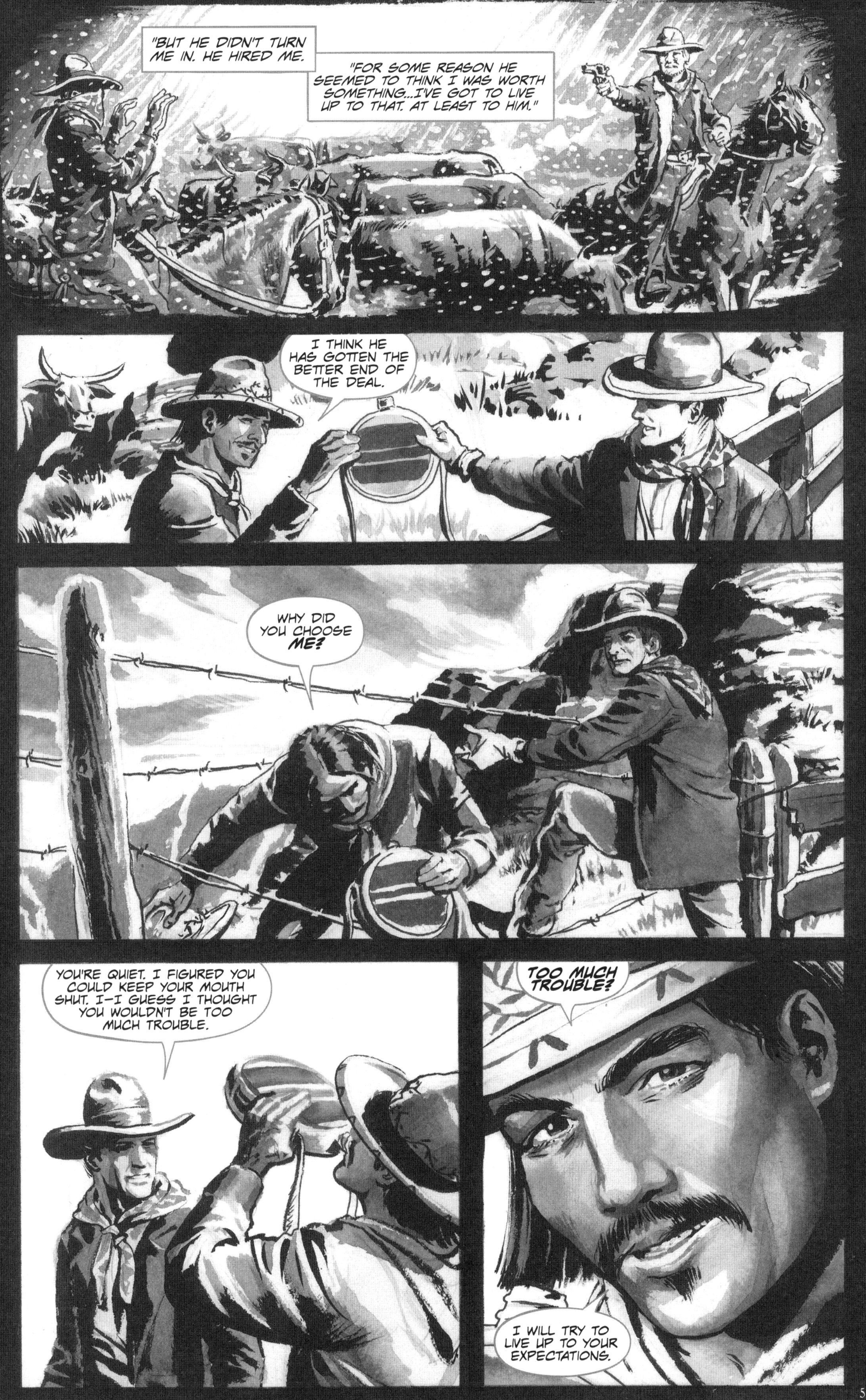
"BUT HE DIDN'T TURN ME IN. HE HIRED ME.
"FOR SOME REASON HE SEEMED TO THINK I WAS WORTH SOMETHING...I'VE GOT TO LIVE UP TO THAT. AT LEAST TO HIM."
I THINK HE HAS GOTTEN THE BETTER END OF THE DEAL.
WHY DID YOU CHOOSE ME?
YOU'RE QUIET. I FIGURED YOU COULD KEEP YOUR MOUTH SHUT. I--I GUESS I THOUGHT YOU WOULDN'T BE TOO MUCH TROUBLE.
TOO MUCH TROUBLE?
I WILL TRY TO LIVE UP TO YOUR EXPECTATIONS.

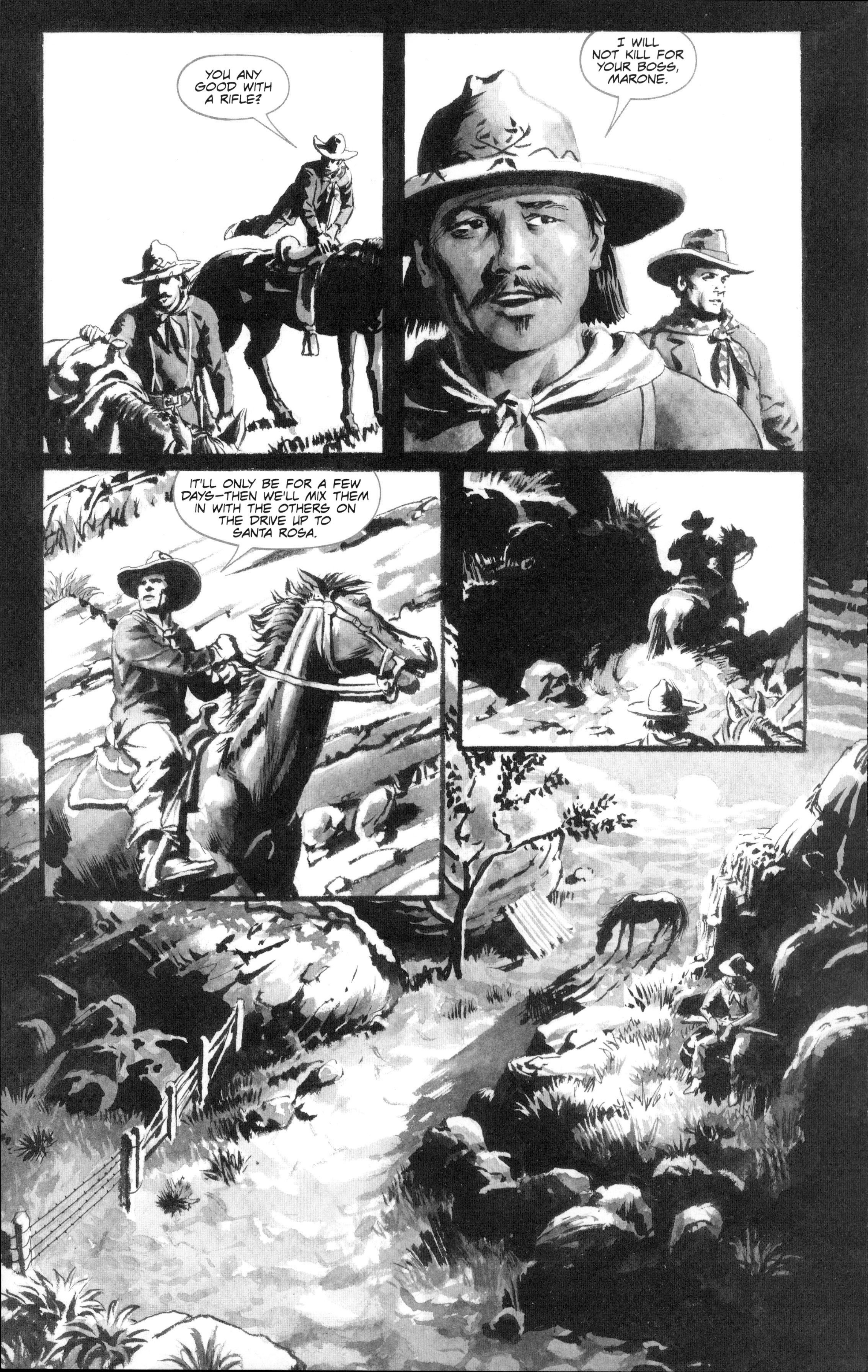
YOU ANY GOOD WITH A RIFLE?
I WILL NOT KILL FOR YOUR BOSS, MARONE.
IT'LL ONLY BE FOR A FEW DAYS—THEN WE'LL MIX THEM IN WITH THE OTHERS ON THE DRIVE UP TO SANTA ROSA.

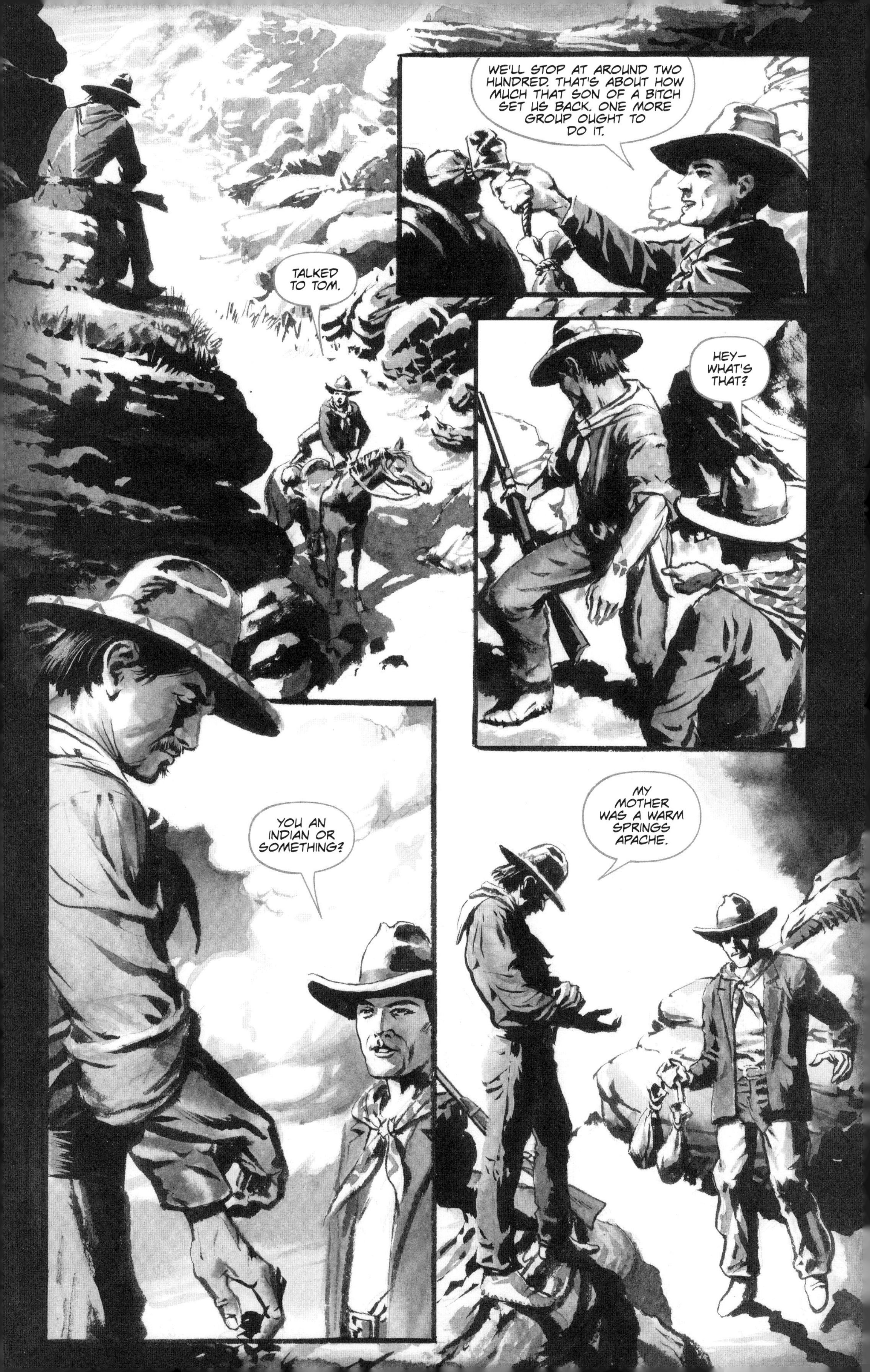

TALKED TO TOM.
WE'LL STOP AT AROUND TWO HUNDRED. THAT'S ABOUT HOW MUCH THAT SON OF A BITCH SET US BACK. ONE MORE GROUP OUGHT TO DO IT.
HEY—WHAT'S THAT?
YOU AN INDIAN OR SOMETHING?
MY MOTHER WAS A WARM SPRINGS APACHE.

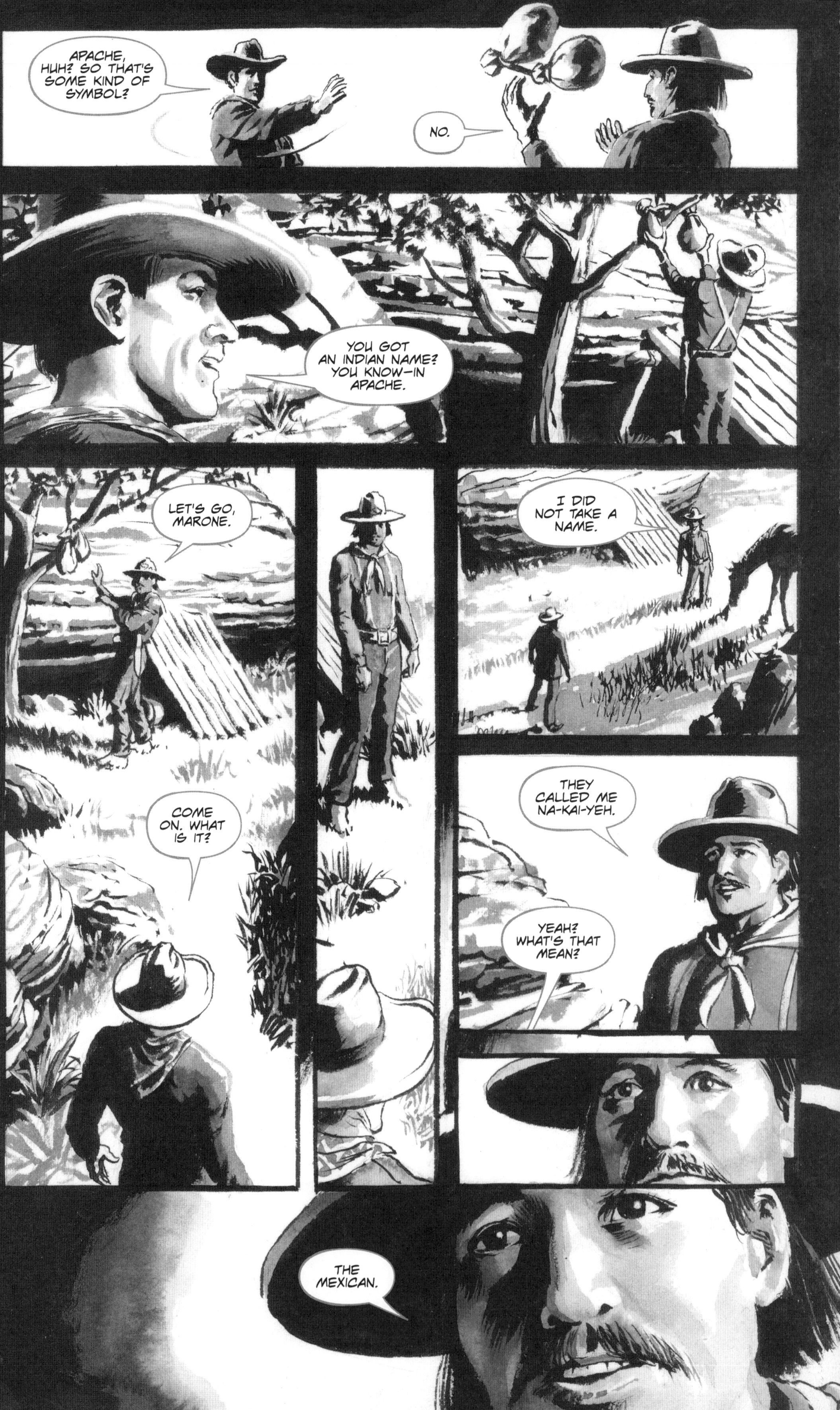
APACHE, HUH? SO THAT'S SOME KIND OF SYMBOL?
NO.
YOU GOT AN INDIAN NAME? YOU KNOW—IN APACHE.
LET'S GO, MARONE.
I DID NOT TAKE A NAME.
COME ON. WHAT IS IT?
THEY CALLED ME NA-KAI-YEH.
YEAH? WHAT'S THAT MEAN?
THE MEXICAN.

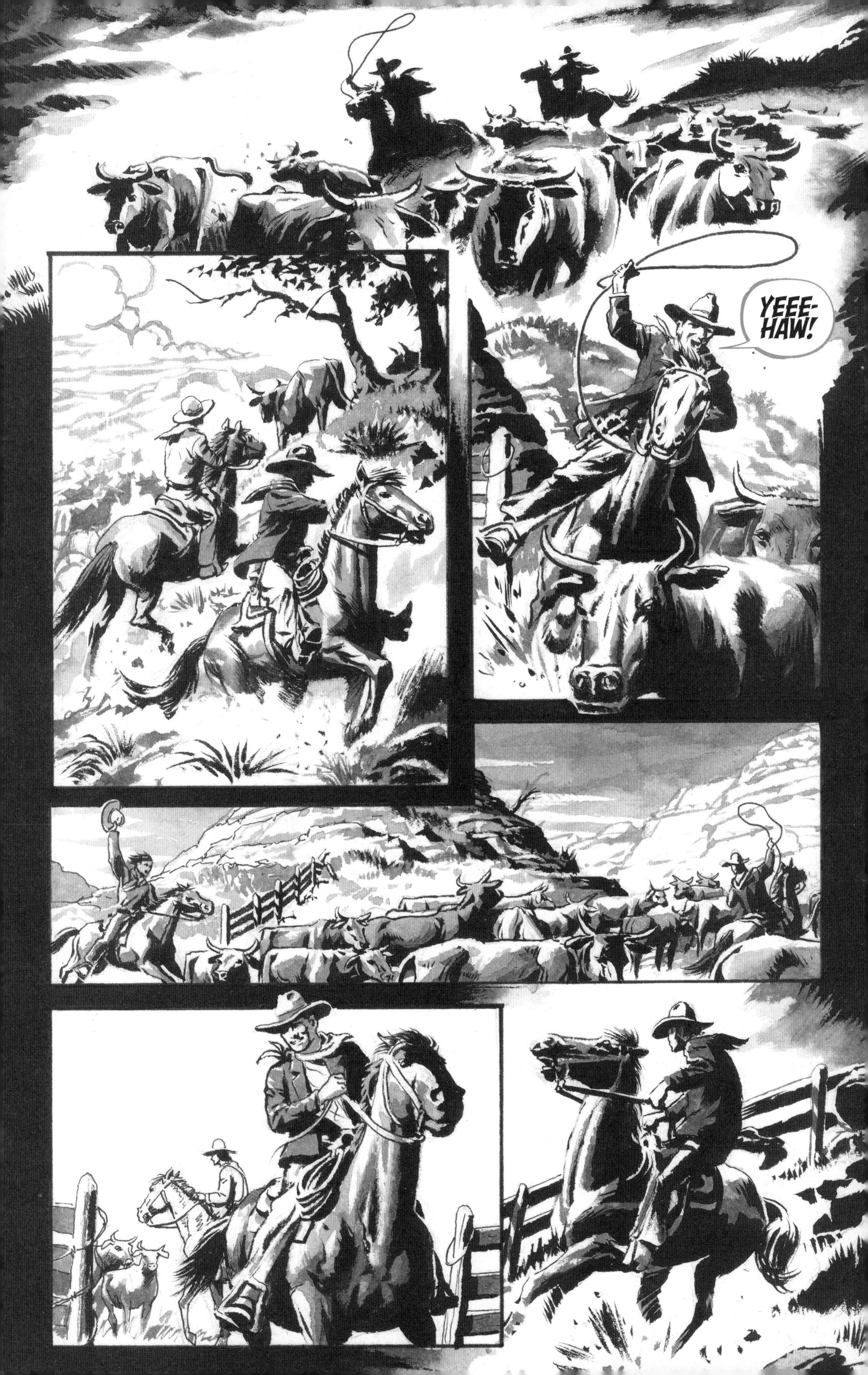
YEEE-
HAW!

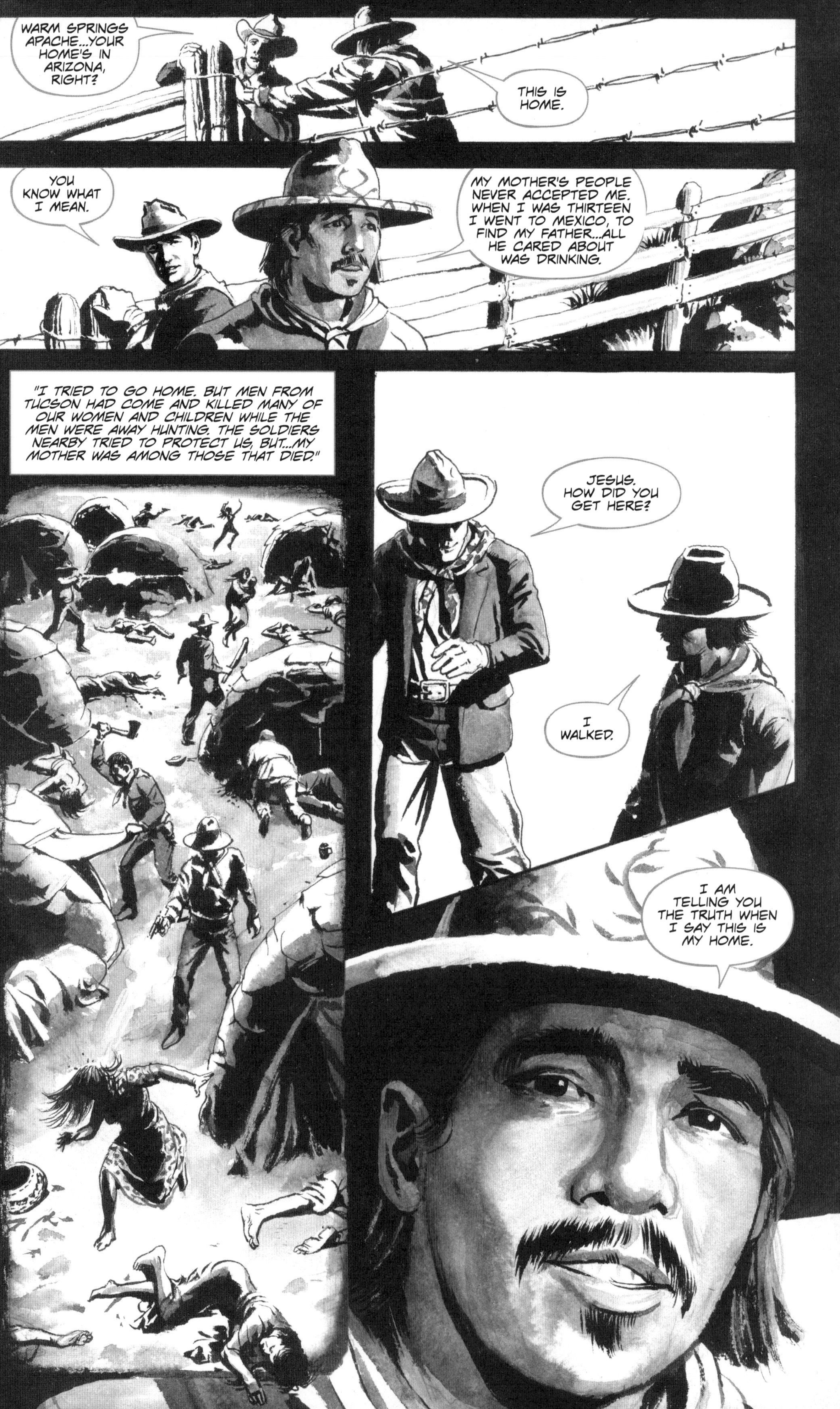
WARM SPRINGS APACHE...YOUR HOME'S IN ARIZONA, RIGHT?
THIS IS HOME.
YOU KNOW WHAT I MEAN.
MY MOTHER'S PEOPLE NEVER ACCEPTED ME. WHEN I WAS THIRTEEN I WENT TO MEXICO, TO FIND MY FATHER...ALL HE CARED ABOUT WAS DRINKING.
"I TRIED TO GO HOME. BUT MEN FROM TUCSON HAD COME AND KILLED MANY OF OUR WOMEN AND CHILDREN WHILE THE MEN WERE AWAY HUNTING. THE SOLDIERS NEARBY TRIED TO PROTECT US, BUT...MY MOTHER WAS AMONG THOSE THAT DIED."
JESUS. HOW DID YOU GET HERE?
I WALKED.
I AM TELLING YOU THE TRUTH WHEN I SAY THIS IS MY HOME.

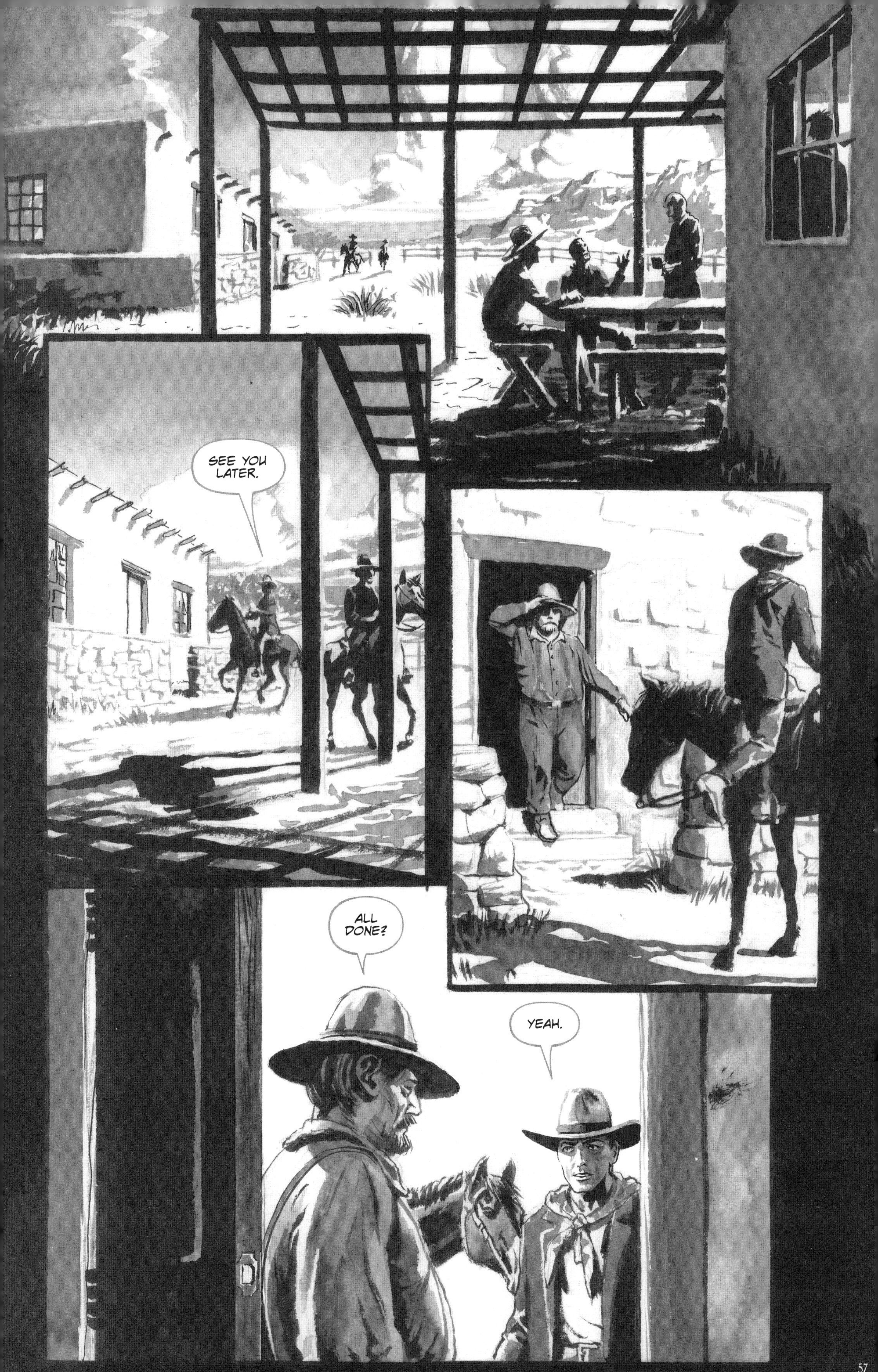
SEE YOU LATER.
ALL DONE?
YEAH.

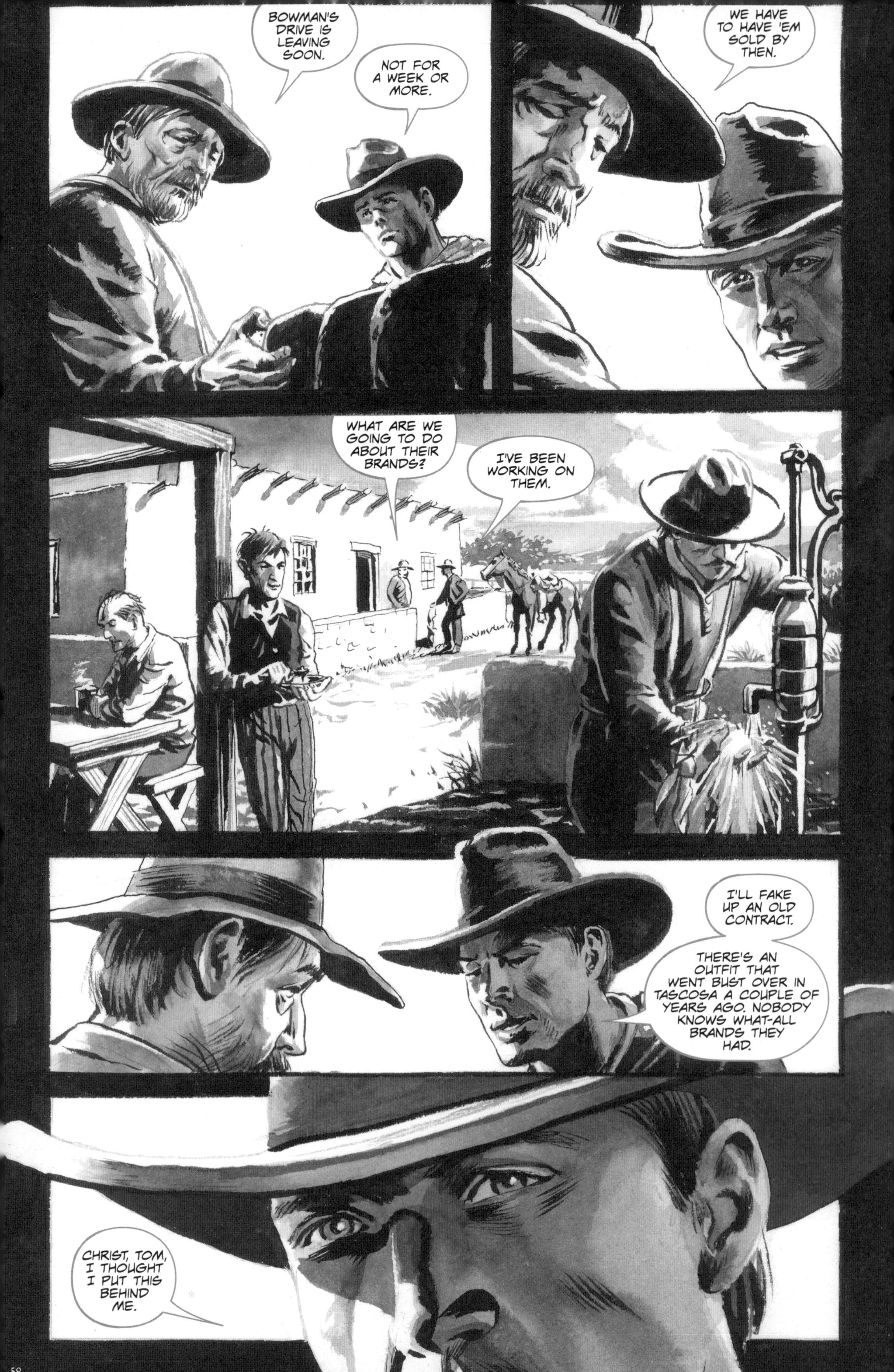
BOWMAN'S DRIVE IS LEAVING SOON.
NOT FOR A WEEK OR MORE.
WE HAVE TO HAVE 'EM SOLD BY THEN.
WHAT ARE WE GOING TO DO ABOUT THEIR BRANDS?
I'VE BEEN WORKING ON THEM.
I'LL FAKE UP AN OLD CONTRACT.
THERE'S AN OUTFIT THAT WENT BUST OVER IN TASCOSA A COUPLE OF YEARS AGO. NOBODY KNOWS WHAT-ALL BRANDS THEY HAD.
CHRIST, TOM, I THOUGHT I PUT THIS BEHIND ME.

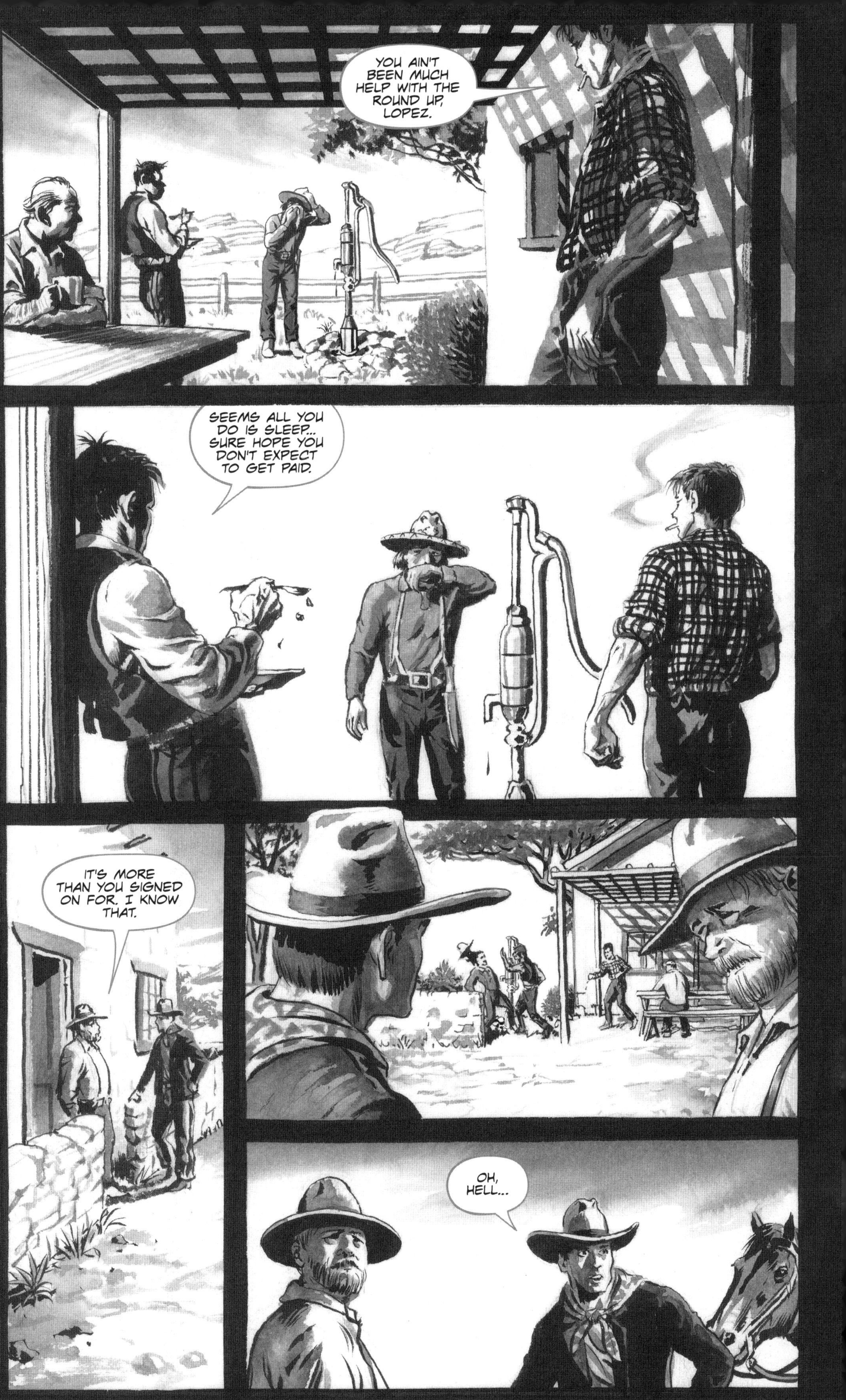
YOU AIN'T BEEN MUCH HELP WITH THE ROUND UP, LOPEZ.
SEEMS ALL YOU DO IS SLEEP... SURE HOPE YOU DON'T EXPECT TO GET PAID.
IT'S MORE THAN YOU SIGNED ON FOR. I KNOW THAT.
OH, HELL...

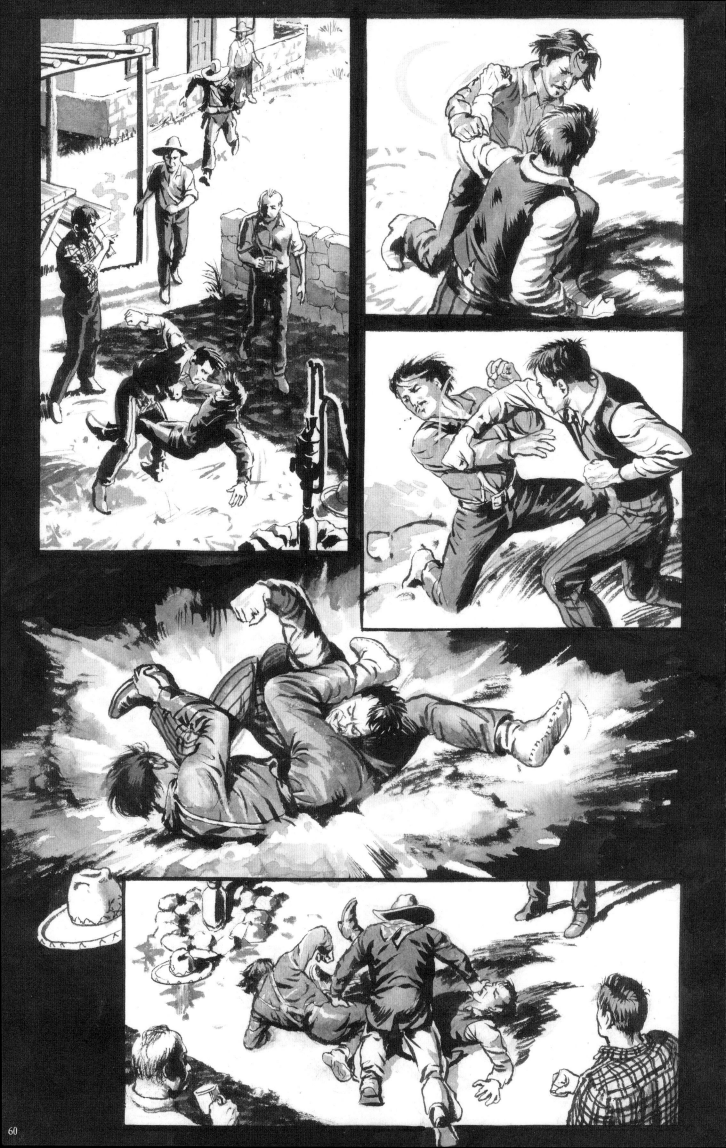

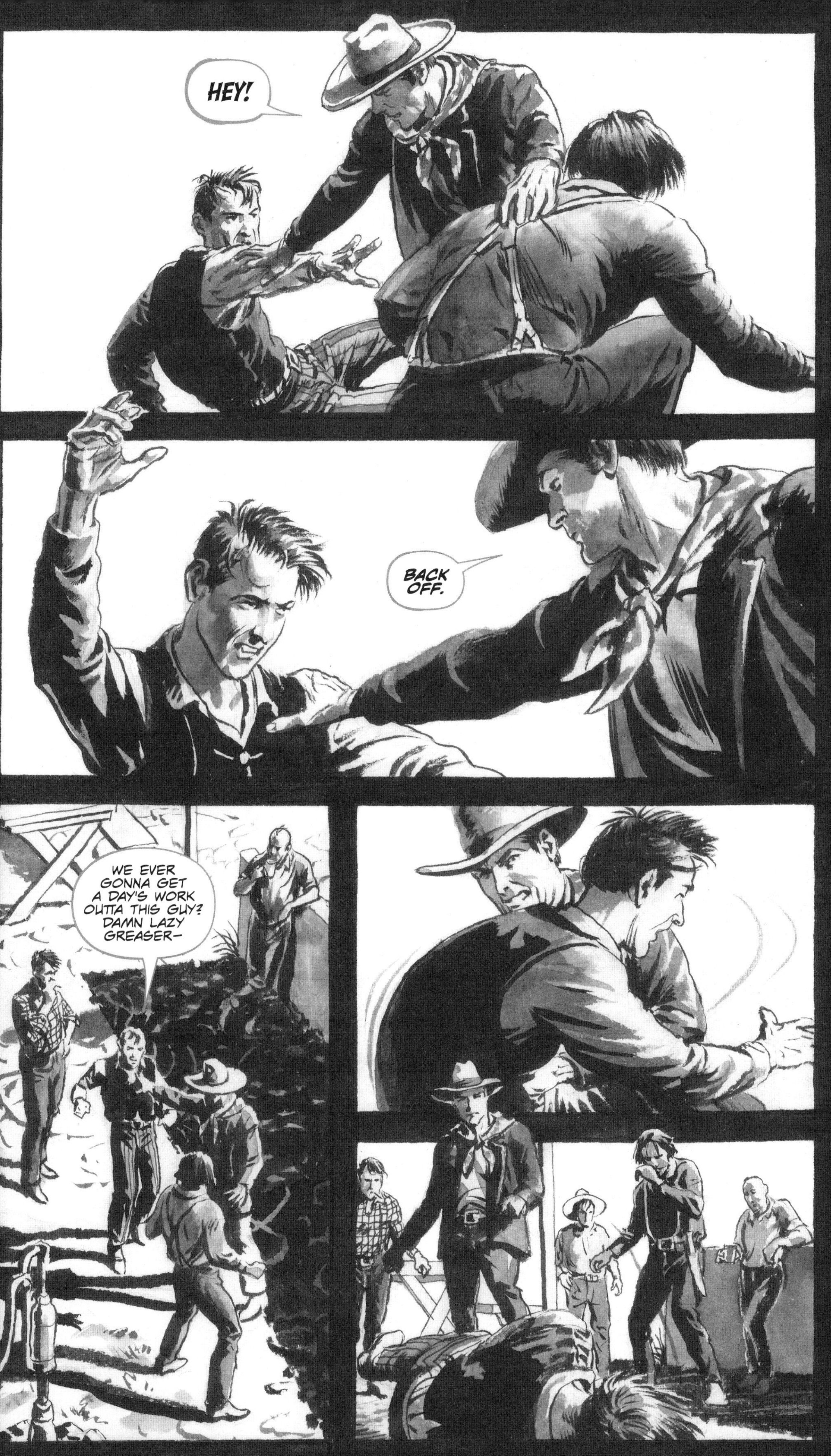
HEY!
BACK OFF.
WE EVER GONNA GET A DAY'S WORK OUTTA THIS GUY? DAMN LAZY GREASER–

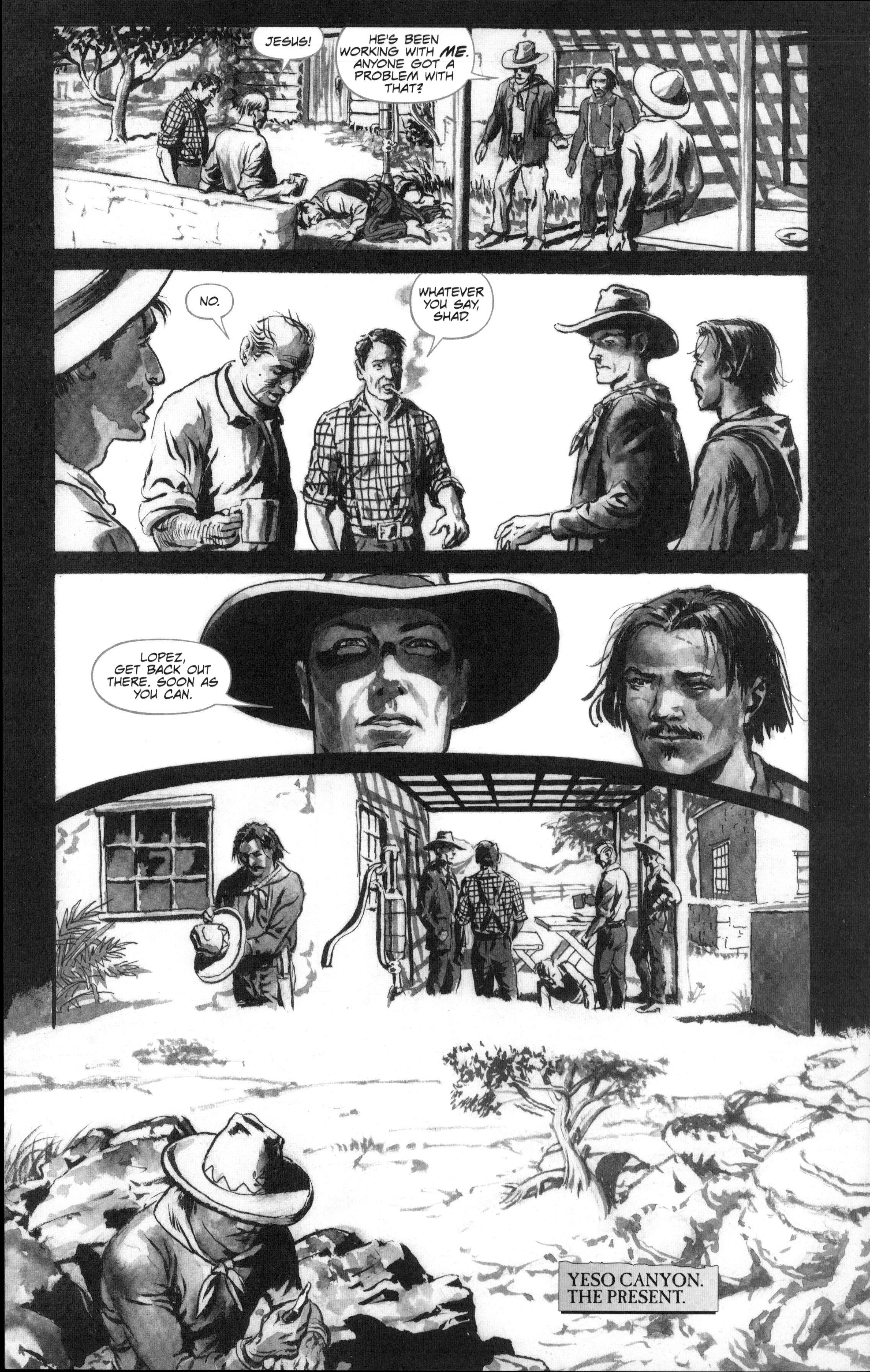
JESUS!
HE'S BEEN WORKING WITH ME. ANYONE GOT A PROBLEM WITH THAT?
NO.
WHATEVER YOU SAY, SHAD.
LOPEZ, GET BACK OUT THERE. SOON AS YOU CAN.
YESO CANYON. THE PRESENT.

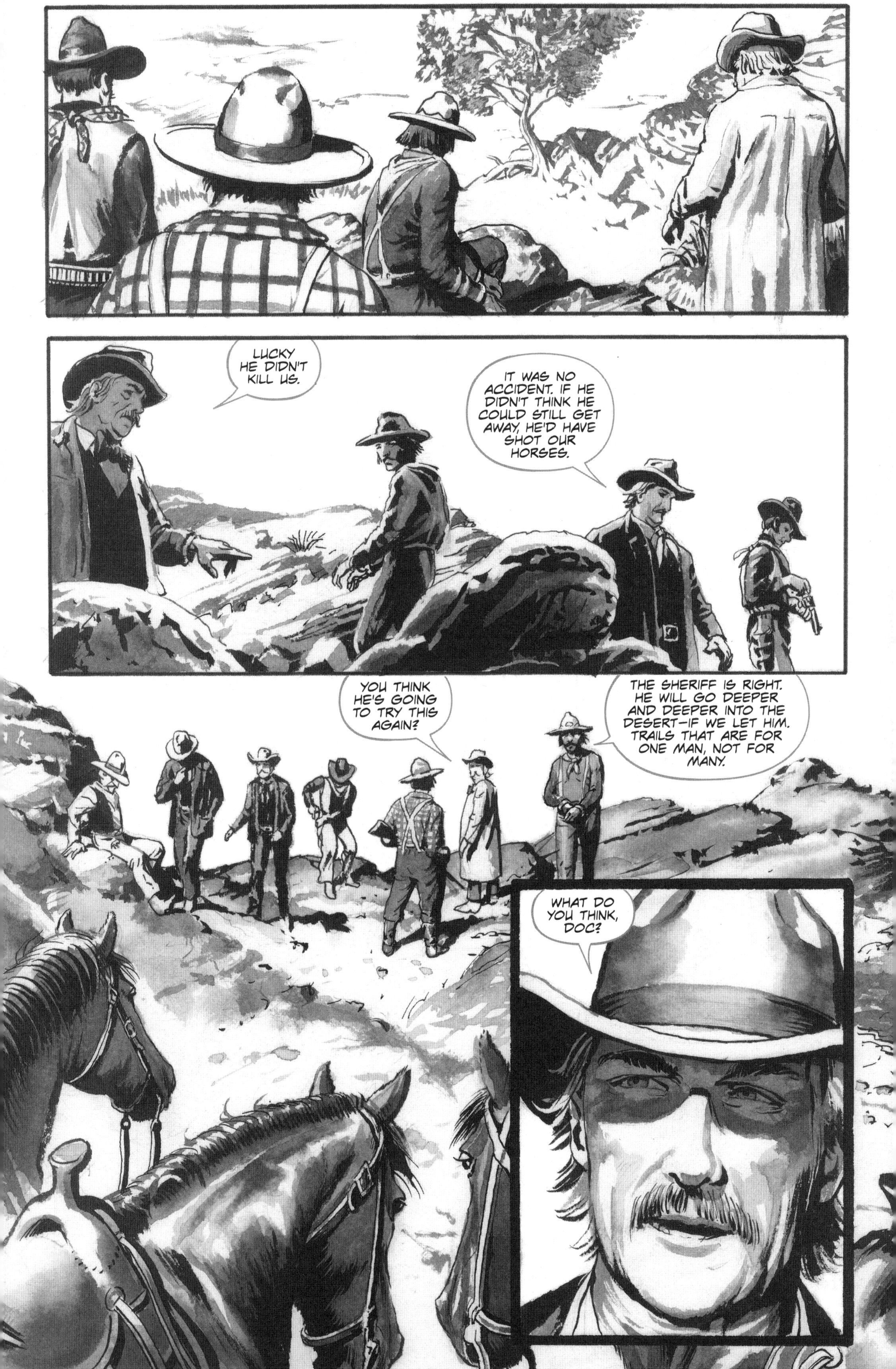
LUCKY HE DIDN'T KILL US.
IT WAS NO ACCIDENT. IF HE DIDN'T THINK HE COULD STILL GET AWAY, HE'D HAVE SHOT OUR HORSES.
YOU THINK HE'S GOING TO TRY THIS AGAIN?
THE SHERIFF IS RIGHT. HE WILL GO DEEPER AND DEEPER INTO THE DESERT–IF WE LET HIM. TRAILS THAT ARE FOR ONE MAN, NOT FOR MANY.
WHAT DO YOU THINK, DOC?

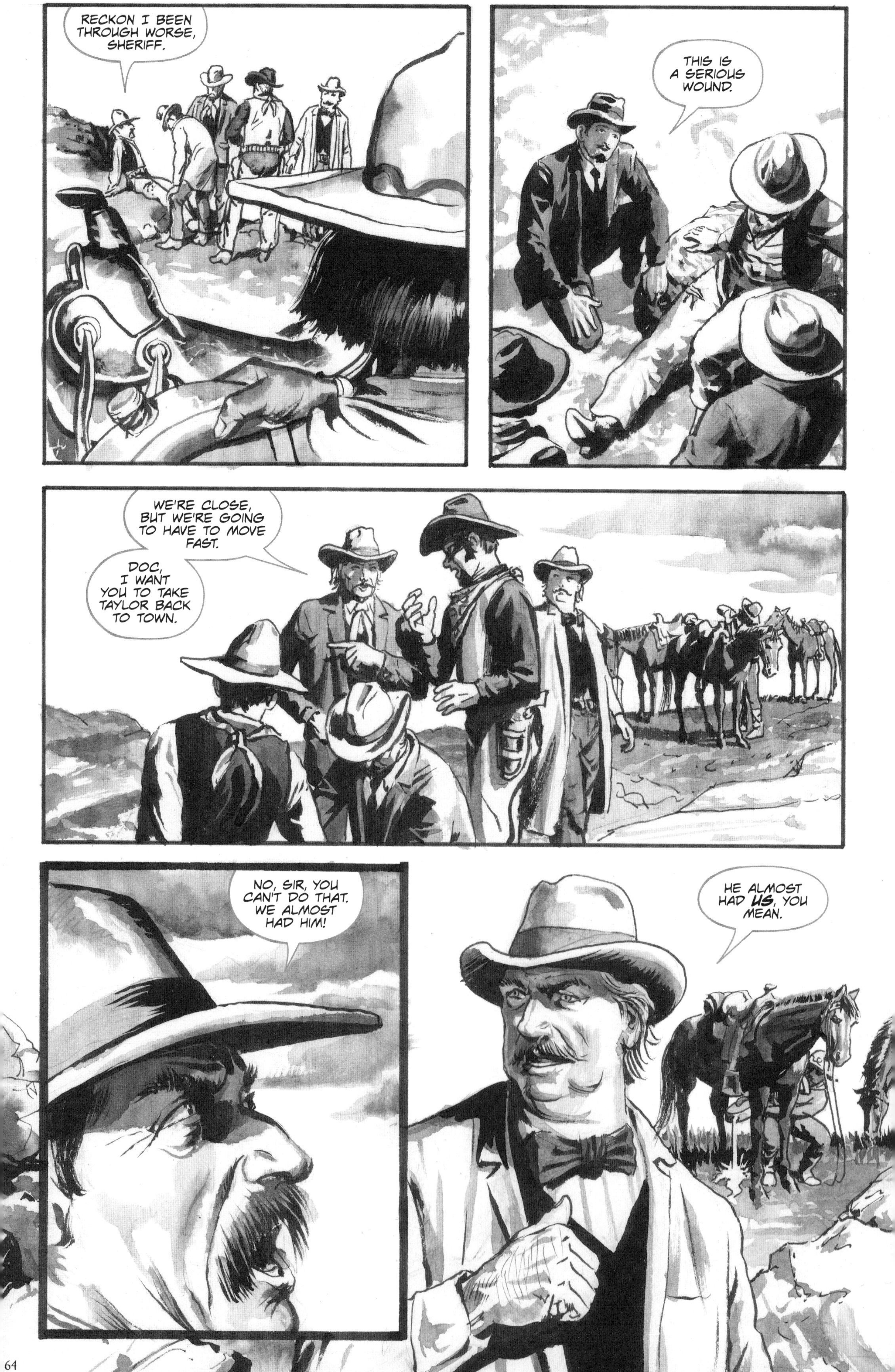
RECKON I BEEN THROUGH WORSE, SHERIFF.
THIS IS A SERIOUS WOUND.
WE'RE CLOSE, BUT WE'RE GOING TO HAVE TO MOVE FAST.
DOC, I WANT YOU TO TAKE TAYLOR BACK TO TOWN.
NO, SIR, YOU CAN'T DO THAT. WE ALMOST HAD HIM!
HE ALMOST HAD **US**, YOU MEAN.

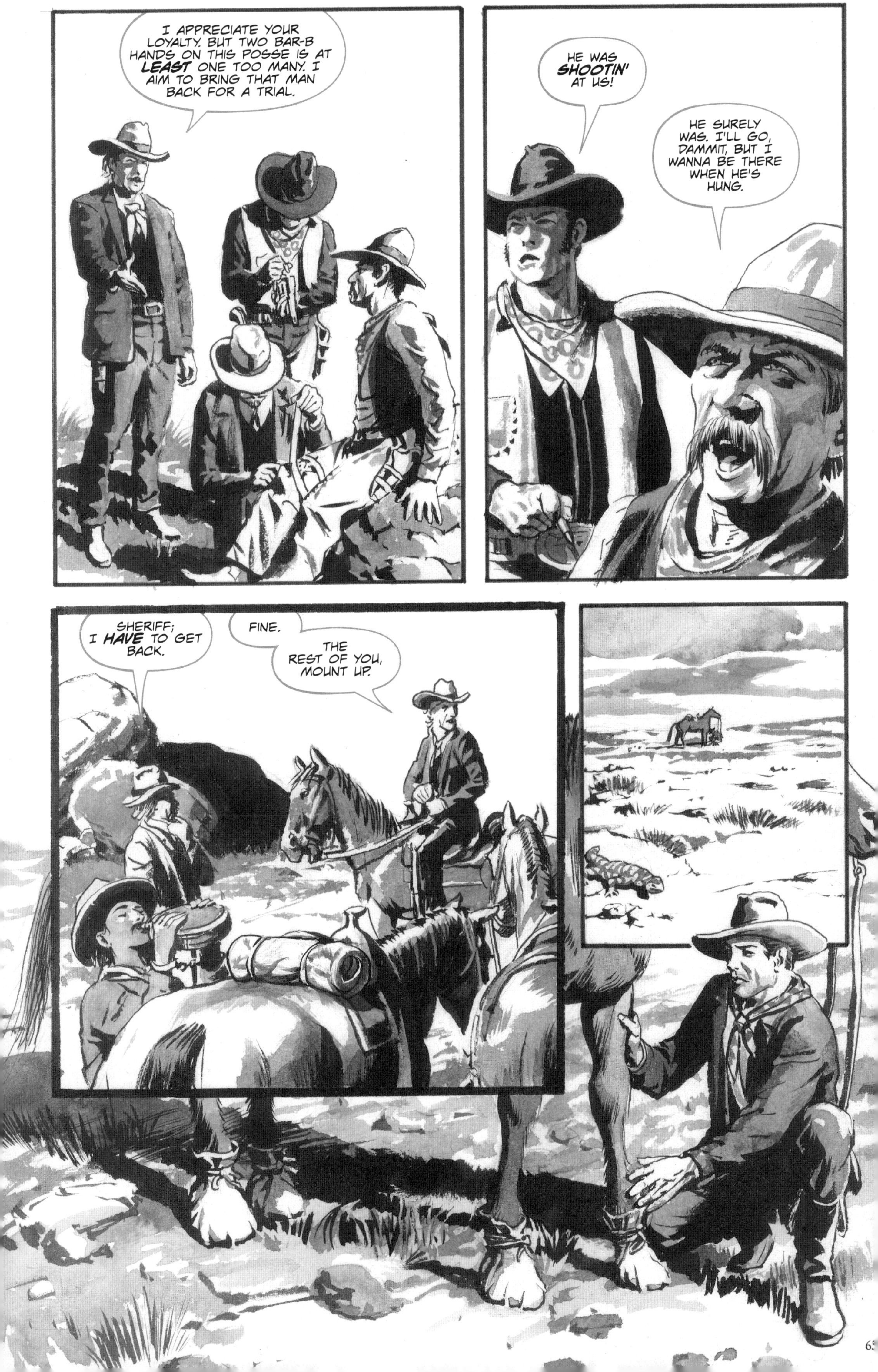
I APPRECIATE YOUR LOYALTY. BUT TWO BAR-B HANDS ON THIS POSSE IS AT LEAST ONE TOO MANY. I AIM TO BRING THAT MAN BACK FOR A TRIAL.
HE WAS SHOOTIN' AT US!
HE SURELY WAS. I'LL GO, DAMMIT, BUT I WANNA BE THERE WHEN HE'S HUNG.
SHERIFF; I HAVE TO GET BACK.
FINE.
THE REST OF YOU, MOUNT UP.

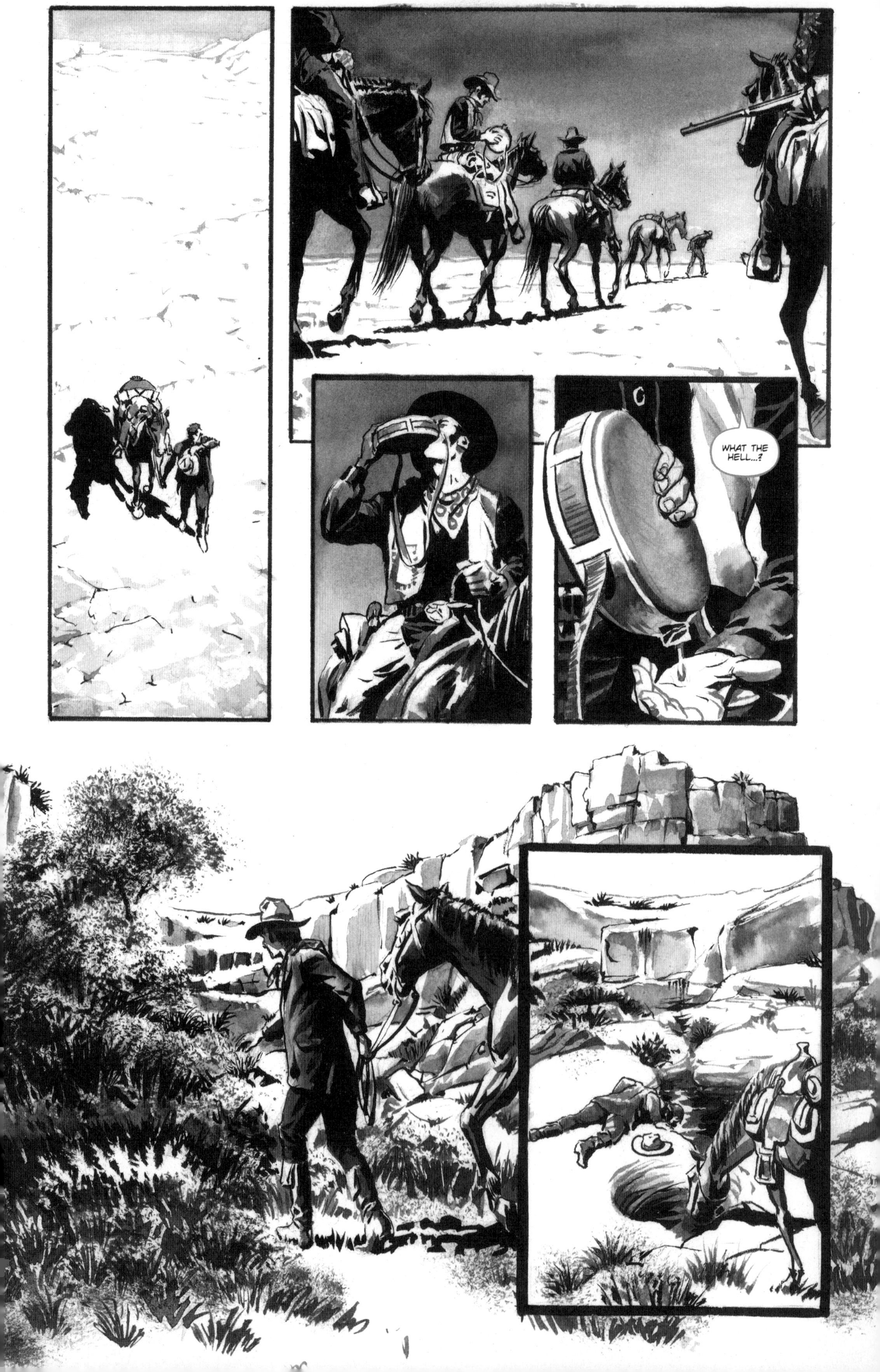
WHAT THE HELL...?

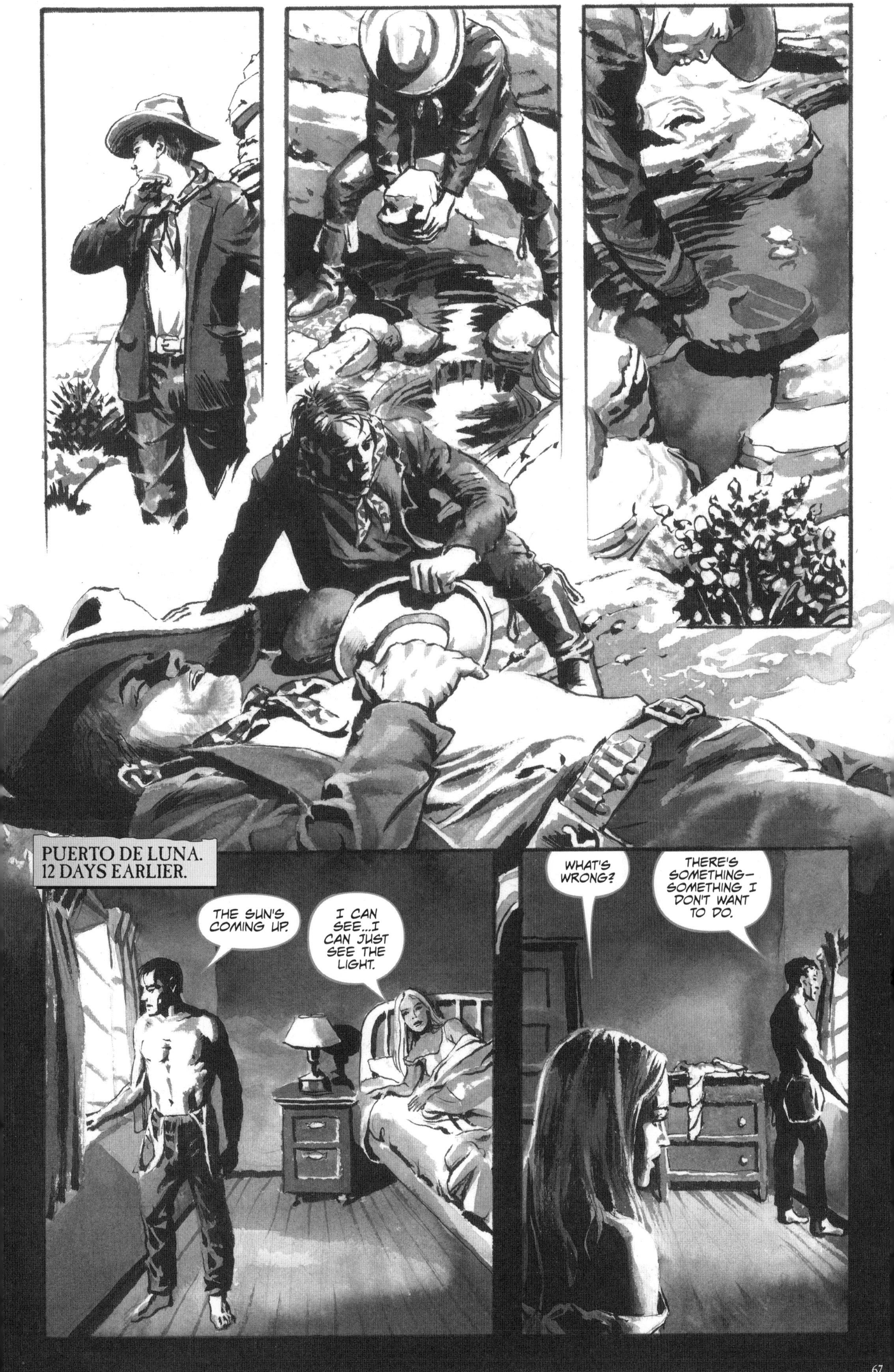

PUERTO DE LUNA.
12 DAYS EARLIER.
THE SUN'S COMING UP.
I CAN SEE...I CAN JUST SEE THE LIGHT.
WHAT'S WRONG?
THERE'S SOMETHING— SOMETHING I DON'T WANT TO DO.

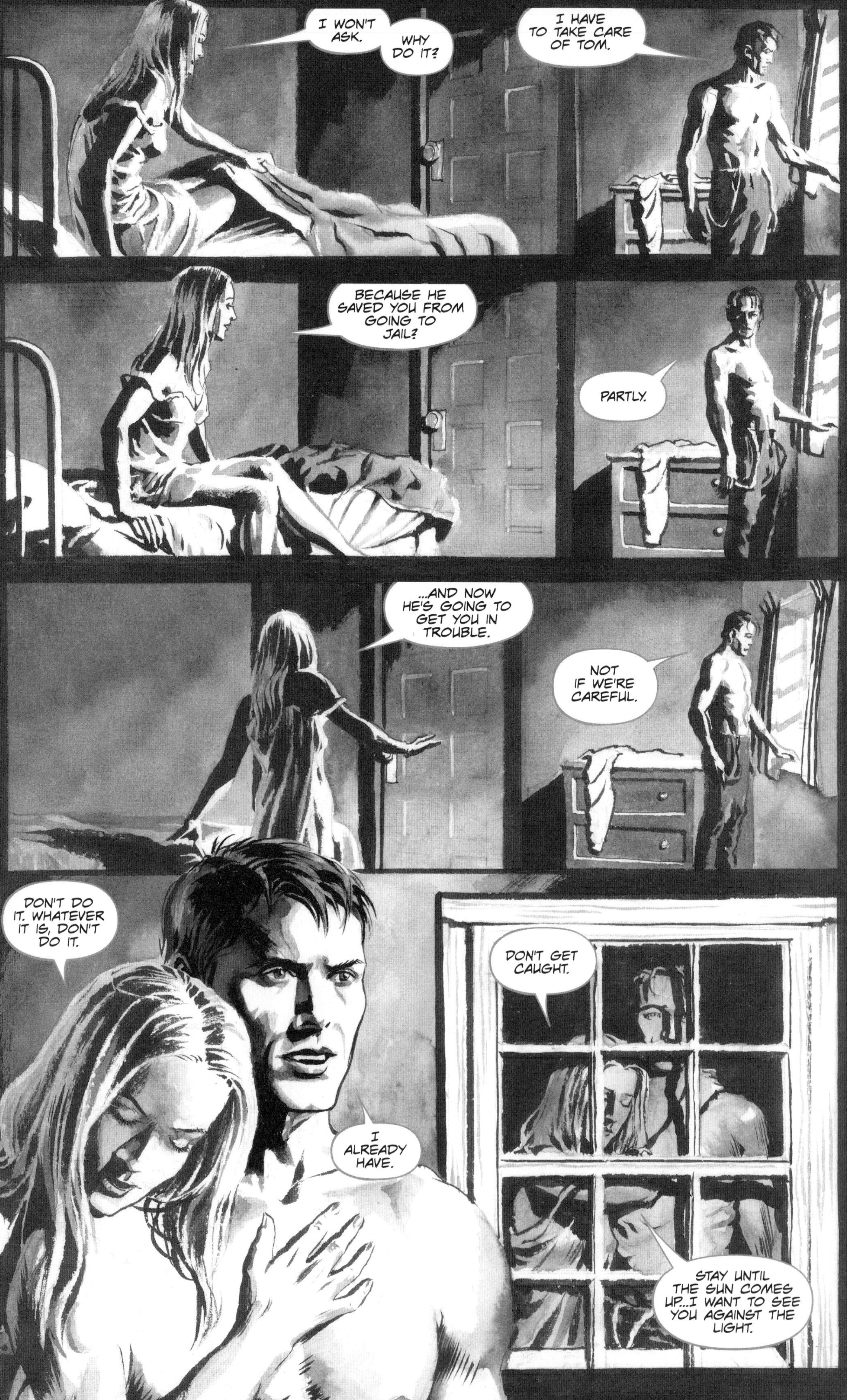
I WON'T ASK.
WHY DO IT?
I HAVE TO TAKE CARE OF TOM.
BECAUSE HE SAVED YOU FROM GOING TO JAIL?
PARTLY.
...AND NOW HE'S GOING TO GET YOU IN TROUBLE.
NOT IF WE'RE CAREFUL.
DON'T DO IT. WHATEVER IT IS, DON'T DO IT.
I ALREADY HAVE.
DON'T GET CAUGHT.
STAY UNTIL THE SUN COMES UP...I WANT TO SEE YOU AGAINST THE LIGHT.

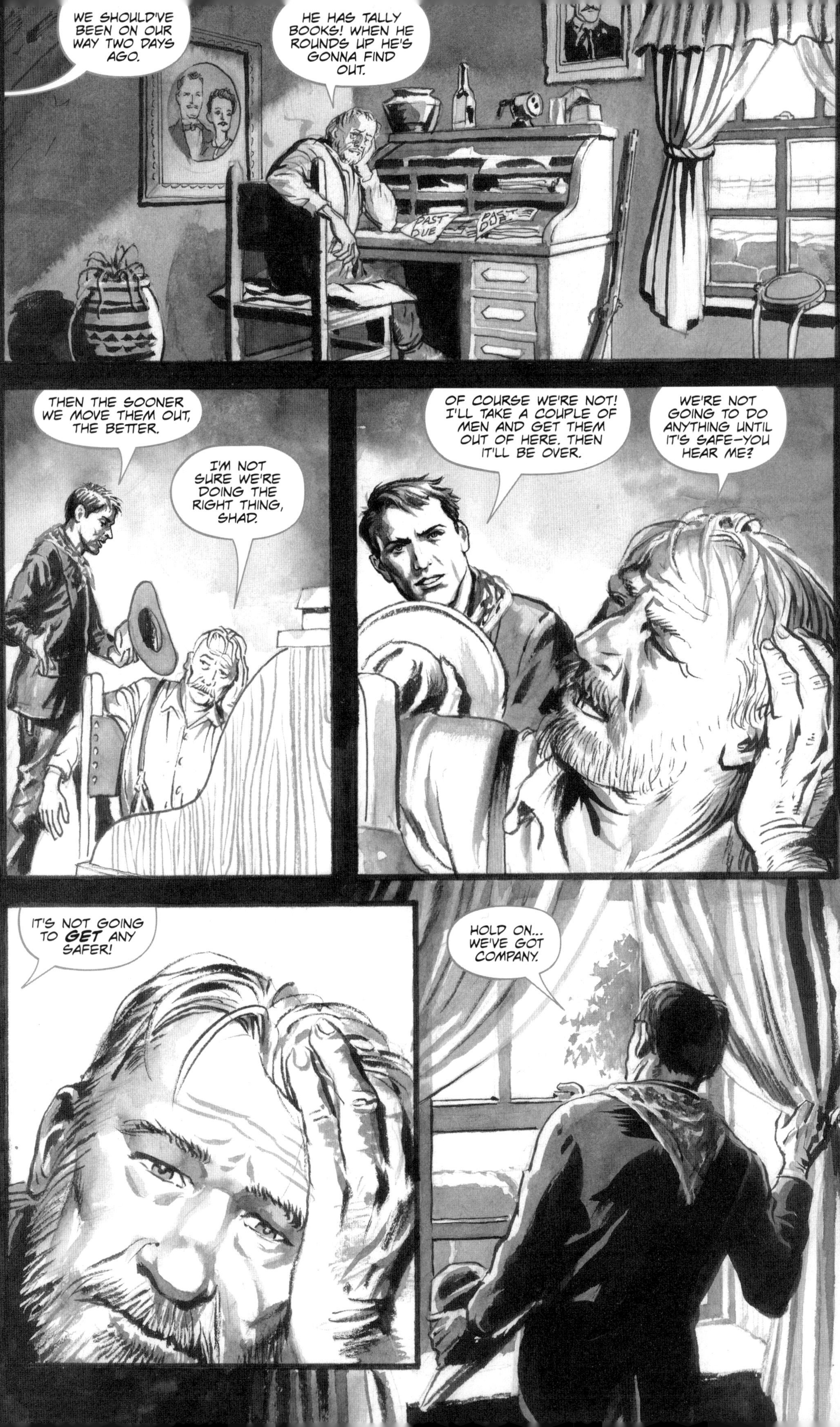
WE SHOULD'VE BEEN ON OUR WAY TWO DAYS AGO.
HE HAS TALLY BOOKS! WHEN HE ROUNDS UP HE'S GONNA FIND OUT.
PAST DUE
PAST DUE
THEN THE SOONER WE MOVE THEM OUT, THE BETTER.
I'M NOT SURE WE'RE DOING THE RIGHT THING, SHAD.
WE'RE NOT GOING TO DO ANYTHING UNTIL IT'S SAFE--YOU HEAR ME?
OF COURSE WE'RE NOT! I'LL TAKE A COUPLE OF MEN AND GET THEM OUT OF HERE. THEN IT'LL BE OVER.
IT'S NOT GOING TO **GET** ANY SAFER!
HOLD ON... WE'VE GOT COMPANY.

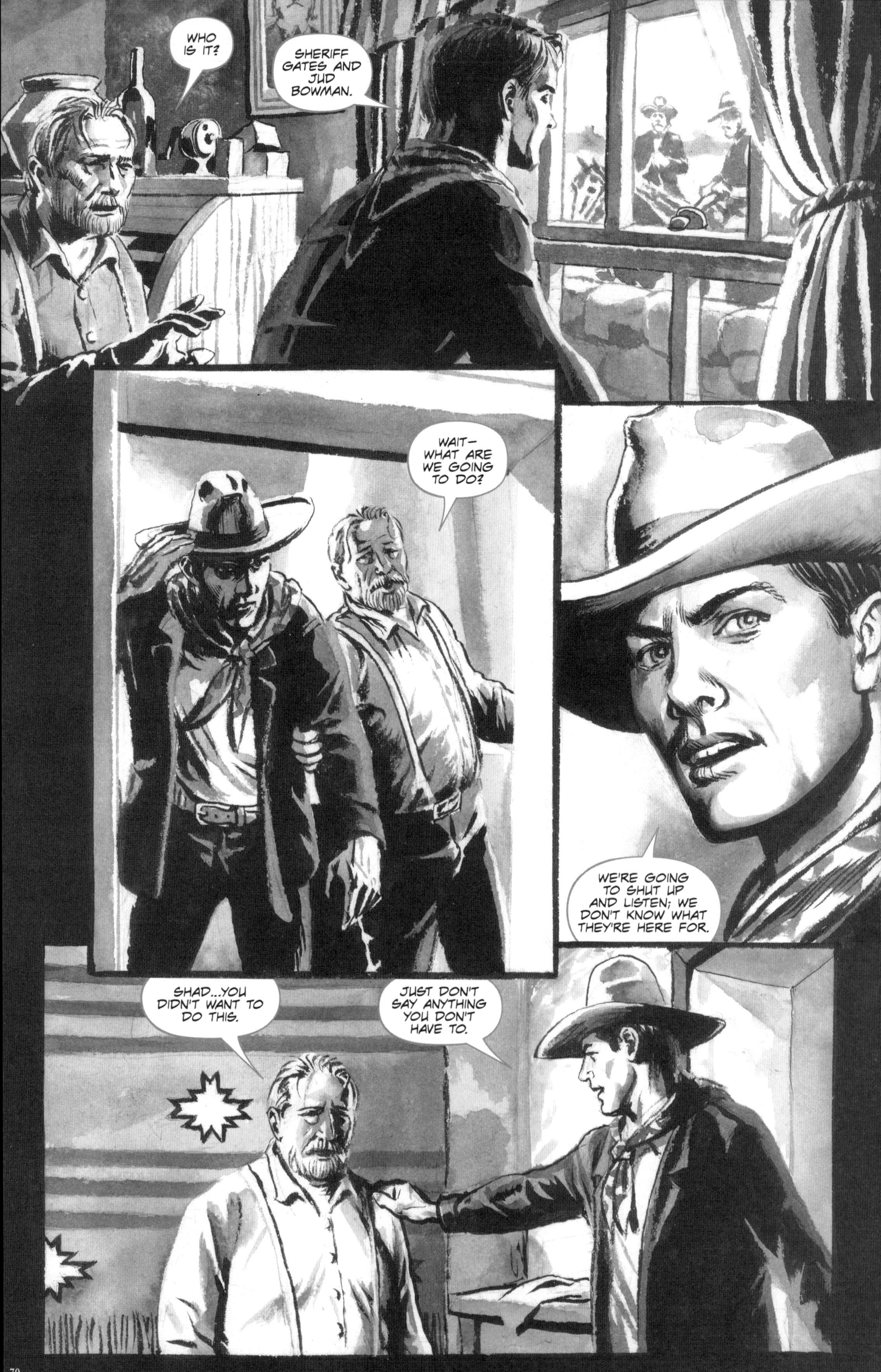
WHO IS IT?
SHERIFF GATES AND JUD BOWMAN.
WAIT— WHAT ARE WE GOING TO DO?
WE'RE GOING TO SHUT UP AND LISTEN; WE DON'T KNOW WHAT THEY'RE HERE FOR.
SHAD...YOU DIDN'T WANT TO DO THIS.
JUST DON'T SAY ANYTHING YOU DON'T HAVE TO.

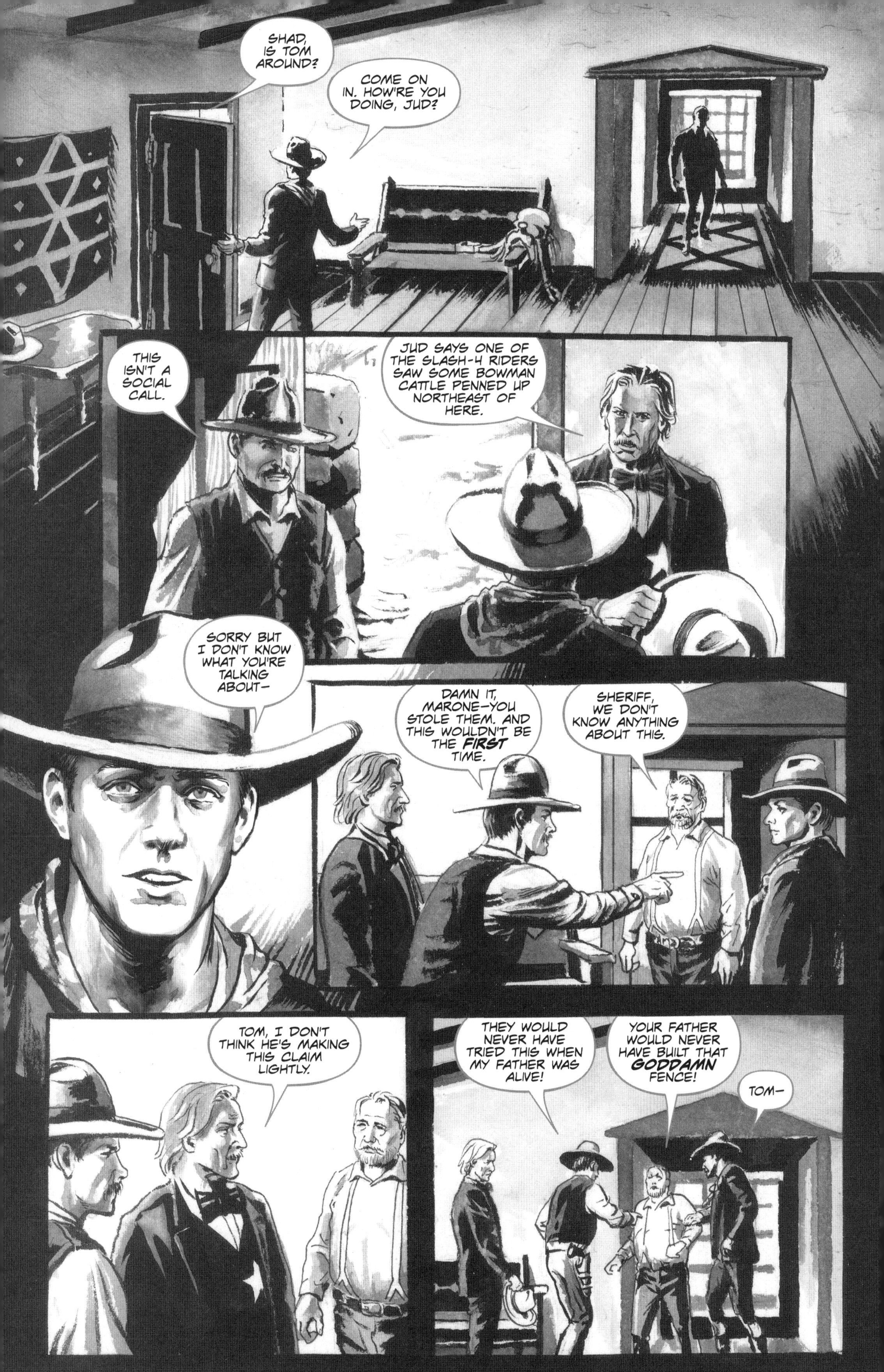

SHAD, IS TOM AROUND?
COME ON IN. HOW'RE YOU DOING, JUD?
THIS ISN'T A SOCIAL CALL.
JUD SAYS ONE OF THE SLASH-4 RIDERS SAW SOME BOWMAN CATTLE PENNED UP NORTHEAST OF HERE.
SORRY BUT I DON'T KNOW WHAT YOU'RE TALKING ABOUT—
DAMN IT, MARONE—YOU STOLE THEM. AND THIS WOULDN'T BE THE *FIRST* TIME.
SHERIFF, WE DON'T KNOW ANYTHING ABOUT THIS.
TOM, I DON'T THINK HE'S MAKING THIS CLAIM LIGHTLY.
THEY WOULD NEVER HAVE TRIED THIS WHEN MY FATHER WAS ALIVE!
YOUR FATHER WOULD NEVER HAVE BUILT THAT *GODDAMN* FENCE!
TOM—

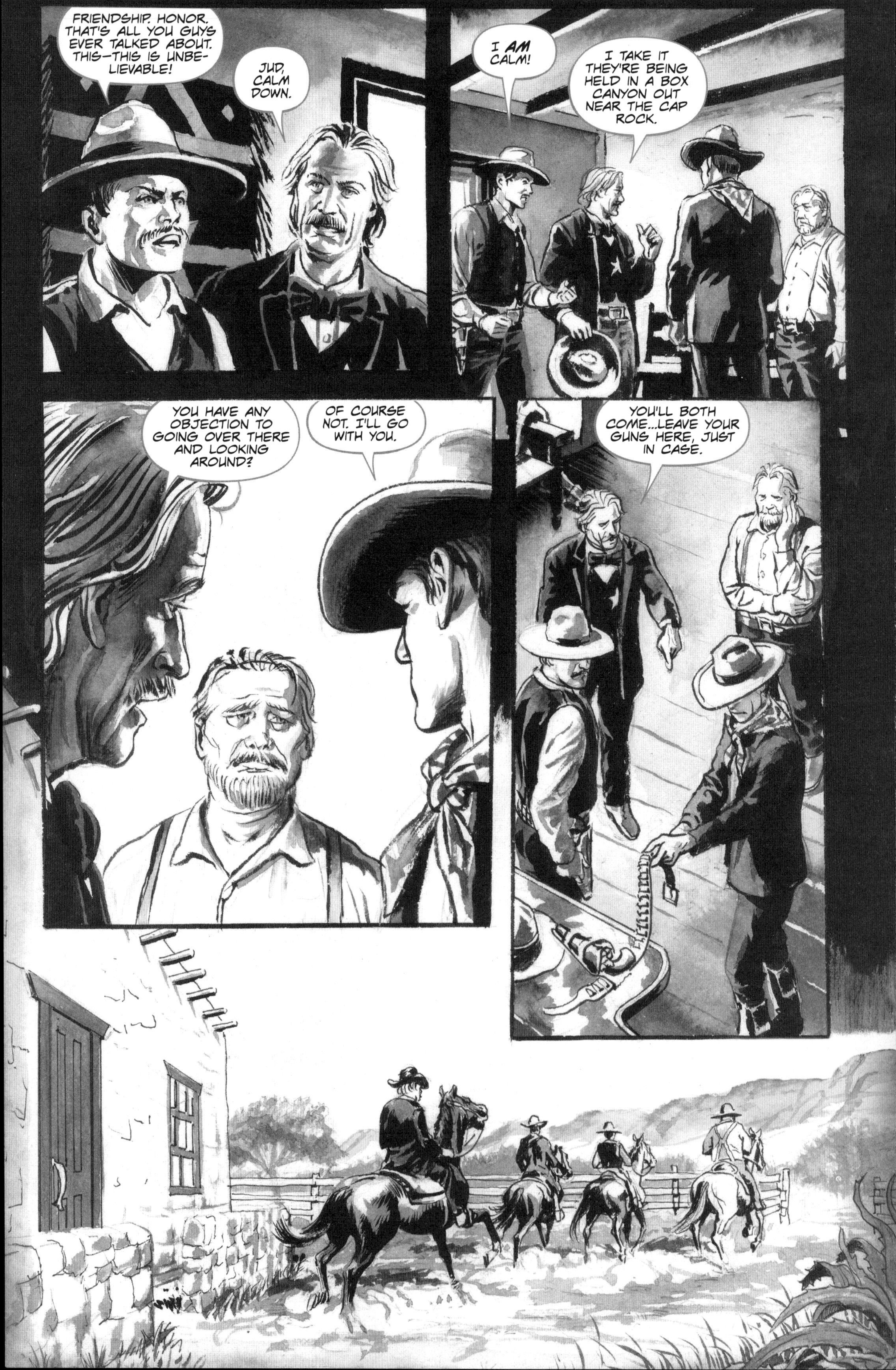
FRIENDSHIP. HONOR. THAT'S ALL YOU GUYS EVER TALKED ABOUT. THIS—THIS IS UNBE-LIEVABLE!
JUD, CALM DOWN.
I AM CALM!
I TAKE IT THEY'RE BEING HELD IN A BOX CANYON OUT NEAR THE CAP ROCK.
YOU HAVE ANY OBJECTION TO GOING OVER THERE AND LOOKING AROUND?
OF COURSE NOT. I'LL GO WITH YOU.
YOU'LL BOTH COME...LEAVE YOUR GUNS HERE, JUST IN CASE.

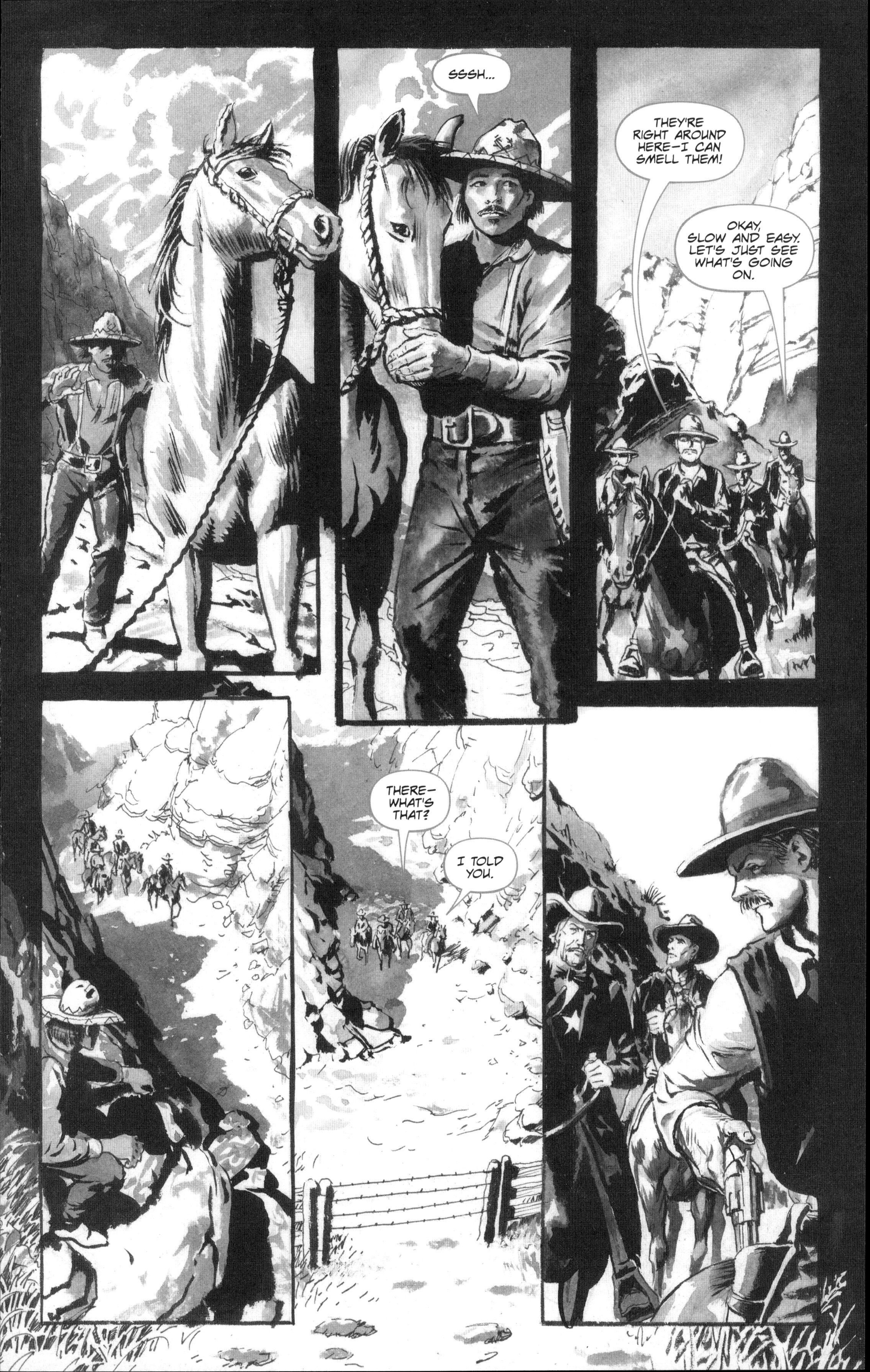
SSSH...
THEY'RE RIGHT AROUND HERE–I CAN SMELL THEM!
OKAY, SLOW AND EASY. LET'S JUST SEE WHAT'S GOING ON.
THERE–WHAT'S THAT?
I TOLD YOU.

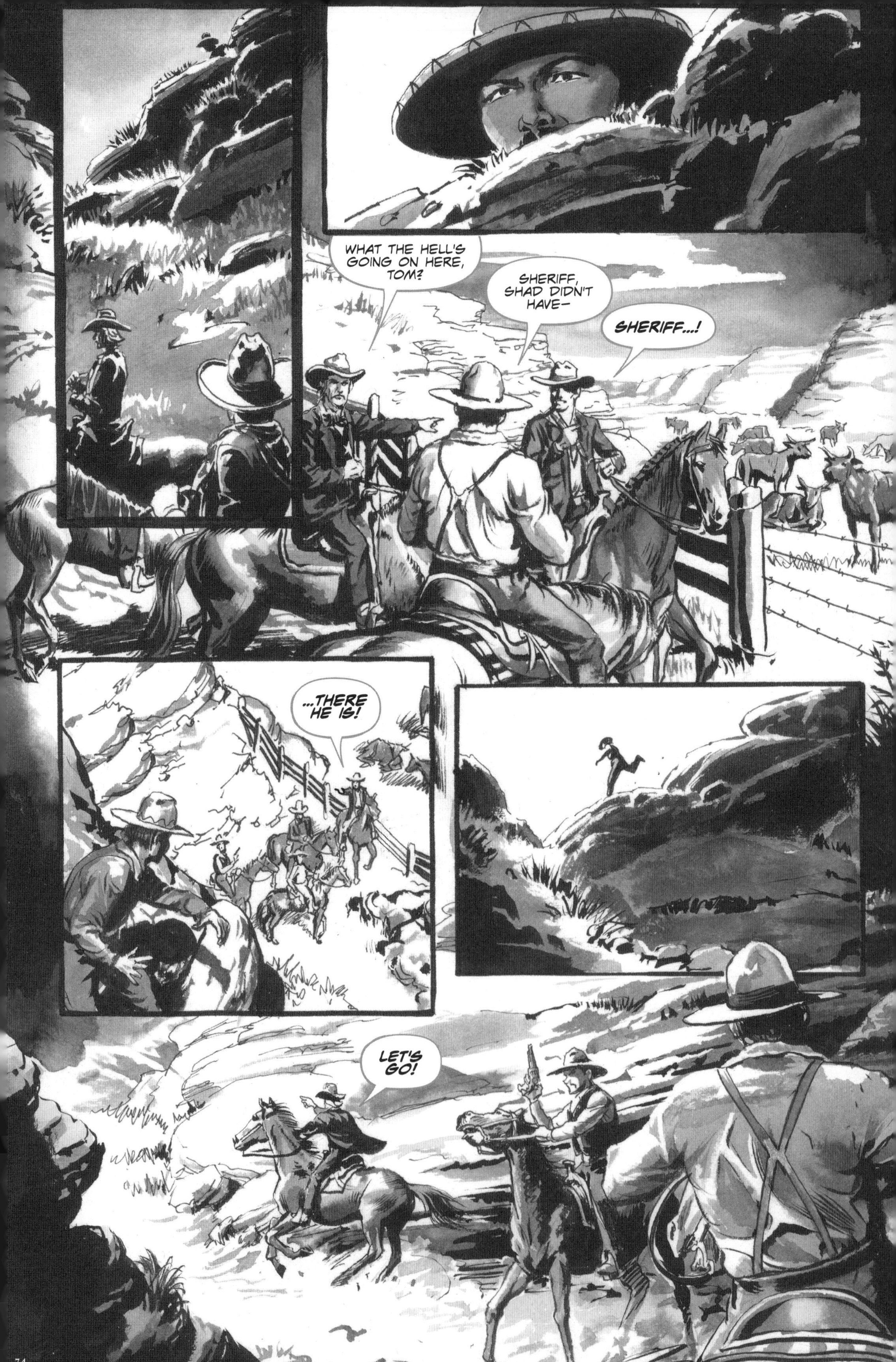
WHAT THE HELL'S GOING ON HERE, TOM?
SHERIFF, SHAD DIDN'T HAVE–
SHERIFF...!
...THERE HE IS!
LET'S GO!

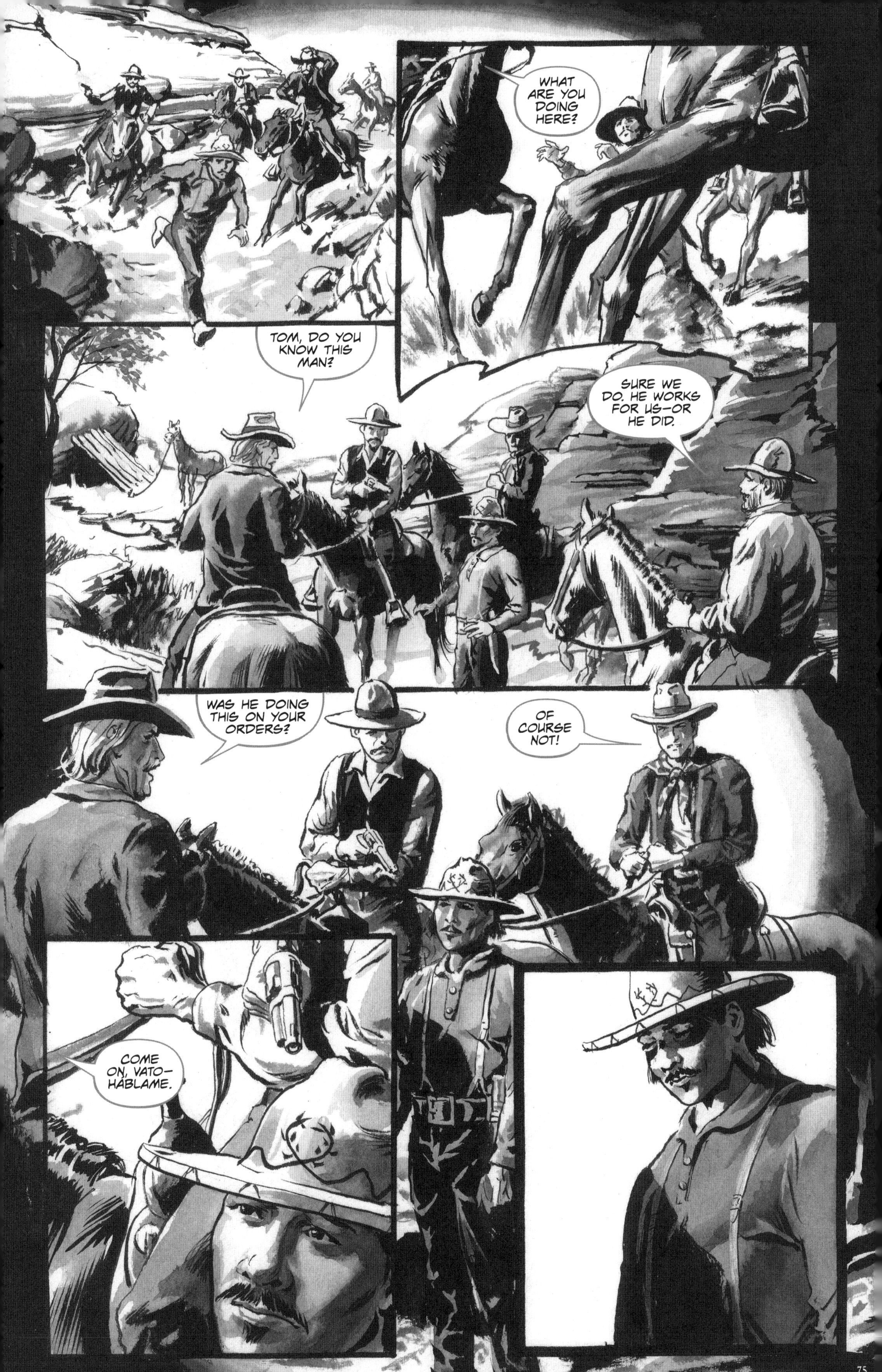
WHAT ARE YOU DOING HERE?
TOM, DO YOU KNOW THIS MAN?
SURE WE DO. HE WORKS FOR US—OR HE DID.
WAS HE DOING THIS ON YOUR ORDERS?
OF COURSE NOT!
COME ON, VATO—HÁBLAME.

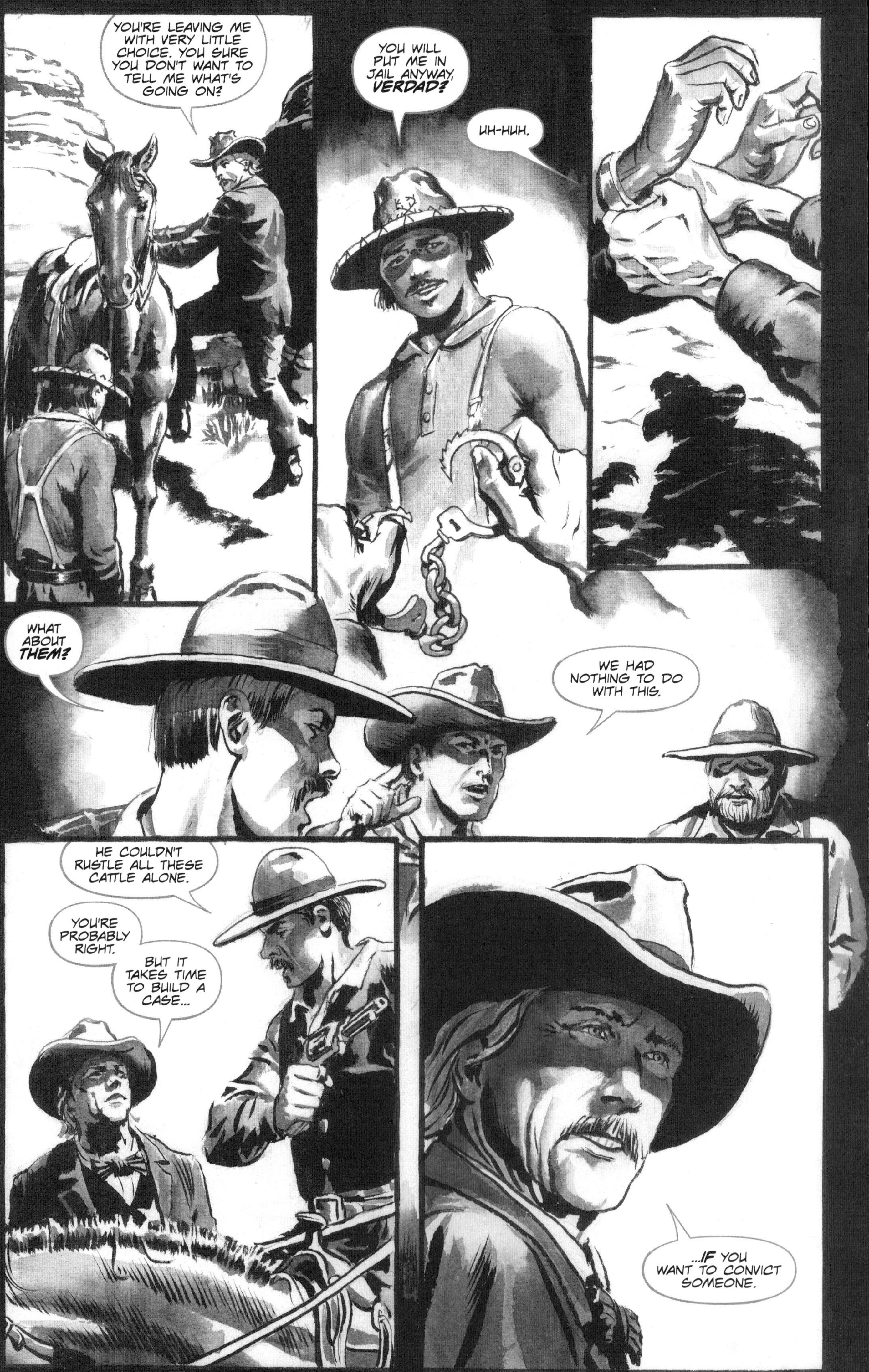
YOU'RE LEAVING ME WITH VERY LITTLE CHOICE. YOU SURE YOU DON'T WANT TO TELL ME WHAT'S GOING ON?
YOU WILL PUT ME IN JAIL ANYWAY, VERDAD?
UH-HUH.
WHAT ABOUT THEM?
WE HAD NOTHING TO DO WITH THIS.
HE COULDN'T RUSTLE ALL THESE CATTLE ALONE.
YOU'RE PROBABLY RIGHT.
BUT IT TAKES TIME TO BUILD A CASE...
...IF YOU WANT TO CONVICT SOMEONE.

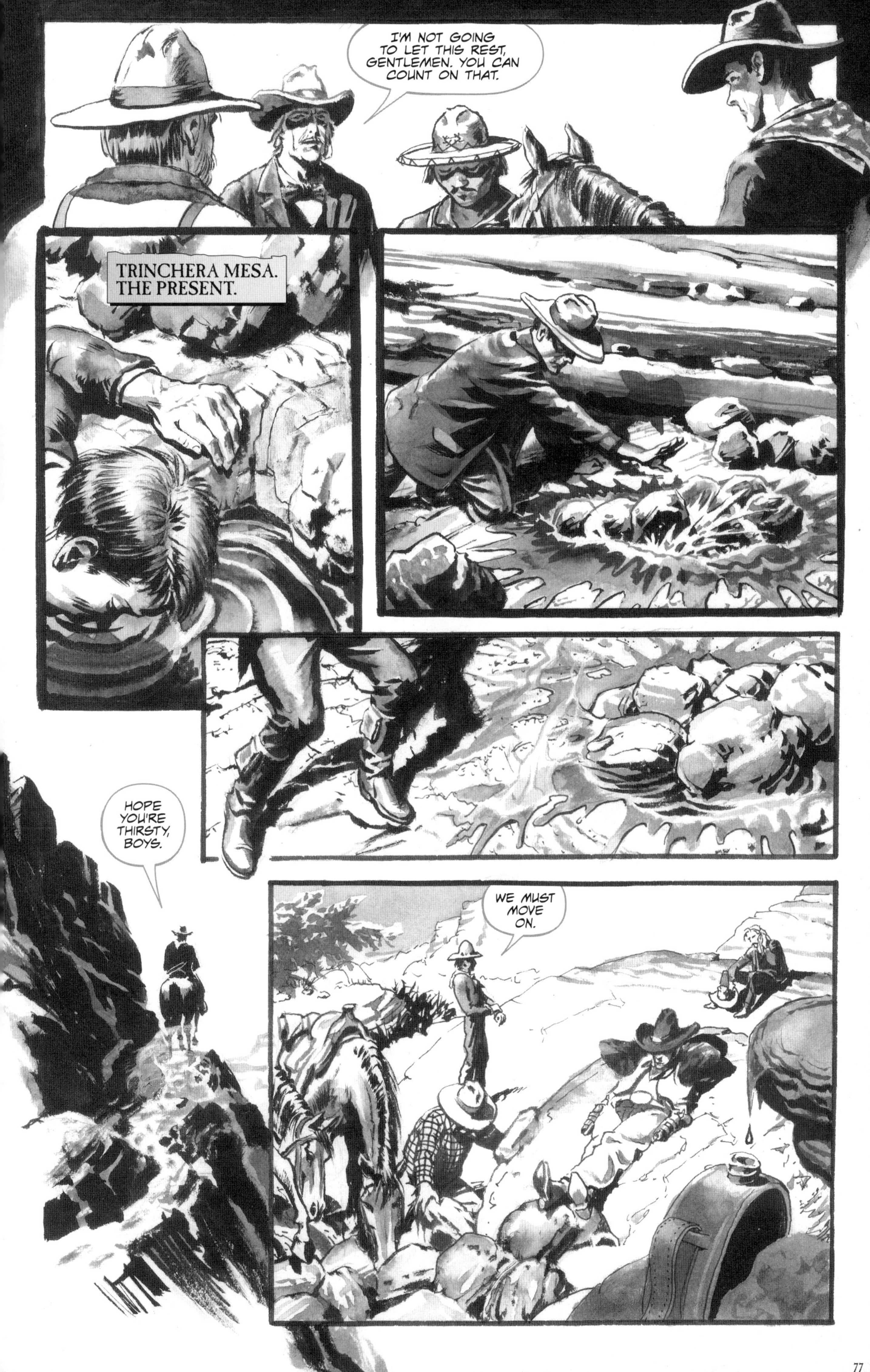

I'M NOT GOING TO LET THIS REST, GENTLEMEN. YOU CAN COUNT ON THAT.
TRINCHERA MESA. THE PRESENT.
HOPE YOU'RE THIRSTY, BOYS.
WE MUST MOVE ON.

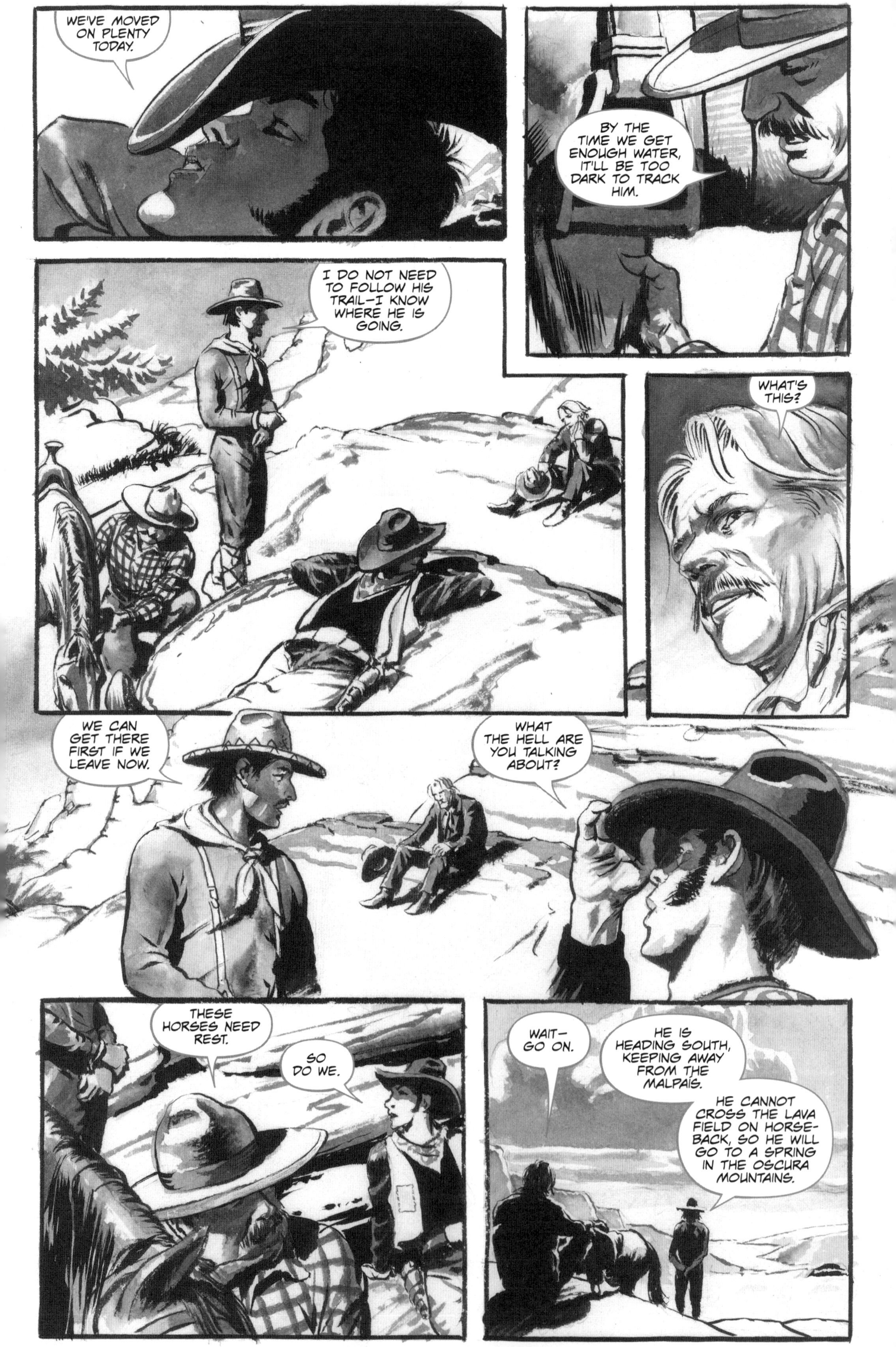
WE'VE MOVED ON PLENTY TODAY.
BY THE TIME WE GET ENOUGH WATER, IT'LL BE TOO DARK TO TRACK HIM.
I DO NOT NEED TO FOLLOW HIS TRAIL—I KNOW WHERE HE IS GOING.
WHAT'S THIS?
WE CAN GET THERE FIRST IF WE LEAVE NOW.
WHAT THE HELL ARE YOU TALKING ABOUT?
THESE HORSES NEED REST.
SO DO WE.
WAIT—GO ON.
HE IS HEADING SOUTH, KEEPING AWAY FROM THE MALPAIS.
HE CANNOT CROSS THE LAVA FIELD ON HORSE-BACK, SO HE WILL GO TO A SPRING IN THE OSCURA MOUNTAINS.

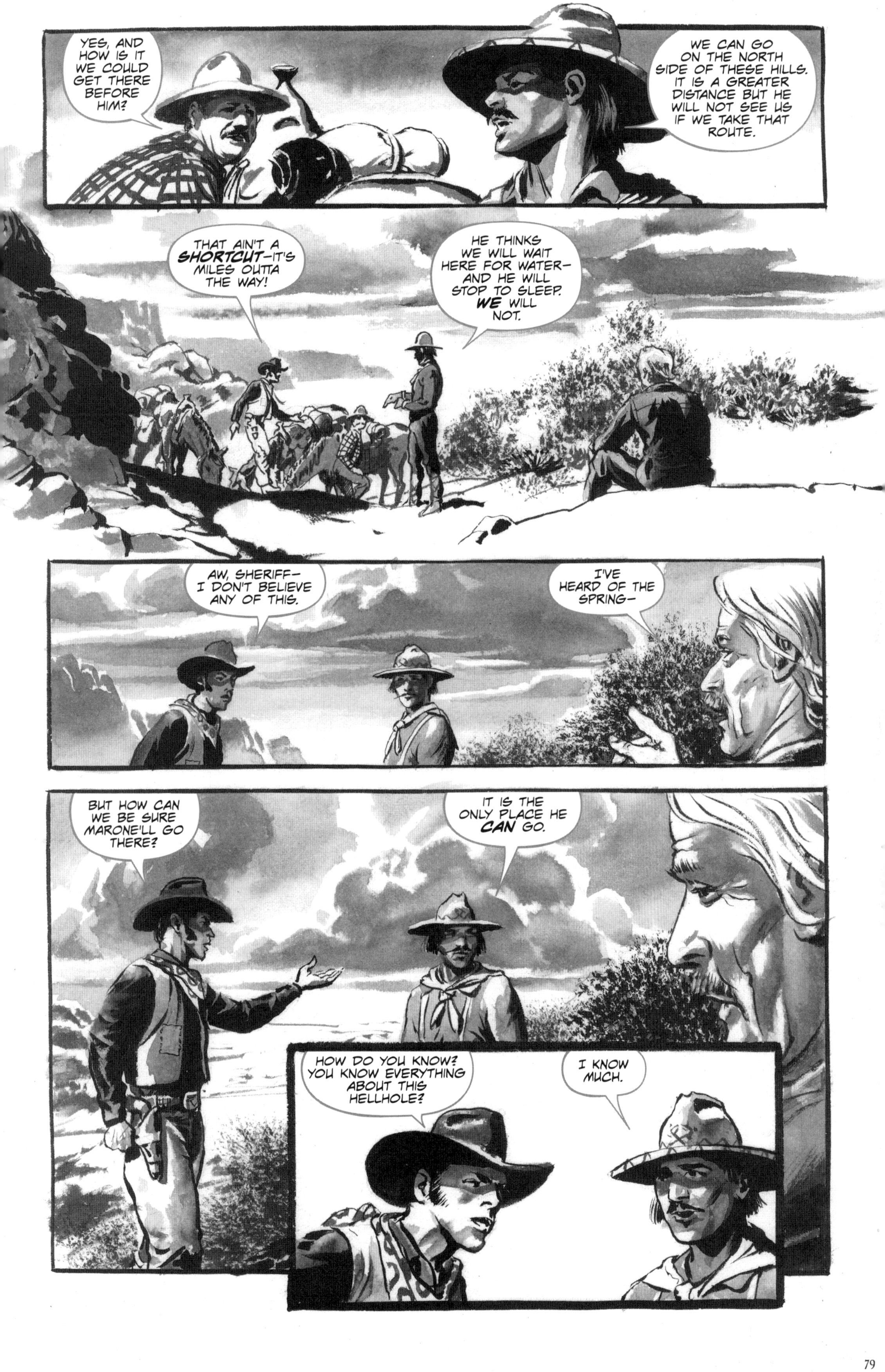
YES, AND HOW IS IT WE COULD GET THERE BEFORE HIM?
WE CAN GO ON THE NORTH SIDE OF THESE HILLS. IT IS A GREATER DISTANCE BUT HE WILL NOT SEE US IF WE TAKE THAT ROUTE.
THAT AIN'T A SHORTCUT–IT'S MILES OUTTA THE WAY!
HE THINKS WE WILL WAIT HERE FOR WATER– AND HE WILL STOP TO SLEEP. WE WILL NOT.
AW, SHERIFF– I DON'T BELIEVE ANY OF THIS.
I'VE HEARD OF THE SPRING–
BUT HOW CAN WE BE SURE MARONE'LL GO THERE?
IT IS THE ONLY PLACE HE CAN GO.
HOW DO YOU KNOW? YOU KNOW EVERYTHING ABOUT THIS HELLHOLE?
I KNOW MUCH.

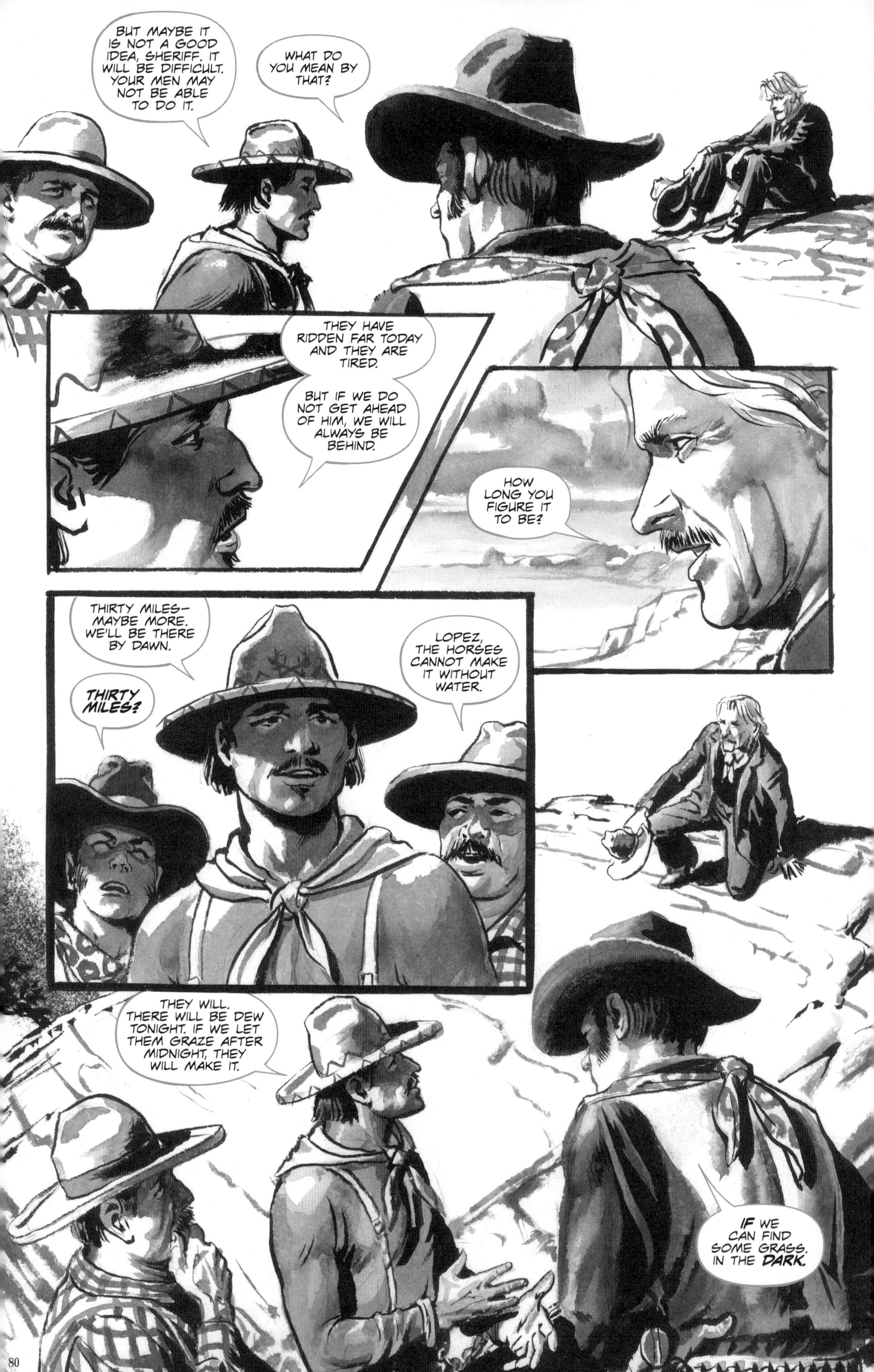
BUT MAYBE IT IS NOT A GOOD IDEA, SHERIFF. IT WILL BE DIFFICULT. YOUR MEN MAY NOT BE ABLE TO DO IT.
WHAT DO YOU MEAN BY THAT?
THEY HAVE RIDDEN FAR TODAY AND THEY ARE TIRED.
BUT IF WE DO NOT GET AHEAD OF HIM, WE WILL ALWAYS BE BEHIND.
HOW LONG YOU FIGURE IT TO BE?
THIRTY MILES— MAYBE MORE. WE'LL BE THERE BY DAWN.
THIRTY MILES?
LOPEZ, THE HORSES CANNOT MAKE IT WITHOUT WATER.
THEY WILL. THERE WILL BE DEW TONIGHT. IF WE LET THEM GRAZE AFTER MIDNIGHT, THEY WILL MAKE IT.
IF WE CAN FIND SOME GRASS. IN THE DARK.

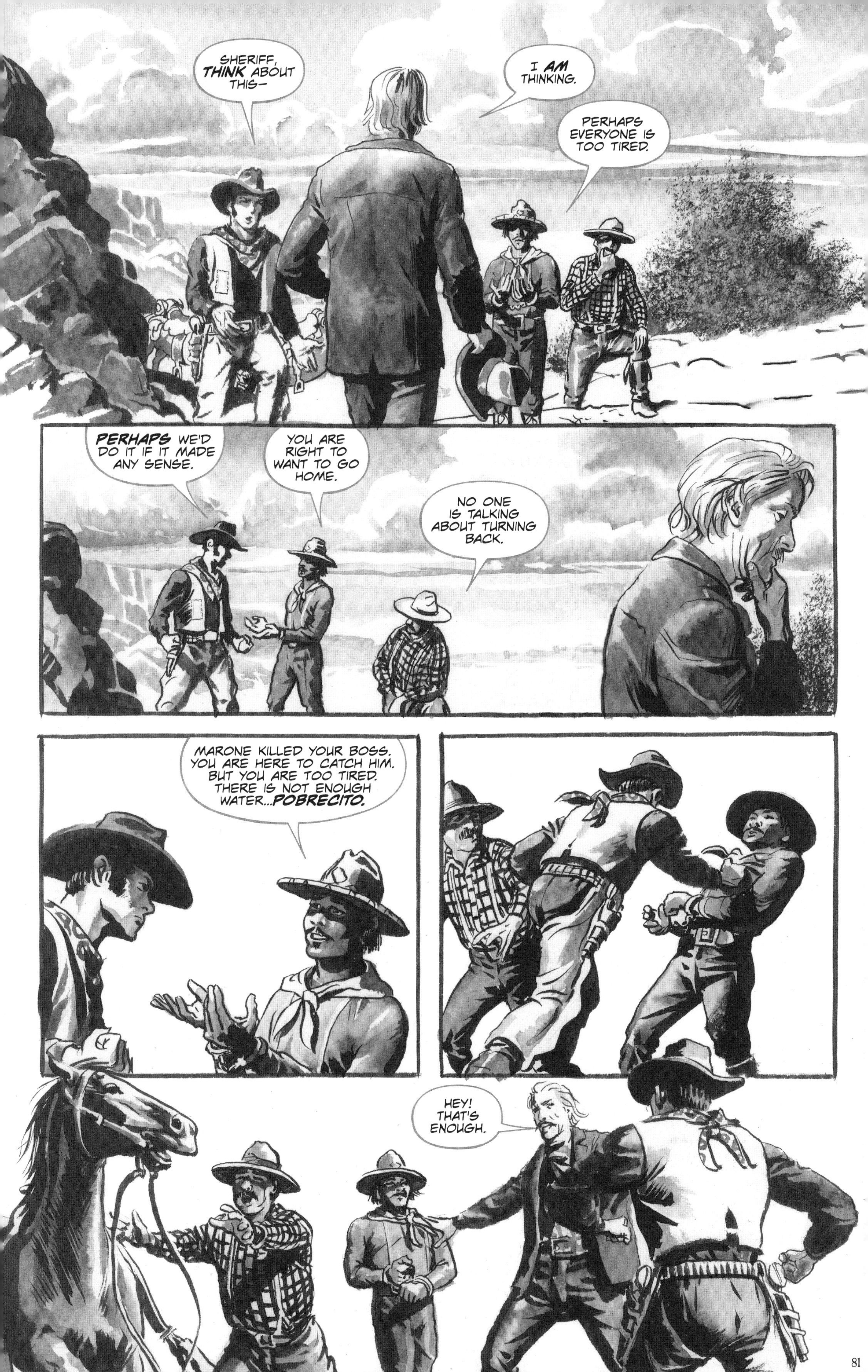
SHERIFF, THINK ABOUT THIS—
I AM THINKING.
PERHAPS EVERYONE IS TOO TIRED.
PERHAPS WE'D DO IT IF IT MADE ANY SENSE.
YOU ARE RIGHT TO WANT TO GO HOME.
NO ONE IS TALKING ABOUT TURNING BACK.
MARONE KILLED YOUR BOSS. YOU ARE HERE TO CATCH HIM. BUT YOU ARE TOO TIRED. THERE IS NOT ENOUGH WATER...POBRECITO.
HEY! THAT'S ENOUGH.

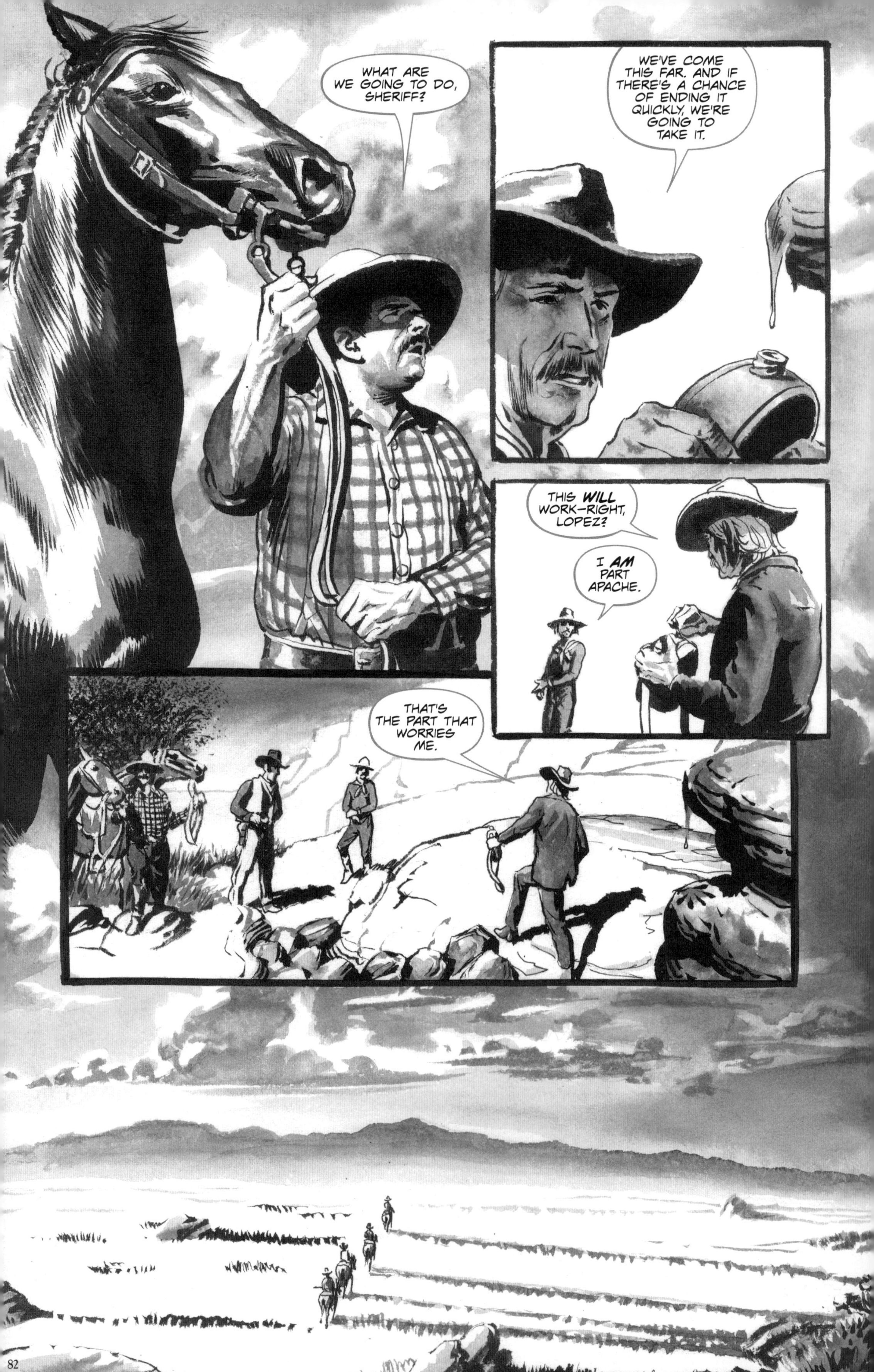
WHAT ARE WE GOING TO DO, SHERIFF?
WE'VE COME THIS FAR. AND IF THERE'S A CHANCE OF ENDING IT QUICKLY, WE'RE GOING TO TAKE IT.
THIS **WILL** WORK–RIGHT, LOPEZ?
I **AM** PART APACHE.
THAT'S THE PART THAT WORRIES ME.

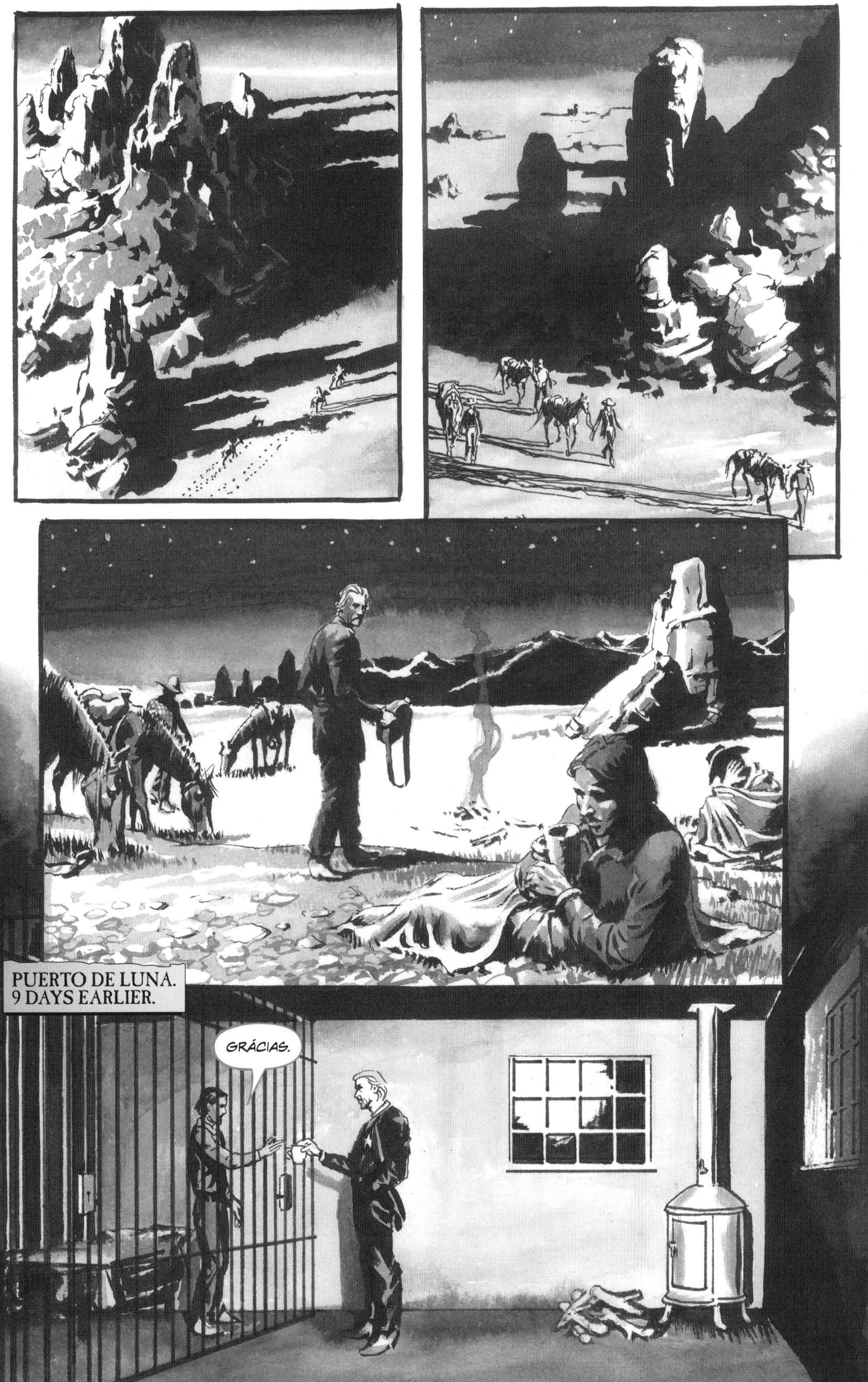
PUERTO DE LUNA.
9 DAYS EARLIER.
GRÁCIAS.

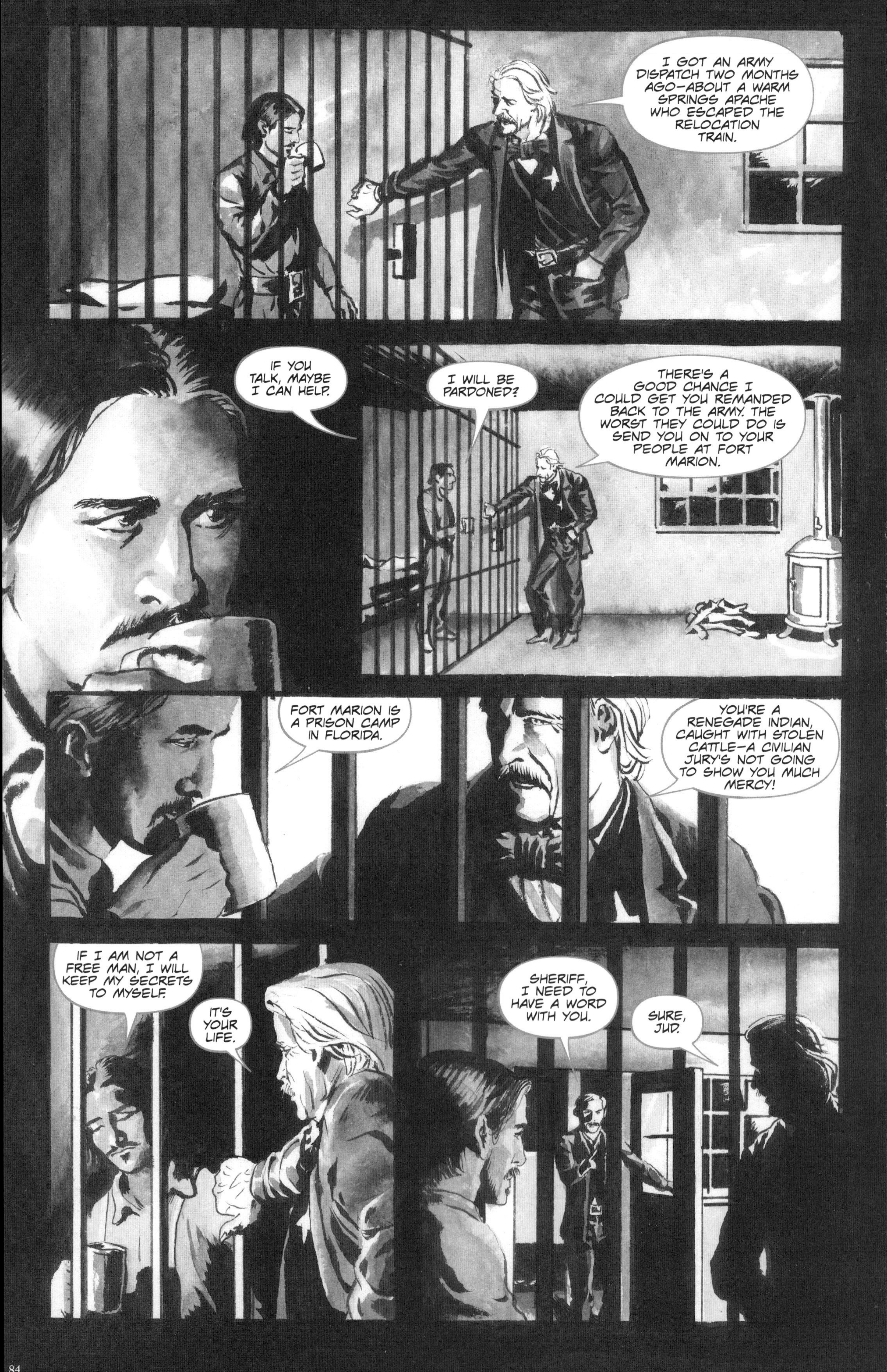
I GOT AN ARMY DISPATCH TWO MONTHS AGO--ABOUT A WARM SPRINGS APACHE WHO ESCAPED THE RELOCATION TRAIN.
IF YOU TALK, MAYBE I CAN HELP.
I WILL BE PARDONED?
THERE'S A GOOD CHANCE I COULD GET YOU REMANDED BACK TO THE ARMY. THE WORST THEY COULD DO IS SEND YOU ON TO YOUR PEOPLE AT FORT MARION.
FORT MARION IS A PRISON CAMP IN FLORIDA.
YOU'RE A RENEGADE INDIAN, CAUGHT WITH STOLEN CATTLE--A CIVILIAN JURY'S NOT GOING TO SHOW YOU MUCH MERCY!
IF I AM NOT A FREE MAN, I WILL KEEP MY SECRETS TO MYSELF.
IT'S YOUR LIFE.
SHERIFF, I NEED TO HAVE A WORD WITH YOU.
SURE, JUD.

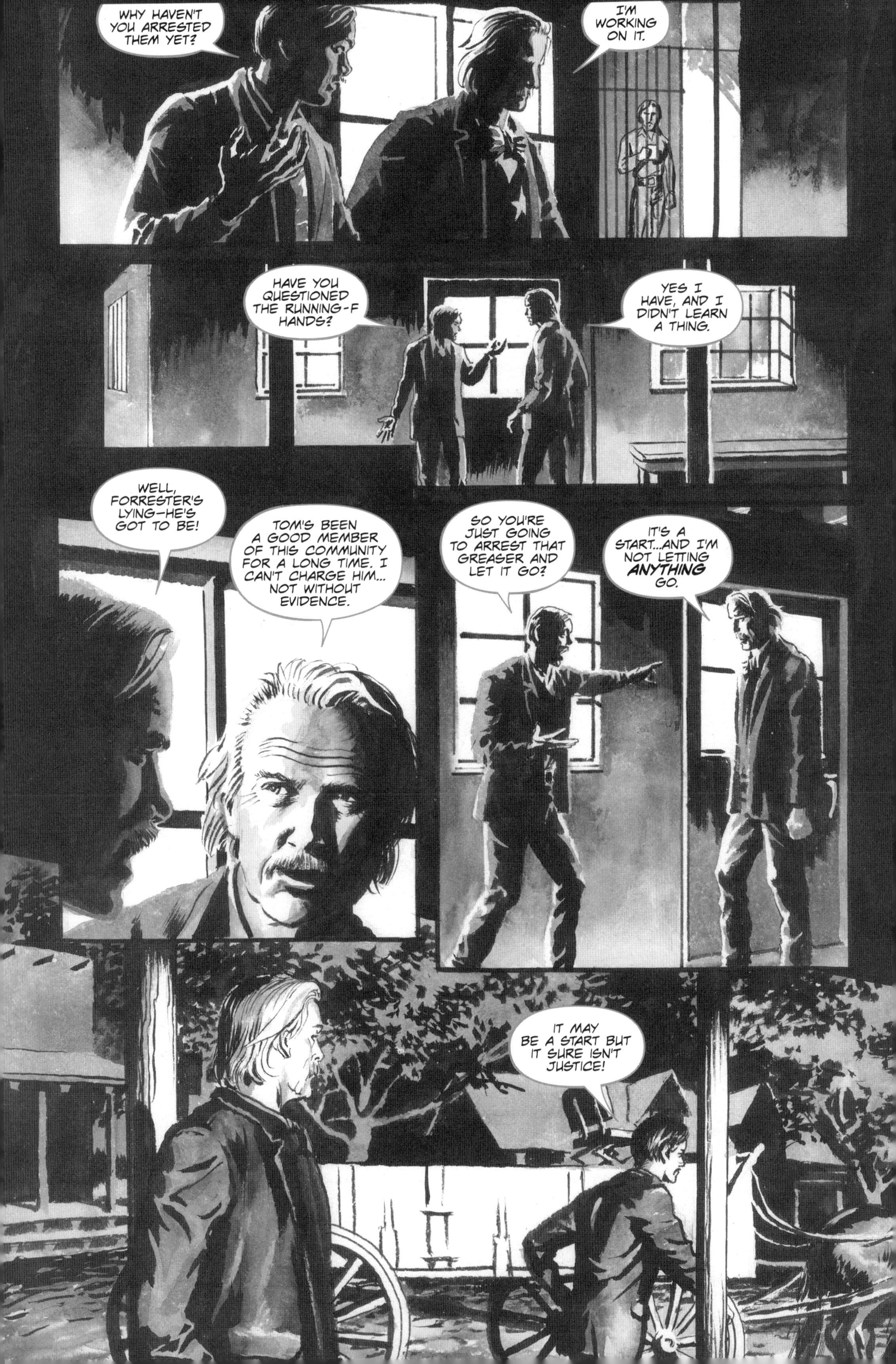
WHY HAVEN'T YOU ARRESTED THEM YET?
I'M WORKING ON IT.
HAVE YOU QUESTIONED THE RUNNING-F HANDS?
YES I HAVE, AND I DIDN'T LEARN A THING.
WELL, FORRESTER'S LYING–HE'S GOT TO BE!
TOM'S BEEN A GOOD MEMBER OF THIS COMMUNITY FOR A LONG TIME. I CAN'T CHARGE HIM... NOT WITHOUT EVIDENCE.
SO YOU'RE JUST GOING TO ARREST THAT GREASER AND LET IT GO?
IT'S A START...AND I'M NOT LETTING **ANYTHING** GO.
IT MAY BE A START BUT IT SURE ISN'T JUSTICE!

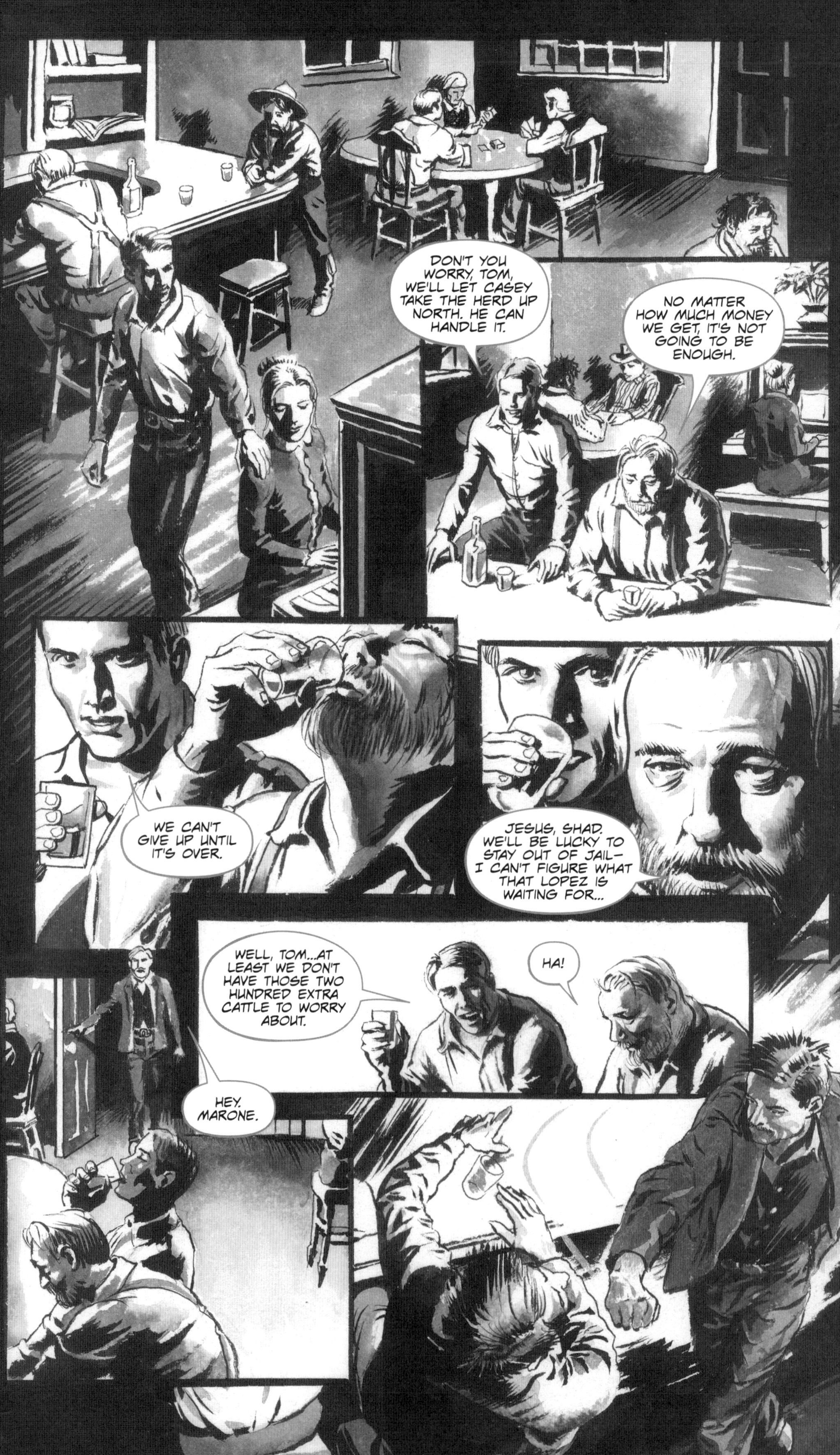
DON'T YOU WORRY, TOM, WE'LL LET CASEY TAKE THE HERD UP NORTH. HE CAN HANDLE IT.
NO MATTER HOW MUCH MONEY WE GET, IT'S NOT GOING TO BE ENOUGH.
WE CAN'T GIVE UP UNTIL IT'S OVER.
JESUS, SHAD. WE'LL BE LUCKY TO STAY OUT OF JAIL-- I CAN'T FIGURE WHAT THAT LOPEZ IS WAITING FOR...
WELL, TOM...AT LEAST WE DON'T HAVE THOSE TWO HUNDRED EXTRA CATTLE TO WORRY ABOUT.
HA!
HEY. MARONE.

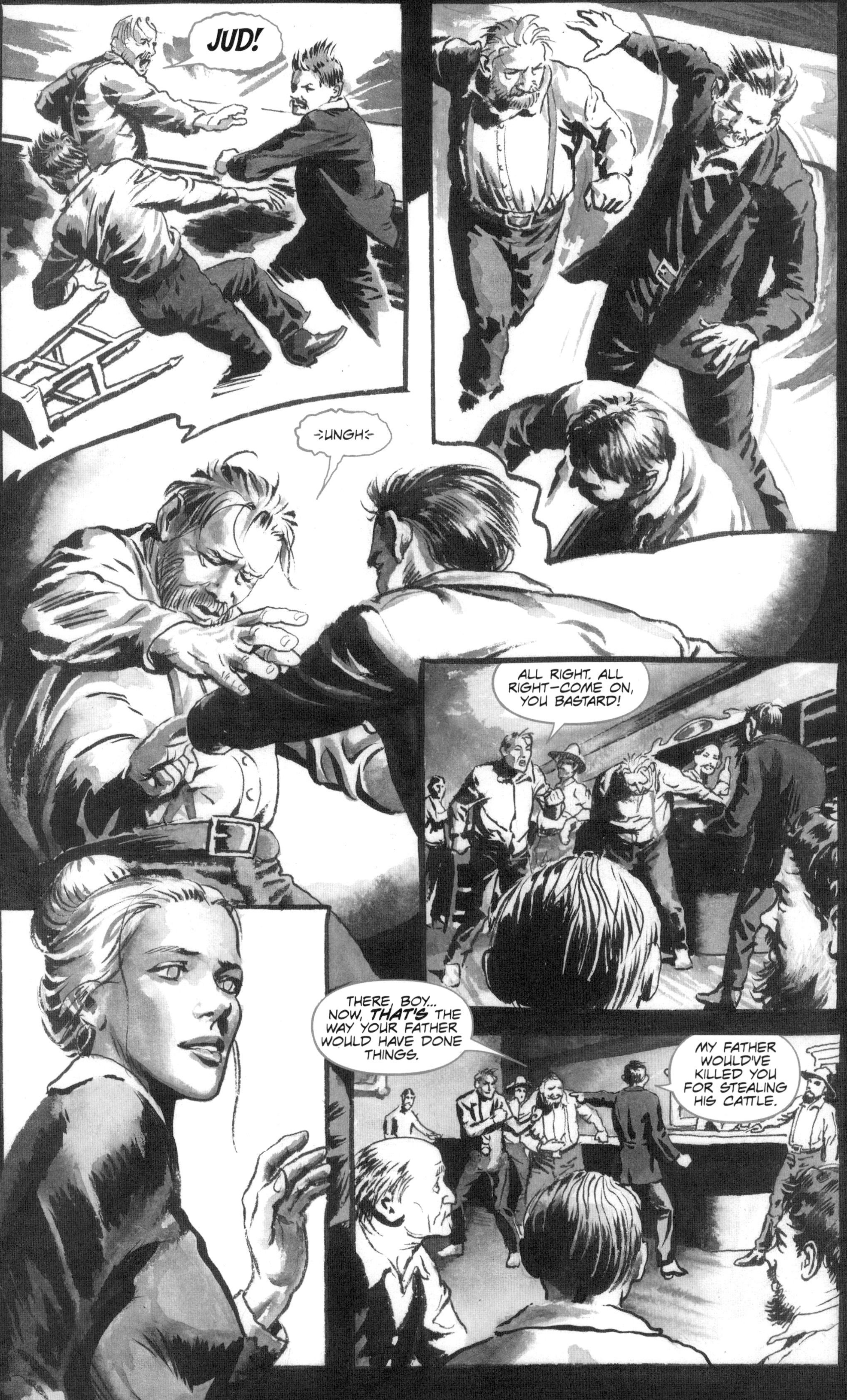
JUD!
UNGH
ALL RIGHT. ALL RIGHT—COME ON, YOU BASTARD!
THERE, BOY... NOW, THAT'S THE WAY YOUR FATHER WOULD HAVE DONE THINGS.
MY FATHER WOULD'VE KILLED YOU FOR STEALING HIS CATTLE.

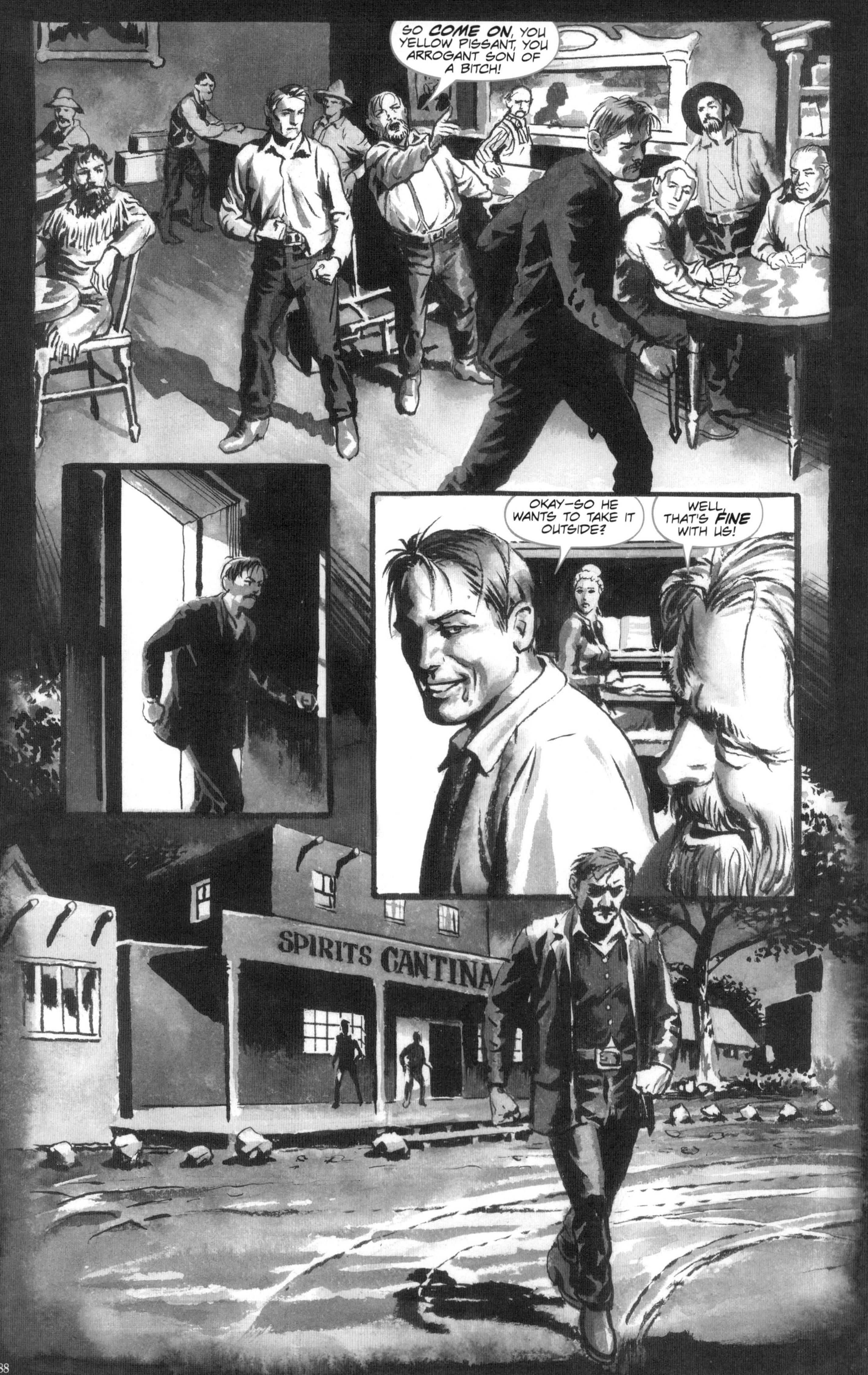
SO COME ON, YOU YELLOW PISSANT, YOU ARROGANT SON OF A BITCH!
OKAY—SO HE WANTS TO TAKE IT OUTSIDE?
WELL, THAT'S FINE WITH US!
SPIRITS CANTINA

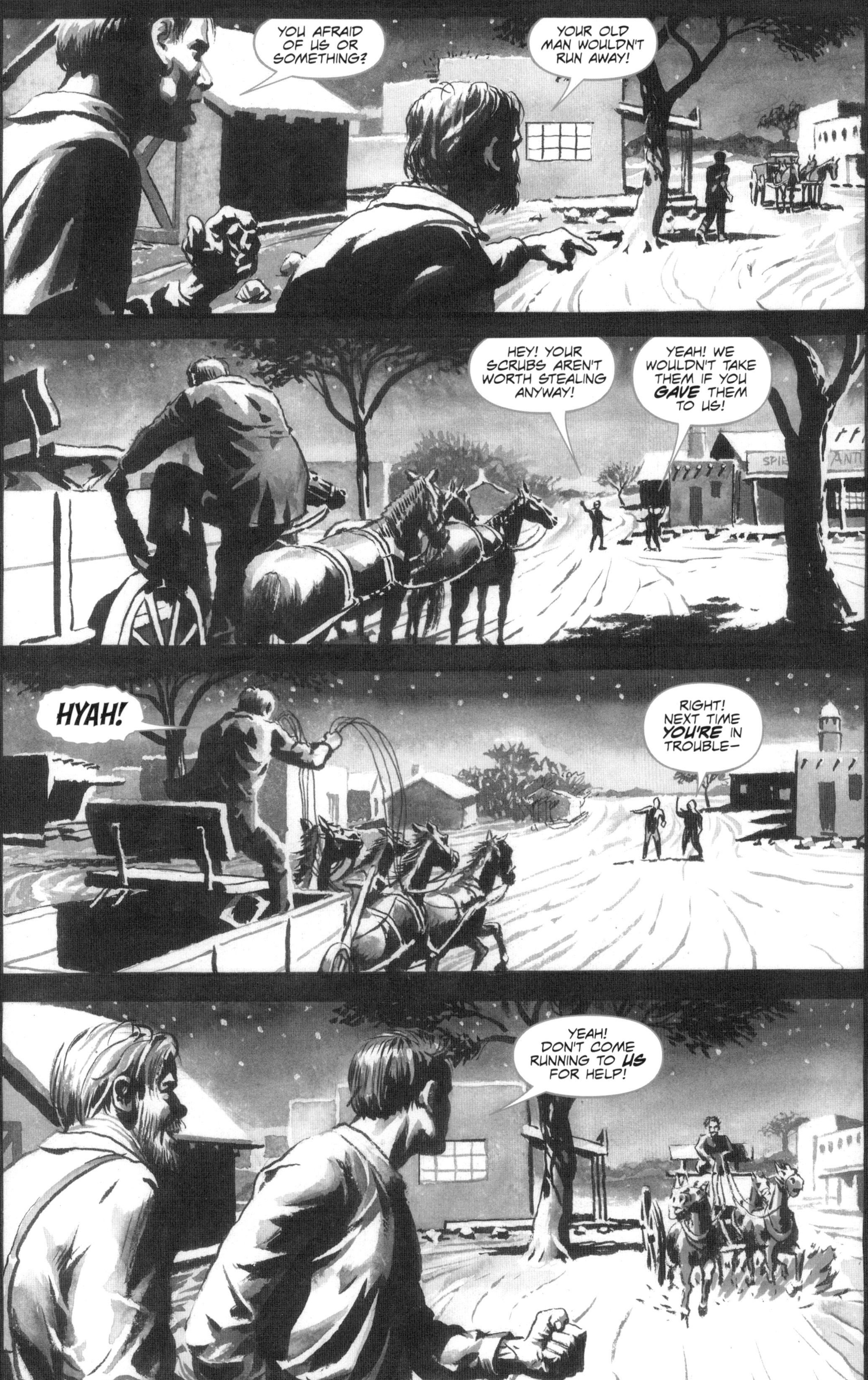
YOU AFRAID OF US OR SOMETHING?
YOUR OLD MAN WOULDN'T RUN AWAY!
HEY! YOUR SCRUBS AREN'T WORTH STEALING ANYWAY!
YEAH! WE WOULDN'T TAKE THEM IF YOU GAVE THEM TO US!
HYAH!
RIGHT! NEXT TIME YOU'RE IN TROUBLE–
YEAH! DON'T COME RUNNING TO US FOR HELP!

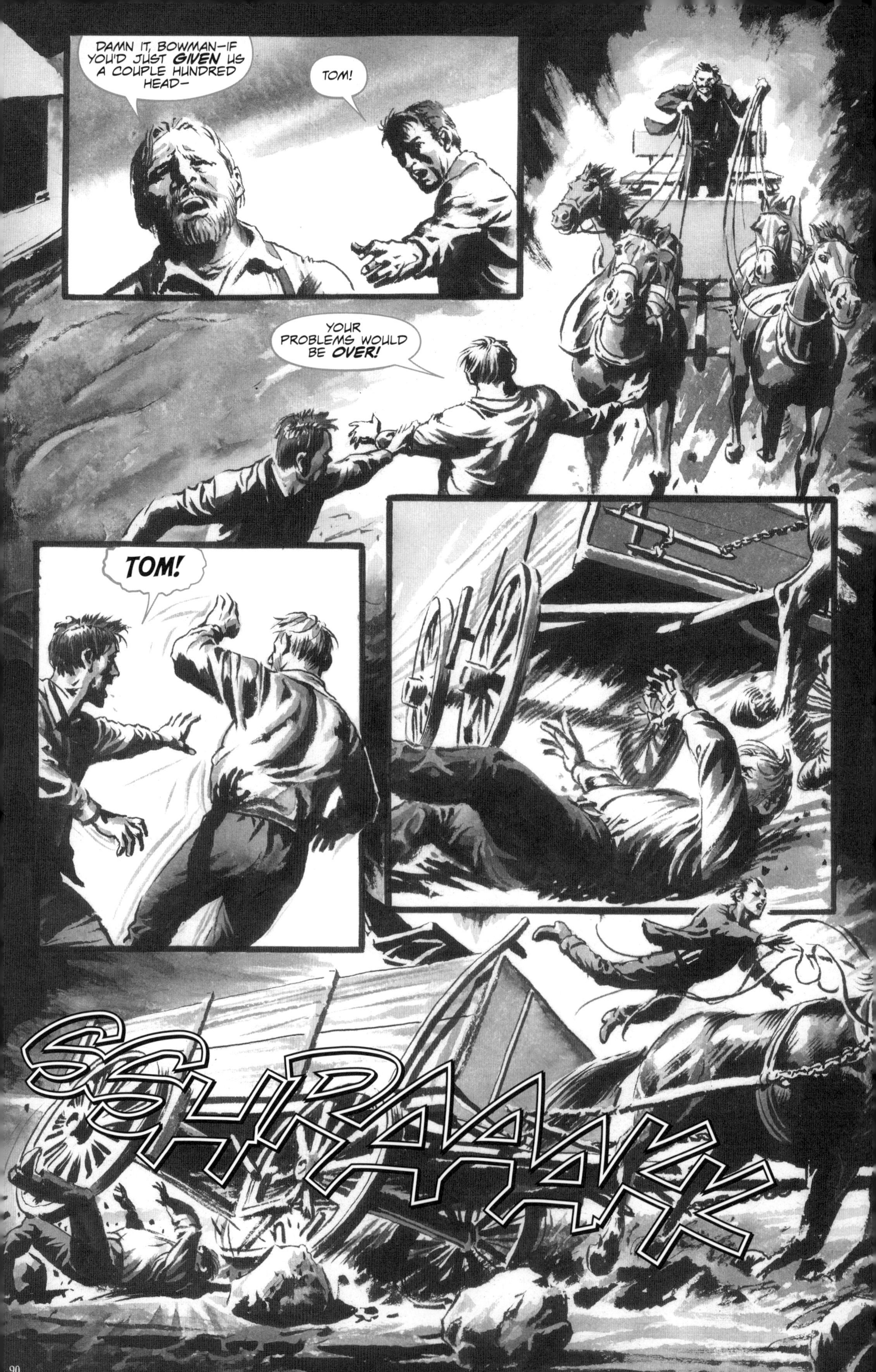
DAMN IT, BOWMAN--IF YOU'D JUST GIVEN US A COUPLE HUNDRED HEAD--
TOM!
YOUR PROBLEMS WOULD BE OVER!
TOM!
SSHRAAAAK

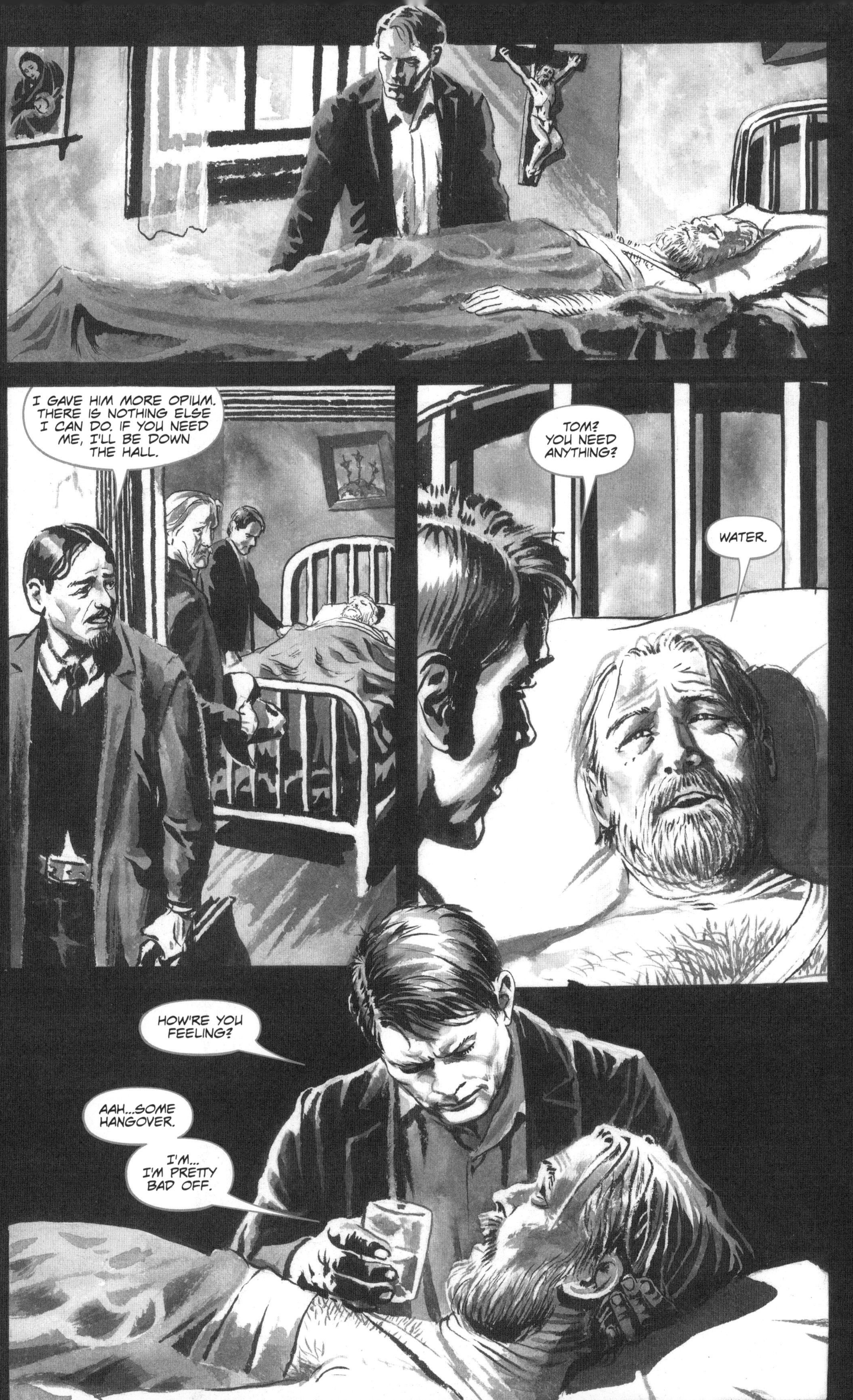
I GAVE HIM MORE OPIUM. THERE IS NOTHING ELSE I CAN DO. IF YOU NEED ME, I'LL BE DOWN THE HALL.
TOM? YOU NEED ANYTHING?
WATER.
HOW'RE YOU FEELING?
AAH...SOME HANGOVER.
I'M... I'M PRETTY BAD OFF.

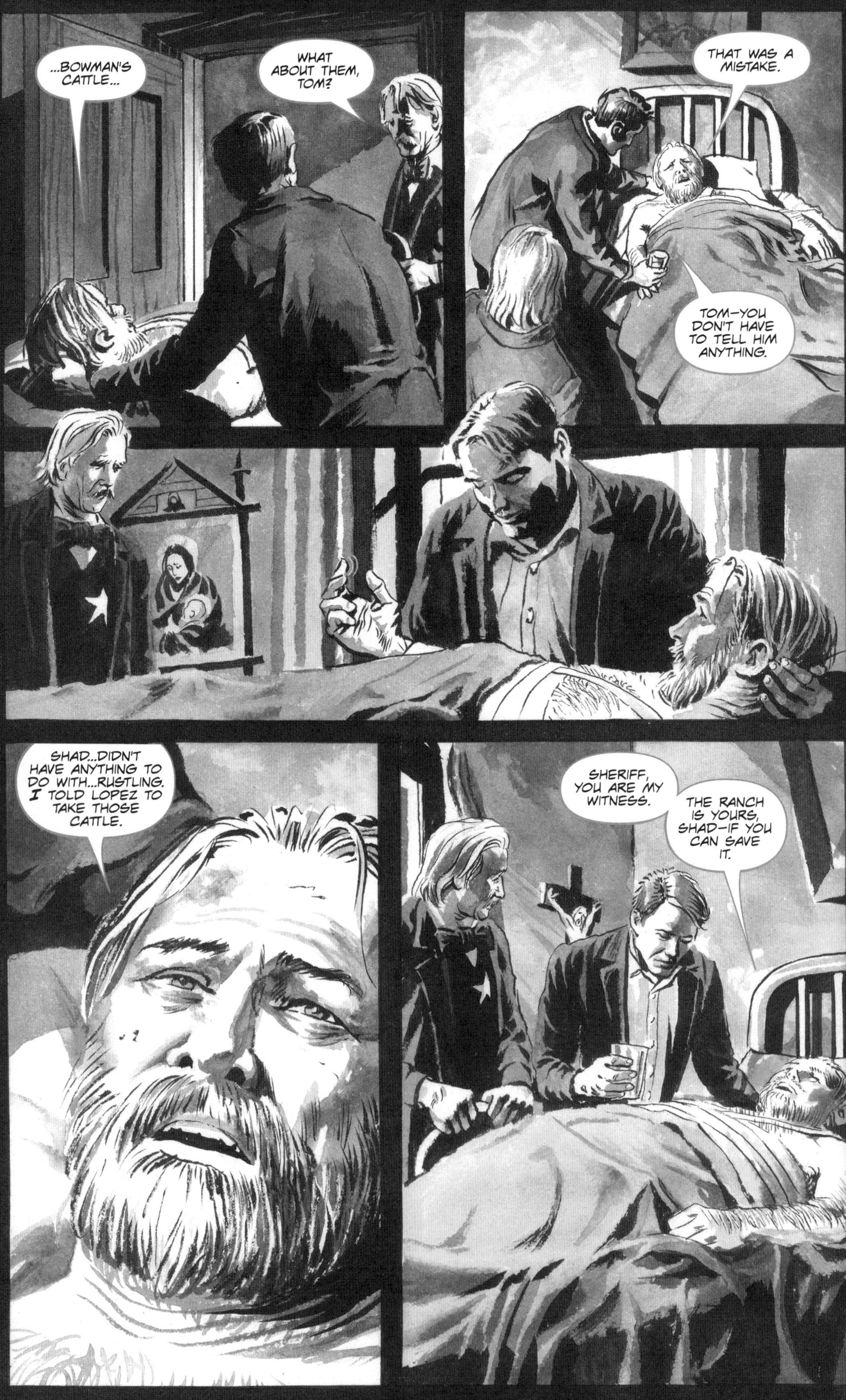
...BOWMAN'S CATTLE...
WHAT ABOUT THEM, TOM?
THAT WAS A MISTAKE.
TOM—YOU DON'T HAVE TO TELL HIM ANYTHING.
SHAD...DIDN'T HAVE ANYTHING TO DO WITH...RUSTLING. I TOLD LOPEZ TO TAKE THOSE CATTLE.
SHERIFF, YOU ARE MY WITNESS.
THE RANCH IS YOURS, SHAD—IF YOU CAN SAVE IT.

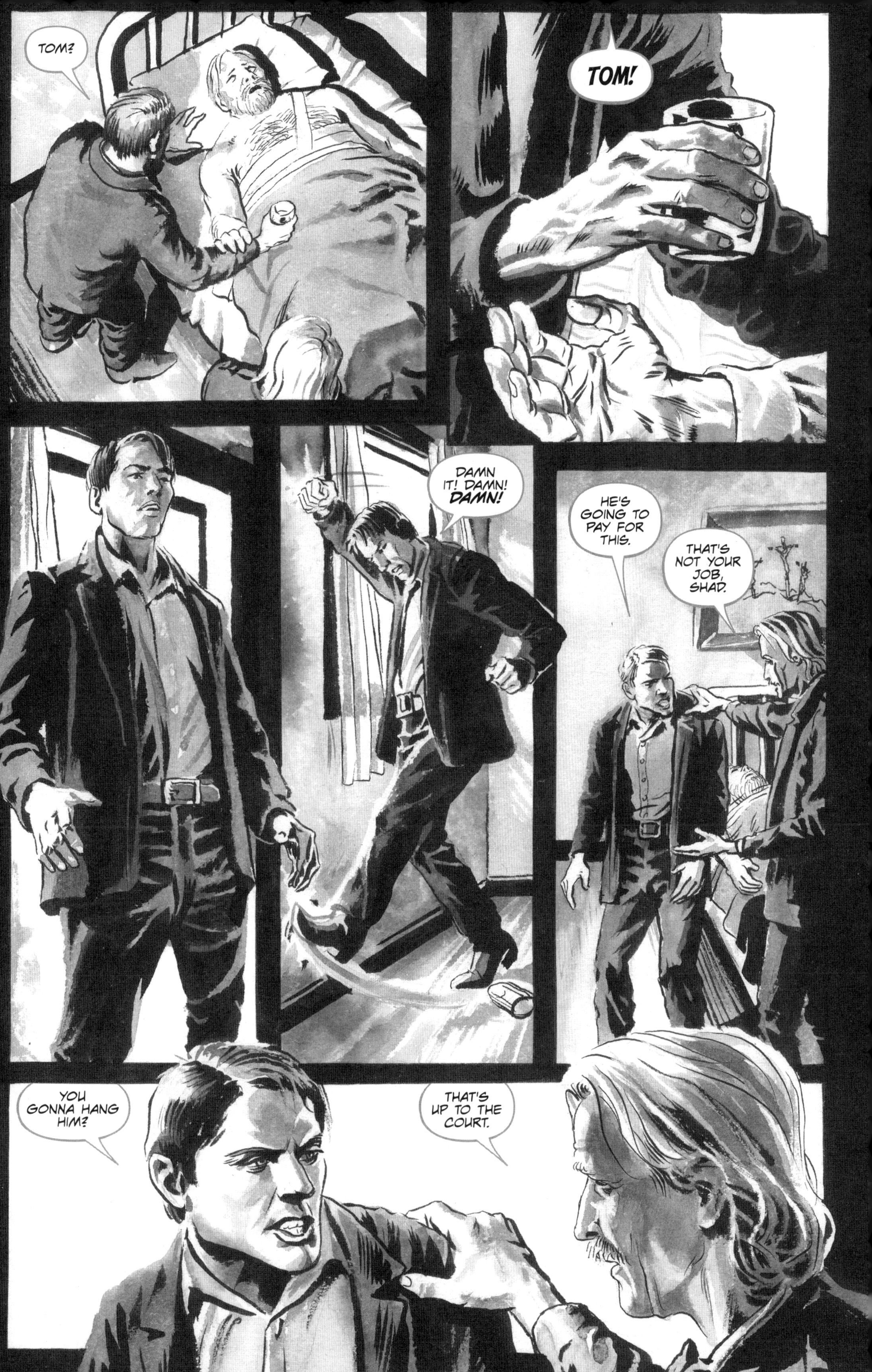
TOM?
TOM!
DAMN IT! DAMN! DAMN!
HE'S GOING TO PAY FOR THIS.
THAT'S NOT YOUR JOB, SHAD.
YOU GONNA HANG HIM?
THAT'S UP TO THE COURT.

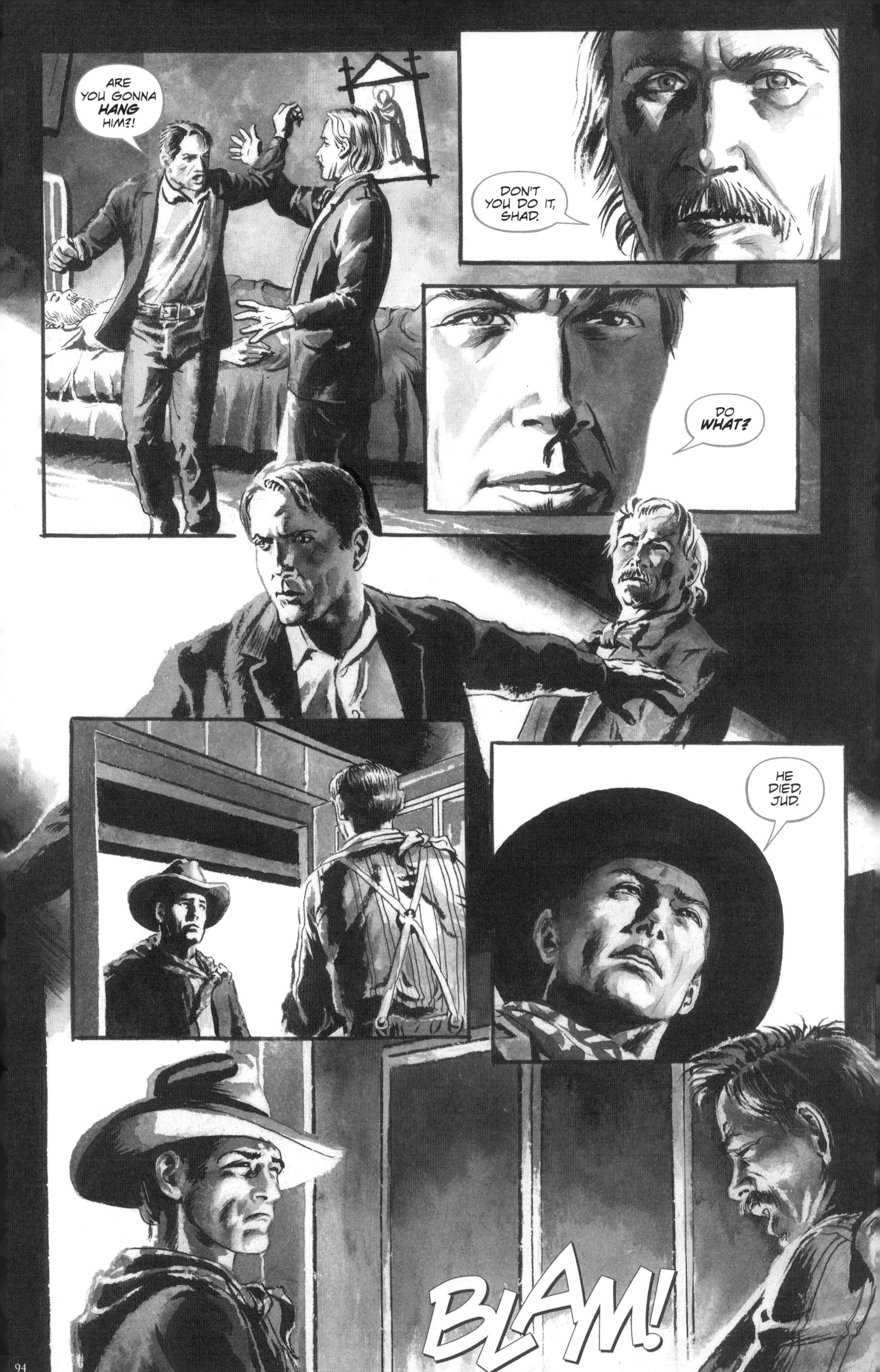
ARE YOU GONNA HANG HIM?!
DON'T YOU DO IT, SHAD.
DO WHAT?
HE DIED, JUD.
BLAM!

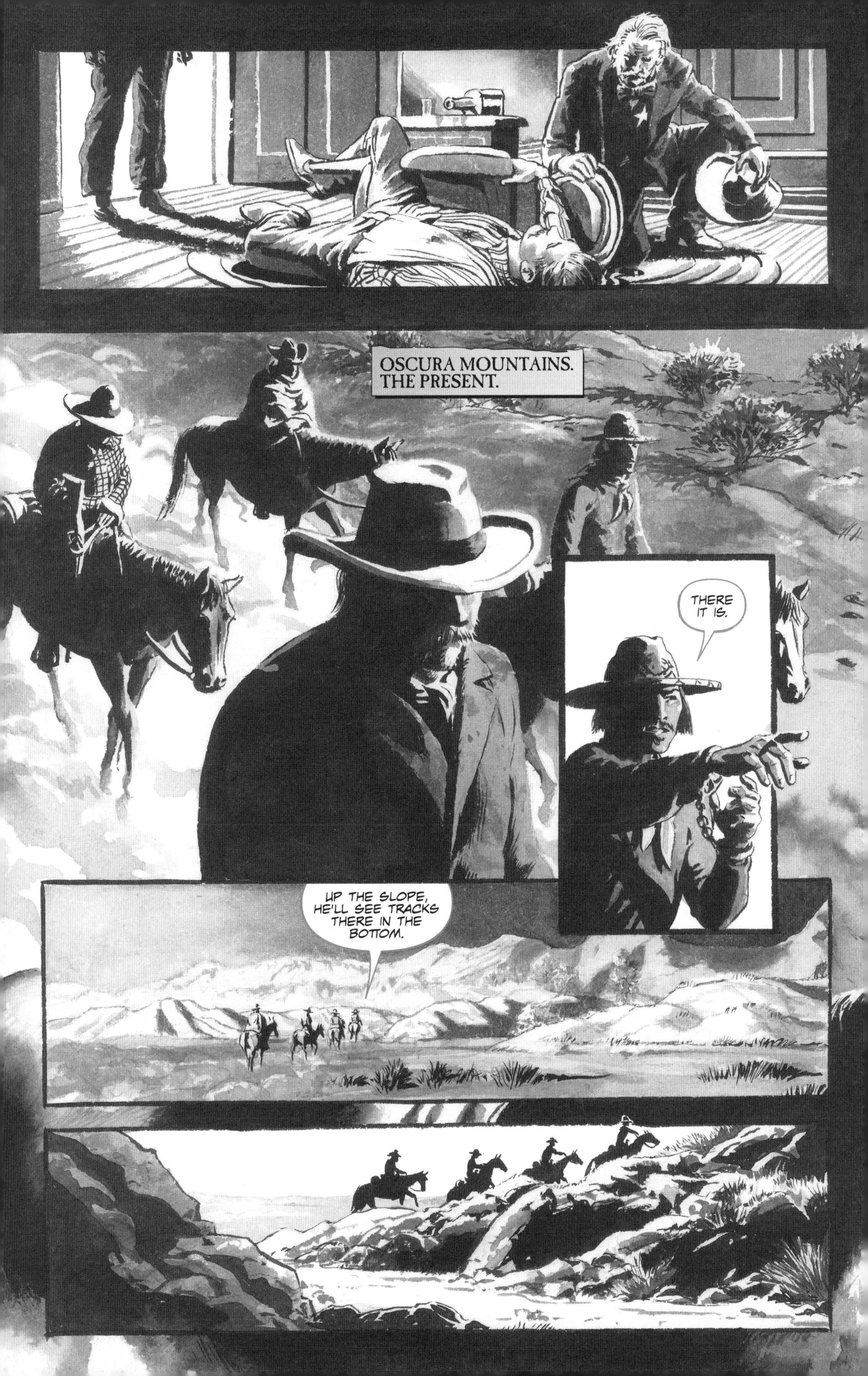
OSCURA MOUNTAINS. THE PRESENT.
THERE IT IS.
UP THE SLOPE, HE'LL SEE TRACKS THERE IN THE BOTTOM.

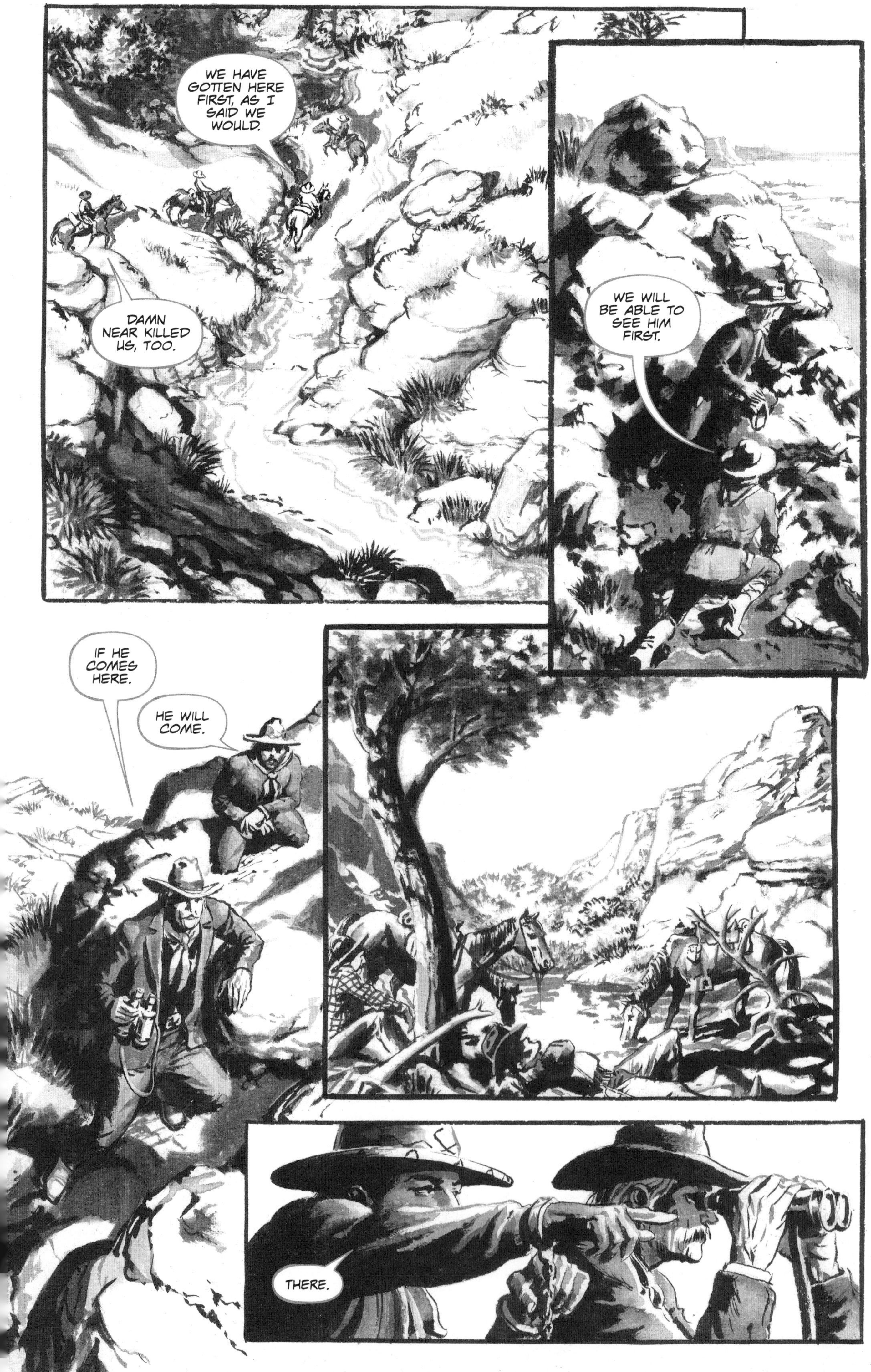
WE HAVE GOTTEN HERE FIRST, AS I SAID WE WOULD.
DAMN NEAR KILLED US, TOO.
WE WILL BE ABLE TO SEE HIM FIRST.
IF HE COMES HERE.
HE WILL COME.
THERE.

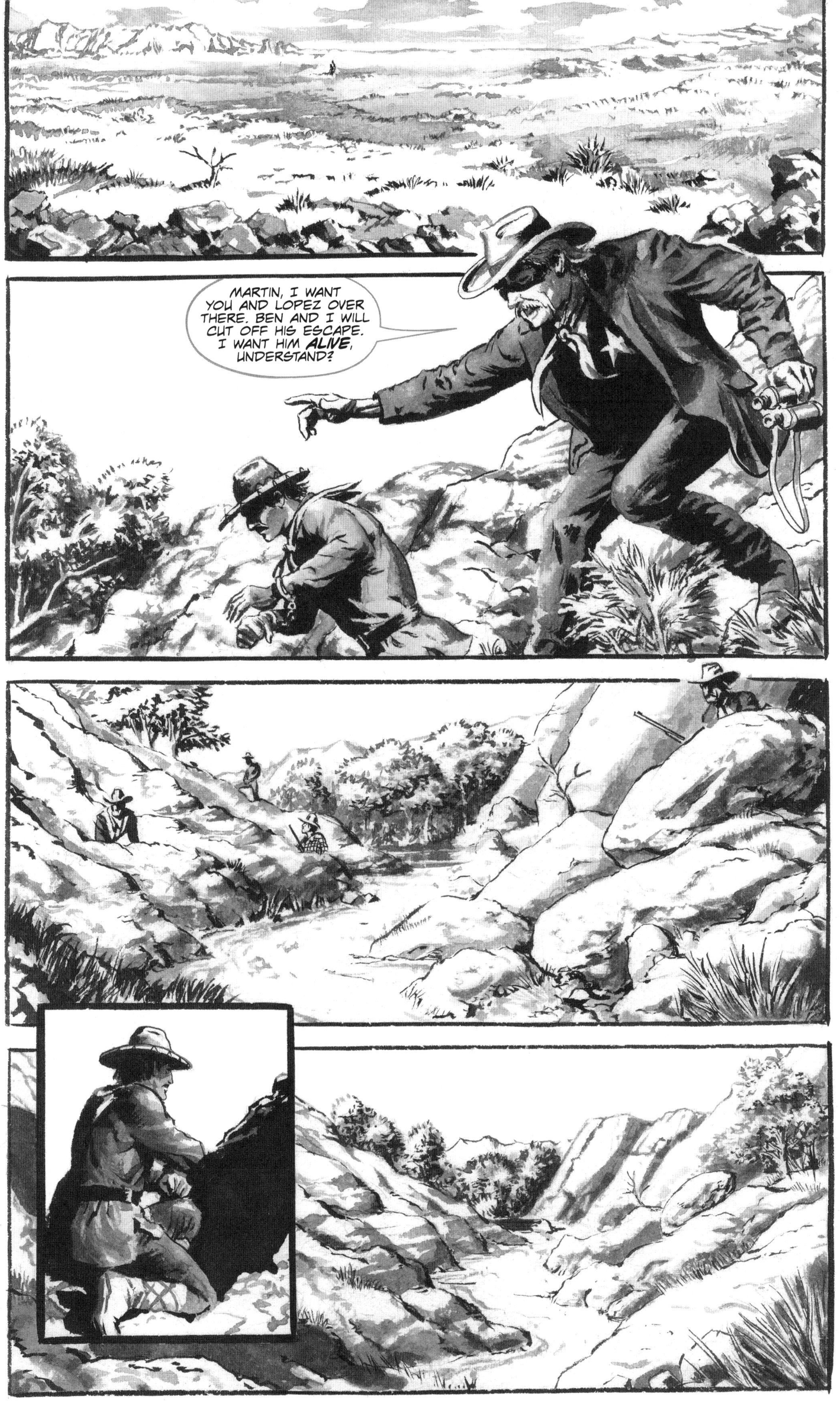
MARTIN, I WANT YOU AND LOPEZ OVER THERE. BEN AND I WILL CUT OFF HIS ESCAPE. I WANT HIM ALIVE, UNDERSTAND?

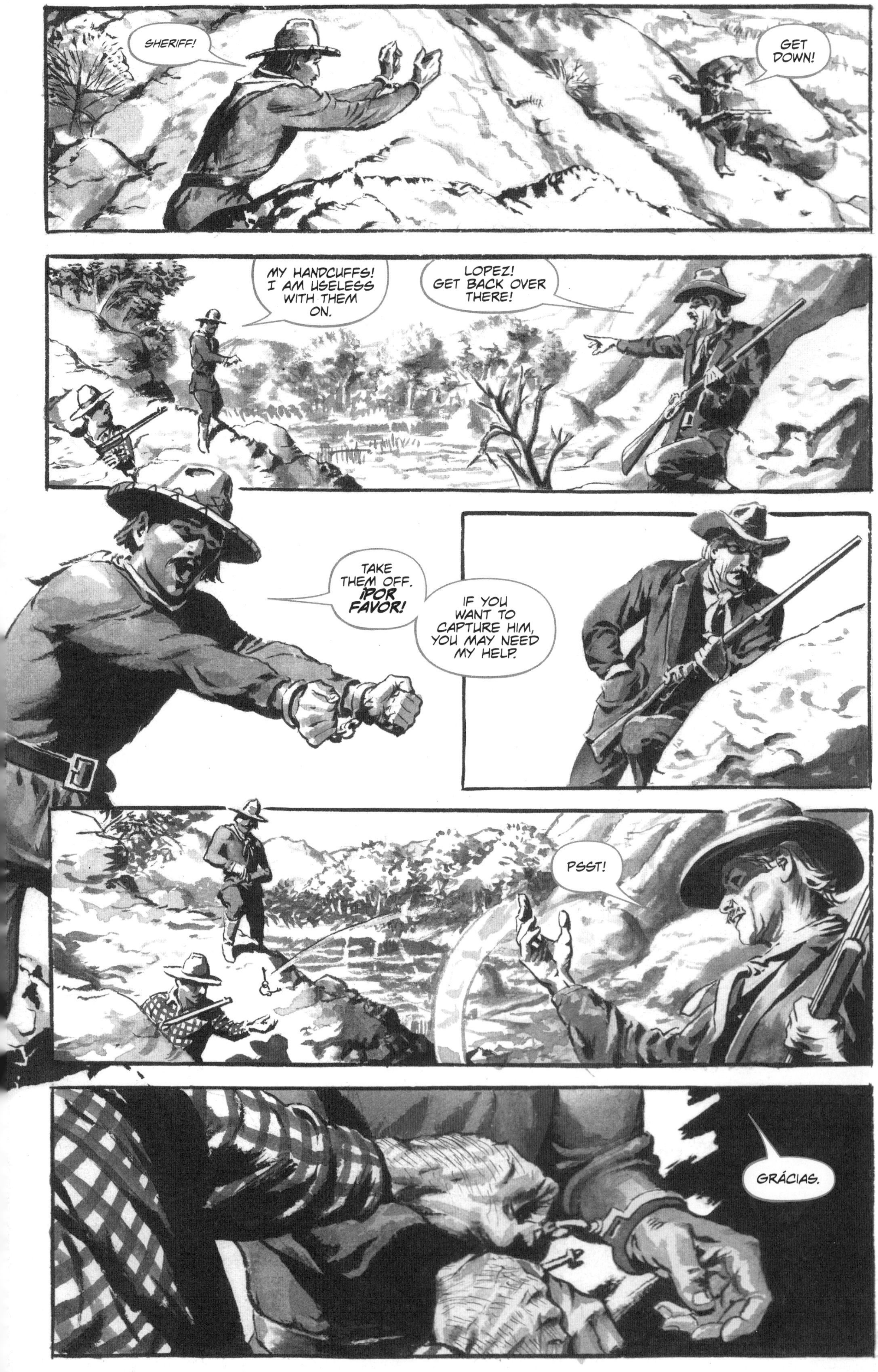
SHERIFF!
GET DOWN!
MY HANDCUFFS! I AM USELESS WITH THEM ON.
LOPEZ! GET BACK OVER THERE!
TAKE THEM OFF. ¡POR FAVOR!
IF YOU WANT TO CAPTURE HIM, YOU MAY NEED MY HELP.
PSST!
GRÁCIAS.

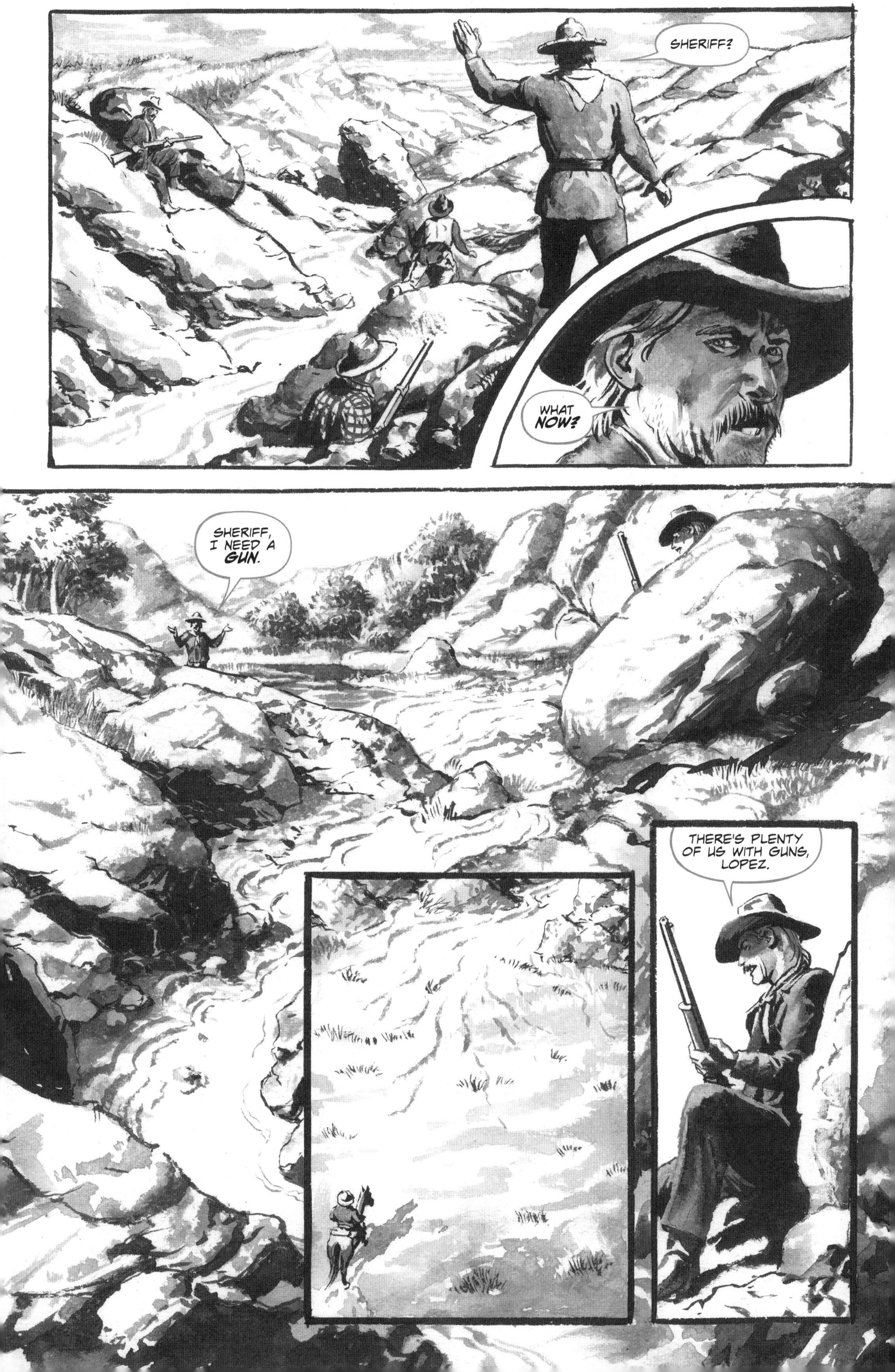
SHERIFF?
WHAT NOW?
SHERIFF, I NEED A GUN.
THERE'S PLENTY OF US WITH GUNS, LOPEZ.

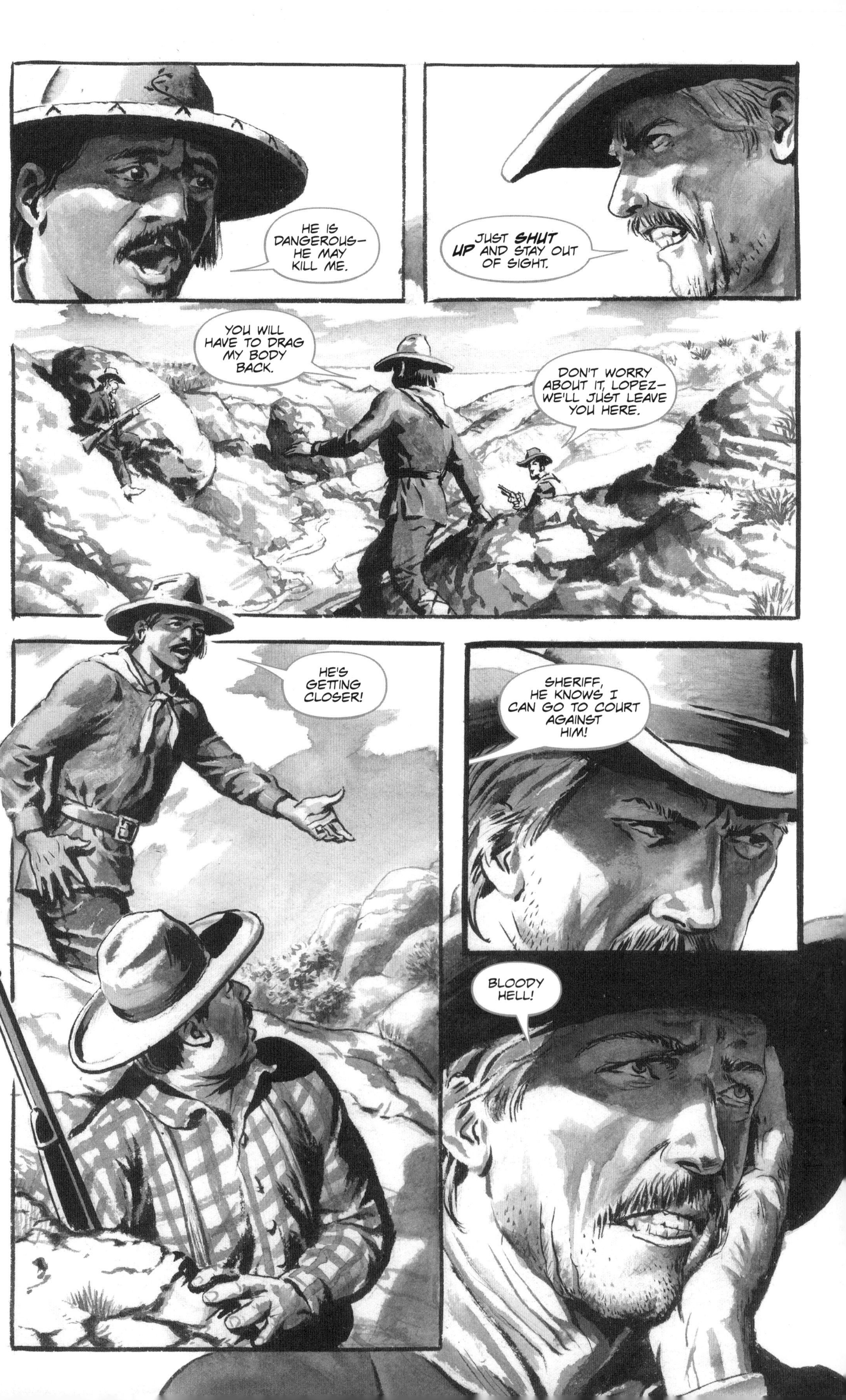
HE IS DANGEROUS— HE MAY KILL ME.
JUST SHUT UP AND STAY OUT OF SIGHT.
YOU WILL HAVE TO DRAG MY BODY BACK.
DON'T WORRY ABOUT IT, LOPEZ— WE'LL JUST LEAVE YOU HERE.
HE'S GETTING CLOSER!
SHERIFF, HE KNOWS I CAN GO TO COURT AGAINST HIM!
BLOODY HELL!

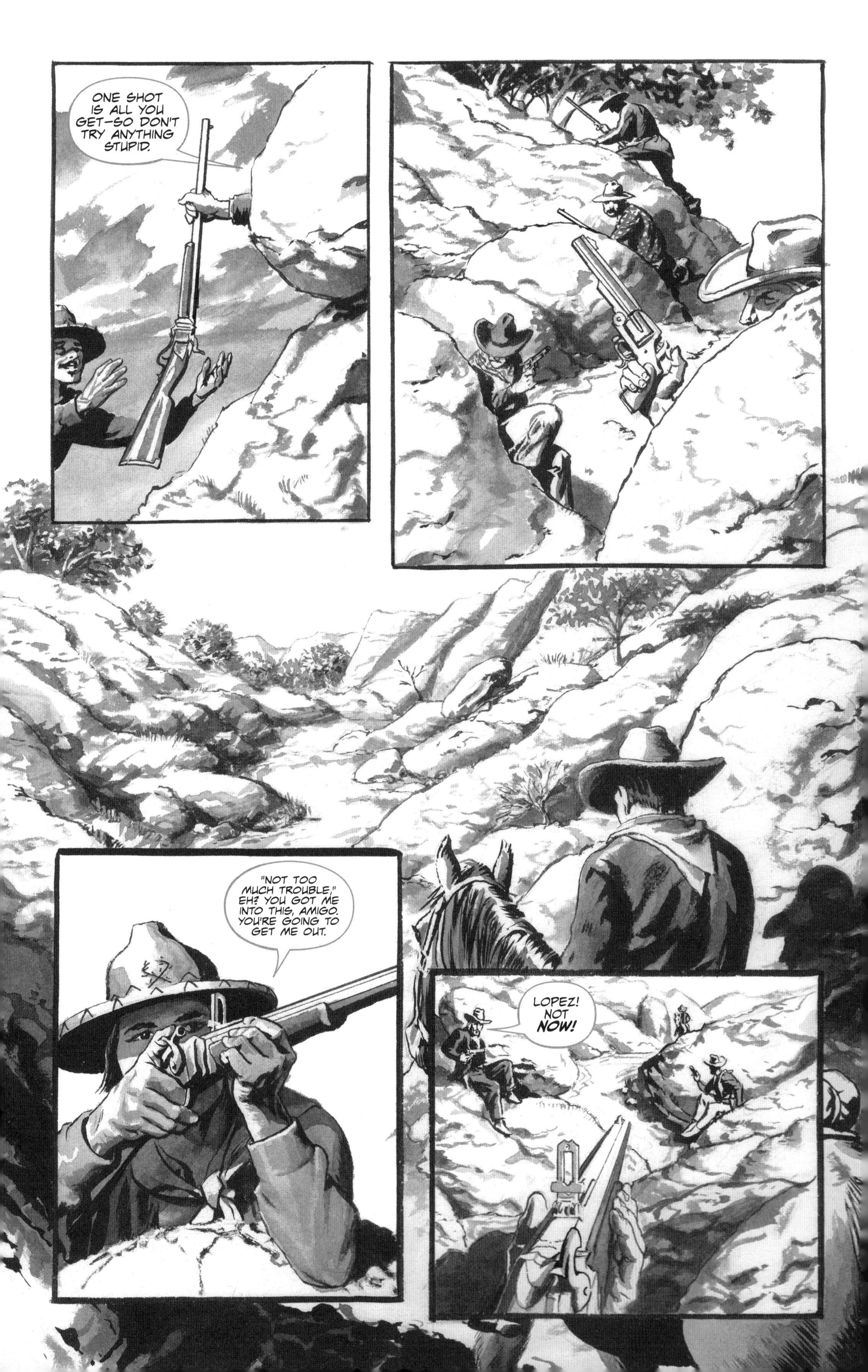
ONE SHOT IS ALL YOU GET—SO DON'T TRY ANYTHING STUPID.
"NOT TOO MUCH TROUBLE," EH? YOU GOT ME INTO THIS, AMIGO. YOU'RE GOING TO GET ME OUT.
LOPEZ! NOT NOW!

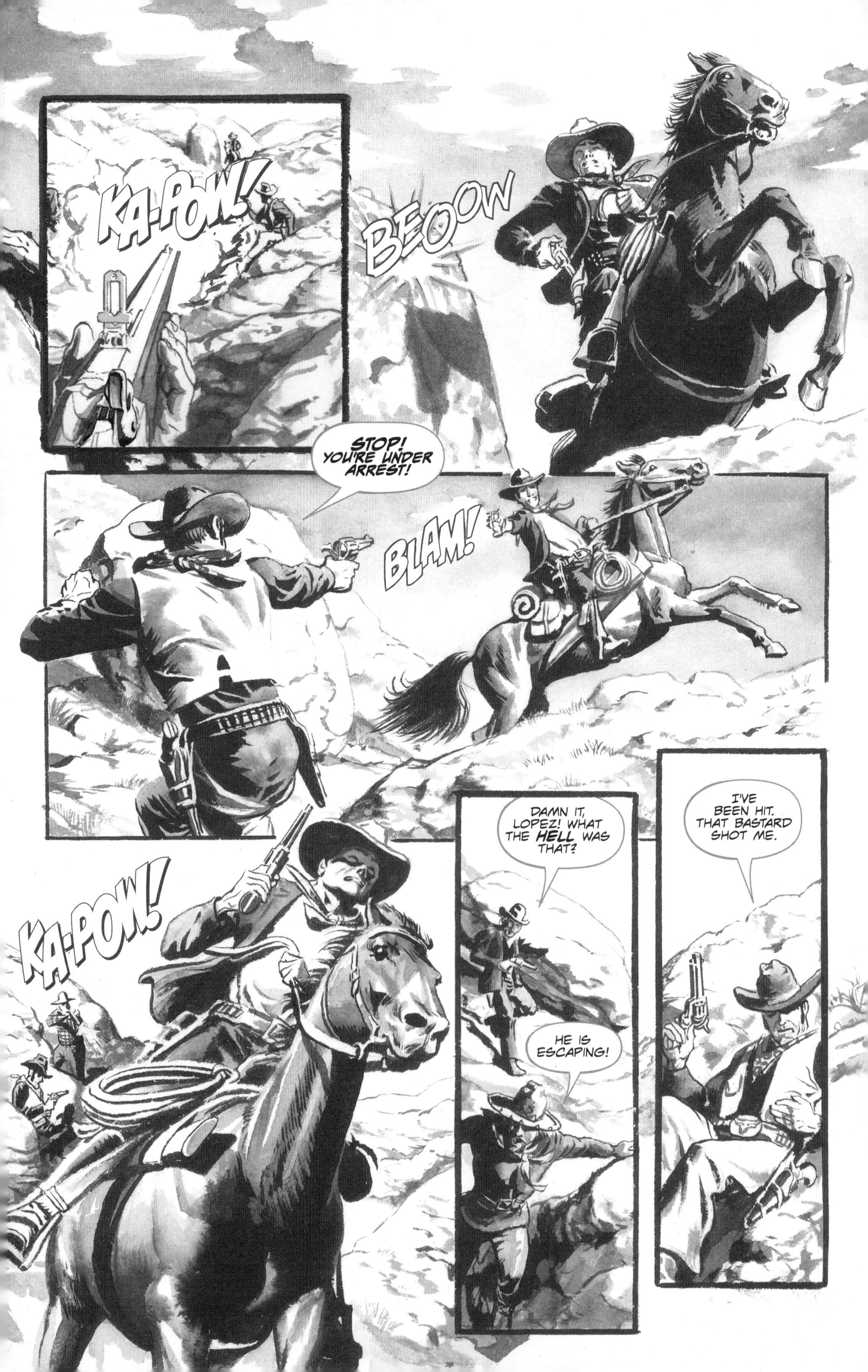
KA-POW!
BEOOW
STOP! YOU'RE UNDER ARREST!
BLAM!
KA-POW!
DAMN IT, LOPEZ! WHAT THE HELL WAS THAT?
HE IS ESCAPING!
I'VE BEEN HIT. THAT BASTARD SHOT ME.

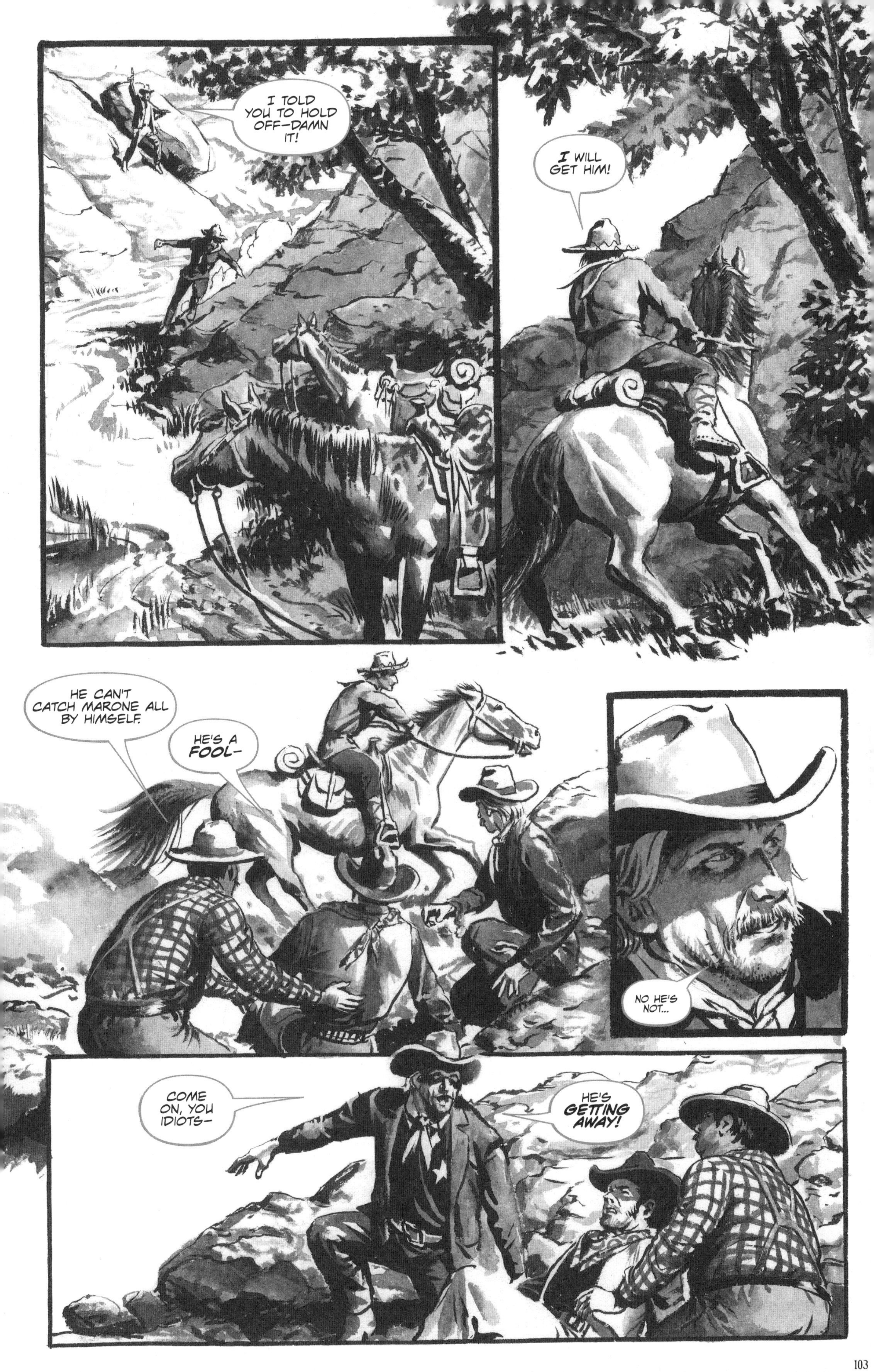
I TOLD YOU TO HOLD OFF—DAMN IT!
I WILL GET HIM!
HE CAN'T CATCH MARONE ALL BY HIMSELF.
HE'S A FOOL—
NO HE'S NOT...
COME ON, YOU IDIOTS—
HE'S GETTING AWAY!

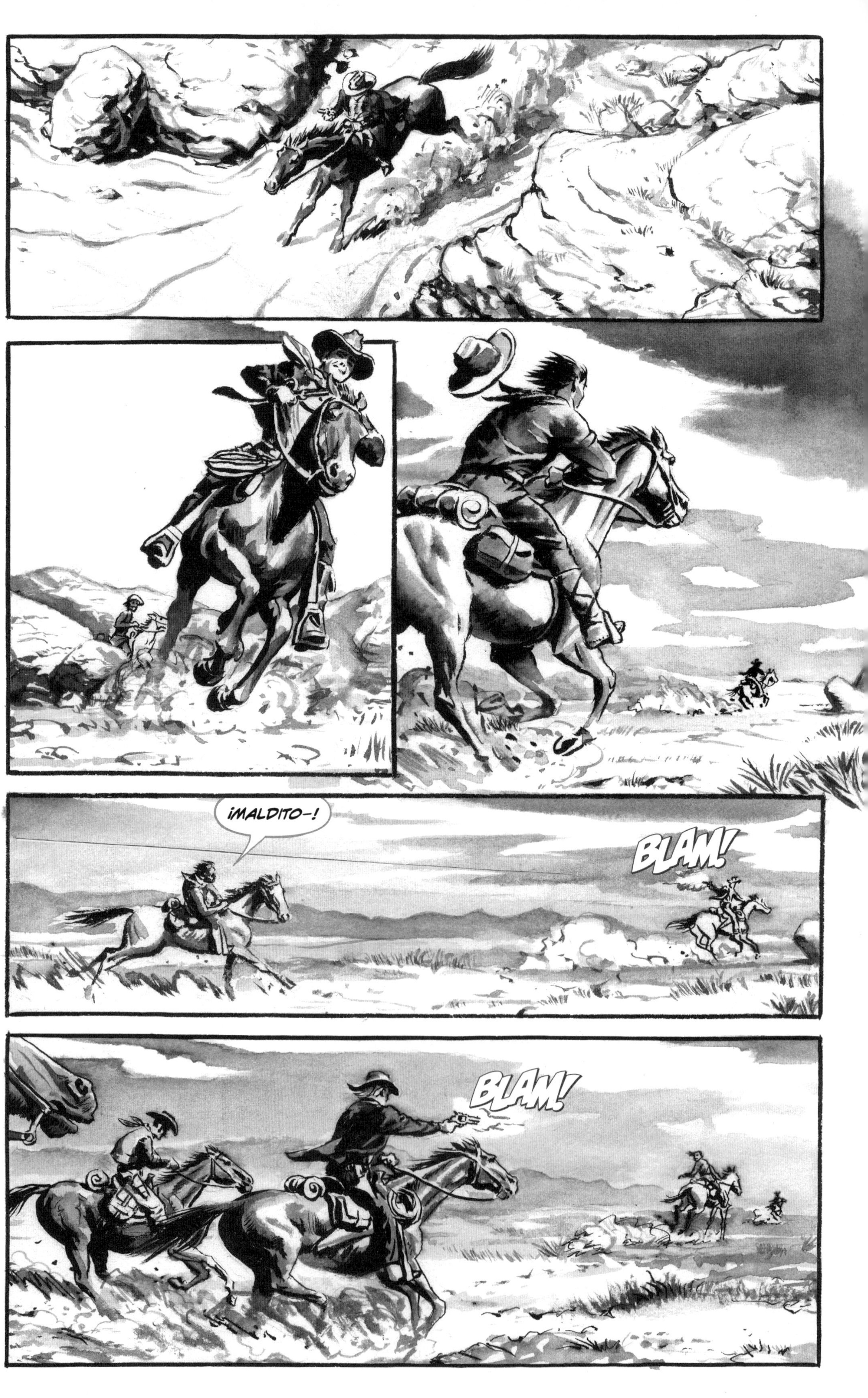
¡MALDITO-!
BLAM!
BLAM!

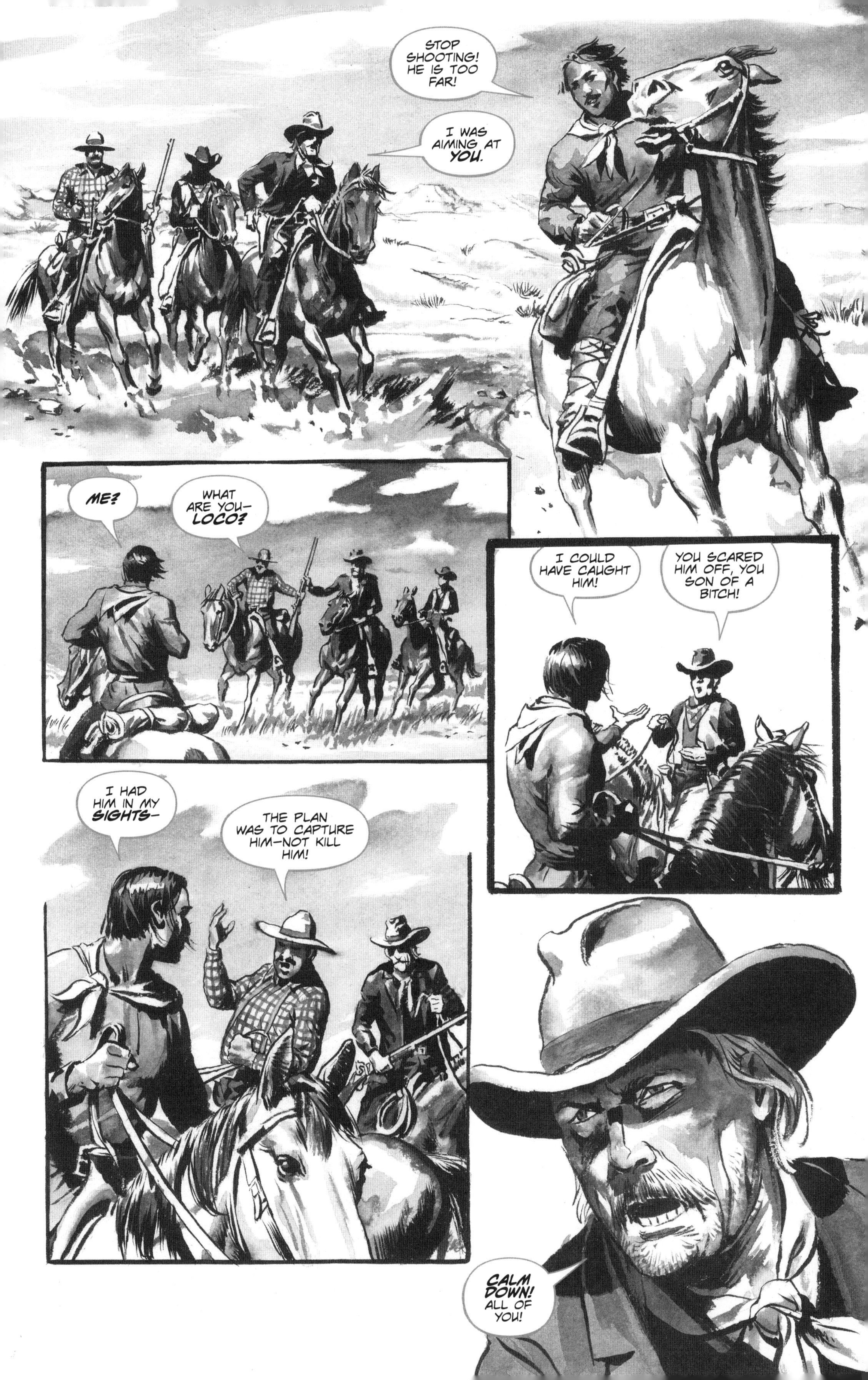

STOP SHOOTING! HE IS TOO FAR!
I WAS AIMING AT YOU.
ME?
WHAT ARE YOU— LOCO?
I COULD HAVE CAUGHT HIM!
YOU SCARED HIM OFF, YOU SON OF A BITCH!
I HAD HIM IN MY SIGHTS—
THE PLAN WAS TO CAPTURE HIM—NOT KILL HIM!
CALM DOWN! ALL OF YOU!

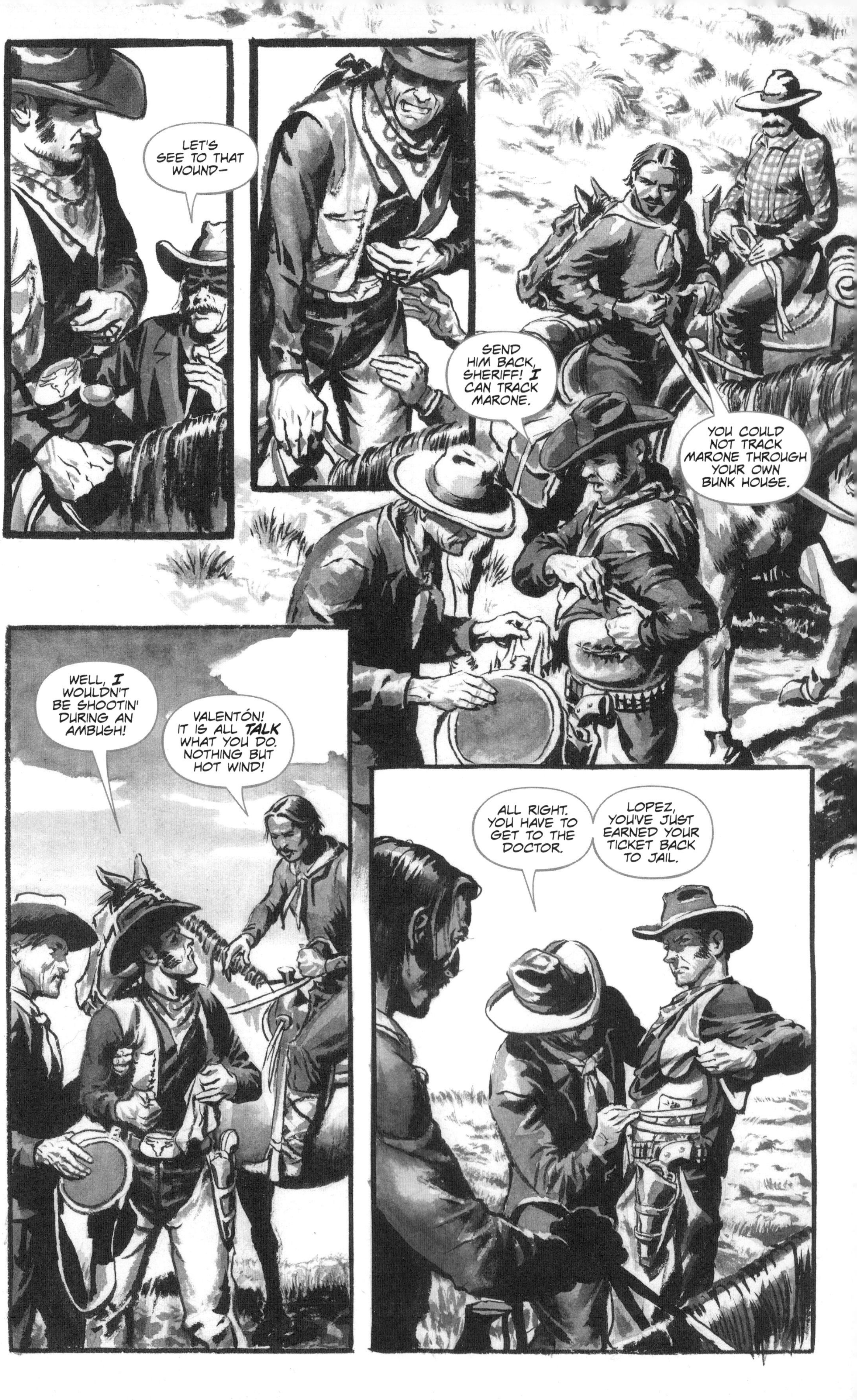
LET'S SEE TO THAT WOUND—
SEND HIM BACK, SHERIFF! I CAN TRACK MARONE.
YOU COULD NOT TRACK MARONE THROUGH YOUR OWN BUNK HOUSE.
WELL, I WOULDN'T BE SHOOTIN' DURING AN AMBUSH!
VALENTÓN! IT IS ALL TALK WHAT YOU DO. NOTHING BUT HOT WIND!
ALL RIGHT. YOU HAVE TO GET TO THE DOCTOR.
LOPEZ, YOU'VE JUST EARNED YOUR TICKET BACK TO JAIL.

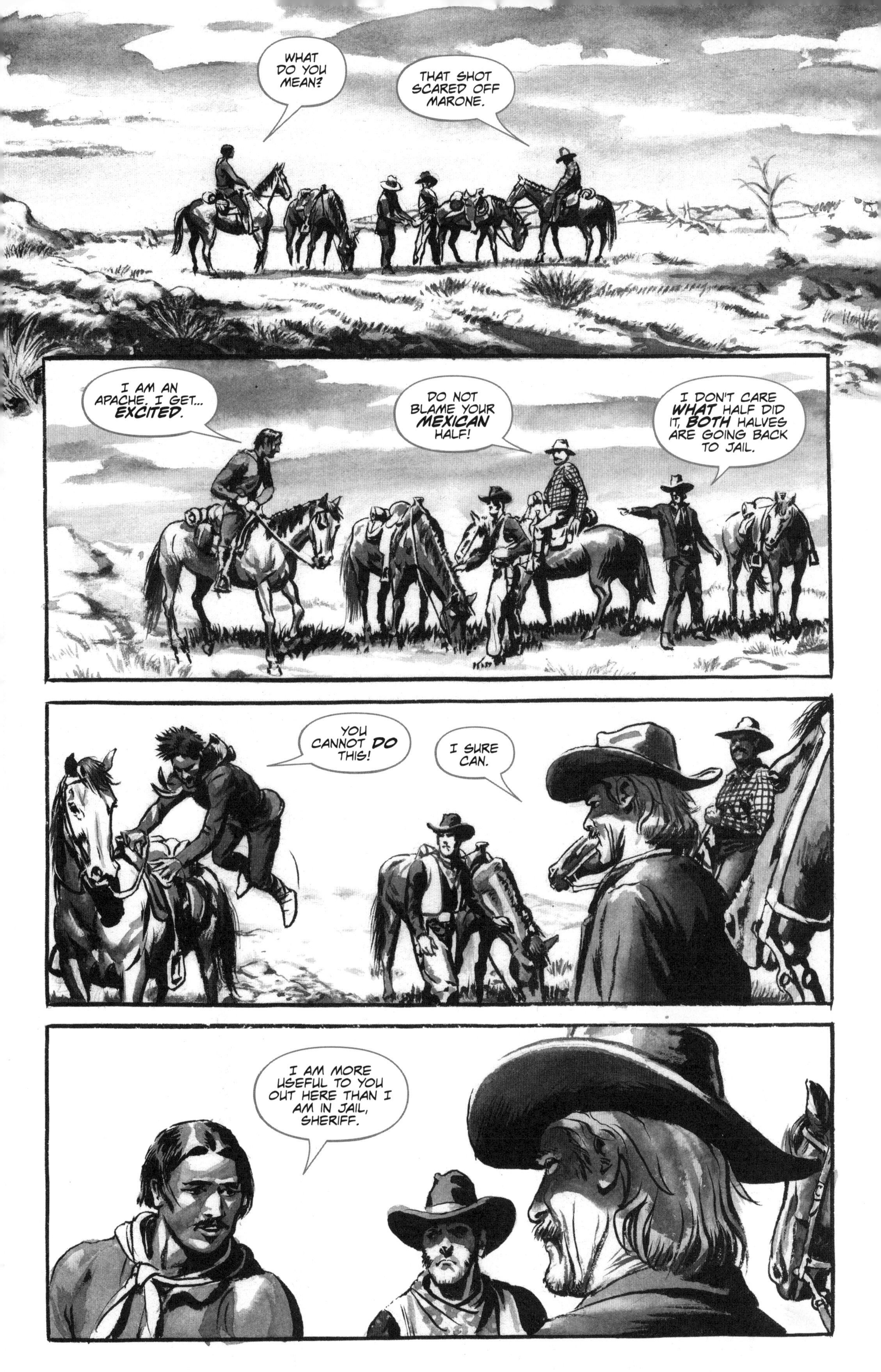
WHAT DO YOU MEAN?
THAT SHOT SCARED OFF MARONE.
I AM AN APACHE. I GET... EXCITED.
DO NOT BLAME YOUR MEXICAN HALF!
I DON'T CARE WHAT HALF DID IT, BOTH HALVES ARE GOING BACK TO JAIL.
YOU CANNOT DO THIS!
I SURE CAN.
I AM MORE USEFUL TO YOU OUT HERE THAN I AM IN JAIL, SHERIFF.

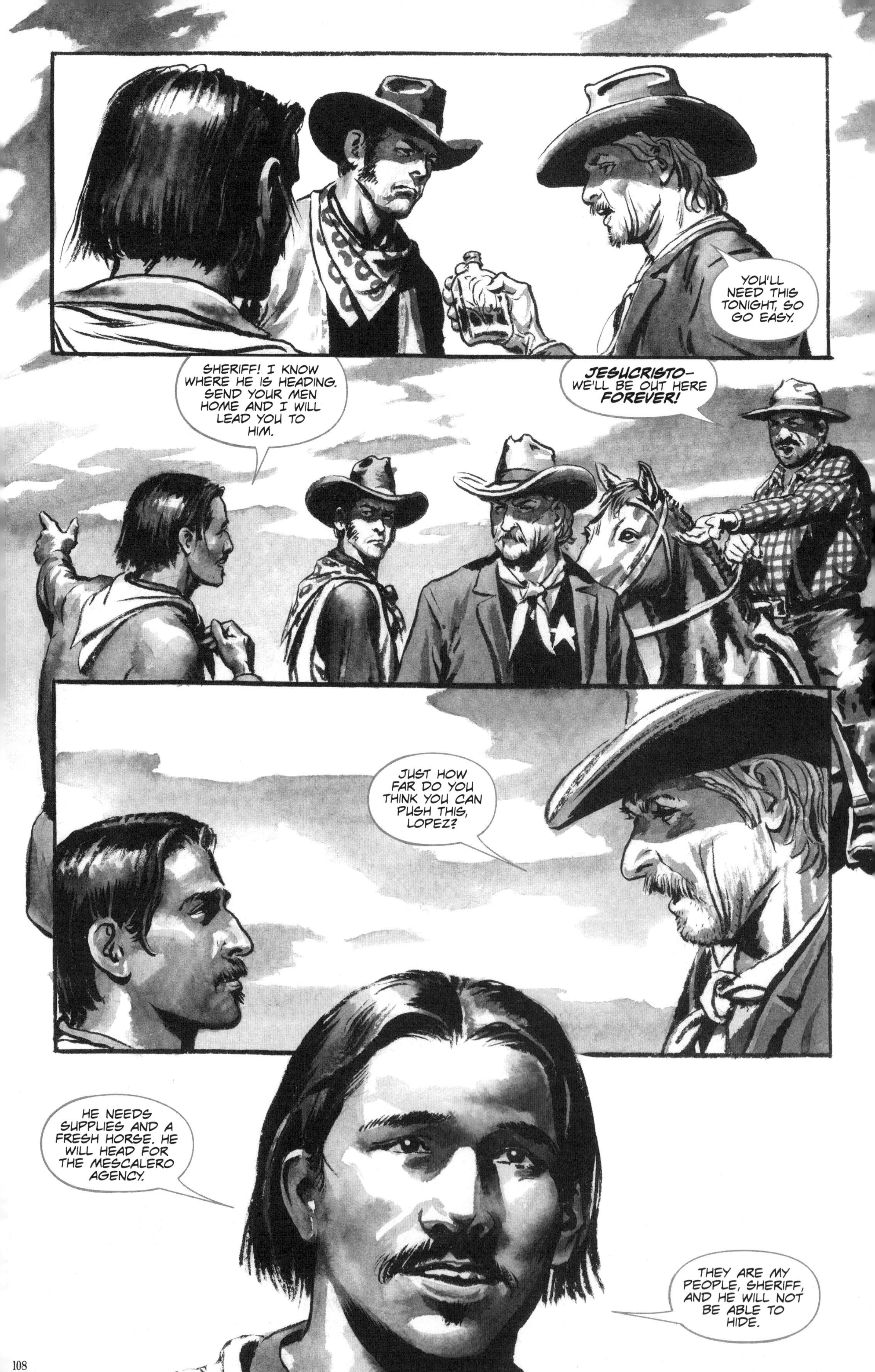
YOU'LL NEED THIS TONIGHT, SO GO EASY.
SHERIFF! I KNOW WHERE HE IS HEADING. SEND YOUR MEN HOME AND I WILL LEAD YOU TO HIM.
JESUCRISTO— WE'LL BE OUT HERE FOREVER!
JUST HOW FAR DO YOU THINK YOU CAN PUSH THIS, LOPEZ?
HE NEEDS SUPPLIES AND A FRESH HORSE. HE WILL HEAD FOR THE MESCALERO AGENCY.
THEY ARE MY PEOPLE, SHERIFF, AND HE WILL NOT BE ABLE TO HIDE.

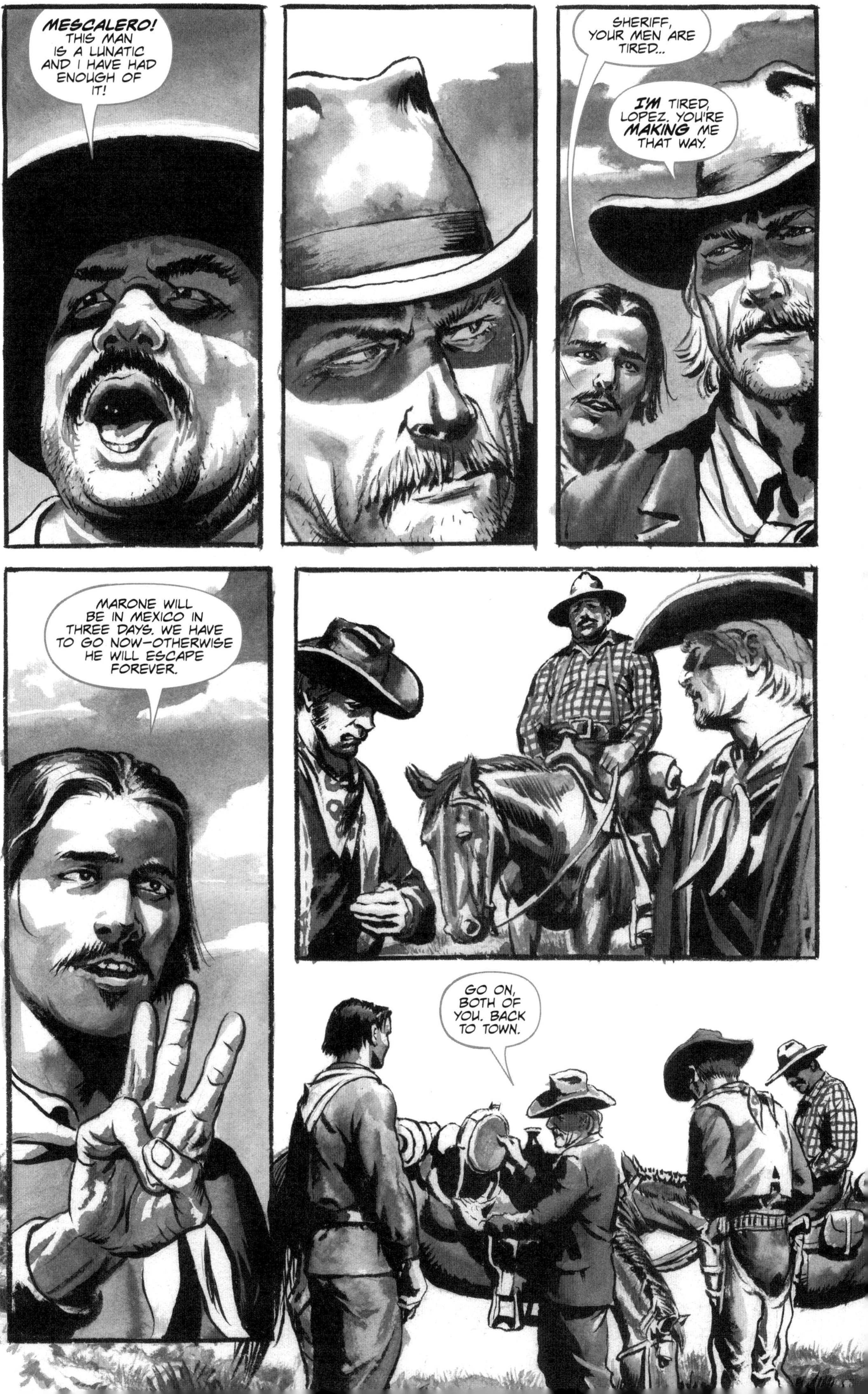
MESCALERO! THIS MAN IS A LUNATIC AND I HAVE HAD ENOUGH OF IT!
SHERIFF, YOUR MEN ARE TIRED...
I'M TIRED, LOPEZ. YOU'RE MAKING ME THAT WAY.
MARONE WILL BE IN MEXICO IN THREE DAYS. WE HAVE TO GO NOW--OTHERWISE HE WILL ESCAPE FOREVER.
GO ON, BOTH OF YOU. BACK TO TOWN.

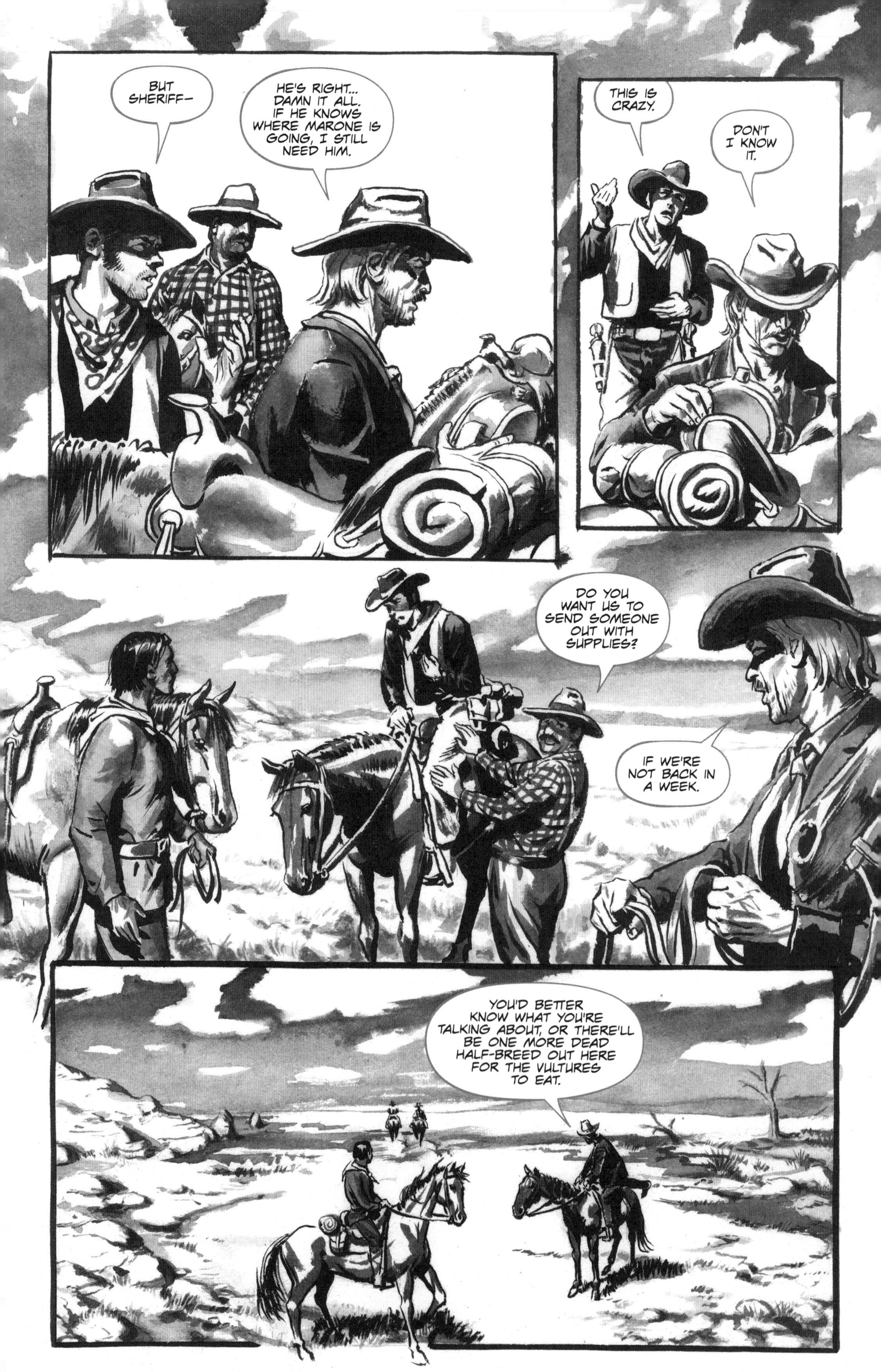
BUT SHERIFF—
HE'S RIGHT... DAMN IT ALL. IF HE KNOWS WHERE MARONE IS GOING, I STILL NEED HIM.
THIS IS CRAZY.
DON'T I KNOW IT.
DO YOU WANT US TO SEND SOMEONE OUT WITH SUPPLIES?
IF WE'RE NOT BACK IN A WEEK.
YOU'D BETTER KNOW WHAT YOU'RE TALKING ABOUT, OR THERE'LL BE ONE MORE DEAD HALF-BREED OUT HERE FOR THE VULTURES TO EAT.

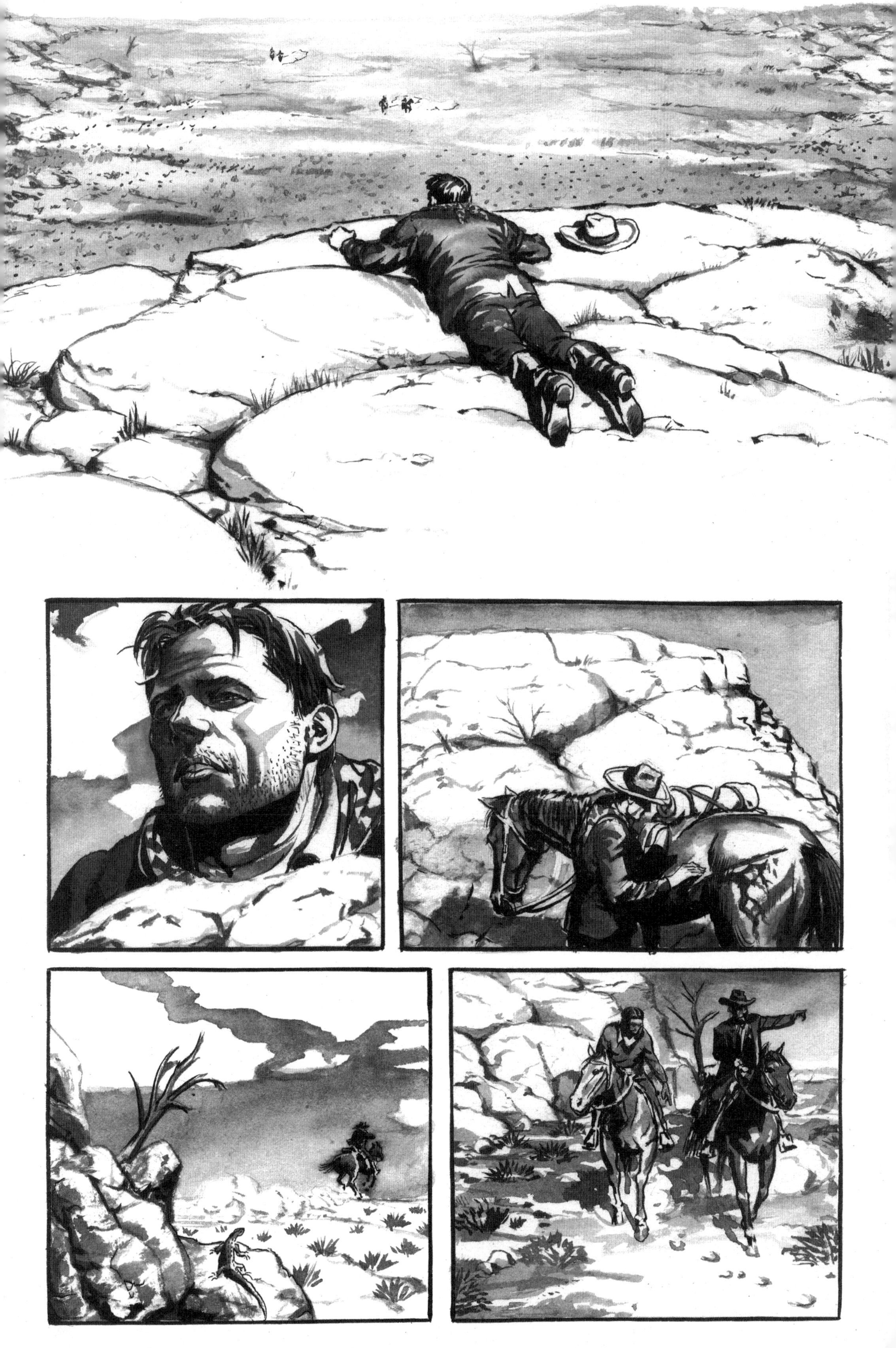

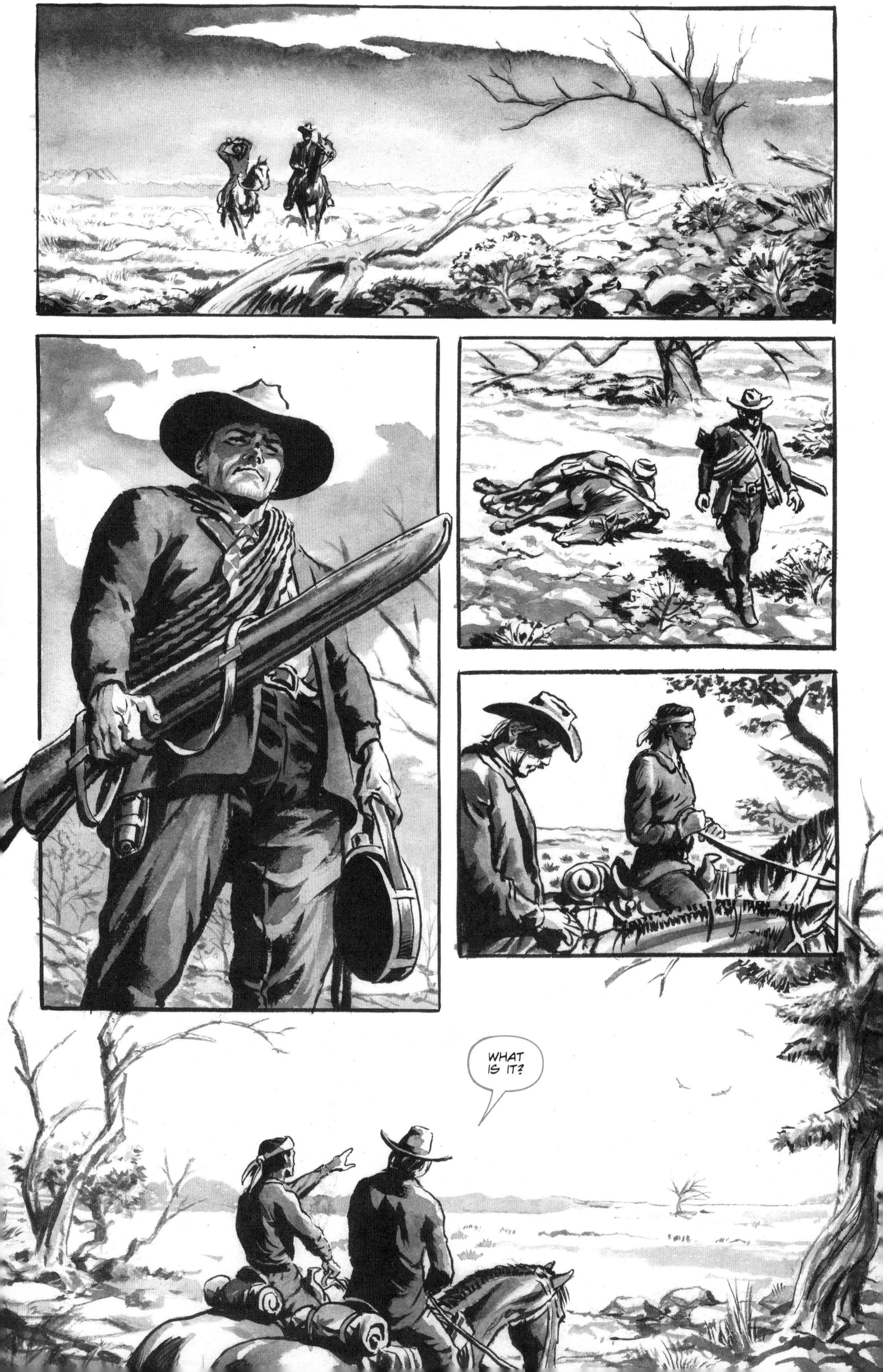
WHAT IS IT?

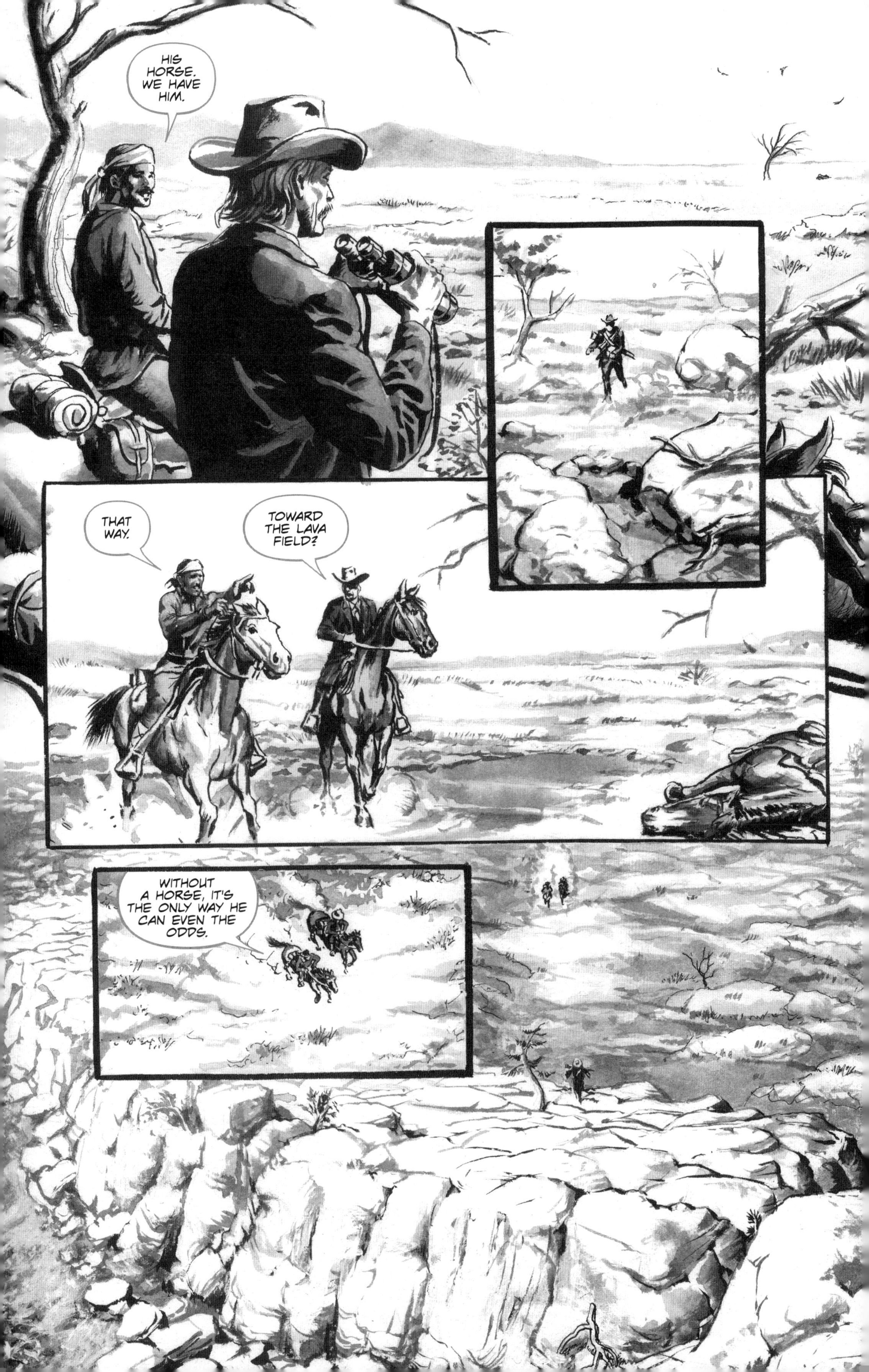
HIS HORSE. WE HAVE HIM.
THAT WAY.
TOWARD THE LAVA FIELD?
WITHOUT A HORSE, IT'S THE ONLY WAY HE CAN EVEN THE ODDS.

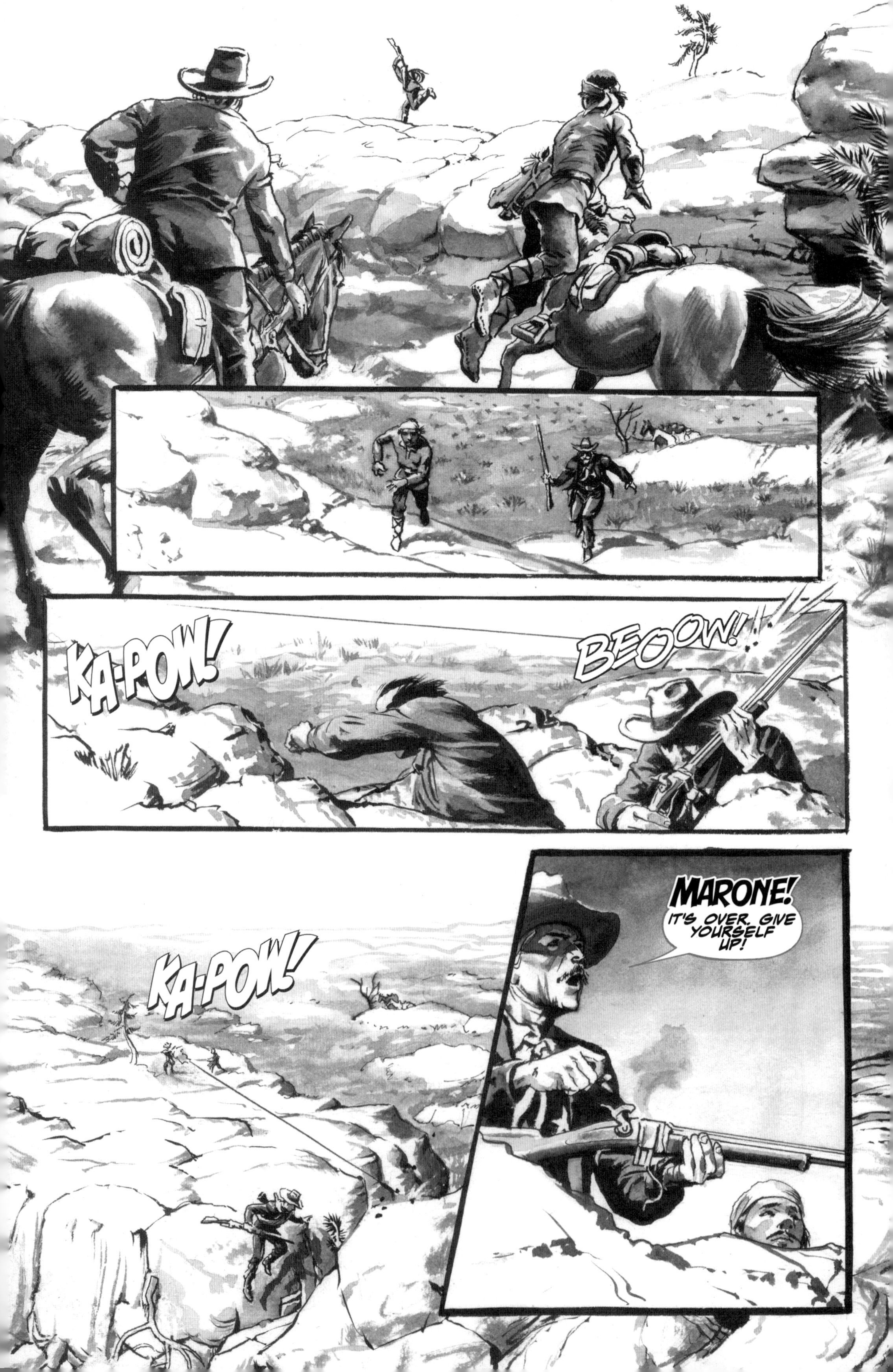
KA-POW!
BEOOW!
KA-POW!
MARONE!
IT'S OVER. GIVE YOURSELF UP!

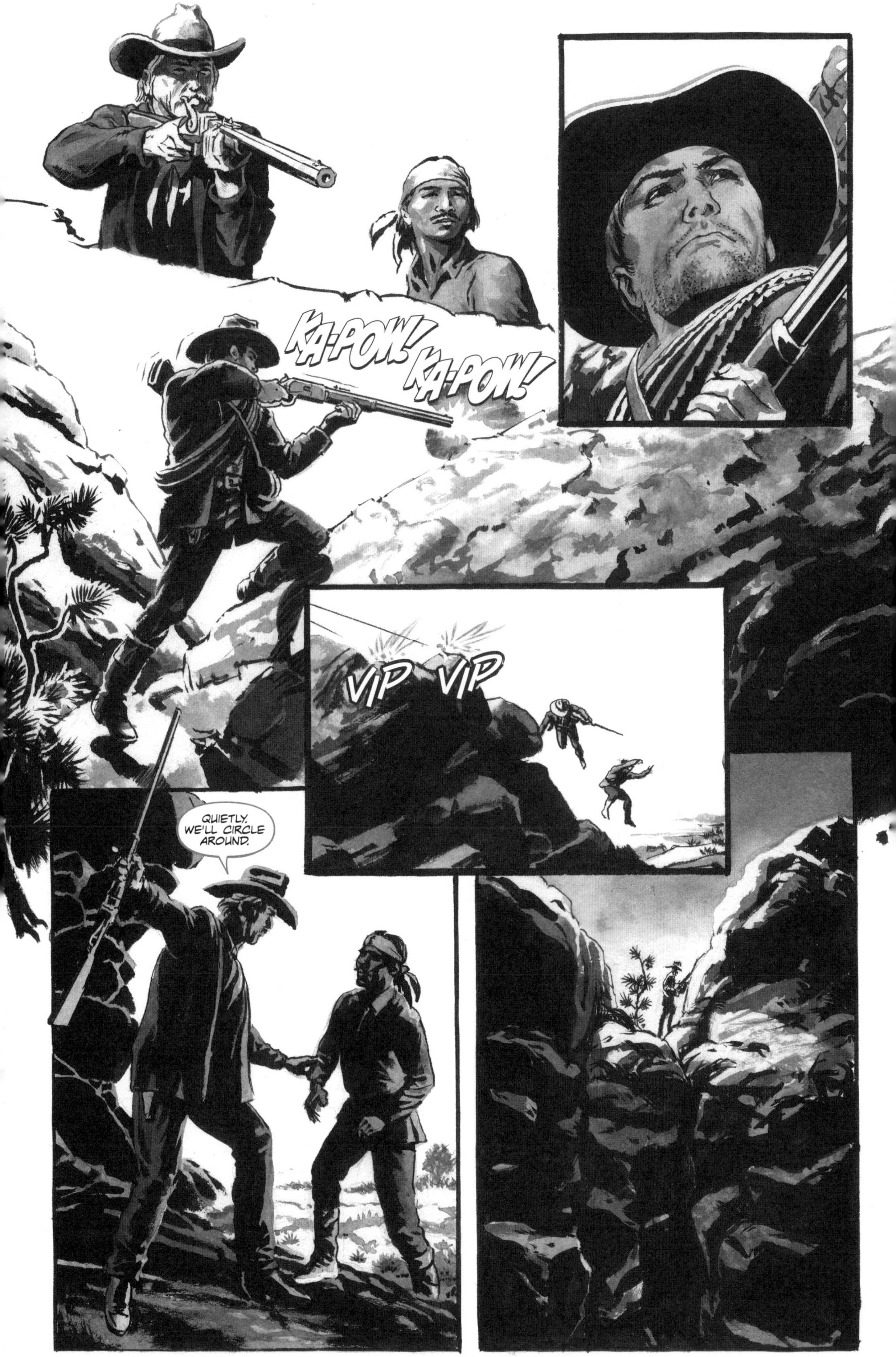
KA-POW! KA-POW!
VIP VIP
QUIETLY. WE'LL CIRCLE AROUND.

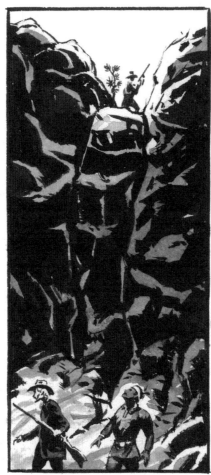

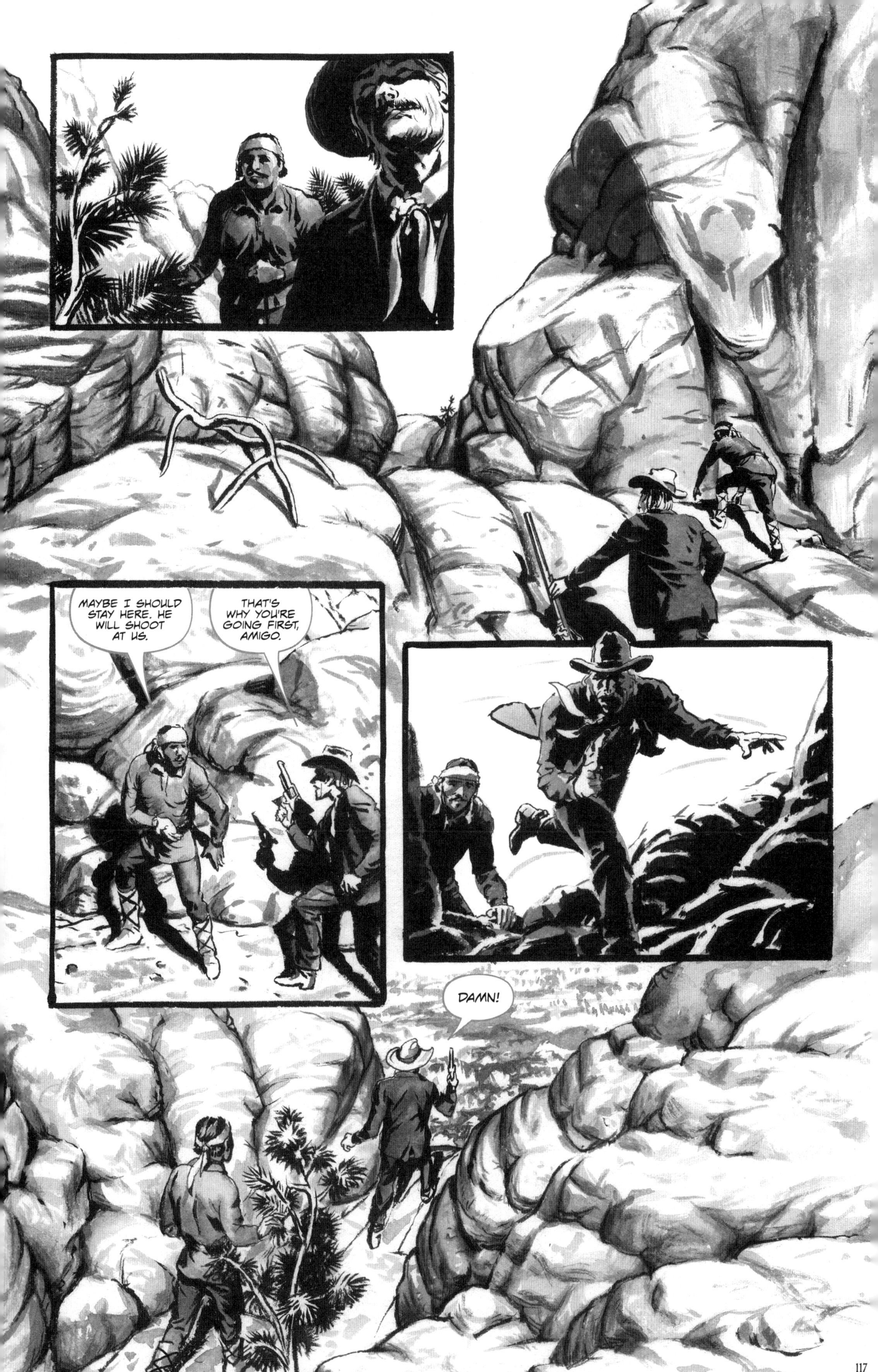
MAYBE I SHOULD STAY HERE. HE WILL SHOOT AT US.
THAT'S WHY YOU'RE GOING FIRST, AMIGO.
DAMN!

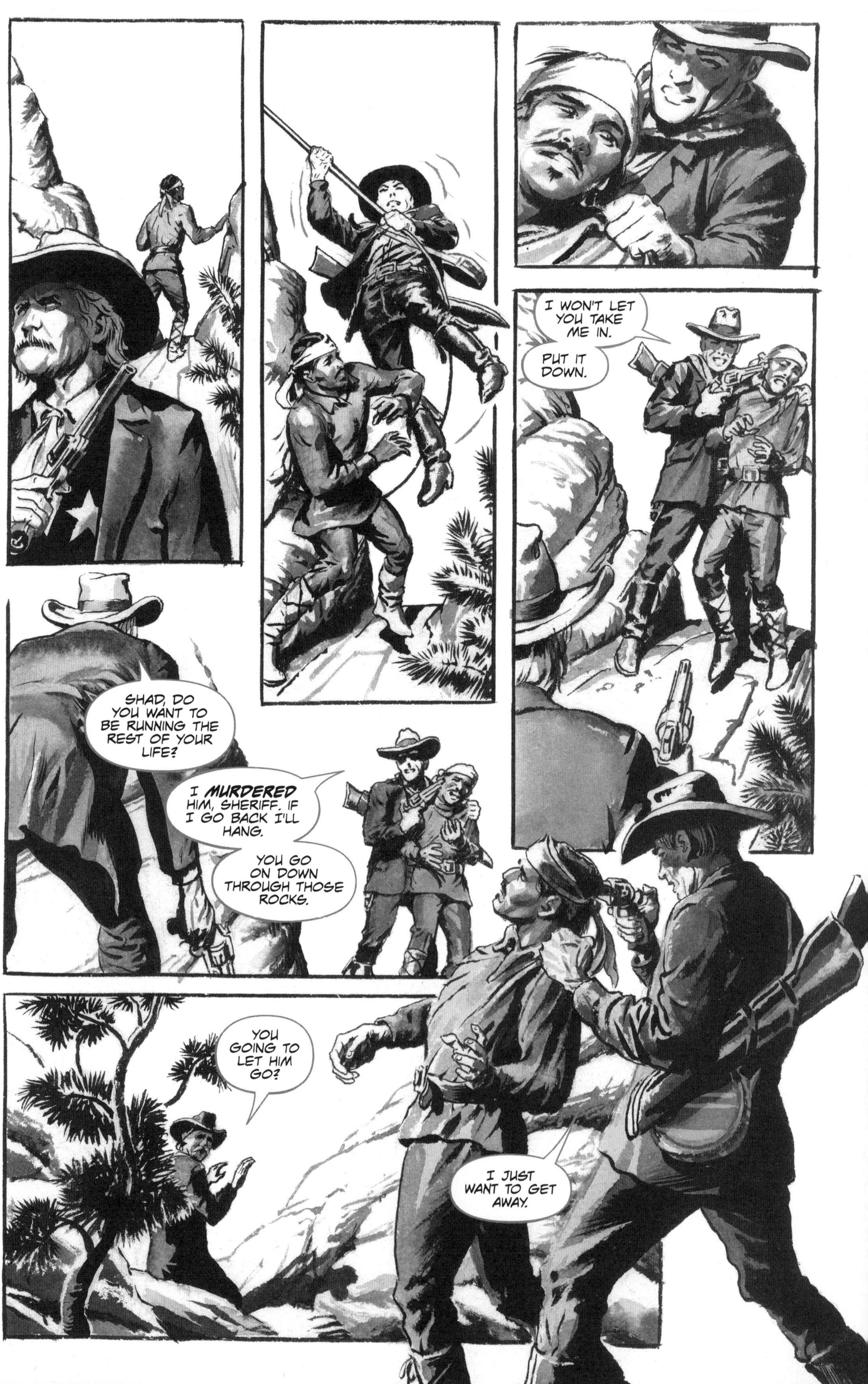
I WON'T LET YOU TAKE ME IN.
PUT IT DOWN.
SHAD, DO YOU WANT TO BE RUNNING THE REST OF YOUR LIFE?
I **MURDERED** HIM, SHERIFF. IF I GO BACK I'LL HANG.
YOU GO ON DOWN THROUGH THOSE ROCKS.
YOU GOING TO LET HIM GO?
I JUST WANT TO GET AWAY.

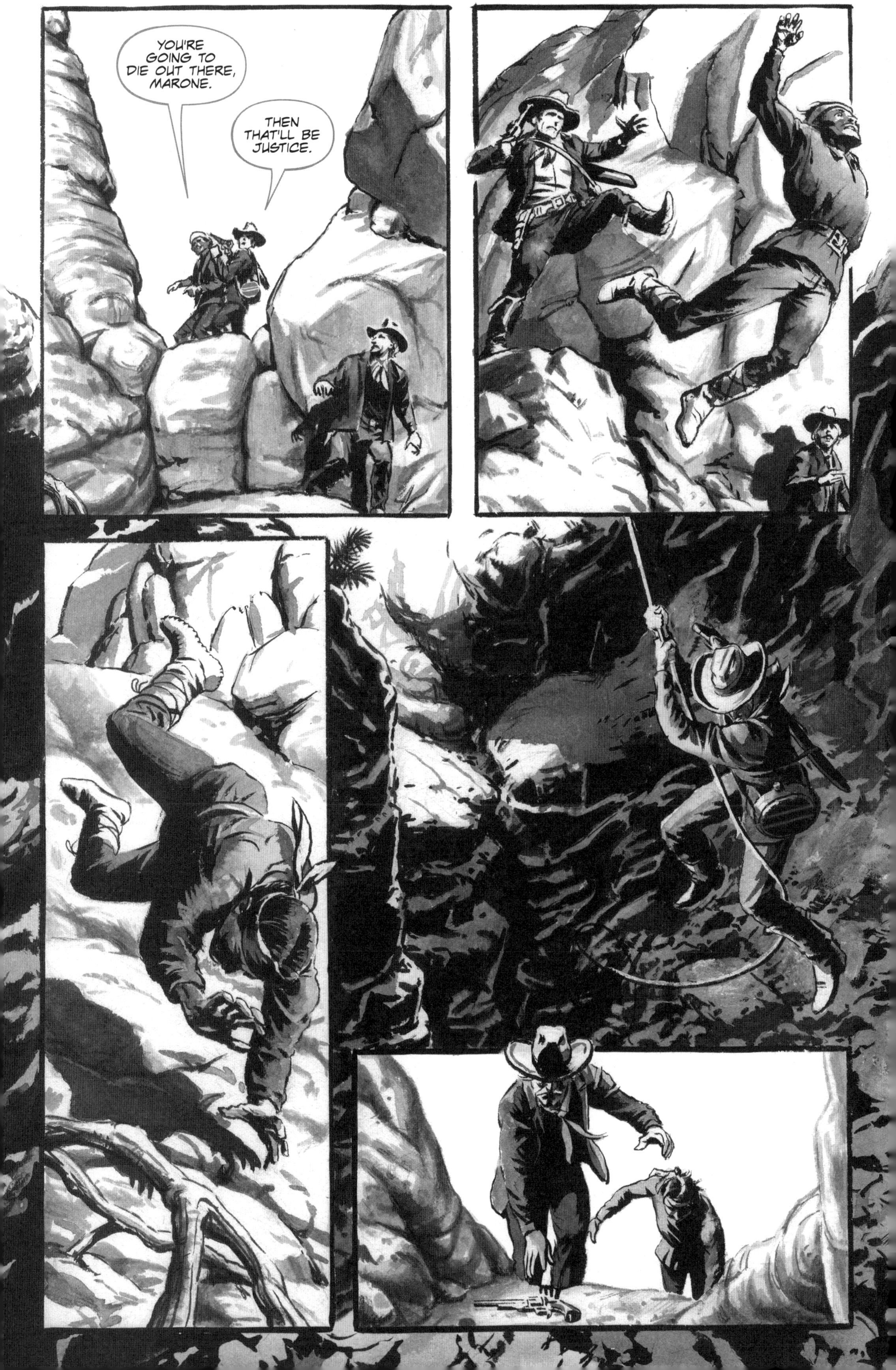
YOU'RE GOING TO DIE OUT THERE, MARONE.
THEN THAT'LL BE JUSTICE.

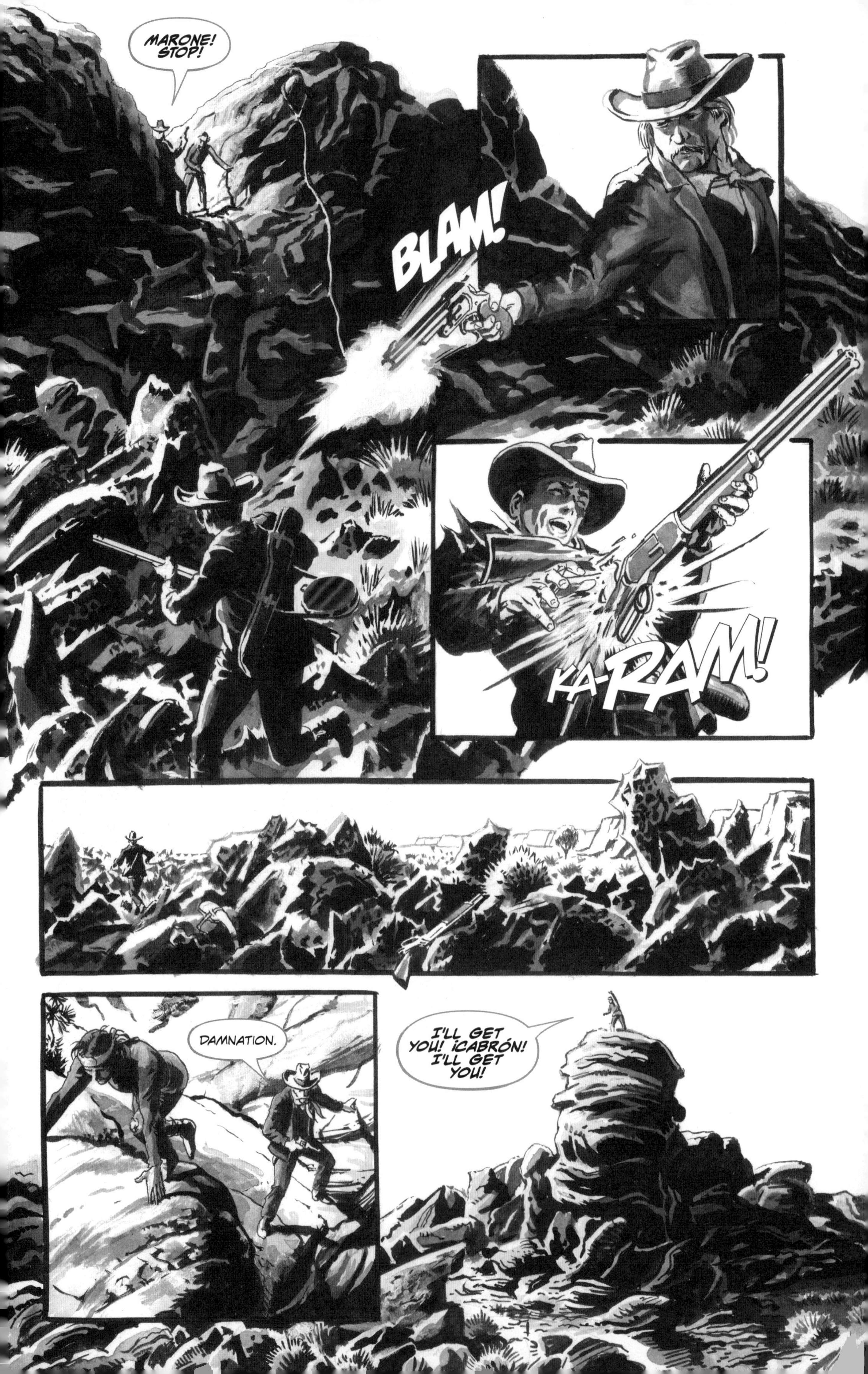
MARONE! STOP!
BLAM!
KA-RAM!
DAMNATION.
I'LL GET YOU! ¡CABRÓN! I'LL GET YOU!

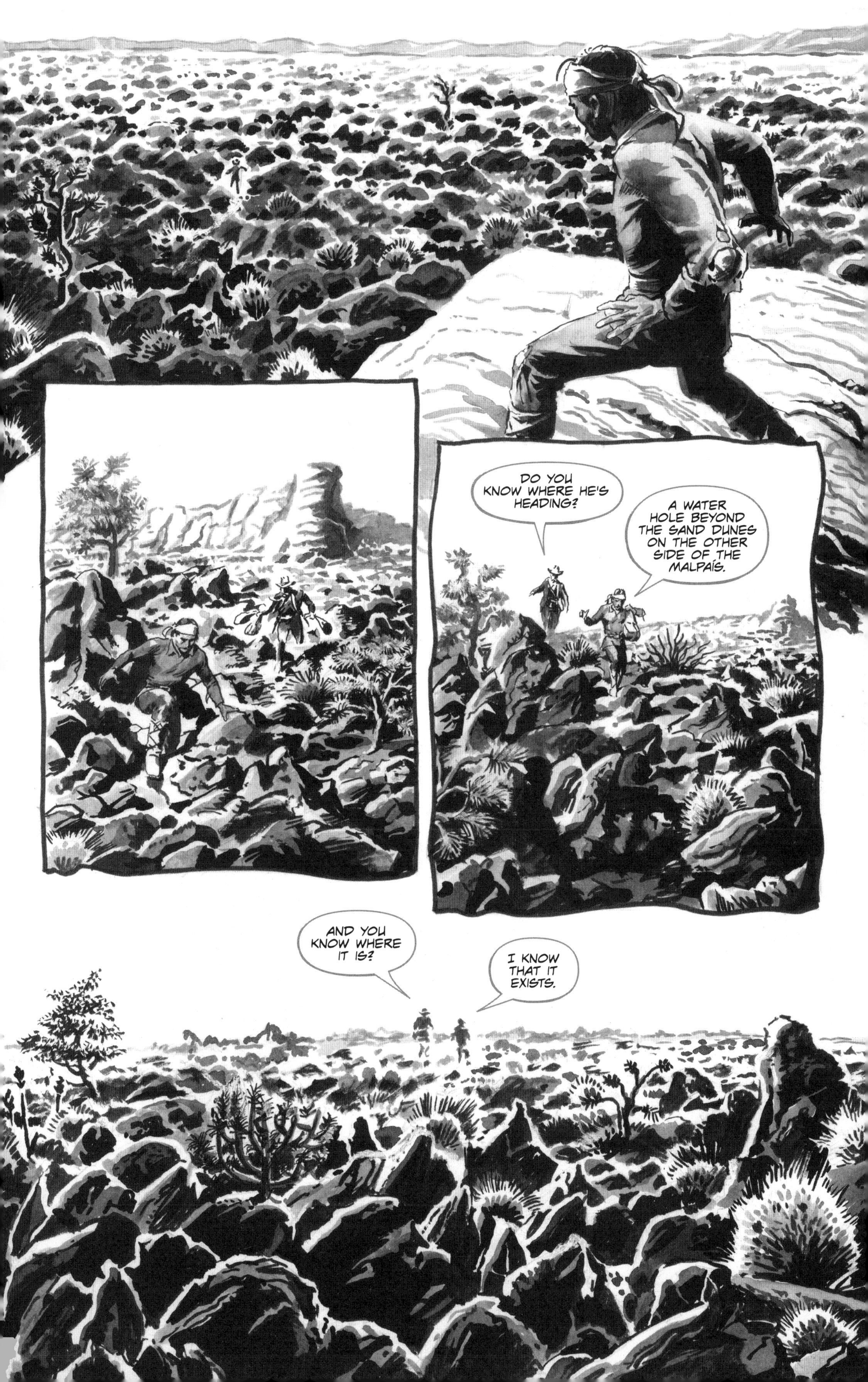
DO YOU KNOW WHERE HE'S HEADING?
A WATER HOLE BEYOND THE SAND DUNES ON THE OTHER SIDE OF THE MALPAÍS.
AND YOU KNOW WHERE IT IS?
I KNOW THAT IT EXISTS.

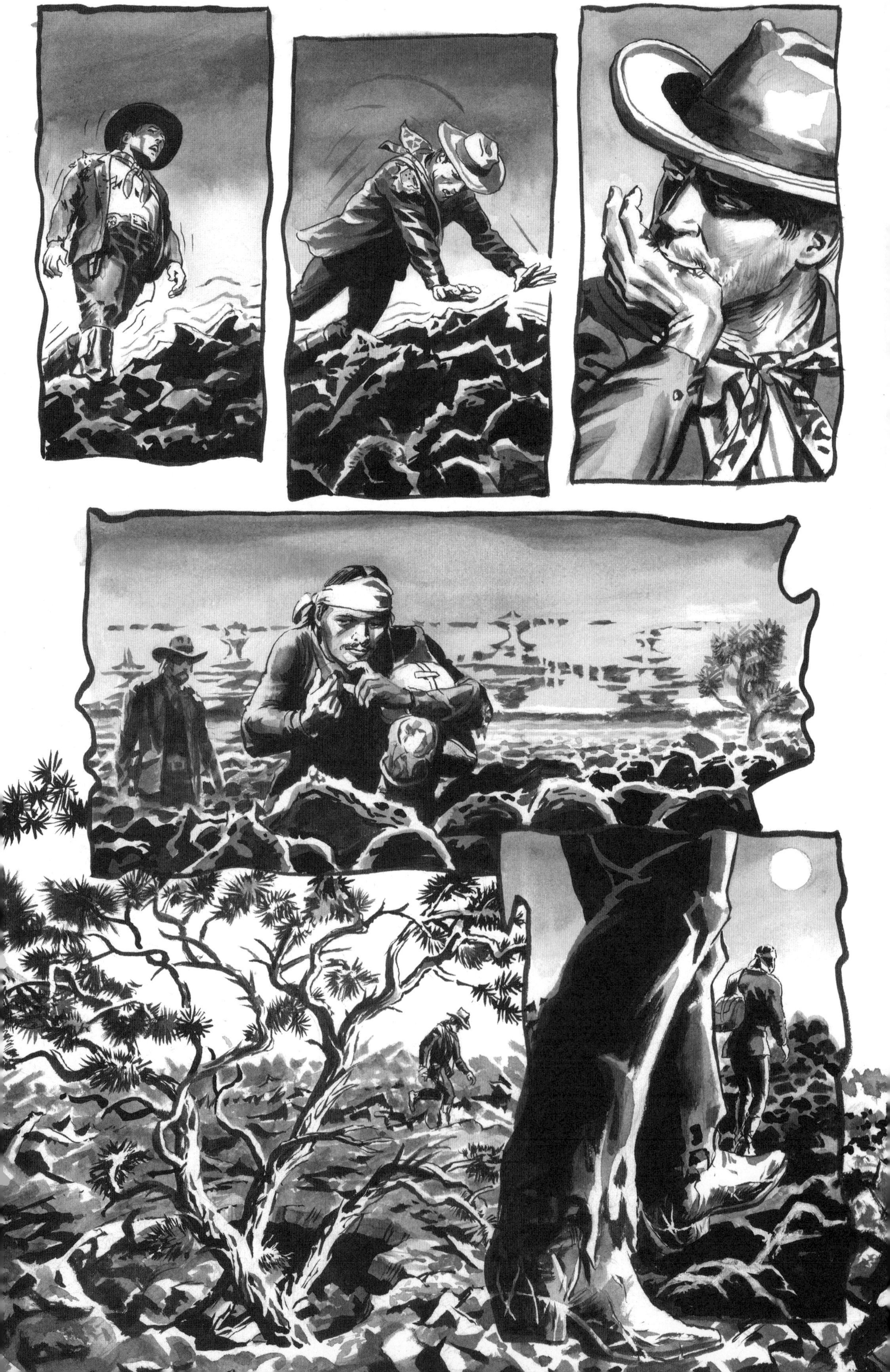

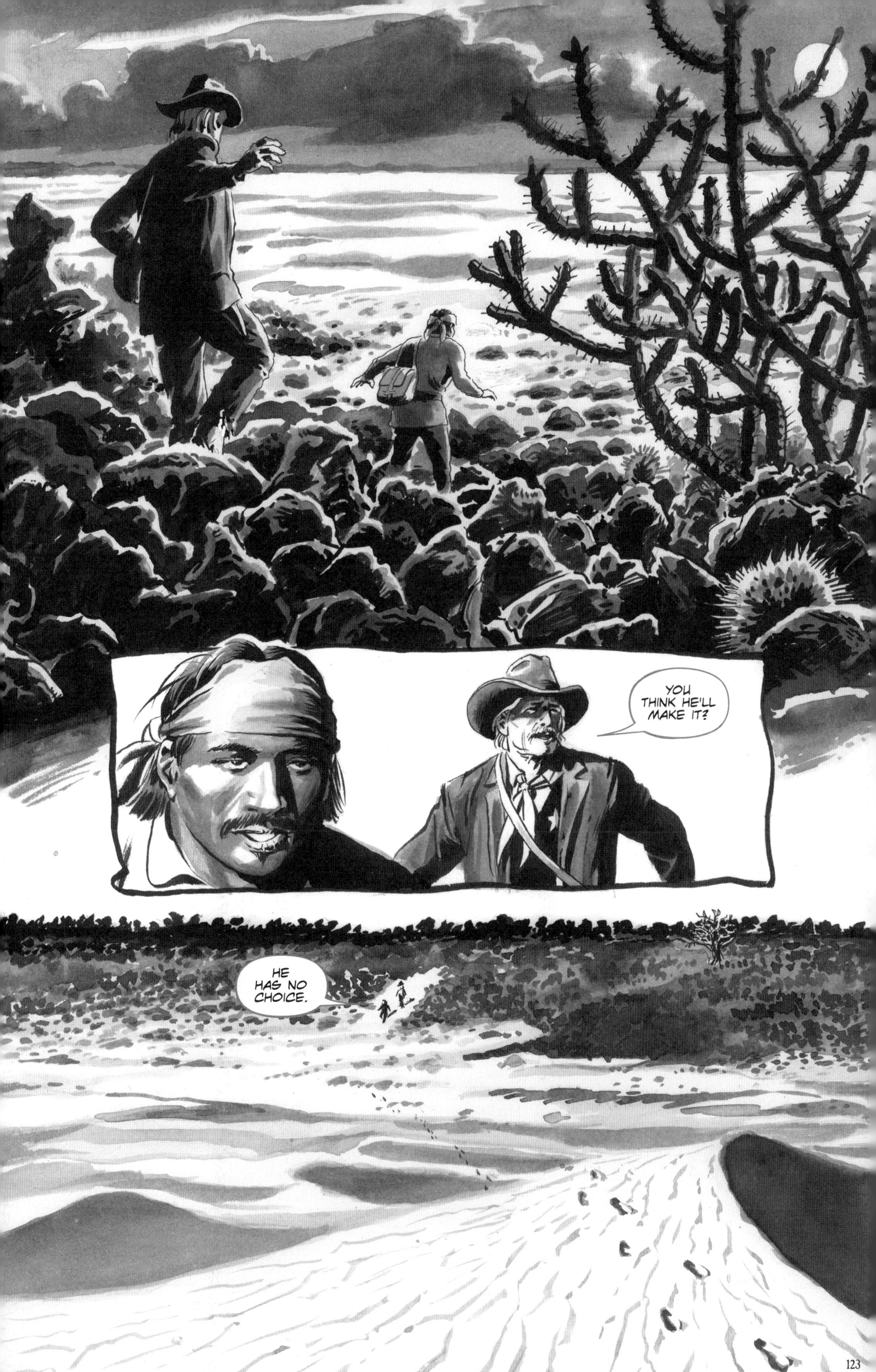
YOU THINK HE'LL MAKE IT?
HE HAS NO CHOICE.

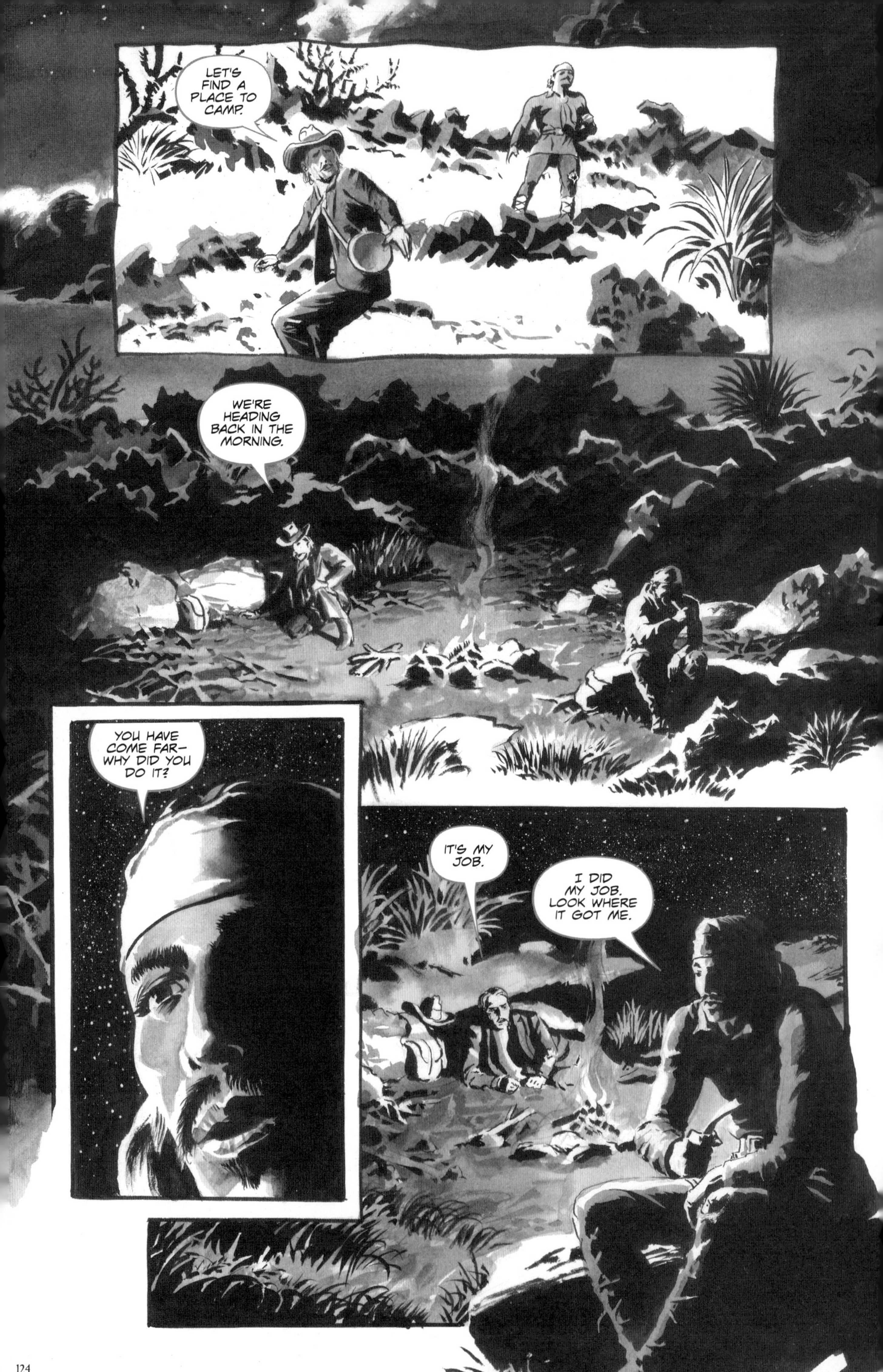
LET'S FIND A PLACE TO CAMP.
WE'RE HEADING BACK IN THE MORNING.
YOU HAVE COME FAR— WHY DID YOU DO IT?
IT'S MY JOB.
I DID MY JOB. LOOK WHERE IT GOT ME.

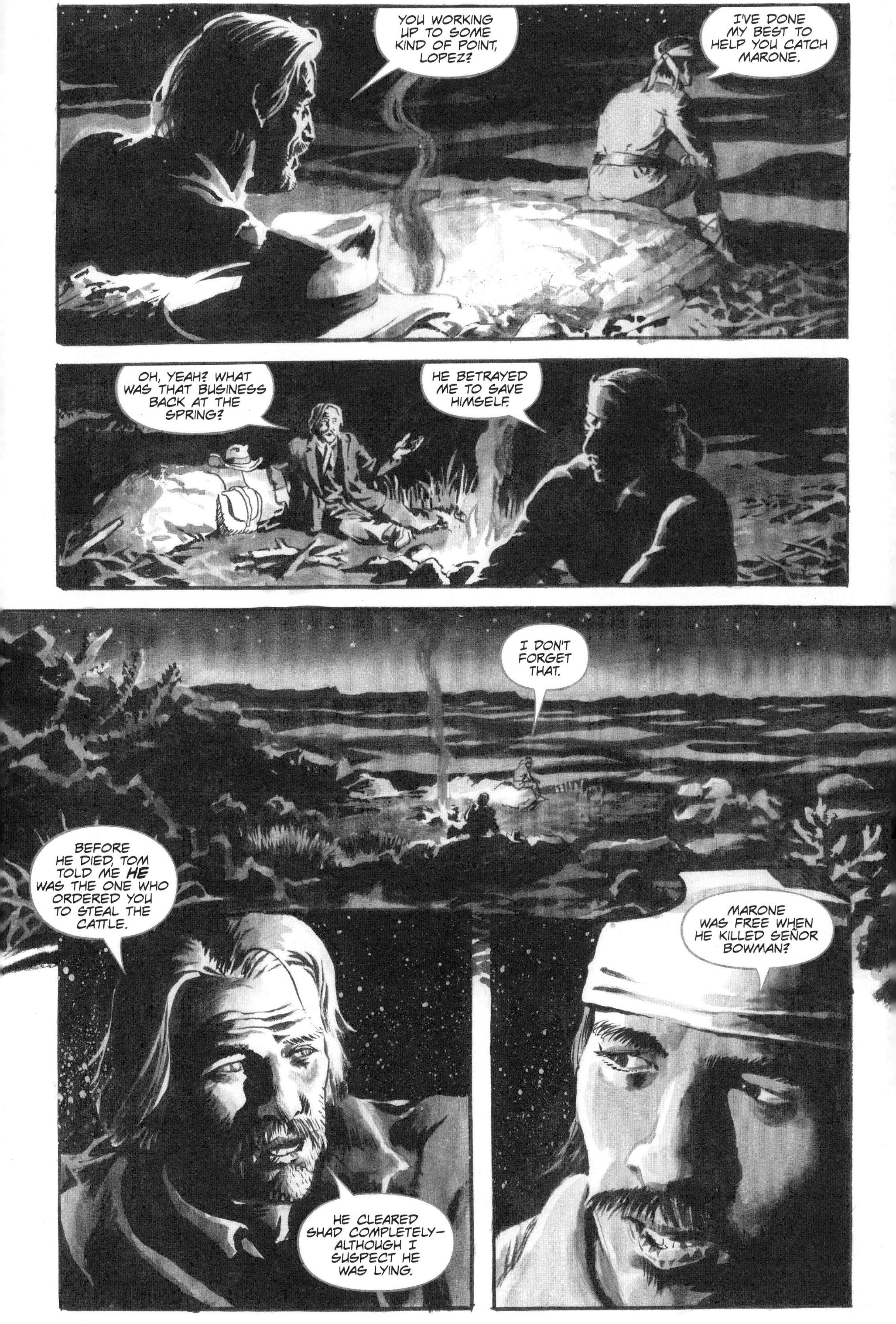
YOU WORKING UP TO SOME KIND OF POINT, LOPEZ?
I'VE DONE MY BEST TO HELP YOU CATCH MARONE.
OH, YEAH? WHAT WAS THAT BUSINESS BACK AT THE SPRING?
HE BETRAYED ME TO SAVE HIMSELF.
I DON'T FORGET THAT.
BEFORE HE DIED, TOM TOLD ME **HE** WAS THE ONE WHO ORDERED YOU TO STEAL THE CATTLE.
HE CLEARED SHAD COMPLETELY— ALTHOUGH I SUSPECT HE WAS LYING.
MARONE WAS FREE WHEN HE KILLED SEÑOR BOWMAN?

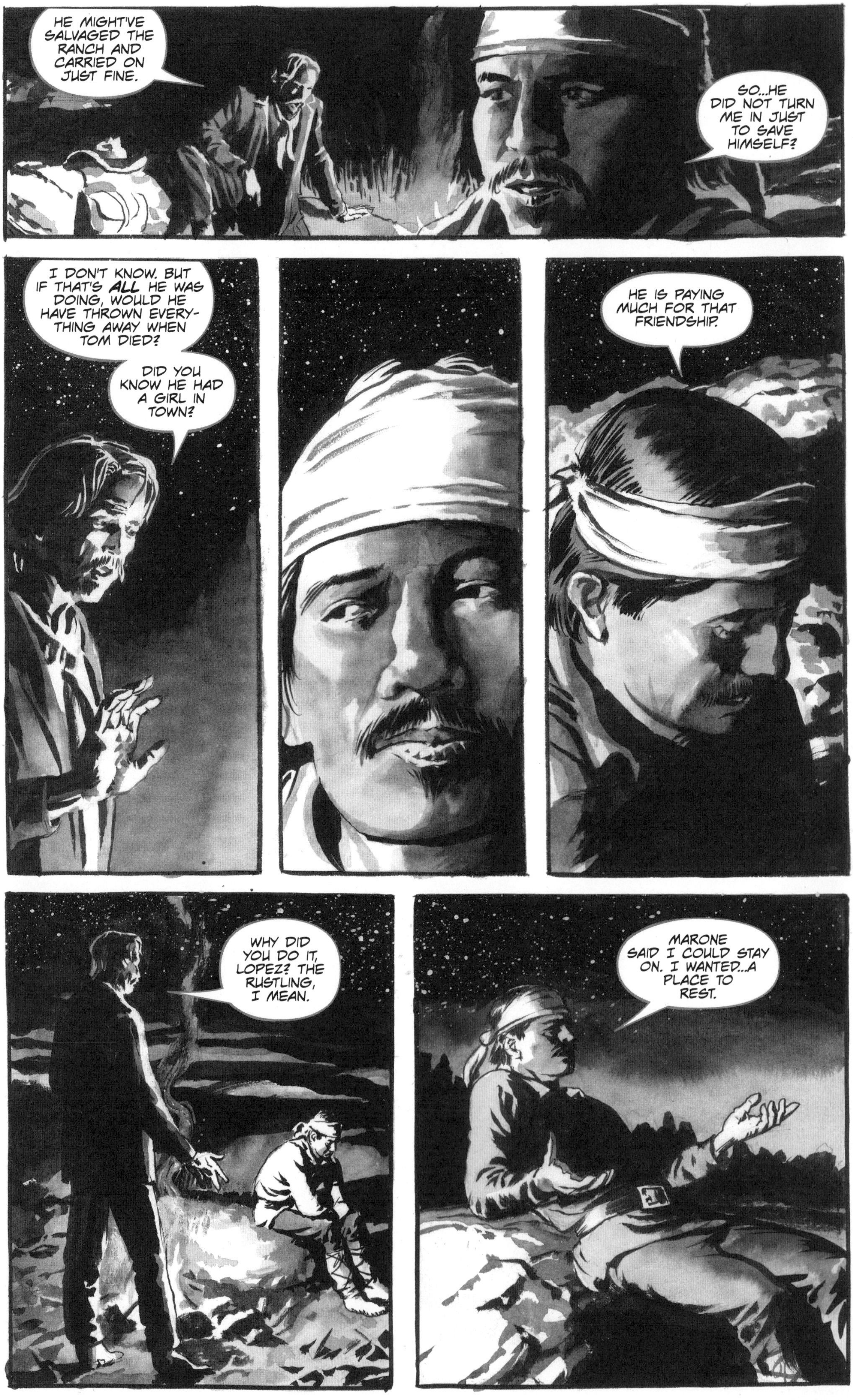
HE MIGHT'VE SALVAGED THE RANCH AND CARRIED ON JUST FINE.
SO...HE DID NOT TURN ME IN JUST TO SAVE HIMSELF?
I DON'T KNOW. BUT IF THAT'S ALL HE WAS DOING, WOULD HE HAVE THROWN EVERY-THING AWAY WHEN TOM DIED?
DID YOU KNOW HE HAD A GIRL IN TOWN?
HE IS PAYING MUCH FOR THAT FRIENDSHIP.
WHY DID YOU DO IT, LOPEZ? THE RUSTLING, I MEAN.
MARONE SAID I COULD STAY ON. I WANTED...A PLACE TO REST.

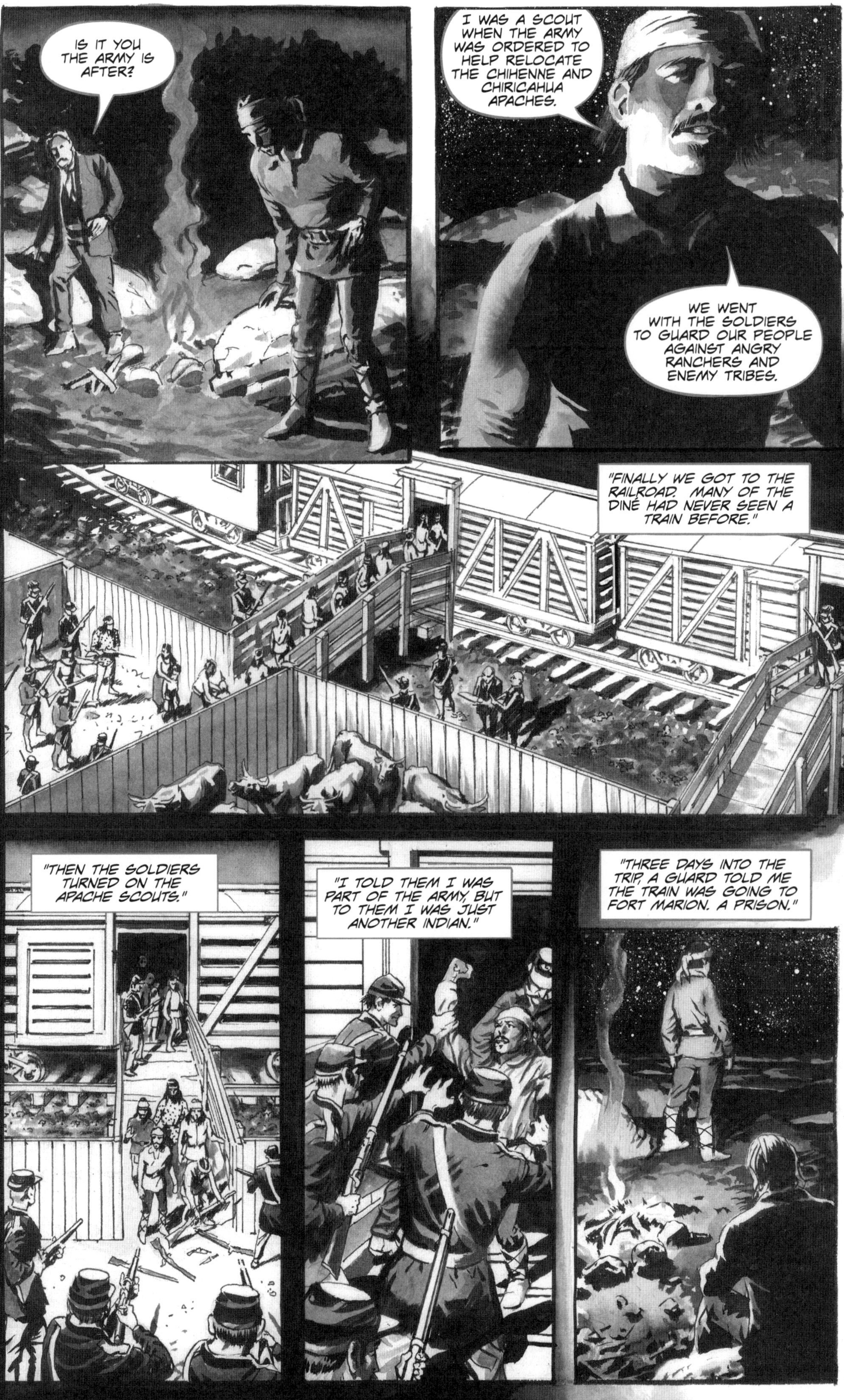
IS IT YOU THE ARMY IS AFTER?
I WAS A SCOUT WHEN THE ARMY WAS ORDERED TO HELP RELOCATE THE CHIHENNE AND CHIRICAHUA APACHES.
WE WENT WITH THE SOLDIERS TO GUARD OUR PEOPLE AGAINST ANGRY RANCHERS AND ENEMY TRIBES.
"FINALLY WE GOT TO THE RAILROAD. MANY OF THE DINÉ HAD NEVER SEEN A TRAIN BEFORE."
"THEN THE SOLDIERS TURNED ON THE APACHE SCOUTS."
"I TOLD THEM I WAS PART OF THE ARMY, BUT TO THEM I WAS JUST ANOTHER INDIAN."
"THREE DAYS INTO THE TRIP, A GUARD TOLD ME THE TRAIN WAS GOING TO FORT MARION. A PRISON."

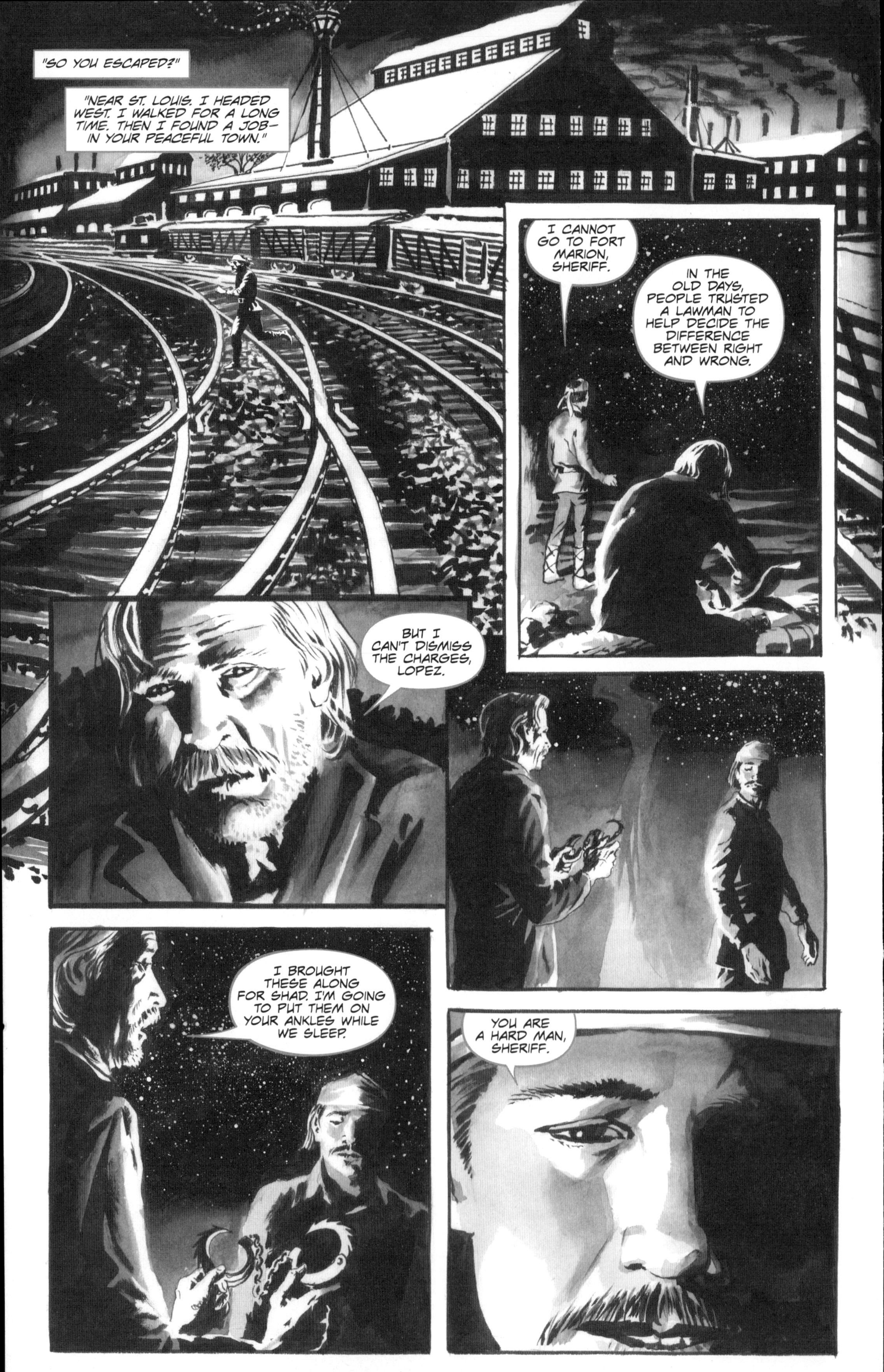
"SO YOU ESCAPED?"
"NEAR ST. LOUIS. I HEADED WEST. I WALKED FOR A LONG TIME. THEN I FOUND A JOB-- IN YOUR PEACEFUL TOWN."
I CANNOT GO TO FORT MARION, SHERIFF.
IN THE OLD DAYS, PEOPLE TRUSTED A LAWMAN TO HELP DECIDE THE DIFFERENCE BETWEEN RIGHT AND WRONG.
BUT I CAN'T DISMISS THE CHARGES, LOPEZ.
I BROUGHT THESE ALONG FOR SHAD. I'M GOING TO PUT THEM ON YOUR ANKLES WHILE WE SLEEP.
YOU ARE A HARD MAN, SHERIFF.

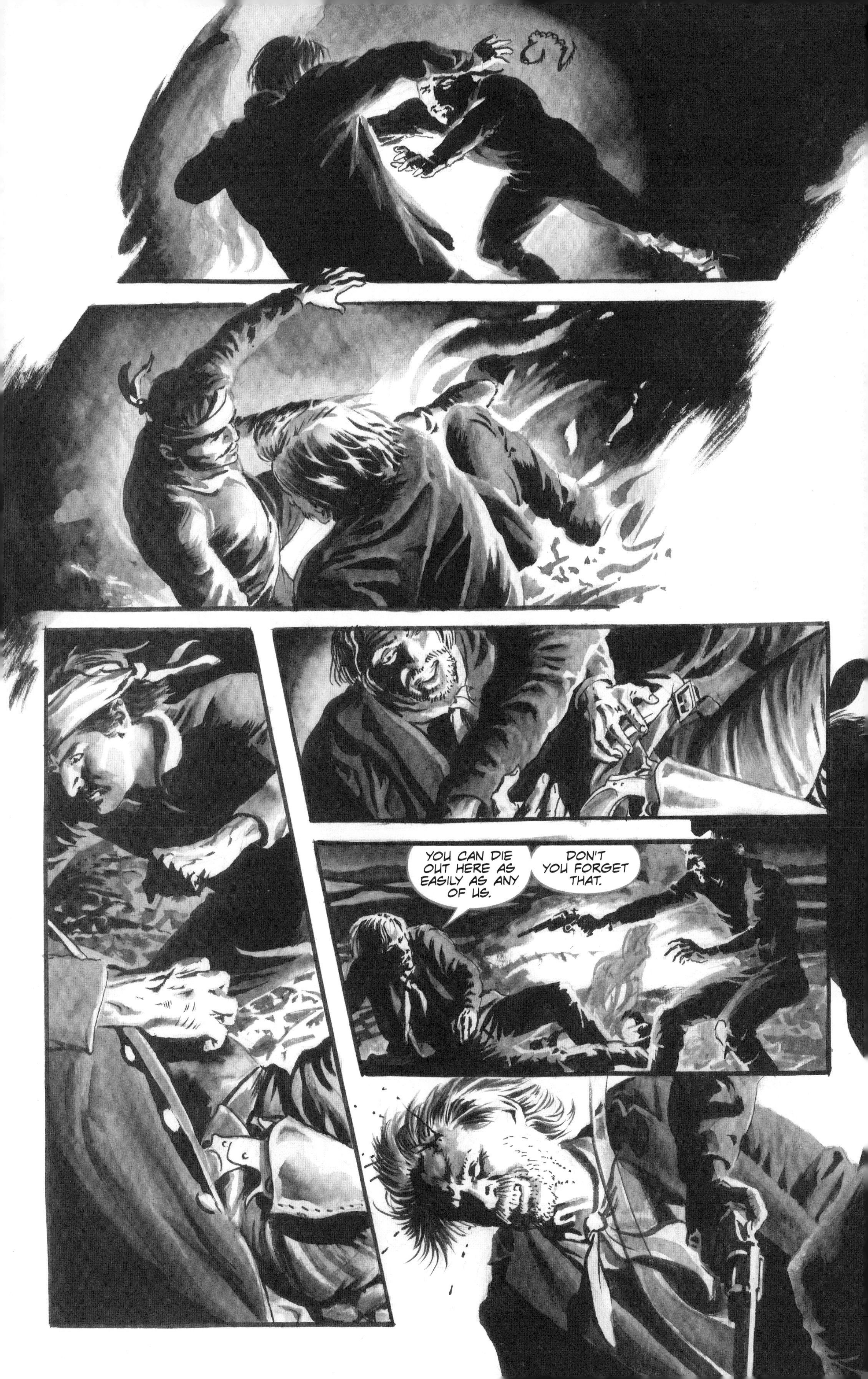
YOU CAN DIE OUT HERE AS EASILY AS ANY OF US.
DON'T YOU FORGET THAT.

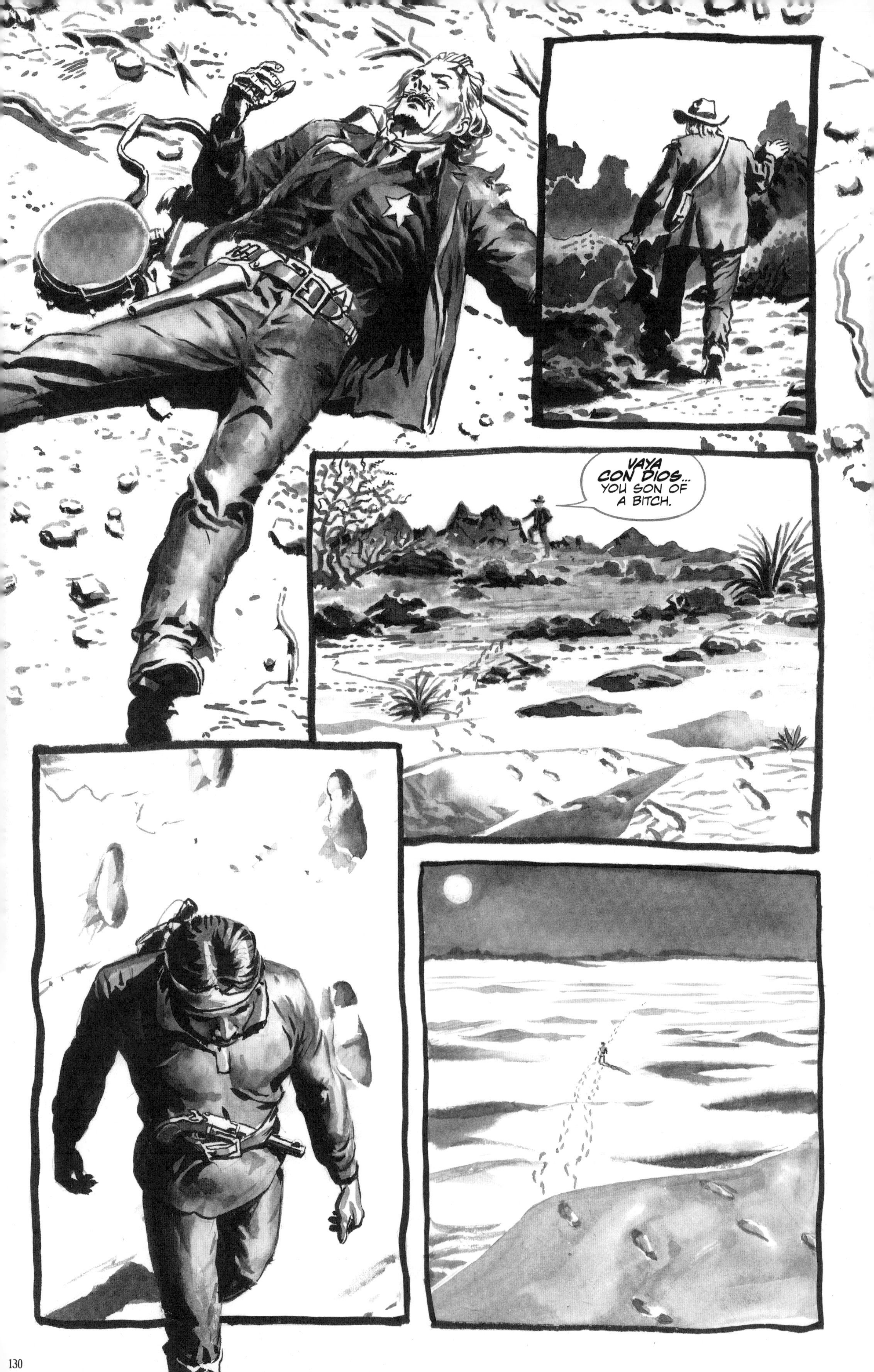
VAYA CON DIOS... YOU SON OF A BITCH.

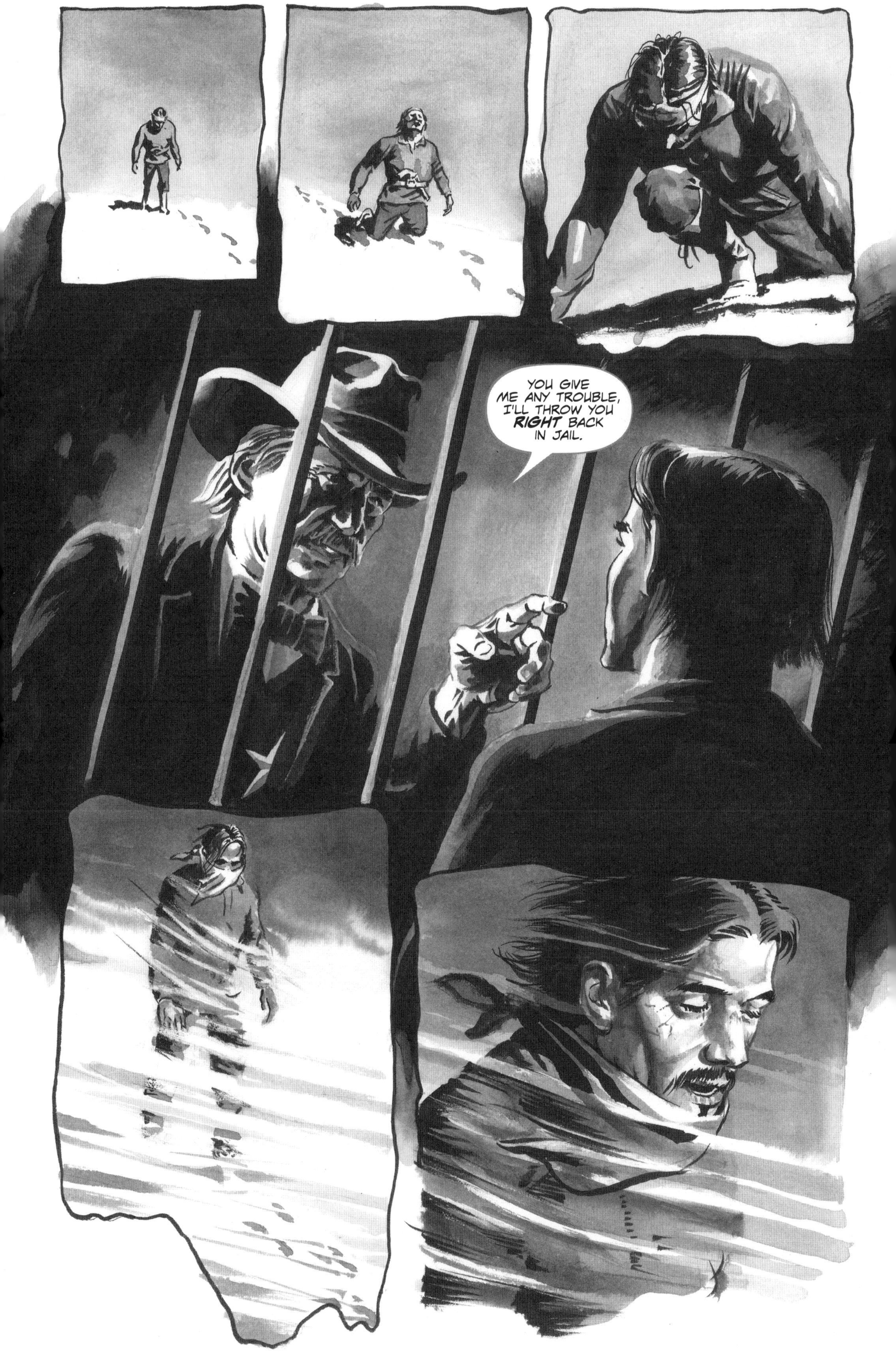
YOU GIVE ME ANY TROUBLE, I'LL THROW YOU RIGHT BACK IN JAIL.

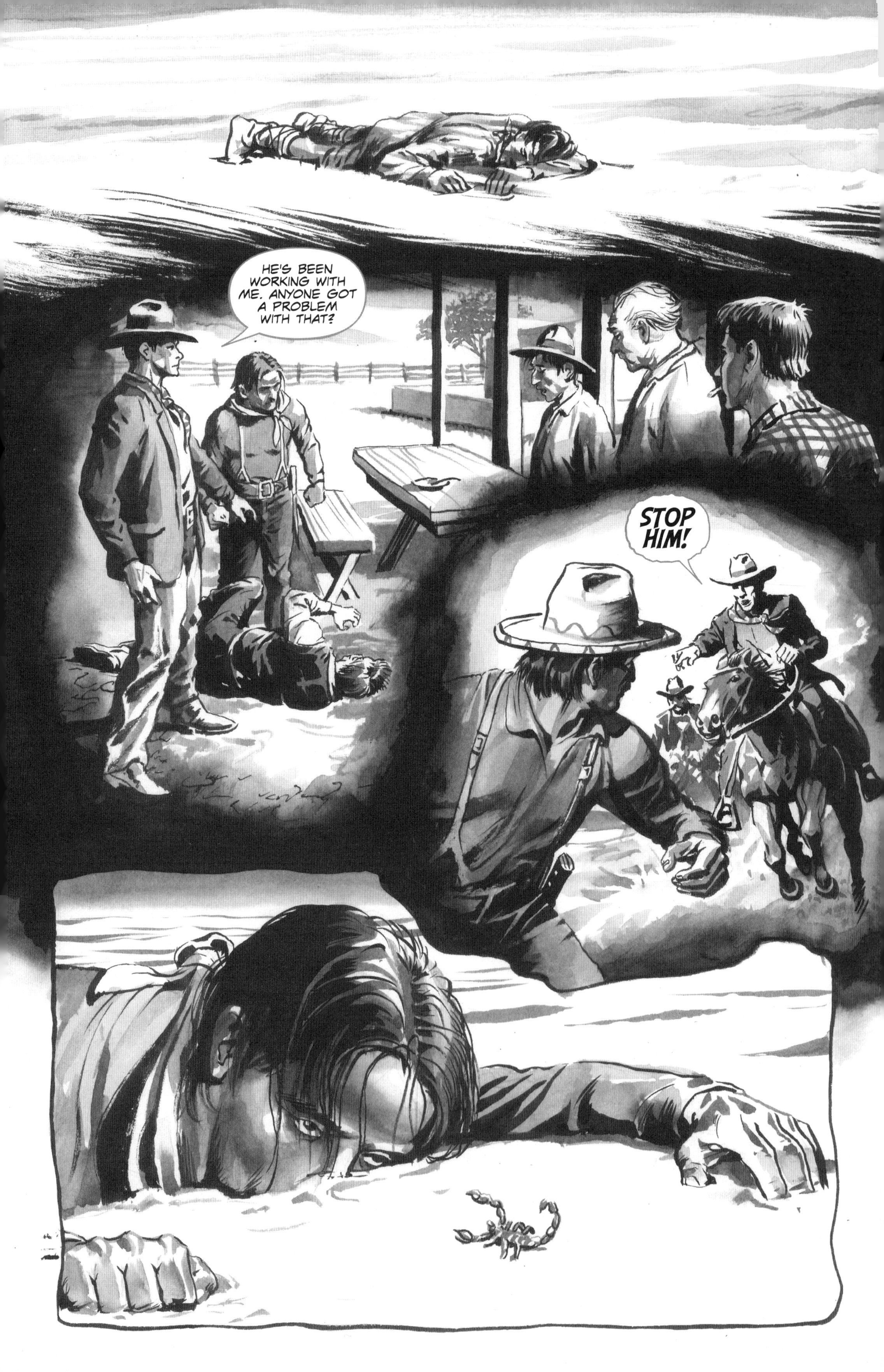
HE'S BEEN WORKING WITH ME. ANYONE GOT A PROBLEM WITH THAT?
STOP HIM!

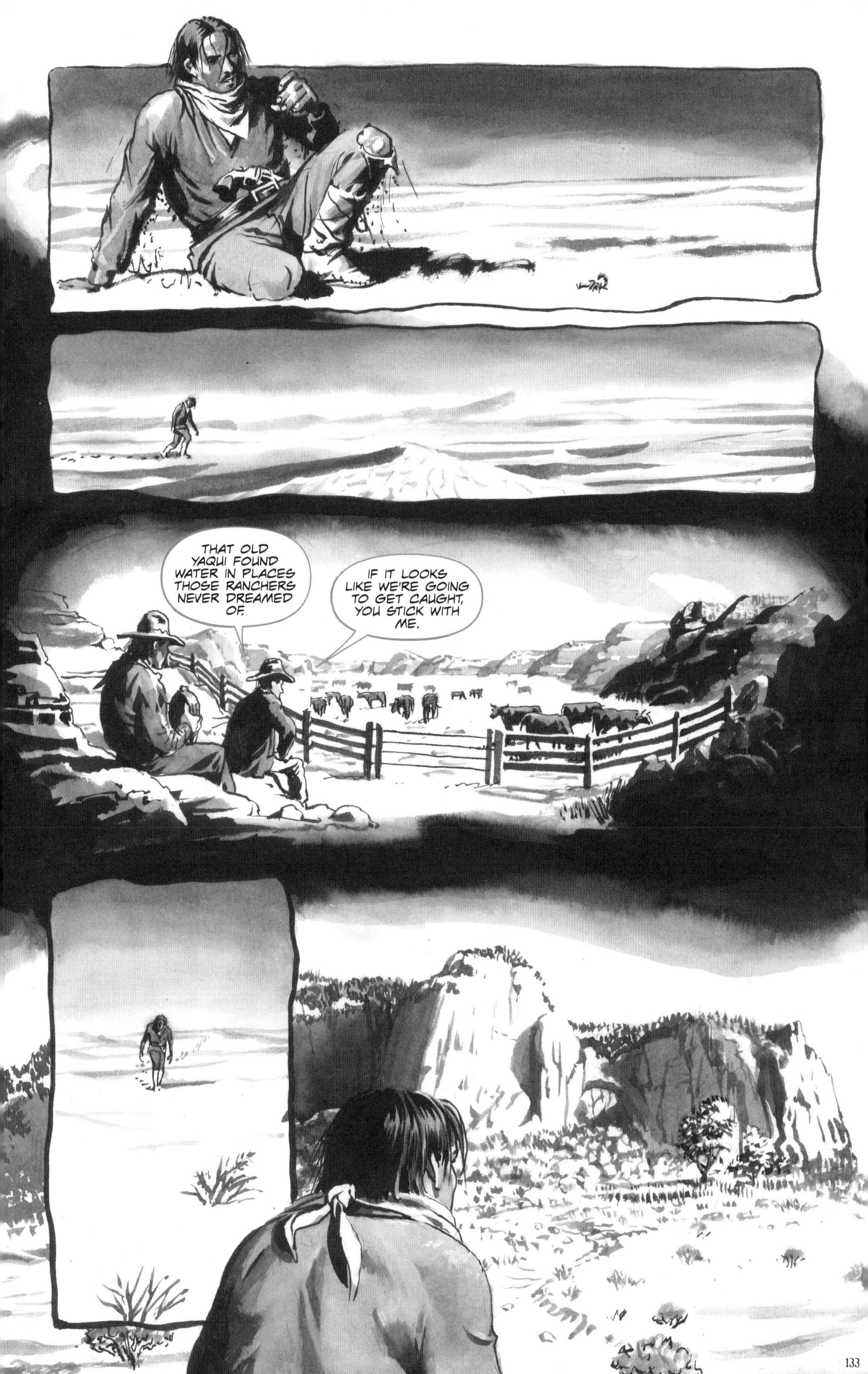
THAT OLD YAQUI FOUND WATER IN PLACES THOSE RANCHERS NEVER DREAMED OF.
IF IT LOOKS LIKE WE'RE GOING TO GET CAUGHT, YOU STICK WITH ME.

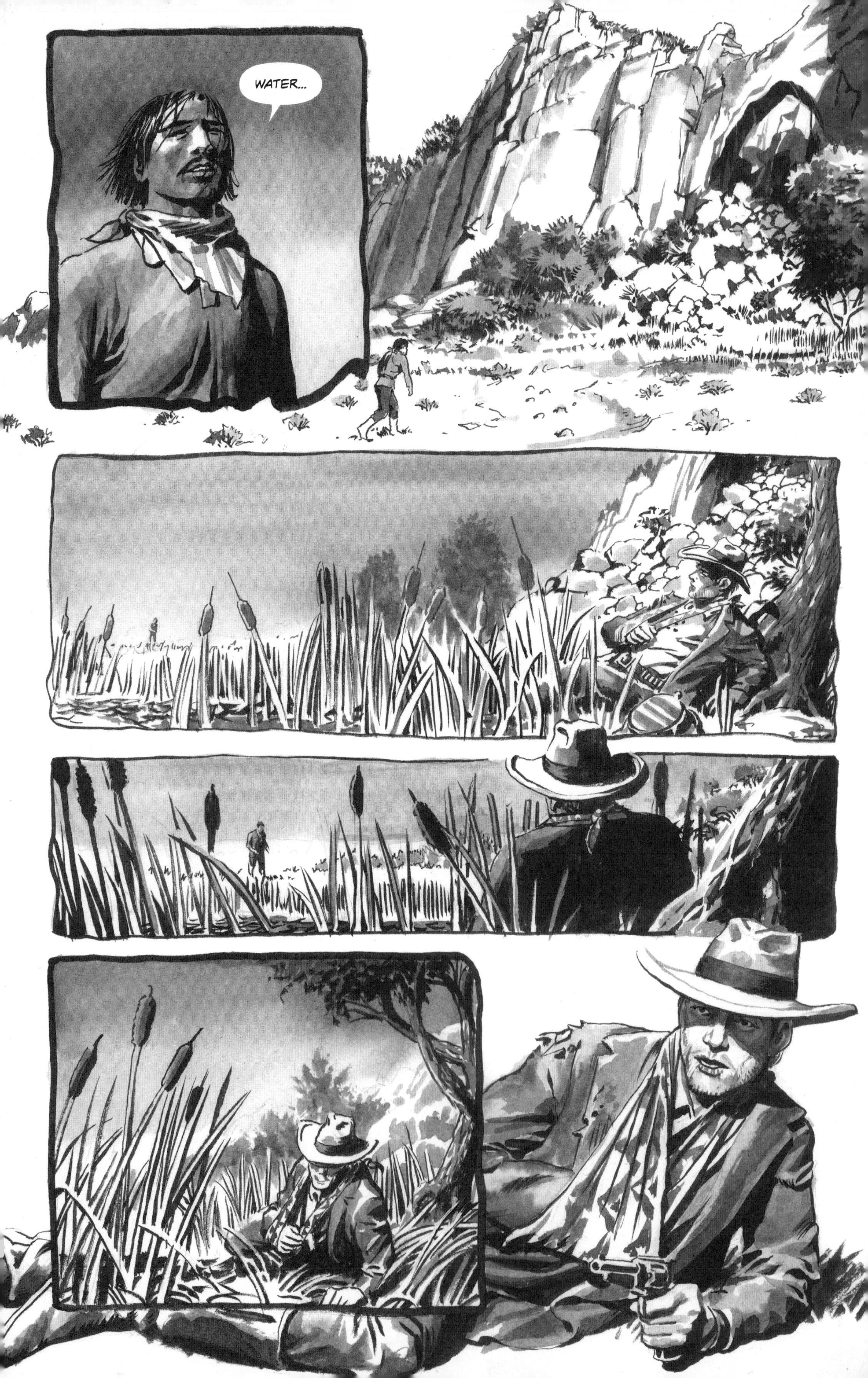
WATER...

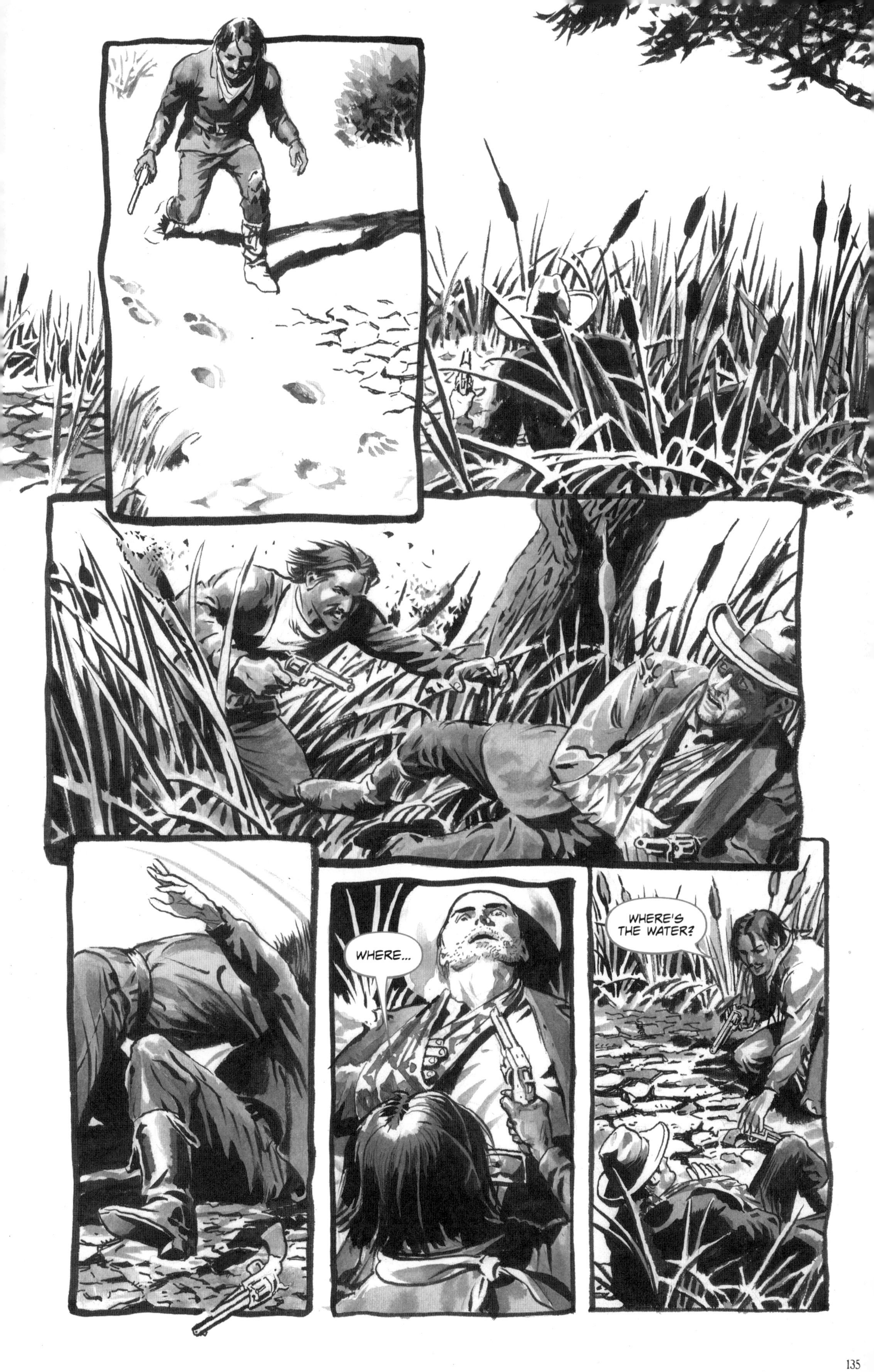
WHERE...
WHERE'S THE WATER?

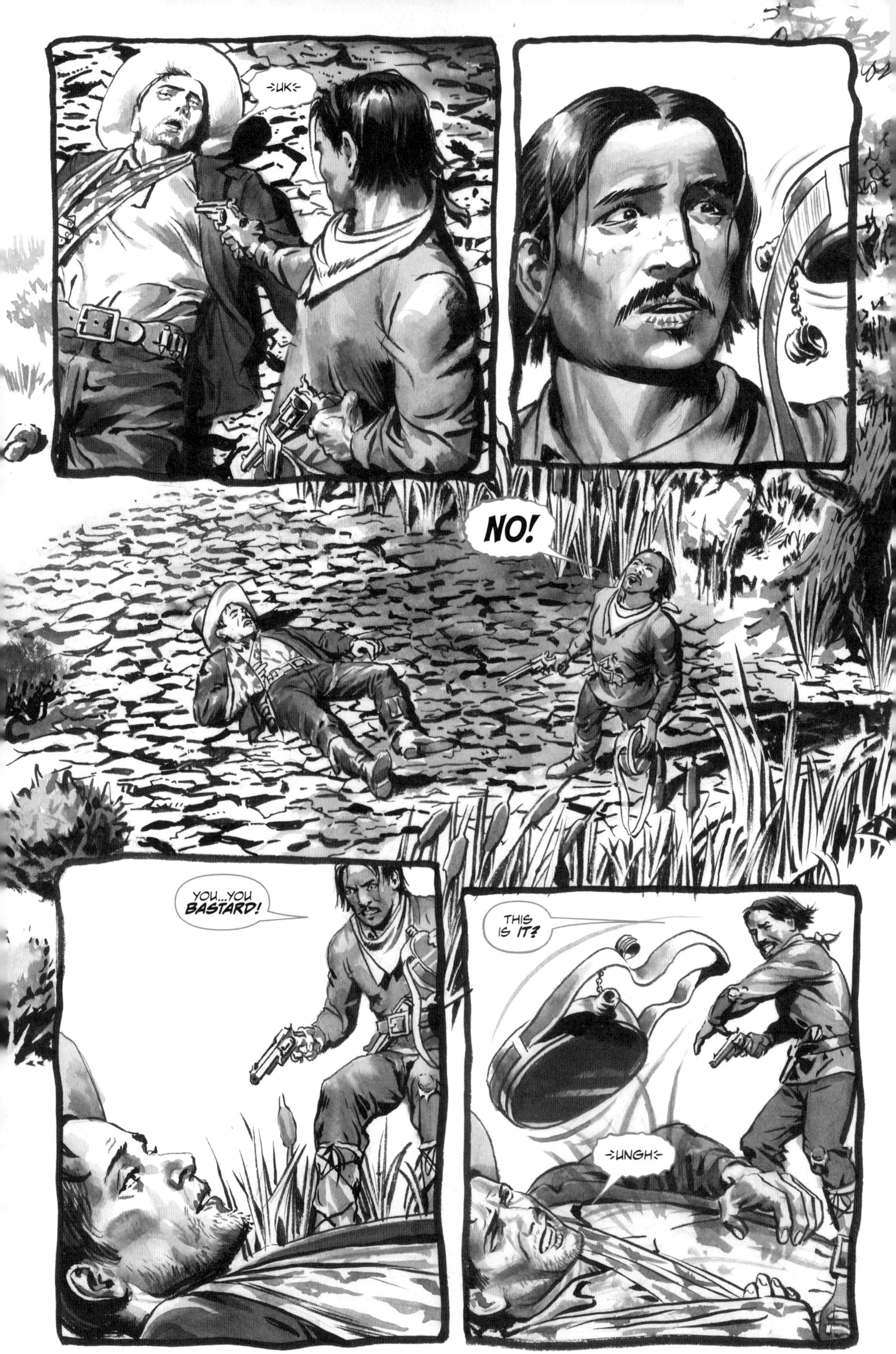

UK
NO!
YOU...YOU BASTARD!
THIS IS IT?
UNGH

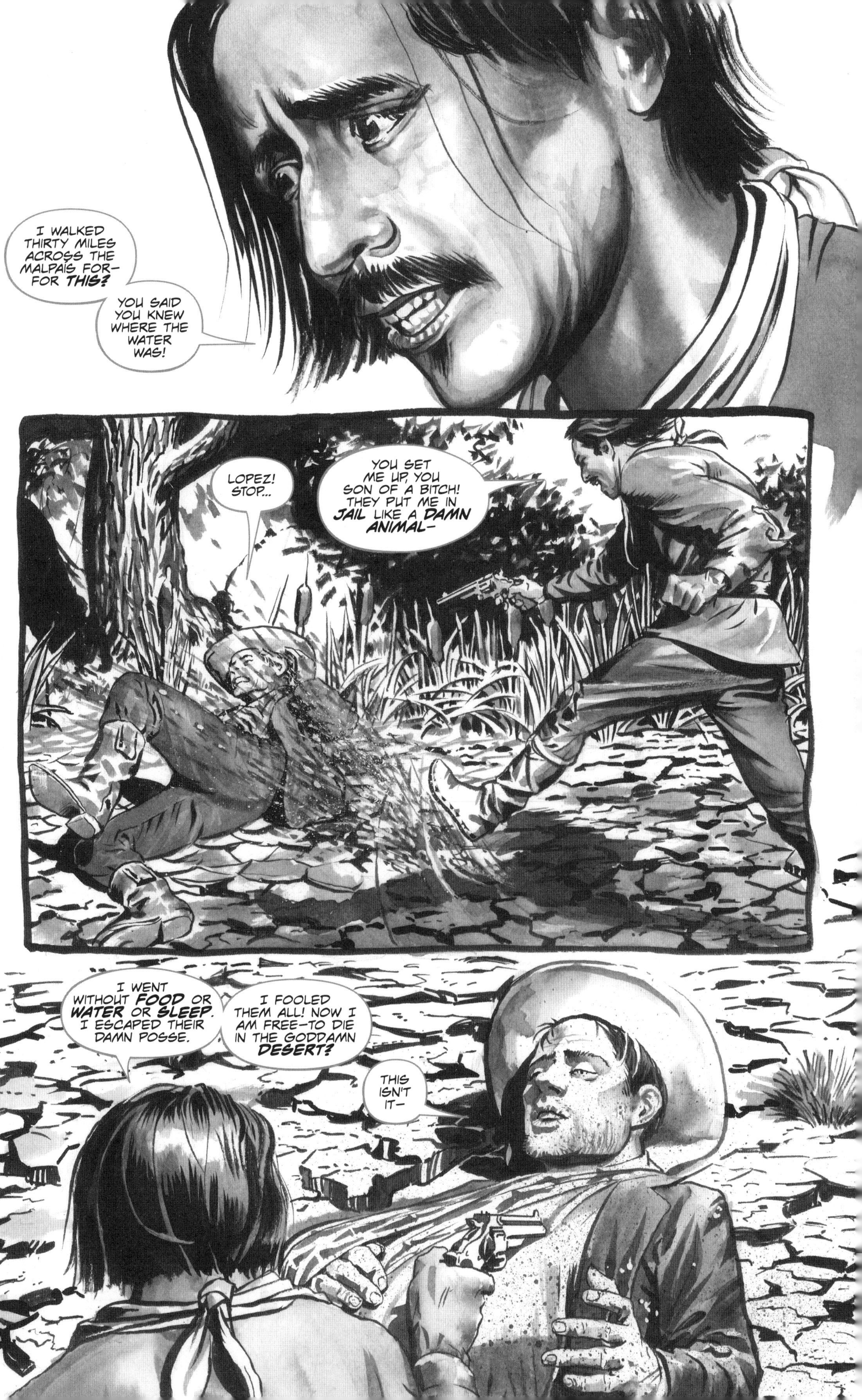
I WALKED THIRTY MILES ACROSS THE MALPAIS FOR-FOR **THIS?**
YOU SAID YOU KNEW WHERE THE WATER WAS!
LOPEZ! STOP...
YOU SET ME UP, YOU SON OF A BITCH! THEY PUT ME IN **JAIL** LIKE A **DAMN ANIMAL**-
I WENT WITHOUT **FOOD** OR **WATER** OR **SLEEP**. I ESCAPED THEIR DAMN POSSE.
I FOOLED THEM ALL! NOW I AM FREE-TO DIE IN THE GODDAMN **DESERT?**
THIS ISN'T IT-

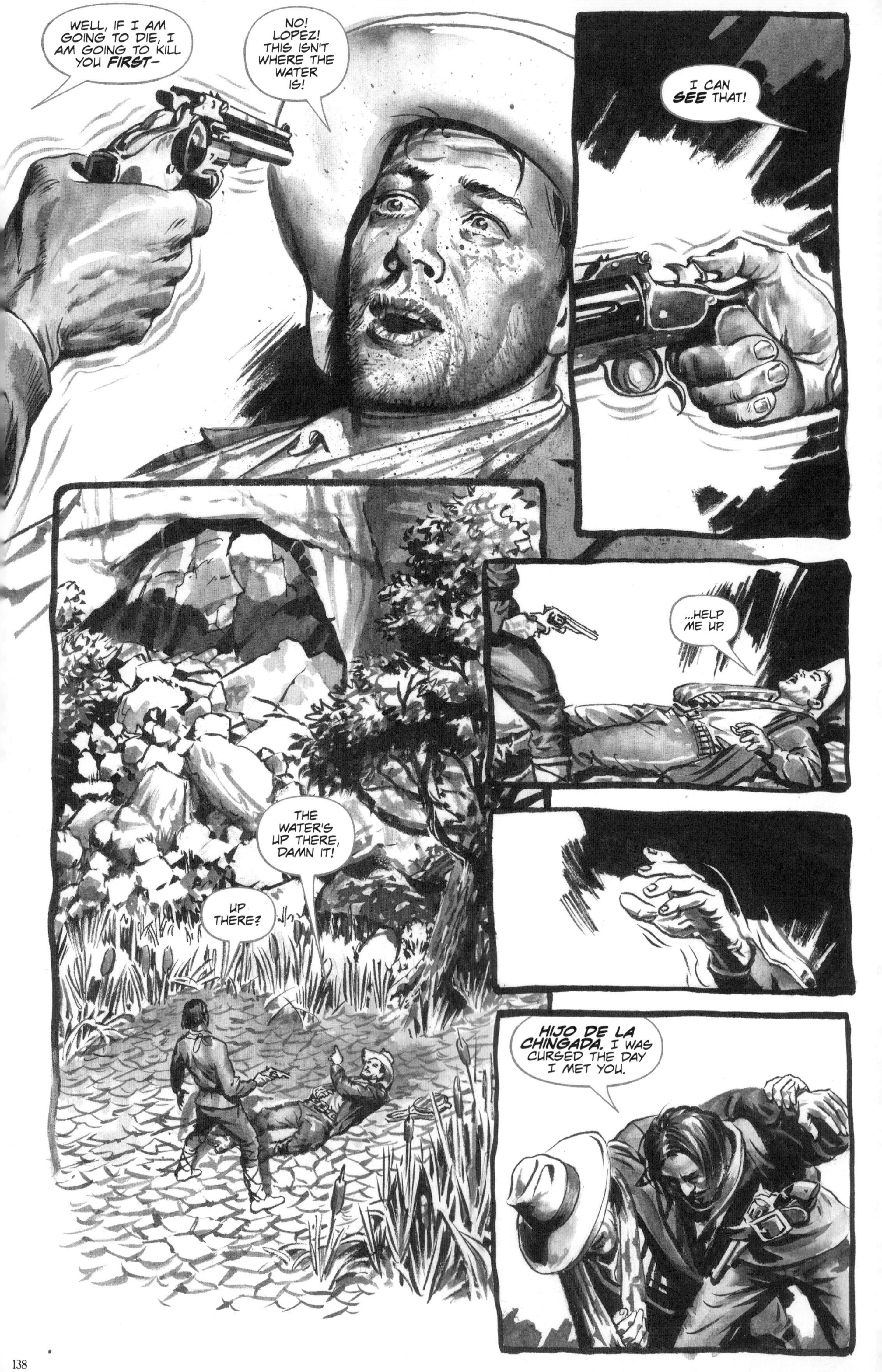
WELL, IF I AM GOING TO DIE, I AM GOING TO KILL YOU FIRST-
NO! LOPEZ! THIS ISN'T WHERE THE WATER IS!
I CAN SEE THAT!
...HELP ME UP.
THE WATER'S UP THERE, DAMN IT!
UP THERE?
HIJO DE LA CHINGADA. I WAS CURSED THE DAY I MET YOU.

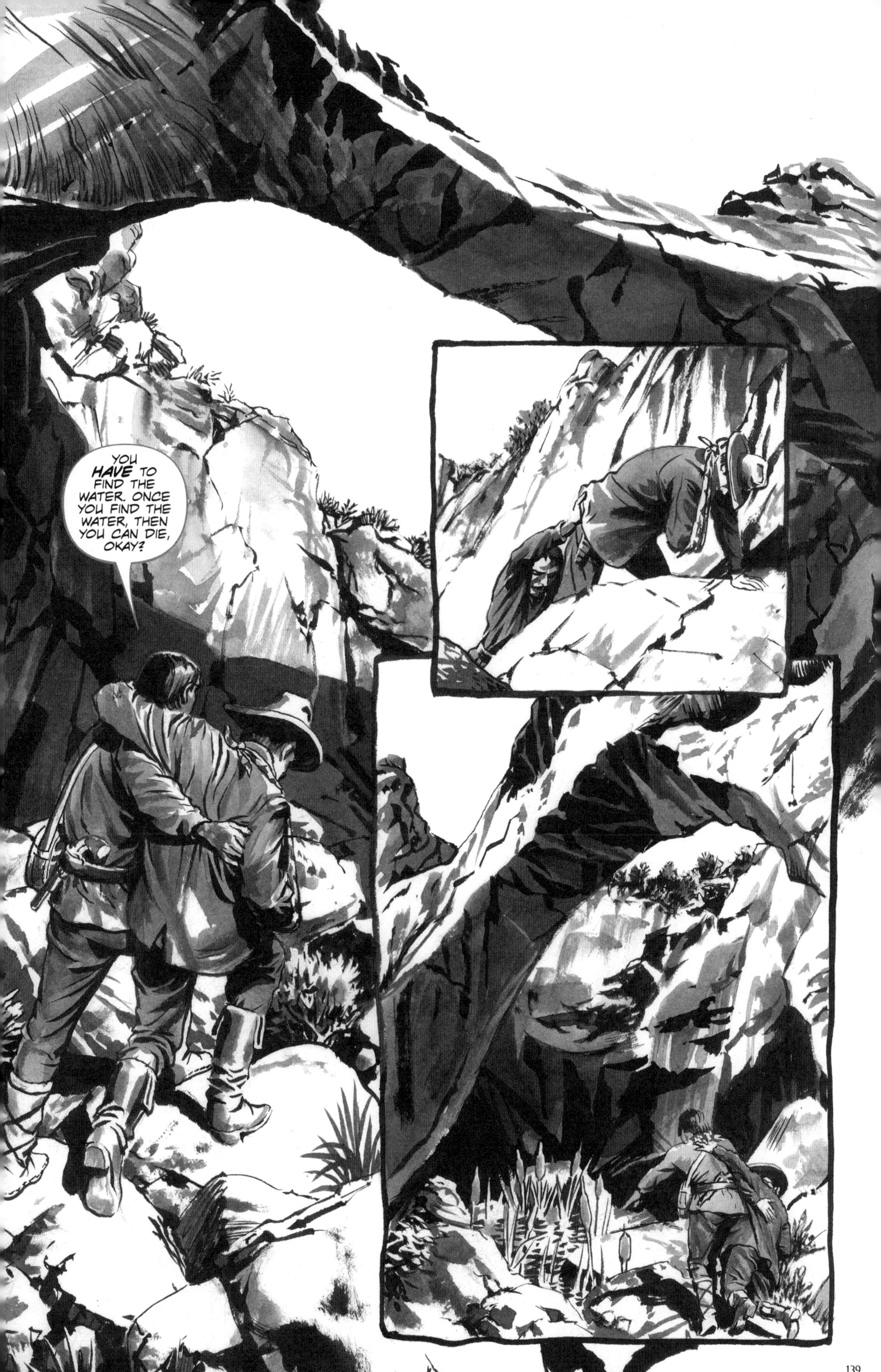
YOU HAVE TO FIND THE WATER. ONCE YOU FIND THE WATER, THEN YOU CAN DIE, OKAY?

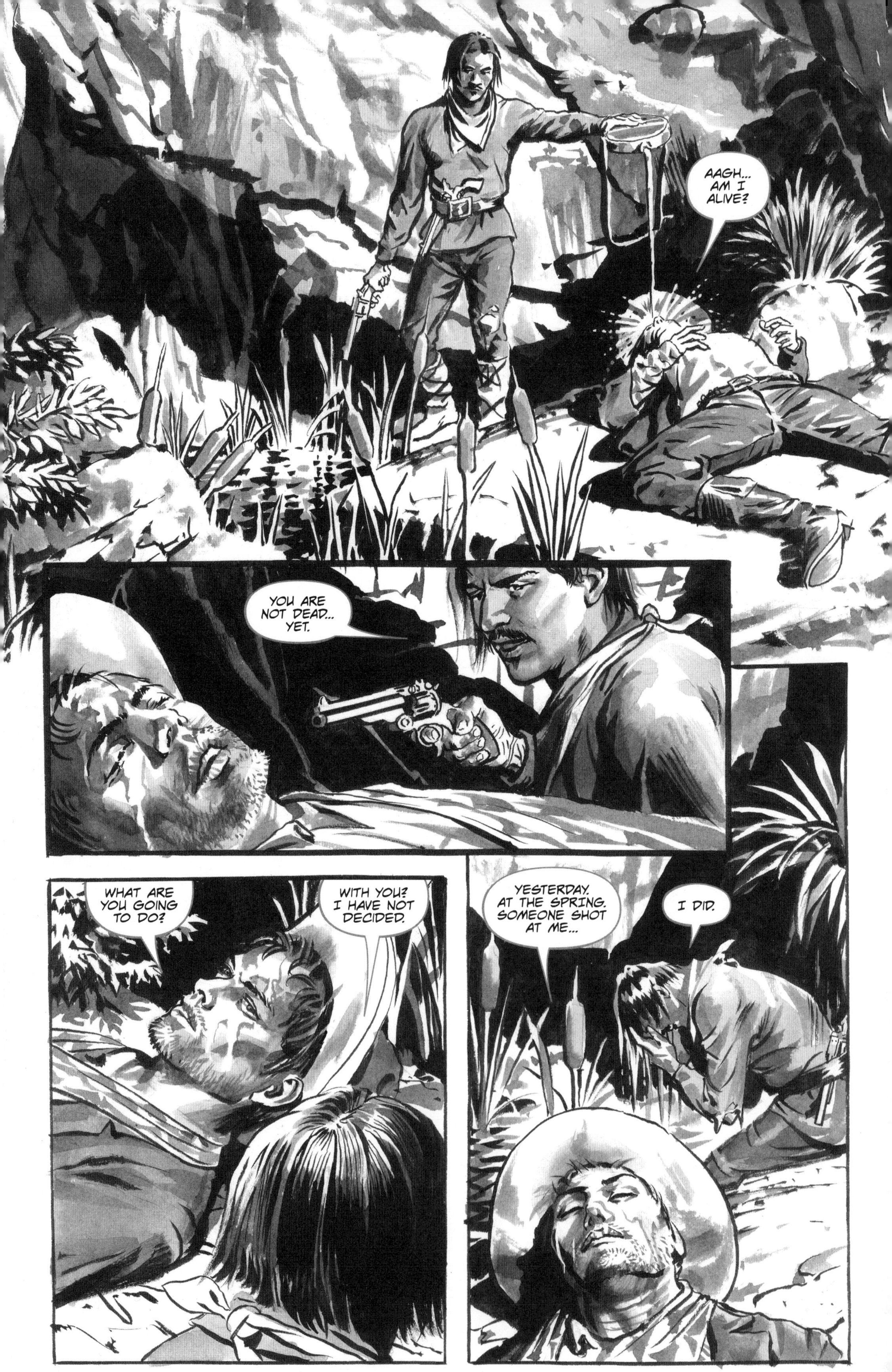
AAGH... AM I ALIVE?
YOU ARE NOT DEAD... YET.
WHAT ARE YOU GOING TO DO?
WITH YOU? I HAVE NOT DECIDED.
YESTERDAY. AT THE SPRING. SOMEONE SHOT AT ME...
I DID.

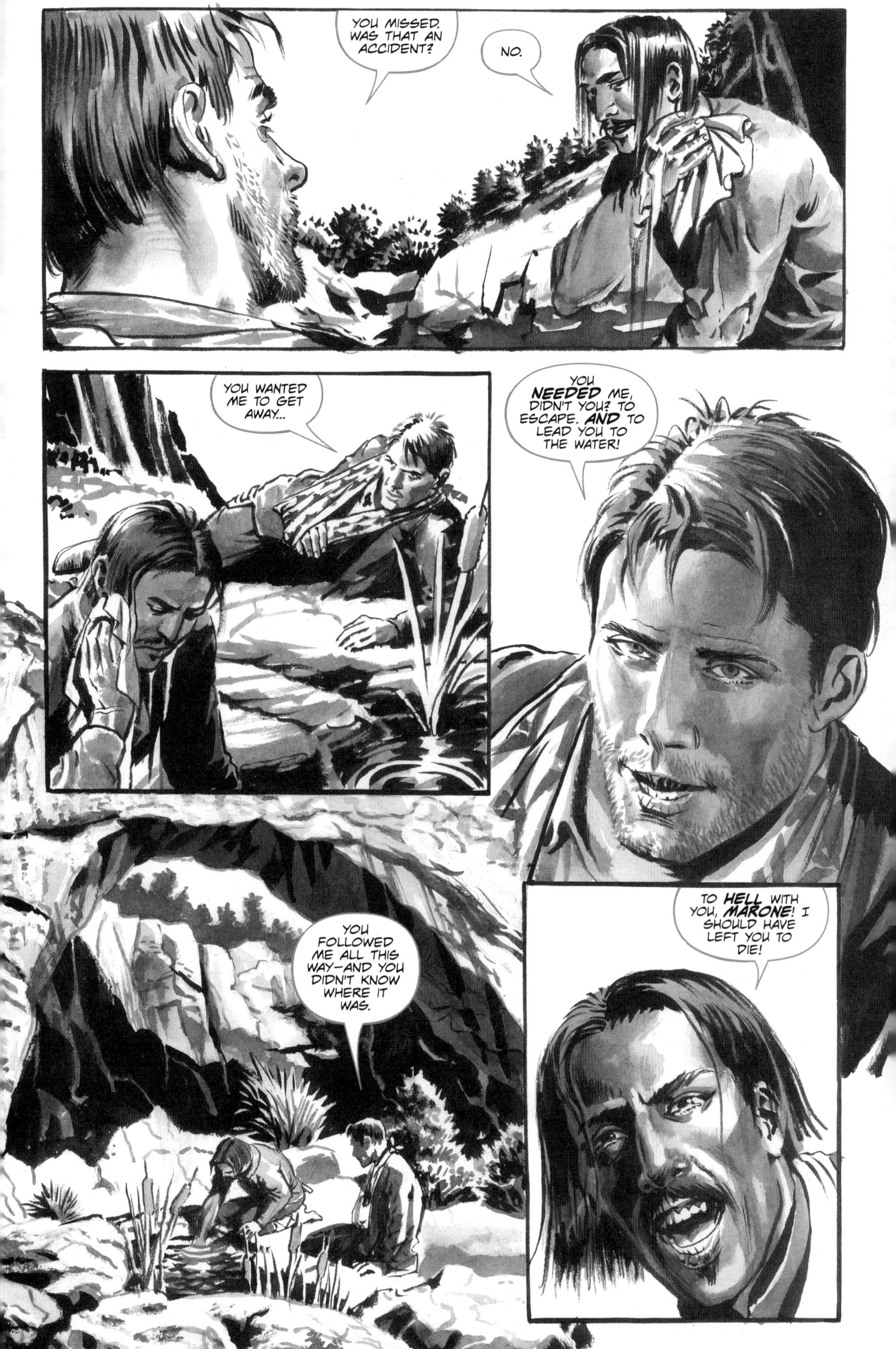
YOU MISSED. WAS THAT AN ACCIDENT?
NO.
YOU WANTED ME TO GET AWAY...
YOU NEEDED ME, DIDN'T YOU? TO ESCAPE. AND TO LEAD YOU TO THE WATER!
YOU FOLLOWED ME ALL THIS WAY--AND YOU DIDN'T KNOW WHERE IT WAS.
TO HELL WITH YOU, MARONE! I SHOULD HAVE LEFT YOU TO DIE!

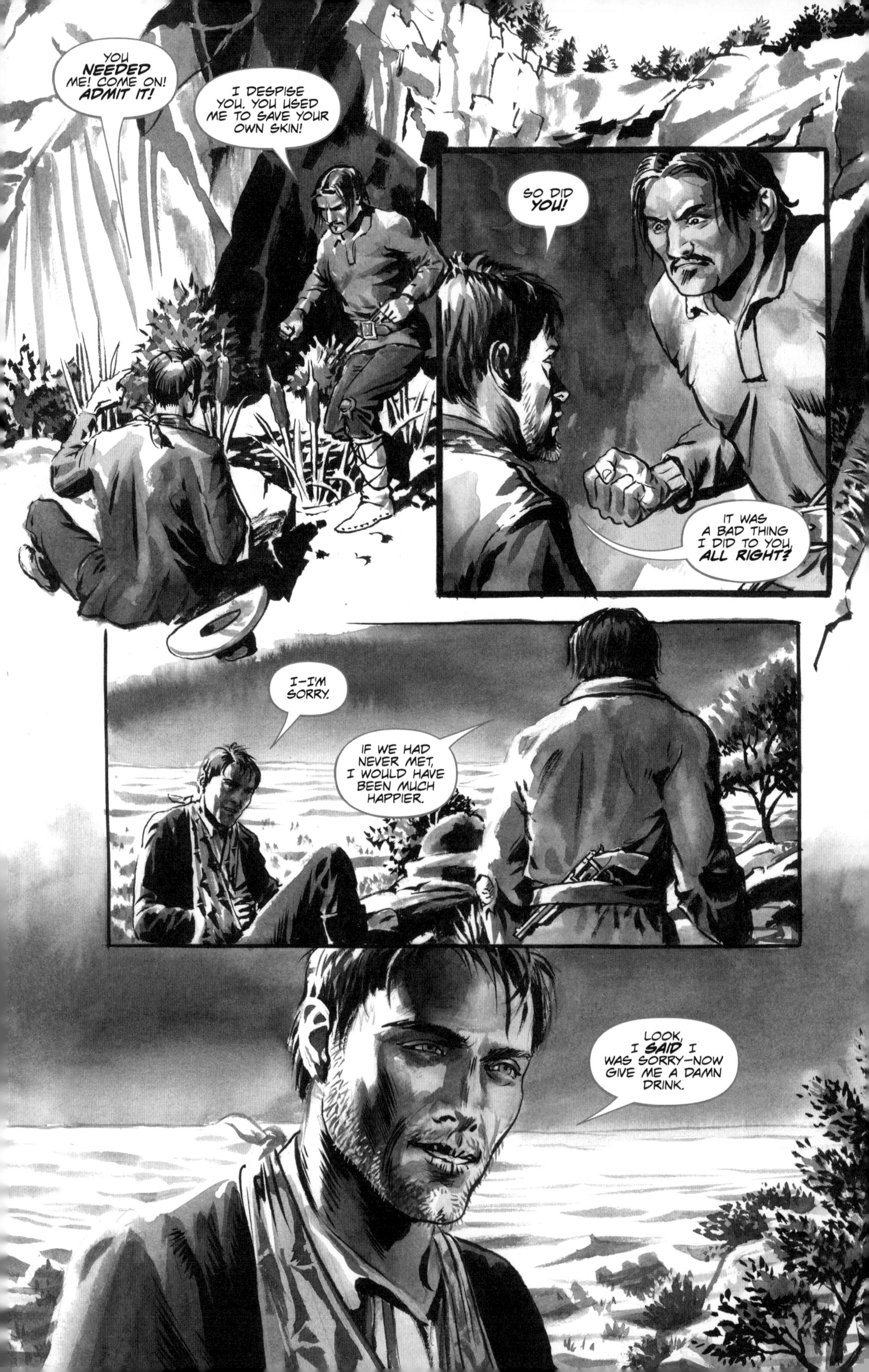
YOU NEEDED ME! COME ON! ADMIT IT!
I DESPISE YOU. YOU USED ME TO SAVE YOUR OWN SKIN!
SO DID YOU!
IT WAS A BAD THING I DID TO YOU, ALL RIGHT?
I-I'M SORRY.
IF WE HAD NEVER MET, I WOULD HAVE BEEN MUCH HAPPIER.
LOOK, I SAID I WAS SORRY—NOW GIVE ME A DAMN DRINK.

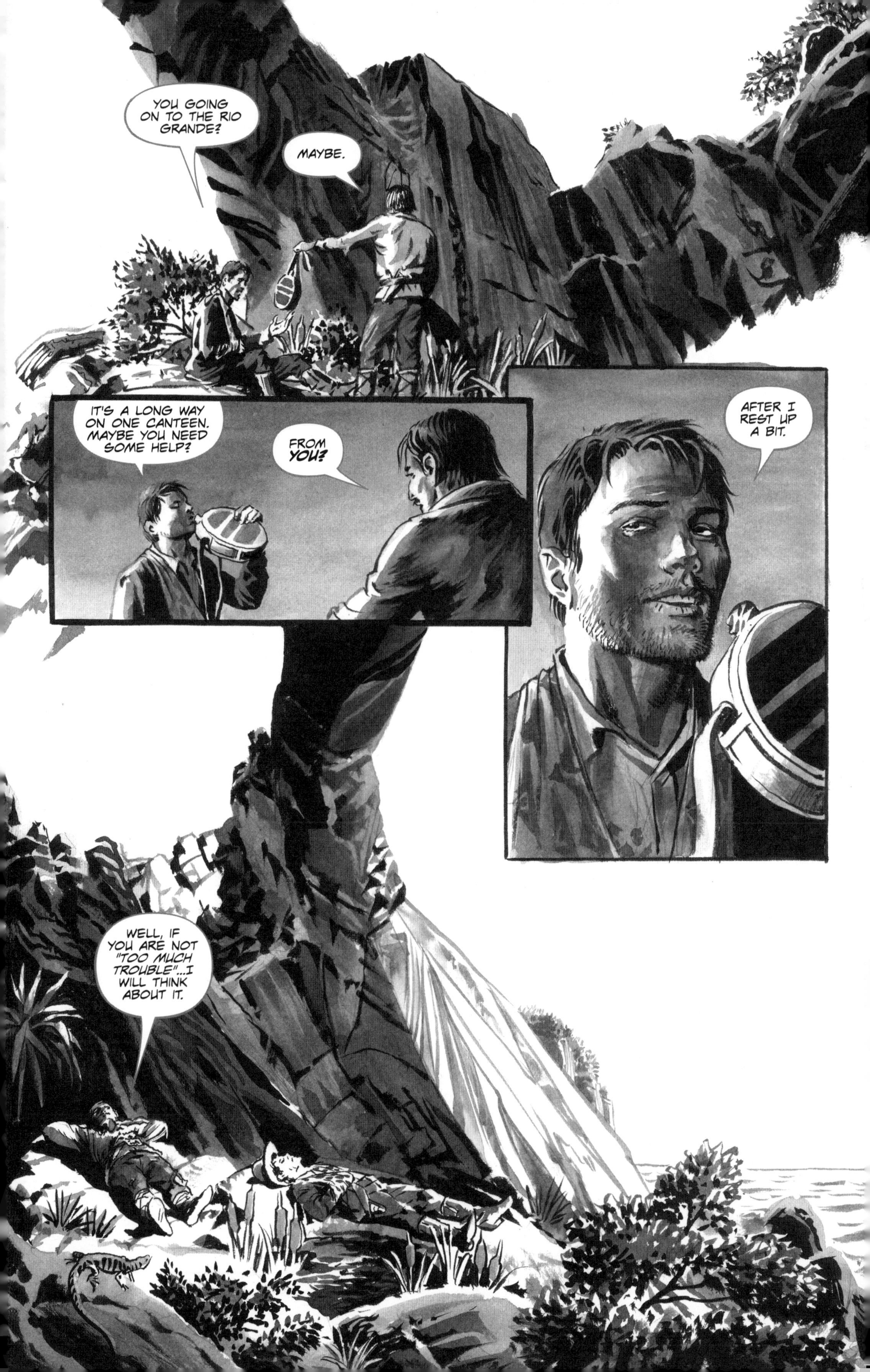
YOU GOING ON TO THE RIO GRANDE?
MAYBE.
IT'S A LONG WAY ON ONE CANTEEN. MAYBE YOU NEED SOME HELP?
FROM *YOU?*
AFTER I REST UP A BIT.
WELL, IF YOU ARE NOT "TOO MUCH TROUBLE"...I WILL THINK ABOUT IT.

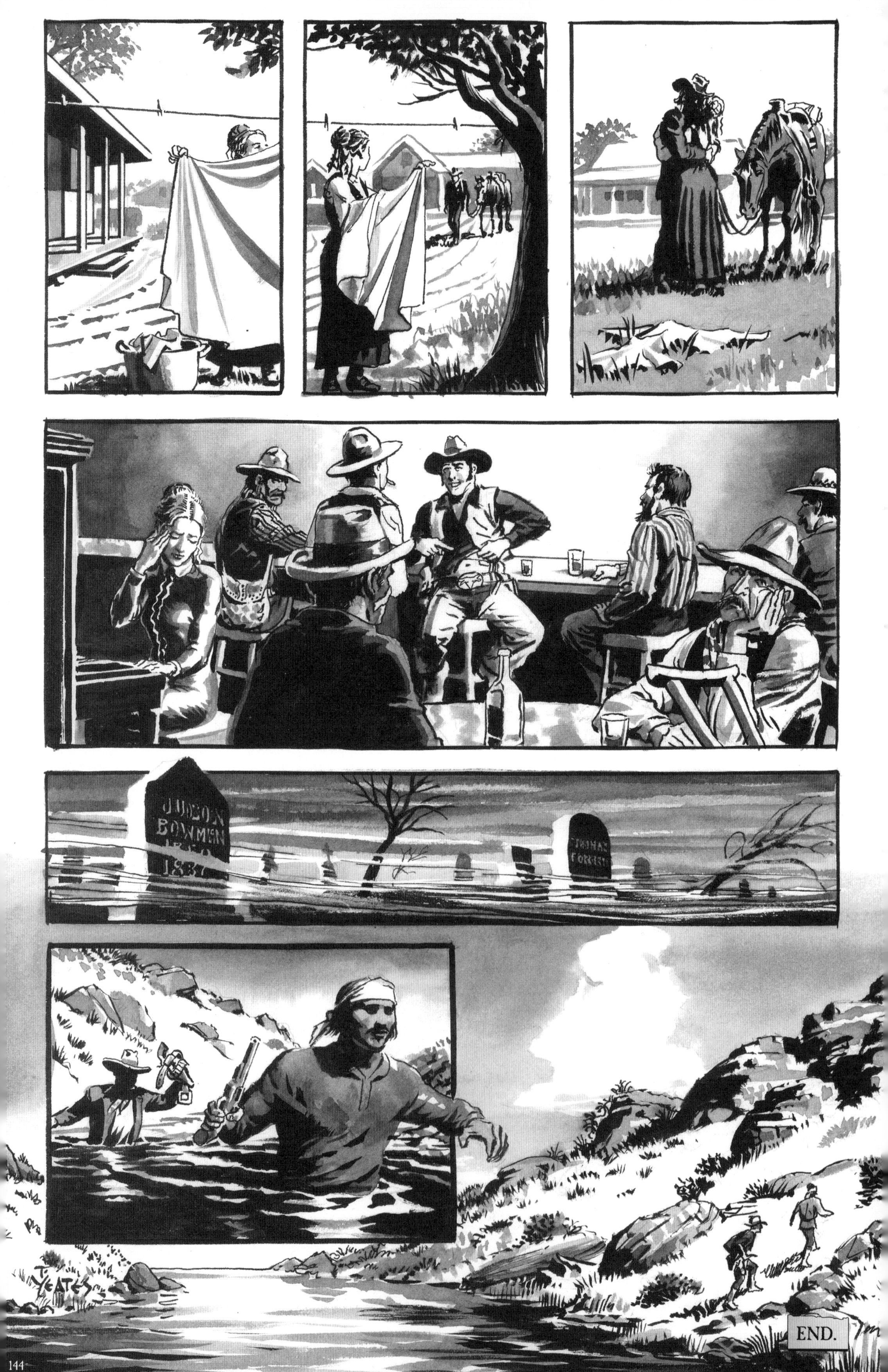
END.

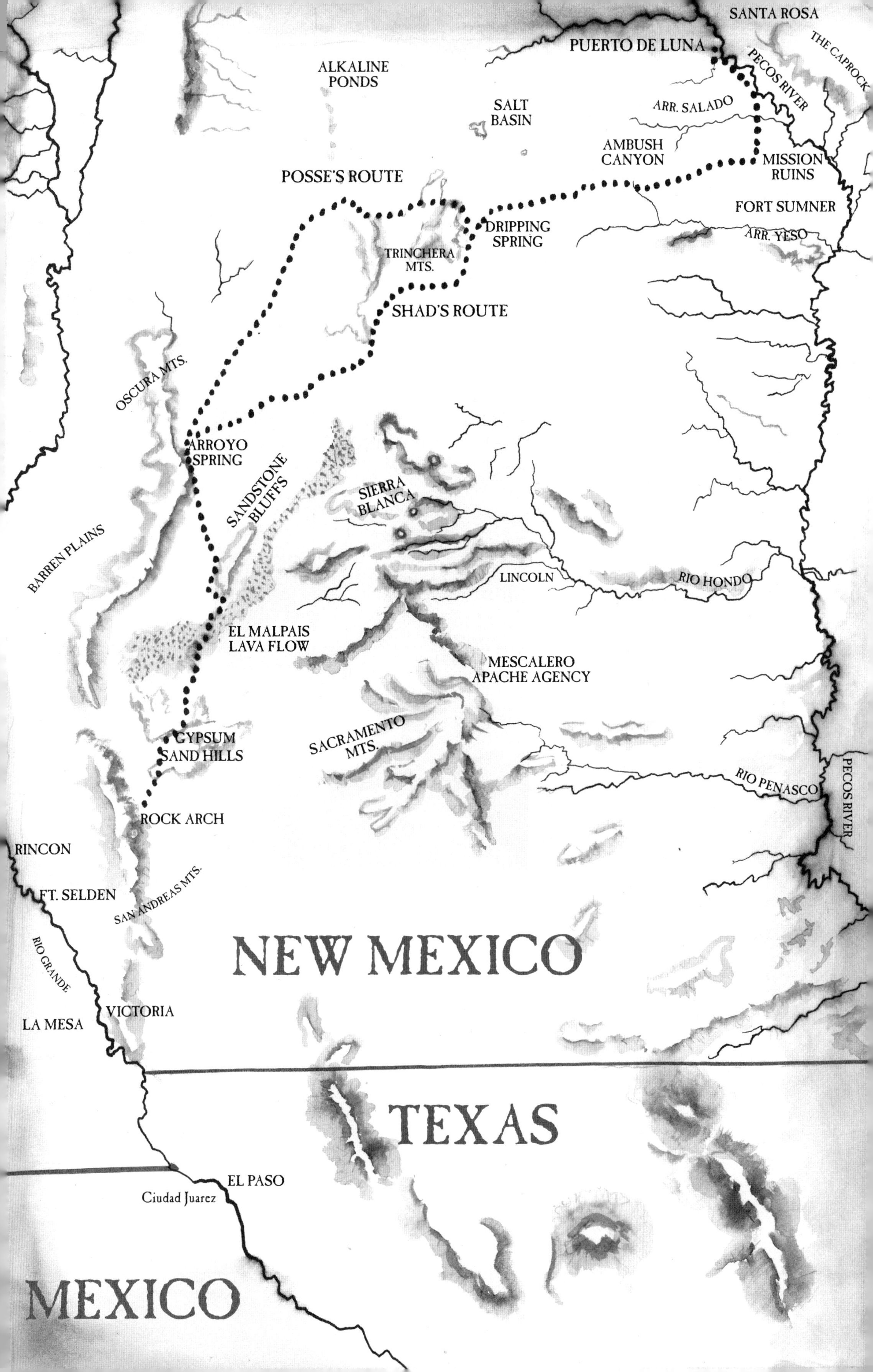
SANTA ROSA
PUERTO DE LUNA
THE CAPROCK
PECOS RIVER
ALKALINE PONDS
SALT BASIN
ARR. SALADO
AMBUSH CANYON
MISSION RUINS
POSSE'S ROUTE
FORT SUMNER
DRIPPING SPRING
ARR. YESO
TRINCHERA MTS.
SHAD'S ROUTE
OSCURA MTS.
ARROYO SPRING
SANDSTONE BLUFFS
SIERRA BLANCA
BARREN PLAINS
LINCOLN
RIO HONDO
EL MALPAIS LAVA FLOW
MESCALERO APACHE AGENCY
SACRAMENTO MTS.
GYPSUM SAND HILLS
PECOS RIVER
RIO PENASCO
ROCK ARCH
RINCON
FT. SELDEN
SAN ANDREAS MTS.
RIO GRANDE
NEW MEXICO
VICTORIA
LA MESA
TEXAS
EL PASO
Ciudad Juarez
MEXICO

The Story Behind the Story

BY BEAU L'AMOUR

DIME WESTERN

The graphic novel of Law of the Desert Born *is quite a bit different from my father's original short story. The tale of how it evolved from the pulp-magazine version that was published in the April 1946 edition of* Dime Western *is a strange chronicle of survival and perseverance all its own.*

My father often told me that his tenure writing westerns dated back to a New Year's Eve party he attended in 1945. He had just returned from France, a miserable, storm-tossed trip aboard the USS *Boise*, and was in the process of being discharged from the army when he was invited to what he described as an "open-house affair" thrown by Standard Magazines' editor in chief, Leo Margulies. That evening Leo gave Louis a fair amount of advice about restarting his career and warned him that the market had shifted. The Standard Group was now interested in buying westerns, and Leo felt Louis had the background to be successful at writing them.

Up until he was deployed to Europe, Louis had concentrated his work in the adventure and crime genres. In fact, *Law of the Desert Born* was just the third western he ever sold. However, after three years of war, America's taste for exotic locales was waning. Too many GIs had returned from traumatic experiences in the Far East or on the high seas, and too many had spent their time on tropical islands or in the deserts of Africa dreaming of home. A new sort of adventure was needed, one located in North America and set reassuringly in the past.

Westerns had been a staple of magazine fiction since the 1880s, but with the ending of World War II their popularity began to grow significantly, a fact that was being noted by Standard and many other publishers. Looking back through my dad's journals and correspondence, I discovered an odd thing...somehow, thousands of miles away, stationed in a drafty ruin in the French countryside, Louis was already aware of that fact. Possibly it was because he was confronted by the same homesickness and exhaustion with the stresses of war as the rest of the population. Maybe he just had a sense of what the collective unconsciousness of his countrymen desired. Regardless, he had begun pecking out westerns months before, almost as soon as his unit returned from Germany and began their long wait to be demobilized in Rouen, France. On New Year's Eve 1945, the time was right; he already had a

drawer full of manuscripts, and he was more than prepared to restart his life as a civilian.

Law of the Desert Born was the first of Louis's post-war westerns to be published. The story was written quickly, one of the half dozen he completed before returning home. Typical of the world of pulp magazines, it was no doubt forgotten just as quickly. At a cent and a half a word, it earned Dad less than sixty dollars and was just one small step in picking up his career and paying his rent. It would be almost forty years before it was revived again, to be used as the title story in a collection published by Bantam Books.

AUDIO DRAMA

One of the more interesting projects that Louis created before he passed away was to work with the audio publishing division at Bantam (now Random House) to produce a series of audio dramatizations, adaptations of his short stories inspired by the great radio dramas of the 1930s and '40s.

...And this is where I came in. Being between jobs and as the member of the family with aspirations in writing and directing for the stage and screen, I ended up being drafted by my father to oversee the adaptation and execution of the audio programs. It was only a couple of years later that Dad passed away and my responsibilities expanded to include reorganizing his entire estate, a process that continues to this day and includes the creation of this graphic novel.

Production of the audios required me to hire whatever writers I could find to create the sixty-page scripts that were produced either by our New York crew or by myself in LA. From out-of-work screenwriters to playwrights to aspiring filmmakers I was always on the prowl for people I could train in the medium and who could be convinced to work on the cheap. Connections at UCLA introduced me to Katherine Shirek (now Katherine Nolan), and I began the process of guiding her through the writing of her first few audioplays. At times I thought she was going to stab me to death with a pencil or bash me with one of the clumsy computers we used back in those days…being a story editor and working closely with writers is a lot like being a director who works closely with actors. It can be a relationship filled with drama. However, over the years, she wrote seven scripts for us, as much of a record as there is in our program. In many ways she was my "go-to writer" for difficult stories.

One summer I was asked by Jenny Frost, then the head of Bantam Audio Publishing, to produce *Law of the Desert Born* as an audio drama. Usually I would pick the titles we worked on, but in this case we had produced two other stories from the *Law of the Desert Born* paperback short story collection and Jenny wanted to offer them together with a third recording as a holiday gift box. It made sense that the third story should be the title story from the collection.

We didn't have a lot of time to put something together for Christmas so I called Kathy and told her we had to get this project out, quick and dirty. All we needed was a program with *Law of the Desert Born* as the title. She and I discussed the story, and I turned her loose on the script. I believe she had around a month to complete it.

About four days before the deadline Kathy called me in a state of panic. She knew the due date for this script was serious; because of the holidays the title was already in the Bantam catalog and recording studio space had been booked. The script was too long, she told me. She had been struggling to cut it but had only been able to get it to around ninety pages, not the required sixty.

One of the reasons that doing the audio dramatizations was kind of tricky was that no matter how long Louis's stories were, from three pages to eighty or ninety, the script had to have a sixty-minute running time. Scripts run about a minute a page, and I always worked with our writers to structure the stories so they turned out between fifty-eight and sixty-two pages and around fifteen to twenty scenes. That could mean cutting the original story significantly or fleshing

out the ideas in the story to get the page count up to what was needed. At eleven pages and with not much plot, none of us had been worried about *Law of the Desert Born* being too long. Foolish us.

Katherine, who usually brought her work in at exactly sixty pages, had done entirely too much of the fleshing out. To my discredit, I had helped her in this; both of us had been worried about not having enough material. But ninety pages was way too long, and I wondered exactly why it was she couldn't make it any shorter. Full of confidence that I could cut anything down to the correct time, I told her I'd meet her the next day, read it, and make it work.

By noon, I, too, was in a panic. She wasn't kidding. Her script really, really couldn't be cut without completely falling apart. I've edited novels, short stories, and movie scripts. For a while we even had a syndicated radio show, and I cut ten minutes out of each of our sixty-minute Bantam audio programs by making hundreds of trims, some even inside music cues (often considered nearly impossible). We never harmed a show, and sometimes we improved them. I pride myself on being able to edit *anything*…except for Kathy's first version of *Law of the Desert Born*, that is. She was right, the damn thing was uncuttable.

We had seventy-two hours. Gulp.

Well, necessity is a mother—or something like that. Pretending a calm I didn't feel, I got out a legal tablet, and I said, "Okay, for this to feel like the original story what's the one thing we have to preserve?"

She said something like, "The ending. The two guys. The hunted and the hunter get together. They become friends."

I wrote that down. "For that to have meaning," I told her, "they have to go through a terrible ordeal." So we had a beginning … or rather an ending. We worked backward, creating an almost entirely new story, imagining each scene based roughly on the one that preceded it until we had a loose structure.

Then I told her to take the tablet and that I would tell the story. I asked her to write down everything I said that was new and different. Everything that just came out on the spur of the moment. Then I took the pad, and she told *me* the story. Each time more material miraculously appeared. We struggled to keep the narrative as lean and mean as possible. Within about five hours, we had all the scenes outlined and about half the dialogue.

Everyone embellishes stories as they tell them. They do it in an unconscious attempt to entertain or satisfy their audience. It may be why eye-witness testimony is so unreliable, but it can also help you in a time of need. It was just a wacky, desperate idea but it worked like a charm. It didn't hurt that Kathy and I were both veterans of one another's work habits; we knew what to expect and how to work together.

I'm convinced that all written material reflects the energy level that the writer or writers put into it. The new audioplay, though still rough, had a vibrancy and a gritty reality that excited both of us. Over the next two days we wrote and rewrote, filling in the gaps and polishing the scenes. I booked us plane tickets to New York, but before we left, I invited a group of actors to my apartment to read through the script so we could see how it sounded.

The reading was both good and bad, like all things that hold promise yet still need some perfecting. But the truly exciting event occurred after we finished the reading and the impromptu cast had settled in for pizzas and Cokes…they started arguing about our story.

I was in the kitchen when Kathy came through the door with her eyes wide. "Go out there," she said. "Go out there and listen to them. It's amazing!"

In the living room a full-fledged debate was raging. Who was the good guy? Who was the bad guy? Whose wrong or insult started the fight? Was it about fathers and sons? Friendship? Loyalty or betrayal? They were discussing our cobbled-together story as if its aspects were real, as if it was events they had been actually and intimately involved in. It was the sort of response you strive for as a writer, but it amazed us that we had actually achieved it.

A day later Kathy and I continued writing in the air. We prepped scenes for auditions and then got to hear fifty or sixty actors read our lines. With that feedback, we sat in our hotel rooms and rewrote again. We also cast the show. The next day was spent in the recording studio as the actors and sound-effects man did their thing. The day after that we were flying home.

It was over. *Law of the Desert Born* was in the can, and we returned to the rest of our lives, families, and even more audios. But we never forgot the explosion of creativity that had lead to this one particular project. In some strange way it both stunned and haunted us.

SCREENPLAY

A year or two later I decided it might be a good idea to have a small catalog of screenplays ready to go on the off chance anyone wanted to make a film of something of Dad's. I chose a traditional western, Son of a Wanted Man, *but additionally I wanted to do something different, something that felt more like an independent feature.*

Law of the Desert Born was still whispering things in my ear. Kathy's too. We kept getting new ideas, and often we'd reminisce about how crazy it had been, how fast we had worked, or what an odd little story it was. Finally, I said that I thought there were still more possibilities lurking in the situation and the characters and that we should turn it into a screenplay. Kathy jumped at the chance.

Besides expanding the story to around one hundred pages I had a couple of very particular goals in mind. One of the best aspects of the audio script was that there were no gunfighters, no hidden treasures, no girl who was the daughter of "the richest man in the county." It was just about working stiffs trying to keep their heads above water and doing a bad job of it. Like our actors in the reading had sensed, there was no clear right or wrong and if there was a hero, he wasn't obvious right at the beginning.

The tone of the audioplay had been very tough, a story about people doing what they had to to survive. The characters were desperately objective, logical, their hard decisions made like they were doing math. It was an extension of our frame of mind when we were rushing, trying to figure out the story and meet the deadline for the audio. Now, I wanted to create a much more emotional script. I wanted a story where the behavior was based on love and friendship, even if the results of those emotions turned out badly.

We started playing with the relationships and the flashbacks. Tom Forrester and Clyde Bowman

(Jud's father) were the earliest settlers and fast friends. Years after Clyde's death, Tom still treats Jud as if he's a boy, but Jud insists on making his own decisions his own way. Shad went from simply being Tom's employee to a young man that Forrester had saved from a life of crime… and his surrogate son. It all created a wonderfully twisted situation when Tom pushes Shad to return to rustling. Will it save his ranch or is it just some petty revenge on a friend's son who seems to have turned against his own father's memory? The answer to that and many other questions is up to the audience to consider.

The western has taken on such a symbolic style in our culture that we often overlook the fact that conflicts like the Lincoln County War (the feud where Billy the Kid made his name and sealed his doom) started because of messy emotions and egotism. Specifically, it was over the *possibility* that there *might* be competing hardware stores in Lincoln County. The "war" developed slowly, beginning with harsh words, petty harassment, and court orders. It ended in county-wide bloodshed. It was an ugly, foolish, and distinctly human event. Kathy and I wanted to look into the confused feelings that set off something of this sort in reality rather than the fetishistically tidy black-and-white-hats approach of a Saturday matinee.

The character of Lopez evolved even further; we based some of his backstory on Massai, an Apache scout who escaped the relocation train bearing him toward a concentration camp in Florida and walked back to New Mexico. We also threw in a bit of the story of the Camp Grant Massacre, where a band of Apaches was slaughtered by a mixed group of white civilians, Mexicans, and members of the Tohono O'odham tribe. Lopez emerged a wonderful, tragic, and funny figure, a trickster, a man who uses his ethnic identity like a cloak of invisibility.

One of the most fun aspects was the almost symbiotic relationship that develops between Lopez and Shad once the posse is on Shad's trail. Lopez wants revenge, but he also wants to escape custody. To create the *possibility* of escape, he has to actually help Shad evade capture. Their fates become more and more intertwined until they are thrown together at the end of a hellish desert crossing, forced to live or die in each other's company.

Finally, I think the greatest challenge was learning to accept that we didn't really have any character development. No one particularly grows or changes in the course of the story. At first this made me frustrated, yet I really liked the story

the way it was. Then I remembered the reaction of our actors at the reading and all the questions and opinions they raised. The answer was clear, if we were successful, it would be the *audience* who grew and changed…as the story unfolded their understanding of the characters might somehow replace the character arc I feared was missing. I only pray we can be that successful!

All in all, I believe we wrote about thirty to forty drafts of the screenplay.

Louis L'Amour around the time he worked bailing hay in Pecos Valley.

THE LIFE OF LOUIS L'AMOUR

It's necessary to make alterations when doing an adaptation, both to focus the story on its new goals and to stimulate your own mind. Whenever I make changes in one of my dad's stories, however, I like to throw in bits of his life, personal details or experiences that even he didn't originally include. I try to turn the adapted work into an alternate reality, the way Louis might have written the story under different circumstances.

Law of the Desert Born begins in eastern New Mexico, with much of the action taking place around Puerto de Luna. It was a locale that Dad knew well from events in his own life. Traveling with his parents and his adopted brother, he

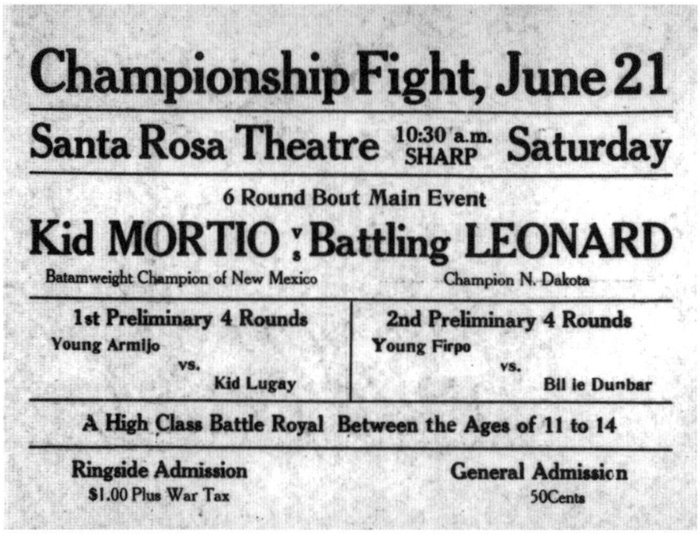
Championship Fight, June 21

Santa Rosa Theatre 10:30 a.m. SHARP Saturday

6 Round Bout Main Event

Kid MORTIO vs. Battling LEONARD

Batamweight Champion of New Mexico — Champion N. Dakota

1st Preliminary 4 Rounds	2nd Preliminary 4 Rounds
Young Armijo vs. Kid Lugay	Young Firpo vs. Bil ie Dunbar

A High Class Battle Royal Between the Ages of 11 to 14

Ringside Admission $1.00 Plus War Tax — General Admission 50Cents

"Battling Leonard" was Louis L'Amour. "Kid Mortio" was a veteran of over 200 fights in Mexico. "I never saw so many gloves in my life," Louis wrote. "It amazes me now that I didn't get an awful beating."

baled hay all up and down the Pecos Valley and even boxed an exhibition in Santa Rosa. It was the 1920s and many of the old-timers were still around. One of the people the Lamoores (Dad changed the name to the French spelling) worked for was Deluvina Maxwell, the woman who had inadvertently sent Billy the Kid to his death. Several of the hardworking senior citizens involved in the harvest had participated, on one side or the other, in the Lincoln County War. And one afternoon, Louis rode horseback from Santa Rosa to Puerto de Luna with a pair of local cowboys who later became the model for his fictional Sackett brothers, ranchers Jud and Red Rasco.

Months later and accidentally separated from his parents, Louis walked and hitchhiked across most of the route that Kathy and I used for Shad's escape. I tried to work in as much of this experience as possible, having the posse follow Shad southwest past the Salinas Missions, then south through the Jornada del Muerto Desert, past the Carrizozo Malpais lava flow to White Sands. It is a landscape that Louis crossed with another pair of brothers and their uncle in a World War I–era Buick touring car...a ride he was desperately lucky to get.

HOLLYWOODLAND

I never felt that any of the producers I dealt with really got Law of the Desert Born, *and I was never really sure why they even wanted to discuss it. Ultimately, I'm very happy I never ended up doing business with any of them.*

In retrospect, the reactions to our script were hysterical, a mixture of scenes from Hollywood send-ups like *The Player* and the classic comedy *Rustlers' Rhapsody* (which should be required viewing for anyone who wants to write a western). The project seemed to confuse everyone, to attract and repel at the same time. An agent told us it might have a chance if I got rid of the irritating flashbacks and just concentrated on the action. One development executive whined at me, "Don't you understand? You *can't* write!" Another invited me to never call again after I refused to water down the beginning by making the first scene between Jud and Shad a typical "western movie" stand-up gunfight rather than a murder. I guess it didn't help that I told him "no" in front of his boss. What did I know? I graduated from art school in an era of independents and auteurs. I eventually learned the hard way that those days were over. If I ever become successful enough to write a Hollywood autobiography, I may have to call it *Learning to Crawl*.

GRAPHIC NOVEL

Very quickly Thomas and Charles and I established a rapport where we could easily change or comment on the other's work while still staying out of each other's way creatively.

As the years passed I would occasionally boot the script up by myself, working on the timing, the humor, adding the character of Rebecca, more members of the posse, Tom's death-bed confession, the ending, and many other things. I probably added a dozen drafts to the damn thing. Once in a while I would call Kathy, who I hadn't seen in years, "I'm working on it again." She didn't have to ask what I was talking about. She was thinking about it, too. The call of the desert. The lava, black in the scorching sun. The wind across the silica sand hills. The endless reams of paper and worn out floppy disks.

I can't say I ever really put it away, but it lived on a sector of my hard drive rarely visited. The first drafts of the screenplay dated back to the later days of Windows 95. Sheriff Gates was named in honor of Bill Gates, though one particularly liberal movie producer reacted in horror at the name. He was not able to separate it from the thought of Daryl Gates, chief of the LAPD during the Los Angeles riots.

Eventually, I met Charles Santino. We were toying with the idea of doing a graphic novel project together and various titles came up, titles like *Hondo* and *Last of the Breed*. But comics projects take a long time to realize. Ultimately, an

artist needs to do five hundred to nine hundred panels and that takes a year or two. Writing a script that I could stand to show to the world would also take a good deal of time and I wanted to get going. We started discussing scripts I had already written.

After reading *Law of the Desert Born*, which, I will admit, was not the first thing I showed him, Charles said something like the following: "Well, they'll never be able to guess what's going to happen next." We made the decision that this was the script we would show, first to Betsy Mitchell at Random House, then to other publishers if we had to. The situation at Random House looked good. Betsy was born and raised in New Mexico and had been a top fiction editor for years. She got it in ways that few others had. I called Kathy and told her that Random House was going to do our script as a graphic novel…as the mother of two teenage boys, she was about to become the coolest mom in the world.

I'd like to say that Random House bought the story and the rest was history, but it really has been a great deal of work. Charles insisted that the script be stripped of all inessentials, and though I imagined that I had done this job years before, I now went at it again with a vengeance. There's nothing like a contract to spur on your creativity and determination! Charles started the process of laying out the panels and pages, forming a new beat of the story (almost a mini-story) from the top left to the bottom right of every pair of pages. We struggled to keep the majority of pages under six or seven panels and the amount of dialogue as evenly dispersed as possible. I'm sure it was just another day at the office for him, but it was fascinating and difficult for me and I wasn't the one doing the heavy lifting.

I started to create a style sheet, a manifesto for how this story would look and feel. I also built an image archive of costumes and locations, props and maps. I didn't know who our artist was going to be, and I was nervous that we'd end up with someone who was stuck in the unreality of western movies or had no knowledge of the American landscape or culture. I gathered together about three hundred photographs, many from the various scouts I had made to find locations when I thought we might make the story into a movie.

Law of the Desert Born is supposed to take place in eastern and central New Mexico, though I romanticized it a bit by using some photographic references from the western part of the state. I wanted the costumes to reflect the 1880s, a time when styles specifically designed for the western market had just started to appear. I wanted the tools and wagons and saddles to reflect the sort of old stuff I had seen and even worked with as a kid, spending a high school summer on a ranch in Colorado.

We finally hired Thomas Yeates to be our illustrator, and with Charles and my old friend Paul O'Dell, who would do our Photoshop work, I had what I started to think of as "the dream team." Thomas was the perfect man for the job. He lived in the west, a guy who had studied in Utah and now lived in northern California. He had spent a fair amount of his youth around horses and didn't imagine the world through the eyes of a city dweller. Even better than that, he had the patience to work with me to get as many of the details right as possible. I can't say that we never diverged from what was authentic, but I can say that it was always a choice we made together for intelligent or practical reasons.

No finished project ever matches your imagination of what it might have been…but the best of all possible worlds is when your collaborators bring so many new and different elements to the party that you never think about "might have been" or worry about "your vision" any longer. The only reality left in your mind is what you are creating together. I suspect that with many of us satisfaction has a lot to do with both the process *and* the outcome. I find myself amazingly happy with both in this case, and I'm very proud and grateful to have been able to work with so many wonderful people. When you do this sort of work on a story, it becomes like a child, starting with the DNA of all its authors yet growing into its own personality. If you are smart and you really listen, it will tell you what it wants to become, not the other way around. We all listened and that's all that matters.

Thank you for reading.

Beau L'Amour
2013, Durango, Colorado

Acknowledgments

If I have learned one thing over the years it is that stories evolve. Some grow and mature, allowing the reader to discover different paths and interests; they resonate with different people in different ways, just like a living being. Over time, each story is different in its themes and content to everyone who experiences it, and even rereading at different ages and under different circumstances can provide a vastly different experience.

When a story is adapted from one form to another, from the spoken word to the written word, from prose to theater, or from fiction to film, new elements are energized in the story. Different media demand different approaches and inspire the writers who take over the tale to discover aspects never imagined in the original telling. My father's short story *Law of the Desert Born* has a long and complicated history. It has been adapted into an audio drama, a screenplay, and now this graphic novel. It has evolved through many drafts and benefited from many contributors.

Obviously the first and foremost of those contributors was Louis L'Amour, who wrote the first version of the story in 1945. However, Louis created more of the context of this graphic novel than by just having written the original short story. His life inspired the entire approach to the retelling of this story because he taught me much of what I know and influenced my vision of western characters and history. He also lived aspects of this graphic novel that he never thought to include back in the 1940s. Clearly, Louis was the creator of the entire environment in which every version of this story exists.

Katherine Nolan and I made our way through several variations of this script over the years, and her enthusiasm and belief that the story always had more to give matched mine at every step. It was her creative energy, dogged determination, and ability to keep reenvisioning the same scenes that pulled us through many rough patches and made all this possible.

Paul O'Dell was there in the beginning and the end, helping with early readings of the script, creating sound effects for the audio production, and now putting the finishing touches on the pages of the graphic novel with his deft Photoshop work.

Along the way there were four casts of actors who helped us workshop the script, two in Los Angeles, one in Santa Fe, and the cast of the audio drama in New York. All helped us refine the story and characters and discover bits and pieces of the form you see here.

Finally, there are those who made up the "dream team" of graphic-novel production.

Charles Santino, who convinced me to take a stab at this style of storytelling, then worked diligently to turn our script into an artful stream of poetic images and to teach me the craft and lore of comics.

Thomas Yeates, who is, first and foremost, the only artist I can imagine illustrating this book and has been the soul of patience and calm while I have struggled to impart the complete vision I have had for this story. We are also blessed that he is a man who has lived his life in the west and has a well-developed sense of its denizens and landscape.

From the Random House team there is Betsy Mitchell, a native New Mexican, who got us started. Tricia Narwani, our editor, who has held our collective hands through times of trouble and saved us from ourselves time and again. Erich Schoeneweiss, the man who knows what can be done and how to do it. Bill Tortolini, letterer extraordinaire, who knows what to put where and has fought the difficult battle between getting the story told and protecting the beautiful art on our pages. And there is Scott Shannon, Irish *capo di tutti capi*, and the man who believed *Law of the Desert Born* would be a chance worth taking.

On the home front, there are Laurel Marlantes and Ron Curmano, who helped create the online "bible" of props, maps, and locations, and Kurt Lancaster, Amy Myers, and their cohorts, who created our promotional videos.

Lastly, Thomas and I both would like to give a nod to his great group of bronc busters and desert rangers: Olivia Yeates, Tod Smith, Ken Hooper, Chris Marrinan, Michael Coy, Pete McDonnell, Debi Sante, Lori Almeida, Sea Dog, and Sheriff Cal Ares. All assisted the process in so many ways.

Thank you,

Beau and the whole family of L'Amours

About the Authors and Artist

LOUIS L'AMOUR, truly America's favorite storyteller, was the first fiction writer ever to receive the Congressional Gold Medal from the United States Congress in honor of his life's work. He was also awarded the Medal of Freedom. There are more than three hundred million copies of his books in print worldwide.

BEAU L'AMOUR grew up among the writers, actors, beatniks, Apache Indians, Asian arms brokers, FBI agents, and members of the Hollywood Ten who were the denizens of his West Hollywood neighborhood and his parents' friends. He graduated from California Institute of the Arts. Over the years, L'Amour has written and produced a series of more than sixty audio dramas and worked in the radio and magazine business, then as a screenwriter and television producer. In the world of book publishing, he has been an art director, literary editor, and ghost writer.

After receiving her MFA in screenwriting from UCLA, **KATHERINE NOLAN** wrote and edited audio dramatizations and screenplays based on the short stories of Louis L'Amour. Traveling the southwest and poring through dusty archives, she worked with Beau L'Amour tracking down the details of his father's extraordinary life. She has published a book of essays and currently works as a writer and editor in various media. Katherine lives in South Pasadena with her husband and two sons.

CHARLES SANTINO scripted the Jack London pastiche "Blood and Ice" for *Savage Tales*, his first pro assignment. With Michael McDowell, he collaborated on the psychological horror novel *Toplin*. Plotting and scripting *Conan the Barbarian* for Marvel followed. He adapted the first graphic novel based on the work of Ayn Rand, *Ayn Rand's Anthem: The Graphic Novel*, with artist Joe Staton. Although he admits that he "can't draw worth a lick," he storyboards his pages before writing a prose script, "so I know it's going to work."

Eisner Award–winning comics illustrator **THOMAS YEATES** is highly influenced by old-guard illustrators like Harold Foster and Al Williamson. Originally from Sacramento, Yeates eventually moved to New Jersey to attend the Joe Kubert School for two years. Since then he has worked as an illustrator, focusing on high adventure in the comic book/graphic novel field. Illustrating a Louis L'Amour western story is a dream job for Yeates. He is currently the artist on the *Prince Valiant* Sunday strip, another dream job.

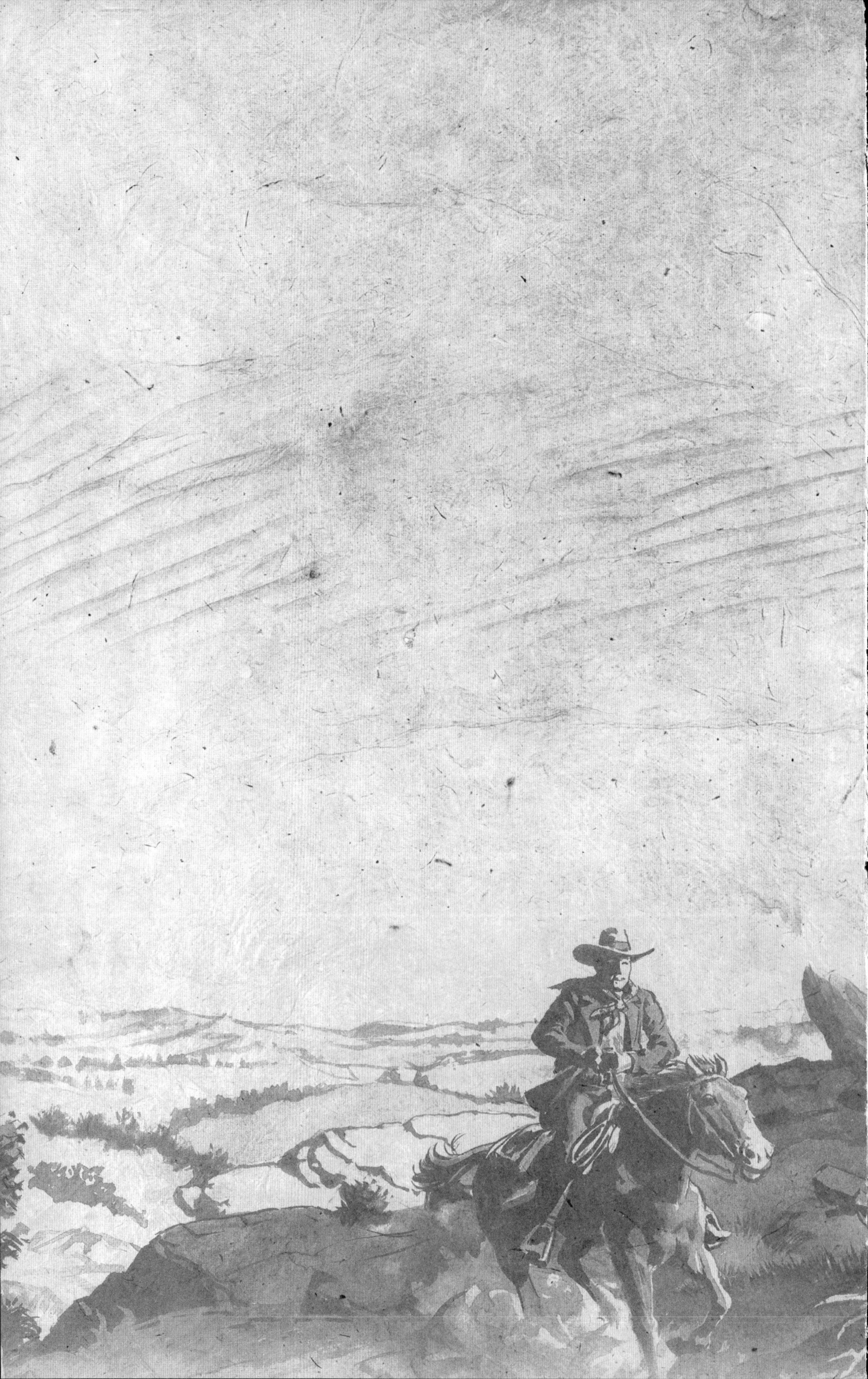